FREEZE
DRY

Forge Books by Corson Hirschfeld

Aloha, Mr. Lucky
Too High
Freeze Dry

FREEZE
DRY

Corson Hirschfeld

A Tom Doherty Associates Book
New York

FREEZE DRY

A Forge Book
Published by Tom Doherty Associates, LLC
175 Fifth Avenue
New York, NY 10010

www.tor.com

Forge® is a registered trademark of Tom Doherty Associates, LLC.

Library of Congress Cataloging-in-Publication Data

Hirschfeld, Corson.
    Freeze dry / Corson Hirschfeld.—1st hardcover ed.
        p.   cm.
"A Forge book"—T.p. verso
    ISBN 0-765-30800-2
    1. Swindlers and swindling—Fiction.   2. Dead—Identification—Fiction.
3. Organized crime—Fiction.   4. Florida—Fiction.   5. Cults—Fiction.
I. Title.
PS3558.I672F74 2003
813'.54—dc21

2003009214

First Edition: October 2003

Printed in the United States of America

0   9   8   7   6   5   4   3   2   1

To Paul, a loyal friend who reads no fiction but
buys my books. (Will he see this?)

PART ONE

The Fall

1

—

T his was to have been a celebratory lunch for Rita Rae and Orlando, but so far there had been no hugs, no making-up-for-lost-time kisses, no feelie-feelie. Spine stiff, Rita Rae had been chilling the air with a grim silence since the taxi from Miami International Airport dropped her off at the South Beach sidewalk café.

She chewed her lip again, slammed a fist into her red Fendi handbag, and finally spoke: "It's that damned dog's fault." At Orlando's bewildered shrug, she snatched the pink flamingo swizzle stick from the Cuba Libre he had ready for her, snapped it in two, and flung the pieces at his chest.

Orlando, lean and dusky with slicked-back hair, ten years younger than Rita Rae's thirty-nine-and-holding, shook the plastic shards from his open-to-the-waist, pink silk shirt. He downed a shot of tequila, locked his dark eyes on Rita Rae's, and, with no music in his voice, said, *"Dime. ¿Qué pasa, guajira?"*

"Pasa this . . ." Rita Rae tilted her head back, coyote-fashion, and shouted, "Shickie Doone. I'll *kill* the little rat."

Conversations died. A roller blader collided into a low rider idling in the Ocean Drive gridlock. Pedestrians and café patrons craned heads, curious to see who wanted Shickie Doone—whoever the little rat was—dead.

To assist them, Rita Rae jumped to her feet, fists on hips. Clad in skin-tight, scarlet leather capri pants and a see-through blouse over a lacy black bra, and at six-foot-five from the top of her shellacked blond beehive to the heel-tips of her Charles Jourdan spike pumps, she was not one to miss.

Spectators developed a sudden interest in anything but the loco blonde with hate-filled eyes. The blue-haired wife of a pear-shaped octogenarian in Bermuda shorts continued to stare, so Rita Rae clarified the message: "You know him, old lady? Shickie Doone, that son of a bitch? That *bastard?* That *motherf—*"

Orlando clamped a hand over her mouth and wrangled her into her chair, simultaneously managing a sideways bow to the elderly woman and another to the restaurant maitre'd fast pacing their way. "So sorry, *señora, señor*—the female problems, she gets like this—"

Rita Rae chomped the side of his palm.

"*¡Coño!*" Orlando lifted the bitten hand to his opposite shoulder in a backhanding windup, but thought better of it when he saw a barrel-chested waiter at the maitre'd's heels.

White teeth flashed from beneath his mouse-tail mustache as he spread his arms, gesturing supplication, and good will. "*No hay problema, señores,* see?" He sat, placed a hand on Rita Rae's and gave her a peck on her rigid cheek. "Is nothing. A lover's quarrel, no more."

Rita Rae offered the management a penitent nod, but when they left, she muttered "bastard" a few more times, and, "I gave the worm nearly a year of my life and he *conned* me. *Me!*"

She shook her left hand as if a wasp had alighted on it, held it out, fingers splayed. "I've been staring at my ring ever since the plane left Knoxville. This is not my diamond. He switched it. Just because I sold his mutt."

"There, there, *mi vida.* Sometimes, you overreact, no?"

"I know how he did it, too. I put it in the ultrasonic cleaner in the bathroom before he left for Vegas. He brought it to me in the bedroom, kissed my wrist like some slick Lancelot, and slipped it on my finger with his ugly mug hovering over my hand so I couldn't see it. Then he smooth-talked me into a roll in the hay. 'One last time,' he says. 'I'm sorry our marriage didn't work out, sweetie. I signed the papers, gave you everything you deserve.' The bastard. Screwed me out of my beautiful ring—switched it, never mentioned the yapper—then screwed *me* for good measure."

"*¡Dios mío!*" Orlando's manicured fingers waved the heavy, cologne-laced air at his chest. "Spare the disagreeable details."

He took her still-extended hand, twisting it so the five carat brilliant-cut stone caught sunlight. Scowling, Orlando removed a collapsible loupe from his leather shoulder bag for a closer look. "Hmmm."

"What the hell's that mean? Is it my ring or not?"

"Platinum mount. The stone is flawless. *Perfecto.*"

Rita Rae sighed. "That's a relief. I was so worried—"

"Full of fire."

"I love my ring."

"However . . ." Orlando lowered his voice. "Your stone had a fault near the base. Now? Gone. And the color? Hmmm. The facet edges? Soft, rounded. The stone has a watery look—"

Rita Rae jerked her hand free. "So?"

"You are wearing a fine cubic zirconia." Orlando set the loupe aside and patted her hand. "Yes, your husband, he tricks you."

"*The bastard!*" Rita Rae bounced an ice cube off the door of a passing cab. "What went wrong? He was making a bundle from that cult of his. Couldn't wait to marry me when he thought I was a 'helpless oil widow.' I put up with his whining about the credit card bills and the rest of it. Even let that mutt sleep on the bed. Hardly saw you at all. Gave it to him whenever he wanted it at first: 'Yes, Shickie, dear. Whatever you say, Shickie. Why don't I wear the cheerleader outfit tonight? Or, how about we play sheep and shepherd?'

"Orlando, I swear, I've still got calluses on my knees. Look." She hoisted a calf onto the table.

Orlando averted his eyes. "*¡Por Dios!*"

"You don't like that? After he left for Vegas, I closed the bank account. It had eighty-three dollars in it. The house? Mortgaged to the hilt. He's in default. Silver's gone. I found the combination to his safe—empty. He's got loan sharks after him—one called this morning. What did I get out of all this? *Debt*.

"I don't know where he is in Vegas. What if he cashed everything in and split to Rio or the Riviera?" Shaking her head. "Like *we* were supposed to?"

More head shaking, "I'd have followed him if I wasn't persona non grata in Vegas. You remember that business with the counterfeit casino chips?" She shook her head again. "Those bastards never forget."

She exhaled, a doleful sigh, pressed palms to her eyes. "God must hate me."

Orlando nodded in sympathy, gave her a long inquiring look. "You are certain of this?"

"That God hates me?"

"No, about your husband."

"Hell, yes. Orlando . . ." Rita Rae leaned over the table, gripped the edges of his blousy shirt and pulled him close, "this was a plot from the start. He's got a bundle stashed somewhere. Swiss account, Grand Cayman, under a rock in the woods. Somewhere. We've got to find him, find our money and my beautiful ring before that loan shark and whoever else he owes gets hold of him."

Orlando began cleaning his already immaculate nails with a six-inch flick knife. "I have friends in Vegas," he said. "We will find him. And if he meets with an accident? Hello, Señor Life Insurance Man . . . yes?"

2

When the ticket for the Vegas junket fell into his hands like sweet manna from heaven, Shickie knew his life was about to change, felt it in every fiber of his stubby body.

The Strip: play hard, win big. Good riddance greedy, divorcing, dog-stealing wife; buzz-off loan shark; adios heartless creditors. Shickie Doone, the Prince of Light, would once again be king of the hill in Gatlinburg, Tennessee.

"You're tapped out, pal," the L. A. mortician said, needling him. "Maybe you oughta go downstairs and play the quarter slots with what you got left." He yawned and stretched, poking skeletal arms from a baggy yellow shirt speckled with cocktail napkin nudes, walked across the room to the wet bar behind Shickie, and retrieved a half-empty bottle of bourbon. "How's about a stiff one, as we say in the trade?" He poured a double shot of booze in Shickie's glass. The mortician, seventeen hundred up, was drinking ginger ale.

On a good day, Shickie, a gnomish man in his late fifties, might have been cast as one of Sleeping Beauty's more chipper housemates. At the moment, however, following two depressing days in the casinos and three and a half hours of punishing seven card stud in a private game ten stories above the Caesar's Palace gaming floor, it appeared some vindictive poker succubus had drained the last breath from his lungs. He slumped in his chair, pale, hollowed, knuckles brushing the carpet, legs extended.

The Doones are cursed, he concluded. Thieving brother Fenster, in the clink more than he's out. Little sister Nell, who ran off at thirteen with a door-to-door Jehovah's Witness. And Ma, mean as a snake, who's never been right since Pa got drunk and fell asleep in the coconut shredder at that bakery. Sheesh. The Doones have always had bad luck, worn it around our necks like albatrosses. And if I don't shake the big bird off my shoulders, I'm burnt toast.

He massaged his temples and took a swallow of bourbon.

"I'll have a refresher myself," said the florist, a dapper eighty-year-old with a silver pompadour, still wearing his sharkskin suit jacket against the arctic chill of the Philly butcher's room. At the start of the game, when his rosebud boutonniere was still fresh, the florist had bragged how he catered flowers to mob funerals. He patted the rim of his glass, said, "Just a taste," to the mortician, and clasped his hands at the edge of the table behind his stake, fat with twelve hundred dollars of Shickie's money. He unpinned the wilted rosebud from his lapel and tossed it onto Shickie's lap. "You're done for, fella," he said with a raspy chuckle. "But before you go, tell us again about that mansion in Memphis."

Shickie sighed. "Gatlinburg, not Memphis. Memphis is where Elvis was from. Gatlinburg is where I'm from. And whilst I was too modest to call it so, mansion is the correct word. The columns on my front porch originally graced the Parthenon—that's a famous temple in Athens, Greece, you Philistine bloodsuckers."

"Philistine?" said the butcher, a ponderous, slow-moving cigar smoker with a florid complexion, brushy brows, and a glossy cranium. His winnings, some twenty-one hundred in casino chips and bills, also Shickie's, were arranged before him in neat stacks like the chops and cuts in his Philly display case. He cocked a furry eyebrow at the other players. "Philistines are the ones in the Bible, had that skin disease, like where their noses fell off and the prophets wouldn't have nothing to do with them, made them wander around with bags over their heads and beg for shekels." To Shickie, he said, "I saw your Parthenon. Think I never travel anywheres but Vegas? Took the wife on a European cruise. Cost me a bundle. Your Parthenon's a pile of fallen down rocks. Whatever you paid for those columns, you got screwed.

"But, what the hell, here's to you." He raised his beer bottle in a toast. "Take a licking and keep on ticking, right?"

Ever the optimist, Shickie blew stale breath through pursed lips, and sat up. "That's right. Me? Pack it in? No way. The good Lord has been testing my resolve, that's all."

"Some test," said the mortician. "All I see is twenty bucks in front of you. That all you got?"

Shickie rummaged through his pockets, retrieved two fives, four quarters, and a twenty-dollar casino chip. "Should'a brought more. Look, I've gotta get right. If one of you gentlemen would consider taking my personal check or I.O.U. . . . ."

The L.A. mortician answered by raising his middle finger, making not only a point, but a show of the star sapphire ring encircling the finger, the ring Shickie had lost three hands ago. He smooched the upraised fingertip, blew the kiss to Shickie, removed the ring, and set it before him.

The blue cabochon stared at Shickie like an unforgiving eye.

"Behold," said the florist. "The Pope's ring."

"One of his favorites," Shickie said. "A gift on account of a favor I did for the Vatican."

"The Pope's ring," said the butcher. He blew a cloud of smoke at Shickie. "You are so full of shit. Kind of like being such close pals with the king of Monaco."

"Not close pals. What I said, was, we watched the Grand Prix together. It was Princess Grace, God bless her soul, I had the relationship with."

"Was probably your good luck at cards what turned her

on," the mortician said, and then, "Listen, friend, I've enjoyed your company, but I want to play cards and you don't have enough for a hand, so why don't you pack it in?"

"Wait." Shickie rummaged under the table, emerged with his shoes. "Italian. Worth near five hundred bucks. Barely worn. Shined yesterday morning. Make me an offer."

"What size?" asked the butcher.

"Tens."

"Too small. I wear twelves."

Shickie held them up to the mortician and florist. "Corinthian leather."

The florist shook his head, but the mortician, "I wear tens," took them, worked the woven hide with his fingers, checked the laces and soles, passed the shoes quickly beneath his nose. He tried them on. "I'll take 'em off your hands as a favor. How about thirty bucks?"

"Thirty? Gimme a break."

The mortician kept the shoes and placed twenty one-dollar bills and a twenty-dollar chip on the table. "There's forty. Not a penny more."

"His generosity is contagious," said the butcher. "Tell you what. That watch of yours? I'll give you, say, a hundred for it."

"Criminy. This is a Rolex."

"You think I'd lay out that kind of mazuma for a Timex?"

Shickie ran his hand over the Rolex and shook his head. "This is my lucky watch, worth fifty times that. No way."

"Okay, how's this? Make it two hundred and call it a loan. You win, you pay me back and walk away wearing it."

"If you take the loan," the mortician added, "win or lose, I'm keeping the shoes." He held them to his chest.

"Who knows? Lady luck could smile at you," said the butcher, chewing his cigar.

Shickie said a silent prayer. Yeah, coupla good hands. Two hundred and ninety-one bucks is enough to put me back in the action. He stared at the watch for five long seconds and shut his eyes. More than enough. "Oh, hell. Here." He unlatched the watch and handed it to the butcher.

The butcher examined the face and the back, the band, put the watch to his ear, showed it to the florist, who scrutinized it and nodded. He counted off twenty ten dollar bills, pushed them across the table to Shickie, and slipped the Rolex over his thick hand. The link band was too small to latch, so he let it hang loose on his wrist.

"Let's play ball." The mortician lifted the shuffled deck. "Same game. Seven card stud. Ante up, five bucks." He added his five to the pot, said, "Third street, coming your way," and dealt two cards down, one up, around the table.

Shickie's up card was a jack of spades; the florist's, a six of spades; the butcher's, a three of clubs; and the dealer's, a ten of hearts.

The players regarded their two hole cards. Shickie curled up the end of his first, a king of hearts. He fought a grin at the second, a king of diamonds. A pocket pair.

The mortician nodded to the butcher's three. "Trey is the bring-in."

The butcher opened for five dollars. The mortician called. Shickie made it ten. The florist played with his lip a moment and called. The butcher re-raised. The mortician called. Shickie capped it. The others called.

The mortician dealt the fourth street cards, calling them out: "Ten of diamonds for the Tennessee wonder, ten of spades for Mr. FTD, six of diamonds for the big man from Philly. Dealer receives a seven of hearts. Mr. Parthenon is high with the jack."

Shickie said, "Bet ten."

"Hey," the florist said. "Tell us again how you broke the bank in Monaco."

"Not now," Shickie said.

"Was a good story. So, screw it. I'll call."

The butcher raised ten. The mortician called. Shickie re-raised and the others called.

The mortician dealt. Out came fifth street, face up. Shickie received a five of diamonds; the florist, a seven of diamonds; the butcher showed another three, a spade; and the dealer received his third heart, a three.

"Bet's to the man from Philly with a pair of treys showing."

The butcher knocked the ash from his cigar and bet out twenty. The dealer, representing a flush, raised twenty. "Forty to you," he said to Shickie, who, concerned about the dealer's possible flush but excited about his own flush draw, called. The florist stroked his chin, stared at the mortician's hearts and the butcher's treys, and said, "Fold."

The butcher banged it again. "Twenty."

The mortician called.

Idly straightening a stack of chips, the florist asked Shickie, "This mansion of yours. How many square feet did you say it is?"

"How many square feet is the White House? Hell, I don't know. Where was I? Uh . . . raise."

The butcher and mortician called.

The mortician dealt the sixth street cards. Shickie received a jack of clubs; the butcher, a five of clubs; and the mortician, an ace of spades. The mortician nodded to Shickie. "Pair of jacks bets."

Shickie, with two pairs now, kings and jacks, said, "Twenty."

"Raise," said the butcher.

"Call," said the dealer.

"Raise again," from Shickie.

The others called.

The florist rose from the table and wandered to the wet bar.

"Seventh street," the mortician said, and dealt the last, or river card, down.

Shickie lifted his card's corner and flattened it fast. He lifted the card again and gave it an appraising look—Thank you Lord! A third king.

He felt a presence at his back, spun his head, saw the florist with the bourbon bottle two feet away, leaning over him.

"Thought you might like a refill."

"No," Shickie said, irritated, pressing the card to the table-top. Had the old man been sneaking a peek, seen the king? Come to think of it, it seemed one of them was always folding early and wandering to the bar at his back. Looking over his shoulder, the bastards. Signaling the other ones? And, what about all the booze they were sloshing his way, while the butcher stretched his beers, the florist sipped watered-down bourbon, and the mortician drank ginger ale? All of them, especially the florist, pressing him to make with the small talk, breaking his concentration. Were they a team? Splitting up their winnings after they'd picked his bones? He had met the old guy in one of the Caesar's bars. Acted, like, senile, a real pushover. Said he knew about a friendly game upstairs, just a few guys like himself. Shickie could practically hear the butcher telling the florist, "Hey, Joe, bring us up a live one."

Were the deals honest? Seemed to be, but with the booze and all the talk, would he have noticed? Sheesh!

He did pull a good hand time to time. Probably bait, to keep him on the line while they bled him, having fun with it, stringing it out.

Shickie scanned the table again. The mortician could have made his flush. The butcher showed a pair of threes, so he filled with another trey down. Neither would beat Shickie's full house. He held a lock this time, for sure.

I'll take this hand, Shickie told himself, pay off the butcher, that son of a bitch, for my Rolex and, before they sucker me back in, I'll wave goodbye and hit the door, a wiser man. Take the pot to Bellagio, jump in an honest casino game, and put myself on the comeback trail.

"Pair of jacks bets," said the mortician.

"Twenty," Shickie said.

"Make it forty," from the butcher, drawing on his cigar.

"Again," said the mortician, drumming his fingertips on the wood, no doubt nervous over the size of the pot, some seven hundred dollars.

The butcher, Shickie considered, just might hold three aces down, giving him a winning full house, but extremely improbable given the ace showing in front of the mortician. "Raise again," Shickie said.

"And again," from the butcher.

"Fold," said the dealer.

What the hell? The mortician raises and folds? What a shitty player, if he didn't have the flush. Unless he had it and got cold feet, which was also stupid this far along. Didn't add up. Maybe the bastard was bumping the pot for the butcher. Sheesh! Shickie rubbed his eyes, confused. Shouldn'a drank so much.

He moved to call, reached for the twenty dollars, and saw he had only sixteen in front of him. "Uh—"

The butcher grinned, showing big Teddy Roosevelt incisors. "You're all in. But, say," he waved the air with his cigar, trailing loops of white smoke, "you're confident, I'm confident . . . how's about I lend you another hundred for a side bet? Up the stakes a bit?"

"Sure," Shickie said, disbelieving. "I'll give you an I.O.U."

"Nah, no need to sign anything. Your word's good enough for me. Although, some collateral would be nice. Up front."

Shickie shrugged. "You vultures cleaned me out. I don't have—"

"I was thinking . . . about the shirt off your back."

"Sheesh!"

The butcher said, "Hey, you believe in your cards? Let's see skin."

Shickie wiped his forehead, nodded, and, resigned, unbuttoned his baby blue silk shirt. He shucked it and passed it to the butcher. "My lucky shirt."

The butcher placed four dollars in the pot and set two stacks of chips, a hundred each, at the side.

The mortician said, "Showtime. Best five, gents," and winked at the florist, expecting to see Shickie go down in flames.

Now it was Shickie's turn to grin. He turned up his pocket cards. "Kings full."

The florist whistled, followed by the mortician's "Sumbitch."

"Well, well," said the red-faced butcher, a hostile edge to his voice. He docked his squat cigar in the ashtray, none too gently. "Would you look at that? Our shoeless, shirtless wonder's luck has finally changed."

"I always bounce back," Shickie said.

"Hell," the butcher continued. "I thought I had a winning hand with that pair of treys showing plus two sixes." He slow-rolled his cards. "Although, wait . . . whaddaya know? It works another way. I had this four and six of clubs in the pocket on third street along with the three of clubs up, then pulled this five of clubs on sixth street, and this deuce of clubs for a river card. Let's see, two through six of clubs. What do they call that? A straight flush?"

He raised a fat palm and slapped high fives with the florist and the mortician. "What did I tell you? The shirt off his back! Both of ya owes me a Ben Franklin."

"NO!" Shickie stared for three long seconds at the string of clubs, and collapsed onto the table, scattering everything on it before flopping via the mortician's lap to the floor.

His sputtering shifted to whimpers and he clutched the butcher's pant leg, trying to pull himself upright. "Criminy," he said to the braying face peering past the big belly, "give me a hand."

Tearing from laughter, the butcher helped him to his feet.

The three players sniggered and hurled taunts as Shickie padded quickly, ignominiously, from the hotel room in his stocking feet.

As he had said, a wiser man.

3

Shickie ran from the butcher's room to snag the closing doors of a plush elevator, joining the more genteel company of a heavy-boned transvestite in a pink sequin cocktail gown and half a dozen inebriated conventioneers throwing her passes. On the way down, he wiggled a toe through one of the holes in his thin silk socks and cursed softly over the gangbang he'd received from the trio in the room above.

Disgorged into the Caesar's Palace lobby, he joined the pressing crowd migrating to the labyrinthine, gonging, dinging, and neon-blinking vastness of the casino.

"Yeowch!" A dagger of pain shot through his foot and up his spine. He grabbed an ankle; fell to the carpet, onto his back. He extracted the quarter-inch post of a cheap, dime-size pearl earring from the flesh of his big toe and flung it in a flash of anger. He drew momentary satisfaction from the yelp of an elderly slots player who swatted her neck and hurled withering looks at a passing Shriner.

Shickie giggled. Out of control, he rocked on his back like a flipped tortoise, nearly wetting his pants, until a deep "Sir?" gave him pause. He cocked an eyebrow at a looming six-and-a-half-foot Roman centurion, bare-breasted as was Shickie, although deeply tanned, far more fit, and carrying a spear to boot. The centurion jabbed Shickie in the ribcage with the spear's rubber point to assure his attention.

Shickie assumed a doleful look. "*Et tu*, Brute?"

The centurion boosted Shickie to his feet. "It's not polite to throw things at our guests, sir. Perhaps we've done a bit too much celebrating? What say we help you to your room."

Shickie tried to shake free. "Fine with me," he said. "I'm at the Kabul Wonderland. How about a piggyback ride over there, since I ripped up my toe on your crummy carpet?"

The centurion gave Shickie's shoulder a meaningful squeeze and nodded toward a distant point in the seemingly infinite arena. "Exit's that way. Best you move along. If you can't make it, I'll see you get some help—understand?"

Shickie left the centurion speaking into his spear handle, and limped through the gamers. He paused to massage his throbbing toe, gave a quick one-finger salute to an eye in the sky, and resumed his trek to a camouflaged exit. He finally emerged from the casino into waning daylight and boarded a raised and canopied moving sidewalk. Under the stony gaze of colossal, ersatz Roman statuary, he glided over an ocean of parked automobiles toward Vegas Boulevard.

At the conveyor's end, he emerged from the sidewalk canopy into late afternoon sunlight. He blinked, stumbled, went afoul of surging pedestrians, and tripped over a stroller. To the sound of parental wails, a toddler rolled west, Shickie Doone, east.

Shickie came to rest, chest to concrete, face over the gutter, nose to a windblown brochure for out-call Asian coeds. Staring at a blurry Filipina bottom speckled with windblown grit and street grime, he sobbed.

"There, there," said a soothing voice. A gentle hand cupped his elbow, helping him to sit, and pressed a religious tract in his palm: *Gamble on Earth, Roast in Hell.* "You look like you could use some guidance, friend."

Shickie squinted at a gathering crowd and, closer, at a rawboned fellow with a toothy smile, a too-small navy suit, a clip-on tie, and a black Bible wedged under one arm. The man spoke again, raising his voice so the gawkers as well as the sinner could hear. "Except a man be born again, he cannot see the kingdom of God. Verily, verily, I say unto thee—"

Shickie interrupted. "Ah, a preacher." He struggled to his feet and shook the extended hand. "I, too," he said, "am a man of the cloth. Indeed, some call me Messiah."

"Blasphemer!" The sidewalk evangelist snatched the tract from Shickie's hand and commenced shouting, scattering onlookers like chickens from a hatchet-happy farmer. "The *beast* and the *false prophet* shall be tormented day and night for *ever* and *ever*. They *shall* be cast into the pit of *fire*." He poked a finger into Shickie's bare chest. "*Thy* end approaches, sinner."

"Sheesh," Shickie sighed, "lighten up." He wriggled away and disappeared into the throng, limping through the shadows of casino towers striping Vegas Boulevard to his hotel, the posh new Kabul Wonderland. Every now and then he hopped and cursed as he stepped on a stone.

Half an hour later he slid the key card through the door lock and entered his voluptuous, comped room. He took a deep breath of cool crisp air smelling faintly of imported soaps. His eyes came to rest on a bowl of fresh fruit and a gargantuan silver chalice chilling a bottle of French champagne. "Ahhh," he said, "home, sweet home." They had even opened the bottle for him. Two Belgian chocolates and a crystal glass rested beside it.

Shickie removed the loosened cork, poured himself a glass, downed it fast, and followed that with a second, savored more slowly. "You deserve this nectar, my boy," he assured himself, "with all those hounds at your heels."

He turned on the TV, set the bottle and glass on the coffee table, sank into a plush divan, and rebounded with an "Ouch!" as the Rolex in his right trouser pocket—deftly recovered from the butcher's wrist during his theatrical collapse—pinched his thigh. Shuffling through his pockets, he retrieved a handful of the players' bills and chips, the watch, and his star sapphire ring.

Alas, Shickie Doone was still up to his chin stubble in debt.

A tad woozy, he toasted a perky Vanna White smiling from a Wheel of Fortune rerun: "All Shickie Doone asks from this world, honey, is to strike it big, get away to a palm-shaded island, and enjoy the good life. What am I doing wrong?"

With a vapid smile, Vanna turned her back to him and spun the big wheel. Shickie lifted the remote and zapped her into the ether. "Philistine."

He swigged a glass of champagne with a chocolate truffle chaser, poured more, and wobble-walked to the wide windows overlooking the rising blaze of the Strip. Beyond, rust-hued smog obscured the distant mountains, dyeing the setting sun an even deeper red. Feeling disturbingly rocky, Shickie gripped the sill with his left hand. With his right, he raised the glass in a disdainful toast to his adversaries, and drank deeply. "Shickie Doone may be down, but he's not out."

"I wouldn't bet on that," someone said at his back.

Shickie spun on his heels. The motion set his head whirling. He tried to speak, but his tongue had turned to cotton. His vision shimmered and dimmed. He sunk to his knees and slumped to the carpet, awash in a midnight sea of vertigo.

4

Ginger Rodgers peered from a thick stand of mountain laurel across the road at the Prince of Light's Gatlinburg home, thirty feet up the mountain. Still only one light on. She moved forward, crouched behind a parked car, well shaded from the streetlamp. "I am *not* a stalker," she assured herself.

Wobbling on the first spike heels she had worn in a dozen years, an image flashed before her eyes of herself at eleven years old, gliding across the linoleum with her mother in their made-over garage rec room. Her father, as usual, had passed out on the recliner, a bottle cradled at his chest. Young Ginger wore the blue satin dance gown her mother had made for her confirmation. She spun on her little girl pumps, wavering as usual, while mommy, in formal Fred Astaire drag, hair slicked back, lifted Ginger's hand and led her into a fox-trot turn.

"Steady, for chrissakes," mommy urged in her Fred Astaire voice. "Don't be such a klutz. Be a *star*, baby."

Ginger did her best. She had the looks, or so men told her, but the rest of it? How many times had she watched those old movies with hopes her namesake's verve would rub off? Maybe that D in Ginger's last name stood for Doomed. Doomed to be a nobody. One letter away from being a star.

Ginger *had*, however, talked herself into tonight's daring adventure, and that counted for something, didn't it?

She had first seen the Prince a scant three Sundays ago during a sermon in the hilltop Temple of Light, a former National Guard armory overlooking touristic Gatlinburg. She knew from that moment their destinies were linked. So far, the nearest she had been to him was forty feet, standing in the third row of the choir loft. Although, during services (and in her apartment, many times since), she had visualized walking right up to him after the closing prayer and telling him, in the same no-nonsense way Madonna told Juan Peron in *Evita*, how very good she would be for him.

The Prince was Ginger's man, her Fred Astaire. He just didn't know it yet.

At eight, Ginger had wanted to become a saint (the not-being-Catholic part seemed less an obstacle than her mother's aversion to "fish eaters"). In high school, she joined every club and activity that would have her. After graduation, she dearly wanted to labor on a kibbutz in Israel with the sun-bronzed Chosen, but her mother put a stop to that ("It's all Jews over there, baby—no gentility.") In college, University of Tennessee, she had thrown herself into T.M., even considered transferring to Marharishi U. She joined the Hare Krishnas, but the chanting and begging had been too embarrassing. She had, in turn, wandered in and out of numerology, reflexology, and astrology, and would have gotten into phrenology if she hadn't been a hundred years too late.

Ginger had yet to become a star, or, for that matter, to find a constellation she could call home. She was twenty-nine. Three months ago, she moved to Sevier County, Tennessee, the birthplace of Dolly Parton, for inspiration. Dolly possessed the sweetest voice Ginger had ever heard, sweeter than any angel in heaven, and Ginger loved to sing. She sensed a connection. Mere weeks ago, she heard about the Children of Light, popularly known as the Fireflies, and their choir, the finest in Sevier County. Ginger promptly joined their number.

The Firefly congregation was over a hundred and growing fast. They believed their leader, the Reverend Shickleton Doone, the Prince of Light, was a great prophet, perhaps the second Messiah. The Prince performed miracles, turned staffs into snakes, produced coins from thin air, even sent a goat to the Holy Land in a poof of smoke. And, wow, could he sing. Ginger knew her destiny and the Prince's were intertwined the moment she laid eyes on him.

The cornerstone of the Prince's message was that the Rapture was imminent. The Rapture: the spontaneous teleportation of the Worthy from earth to heaven—leaving clothing, possessions, pets, undeserving friends and family, and sinners of every stripe behind, to face seven hard years of the Tribulation, the rise of the Antichrist and, ultimately, Armageddon, the final battle between good and evil. As the Prince had so often reminded his congregation, he knew all along the Rapture would occur not at the turn of the millennium, as so many had expected, but later, at the convergence of strange weather, a shooting star, and trouble in the Middle East. And, in Gatlinburg, Tennessee.

Ginger tugged unconsciously at her micromini and adjusted her bra, smoothed the snug white cashmere sweater, refluffed her long, wavy blond hair and, Good Lord, there he was. The Prince of Light himself. Standing on the narrow walk across the street, admiring his house. As well he might, Ginger thought. Graceland itself was hardly more impressive. The Prince's home looked like something out of *Gone with the Wind*, almost.

Although the two-story house had been built along the lines of a Swiss chalet by a once flush, now gone-bust used car salesman, the Prince had added four impressive, fifteen-foothigh white fiberglass columns and a long plantation porch across the front.

The Prince approached the wide central stairway, casting

wary looks left and right. Surely, he didn't know she was here, did he?

Time to move, Ginger told herself, before he gets to the door and disappears inside.

High above, a dark cloud scudded across a crescent moon, drenching the landscape in ink. One of Ginger's hands went to her hair and worried an errant wisp as she remembered the words her mother had repeated over and over: "Men are lecherous bastards, baby. Stay away from them."

Ginger shook away the memory, took a deep breath, clacked the heels of her red pumps together three times for luck, and stepped from the bushes. She wobbled across the asphalt, accelerating, because the Prince was already halfway up the stairs.

The plan called for this to be a coincidental meeting. As the Prince worked the key in the lock, Ginger cleared her throat, wondering if the "I could be good for you" line might be premature.

Startled, he wheeled to face her. "Who the hell are you?"

A mere two paces away, Ginger lost her nerve and her voice. She blinked, rocked on her heels, and stared at the porch floor.

She forced herself to look up. "Uh . . ." He was shorter than she remembered, although it was difficult to judge during service at the Temple of Light, because he usually stood alone. He looked younger in person, too. Not Rhett Butler, but not unattractive either with the long hair, although his nose looked bigger this close, and it had a wart on the side, and there was another one in his eyebrow, making the hair stand out funny, and . . .

The Prince looked angry. "I said, 'Who the hell are you?' Are you alone?" He looked both ways along the porch, anxious, peering into the darkened street, and back at Ginger, accusing.

She curtsied. Curtsied? Difficult in the tight skirt, but it seemed appropriate. She wrinkled her nose at the strong, distinctive scent of Old Spice. "I'm . . . from the choir. Ginger Rodgers—that's Rodgers with a D. I was just passing by, and I saw you, sir, and I thought I'd say Hi. I know we've never been introduced, but . . ." Her voice trailed off.

The Prince's face softened. "Ah, I see." He gave her an appraising look. Admiring, no question of that, as his gaze dropped from her face to the snug sweater, the top two buttons open to reveal cleavage nicely assisted by a lacy push-up bra. Lingering, now studying the miniskirt and Ginger's legs. Good legs—she was confident of that—as good as those of the original, if not as stable. Back up to her blue eyes. Smiling now. "Never met, huh? Just wanted to say Hi?" Another glance at the street and the Prince turned the key, opened the front door, called inside, "Hello? Anybody home?"

The *wife*. Ginger hadn't thought of that. Her fleeting fear turned to anger. The witch. The ungrateful bitch. The woman who, everyone knew it, was divorcing the poor man.

One more Hello from the Prince. No one answered. Betsy, Ginger's new friend from the choir, was right. The wife must have left him already. Ginger and the Reverend were alone. Be bold. The Prince is lonely and needs companionship. No, not merely companionship, a partner, a confidant, a good woman to help him through these troubled times. In a word: me.

Apparently satisfied the house was empty, the Reverend Doone held open the door, raked the wall for the light switch, and waved Ginger inside.

She took three steps into the atrium and fell to her knees, so overwhelmed was she by the myriad spotlights bursting like lasers off polished brass, refracting through cut crystal, reflecting and re-reflecting across mirrored walls. The cold alabaster at her kneecaps nearly glowed from a heavenly white light suffusing from the high-domed, trompe l'oeil ceiling twenty feet above. She raised her eyes to cotton candy clouds and golden angels flanking a magnificent larger-than-life Michelangeloesque rendering of God, His right arm outstretched, curling forefinger about to touch an equally impressive image of the Prince of Light levitating at the other side of the dome. The resemblance was passable, if muscularly and cosmetically enhanced.

The in-the-flesh and noticeably shorter original stood at the kneeling Ginger's back, a beneficent palm cupping her blond curls. Ginger closed her eyes in anticipation of a blessing, words of welcome to the princely abode. Silence. She pressed her palms together at the point of her chin and squeezed her lids shut, awaiting a prayer. Still nothing.

The fingers tightened, rotated Ginger's head, toward Doone's right hand . . . which had unzipped his fly. Good Lord, he was waving his, his . . .

"NO!" she said.

Ginger drew a sharp breath, immediately regretting the outburst. It wasn't the prospect of sex that precipitated her exclamation—seduction was the reason for the trashy get-up, after all. But, six feet inside the door? On her knees, on hard marble, and spot-lit, with God watching from the painted clouds overhead?

This wasn't how the scenario had played out in Ginger's mind. A house tour first, perhaps a prayer, a beverage, a gentle touch leading to hesitant foreplay. Ginger mouthed another, silent No. If she acquiesced here—to this—what would it get her? A pat on the head, a breath mint, and cab fare home, while the sated Prince retired to his bed, alone, with no more than a fleeting memory of the top of Ginger's head in the morning.

"No?" Doone repeated from three feet over Ginger's head with a touch of disappointment. His left hand dropped to his waist, his right still gripping the princely staff.

Ginger looked up, chagrined, confused, fearful he would point to the door, still ajar, and send her into the night. Her plan included more than doing the deed with the Prince: she planned to do it so well she would not merely spend the night, but capture his heart, install herself at the nexus of his spiritual empire, a partner at the side of the Second Messiah. Ginger would become the Princess of Light. The star her mommy always wanted her to be.

"What I meant, your Lightness," she said, exuding contrition but surprised at his lustiness (wasn't this the man who preached moderation in all things but giving?), "I meant, uh, not *here*. I need to freshen up." She rose, stood, a head taller than the Prince, nibbling her knuckle, delaying, trying not to stare at what the Prince was still holding in his right hand. Staring anyway. Her eyes moved to the stairway, traced the runner up, toward what must be—"The bedroom. I'll go to the bedroom. You stay here."

"Freshen up?" The Prince's face brightened. "Sure."

"Which way?"

He waved the air impatiently. "Uh, go on up. You'll find it."

Ginger kissed him gently on the top of the head, catching another glimpse of the Prince's holy member, alert, eager. "Wait till I call," she said, and bounded up the stairs. She nearly stumbled entering the master bedroom, so impressive was its opulence, the flocked wallpaper, cushy carpet, round king-sized bed, the huge TV. And mirrors on the ceiling. Humbled, reminded of her modest origins, Ginger bowed her head and mouthed a short prayer to her namesake for confidence and a convincing performance.

With a guilty glance at the door, she stole an irresistible peek in the walk-in closet, that revealed only the Prince's clothing. The rumored-to-be domestically inattentive, harpy wife had either moved out or had a separate bedroom.

Ginger disrobed, folded her clothes neatly on a rococo armchair, removed from her purse a silky, micro-babydoll, pink chemise with tulle ruffles, carefully selected from a Victoria's Secret store in Knoxville. She trotted to the bathroom. A tinkle, wash-up, cosmetic check, hair combing, a spritz or two of perfume in places the Prince would appreciate, and she returned to the bed. Committed, Ginger turned down the spread. She couldn't resist a girlish bounce on the thick mattress before climbing between the slick silk sheets.

She lay still for a moment, heart racing, arms pressed to her sides, sheet top ticking her chin, legs stiffly together. Loosen up! She rearranged herself, opting this time for stacked, fluffed pillows, sheets loose at her waist, and a side-ways, legs-and-arms-akimbo pose. She regarded herself in the ceiling mirror. Better. She adjusted her curls on the pillow and took a deep breath, wondering whether the Prince would be disappointed.

Who would have thought the tall, dark, and handsome Prince Charming of her youth would turn out to be the not-so-tall, not-so-handsome Prince of Light? Ginger made a final adjustment to the sheets, hiked her chemise higher than thigh-high, moistened her lips, cleared her throat, and called down-stairs. "Yoo-hoo, I'm reaaa-dy."

5

oone's gaze skipped by the young woman's rocking ankles as she climbed the stairs and glided up her oh-so-long legs to barely hidden cheeks, rolling like two mega Ben-wa balls under her snug miniskirt. He whistled softly. The moment she disappeared into the second floor hallway, he wrestled his boxers over his still-saluting erection, kicked off his shoes, removed his socks, shed his shirt, and loosened his trousers, dropping them and his boxers to his ankles.

"Let me tell you, brother," he said, standing in the buff over the jumble of clothes at his feet, the Las Vegas incident forgotten, "*this* is some homecoming."

He rocked, shifting his weight from one bare foot to the other, awaiting the call from above the stairs. He checked the Rolex on his wrist. Three minutes. Another minute passed, yet another. How could the girl take so long to get out of that skimpy skirt and sweater and pull down the sheets? He could have her stripped and on her back in twenty seconds, tops. He tap-tapped the crystal of the watch impatiently.

"Yeowch!" said an electrified Doone, as a pair of vice-grips clamped his elbows and lifted him, kicking and protesting, six inches off the marble floor.

"Quiet," said a compelling voice at his ear. "Mr. Trout wants to talk to you about the money you owe."

"Who?" Still kicking, twisting to see *who* the hell held him, *who* had spoken. Three men. Young. One, skinny and pimply, with weasel's teeth, a see-through goatee, and a shaved head. Beside him, a short, fat, freckled, country boy with bowl-trimmed red hair, the stick of a lollipop protruding from his chubby pink lips. The third, a poster boy for anabolic steroids, the one who held him, standing well over six feet. A dark pony tail swished half way down the man's back as he spun Doone toward the door and lock-stepped him outside, followed by the other two. Acne-face closed the door, which, in Doone's earlier eagerness, he had regrettably failed to close and lock.

The skinny one mocked Doone's "Who?" question in a whiny voice: "'Who-oo?' Like you don't know Thadeus Trout, huh, Doone?"

"'Trout?' Never heard of him. Let go of me, you goons." He cast a woeful glance over his shoulder in sad remembrance of the long-legged choirgirl, apparently still fooling with her lip-stick or the sheets or whatever, upstairs. "You've got the wrong man, whoever you are."

"'The wrong man?'" the whiny voice repeated. He elbowed the giant in his stomach, rippling beneath a fishnet muscle shirt. "That's what they all say come payback time. Or . . ." he poked his round companion in his soft gut with a forefinger, "How about this, Peaches? 'I've got the money, but I can't get it till tomorrow?'" He followed that with a mean squeaky chuckle. "Tell it to my old man, Doone."

"Let me go," Doone said, wriggling. "No shit, I'm not who you think I am."

"No?" the pimply-faced kid said, as they neared the side-walk and a hulking eleven-year-old Buick. "You're not Shickie Doone, the preacher-man? What are you doing in his house, then? Maybe you're the mailman, were gonna make a night deposit in your mailbox upstairs, huh? Or should I say *fee-male* box?" His buddies got a chuckle out of that.

"I'm . . . I'm an interior decorator," Doone said. "Checking out the decorating. Pierre LeFay, that's me. People whose house this is, they're on vacation, gave me the key."

"A decorator. Buck naked. You and your babe was gonna do the bedroom over, huh?" More guffawing.

"We're engaged. I know it's not right in somebody else's house, but, hell, you boys have fooled around like that, haven't you? I swear, I'm not—who is it?—Sticky Dune? I swear on my mother's grave. . . ."

Peaches, the pink pudgy one, pulled the sucker from his lips. "Should I cut his ear off, Junior?"—referring to Junior Trout, the skinny one giving orders. Peaches withdrew a thirteen-inch bowie knife from a sheath at his waist and sliced air.

Junior gave him a look. "What did my old man say? 'Bring him back in one piece.'"

Junior paused at the rear door of the Buick, considering what his father had really said: "Get Shickie Doone from this address, and don't fuck up."

"Just to be *sure* we got the right man this time," Junior said to Peaches. "Run back in and get me his wallet. Doone's pants was on the floor." He turned to the giant. "Hold Doone's arm out, Six-pack." Anticipating the breaking of a radius or ulna, Six-pack, the new man of the trio and anxious to please, complied, but Junior merely relieved Doone of his Rolex. The star sapphire ring was too big for Junior's spindly fingers, so he placed it on his thumb.

While Peaches rooted through Doone's trousers inside, Six-pack, pinioning Doone against the side of the Buick, added, "Best be sure. If we fuck up again, your father swore he'd run our hands through the taffy masher."

Junior gave Six-pack his practiced Clint Eastwood stare. "That wasn't our fault. The other time neither, so don't say 'fuck up' or you're gonna piss me off."

"You're fucking up again," Doone said. "Because I'm not your man."

Peaches returned with the wallet. Junior stuffed the bills in his pocket. "Thanks," he said, "I've had my eye on a Hard Rock Cafe leather jacket, and this'll just about cover it." He flipped open the wallet and perused the contents. "Credit cards, the rest? Every one says Shickleton Doone. You little shit." He hit Doone across the back of the head.

"Ouch! Look, I swear, this is a mistake—"

Six-pack pitched him unceremoniously onto the back seat. Junior took shotgun, Six-pack curled an arm around Doone's shoulders, while Peaches drove.

.

"Hell-o-oo . . . Your Lightness?" Ginger yoo-hooed again from the master bedroom; her chemise, the sheets, arranged just so.

No answer, no padding footsteps on the carpeted stairs, no heavy breathing at the door. Ginger felt her leg twitch, watched her carefully positioned fingers atop her thigh form a nervous fist. Perhaps her lover-to-be was in the little boys' room downstairs, washing up, checking himself in the mirror. Probably standing on tippy-toes, trying to look taller. Ginger giggled at that. Shame on me, she thought. Be positive, Ginger. He's no Tarzan, but does have that pretty, long black hair. His sermons are better than those screamers on TV, and the man sings like an angel. He's an inspiration to the congregation and choir. And . . . he *is* the Prince of Light.

Her palms grew moist at the thought of coupling with the second Messiah. She shifted in the big cushy bed and called once more, louder. "Your Lightness?"

Nothing.

"YOUR LIGHTNESS?" She sat up, threw her bare legs over the edge of the bed, and gazed at the silent hallway. Ten long seconds passed. What if he had changed his mind? Ginger stood, wrapped her sweater around her shoulders, and took tentative steps toward the door. She poked her head into the hallway and looked both ways. No Prince. "Your Lightness?"—toward the stairwell. No answer.

She tiptoed to the head of the stairs and peered down. Clothing. The Prince's. Heaped in a pile on the marble floor where she had left him waiting. Ginger trotted down the stairs, her heart thumping, and called again, knowing there would be no answer. The front door was closed, the house empty. Ginger was alone. She stared at the boxers, the shoes, socks, trousers, and shirt, lying where they had fallen, and realized what had happened. She put a hand to her mouth, fell to her knees, and gaped at the ceiling's trompe l'oeil heaven.

"Good God!" she said, less as an exclamation than an incantation. "The Rapture has begun."

6

Jimmy Feather sat on the roof of his thirteen-year-old pickup, his worn boot heels hooked over the rim of the galvanized cattle trough in the truck's bed. In the dimming light he watched the Clarion Grampus, a three-foot reddish porpoise, circle the confines of the saltwater tank, swimming round and round, as it had since its capture the day before. "No way out, little guy," he said.

As it had done each time Jimmy spoke, the Grampus stopped its circuit, poked its blunt snout from the water, stared at Jimmy intently, and chattered: a staccato series of whistles, pops and crackles as mysterious and unintelligible as alien broadcasts from deep space.

"Sorry, I no speak porpoise," Jimmy said with an insincere chuckle. He raised his eyes to the gray clouds and buttoned his Levi jacket against the chilling air. Jimmy had a pretty good idea what the Grampus was trying to tell him.

The red globe of the sun, momentarily visible through a hole in the overcast western sky, sputtered as it dropped behind pines silhouetted on a distant ridge overlooking the Pacific. In the darkened valley below, two pale yellow rectangles defined the cabin where Jimmy's friends, nine young

Mahak Indians, argued over the form of the approaching ritual—a ritual they imagined their forefathers might have followed a century before at the conclusion of a sea hunt.

Jimmy, being Indian, a brother under the skin, but of
uncertain origin, was excluded from the inner sanctum and
served as guard tonight. His pickup, housing the Grampus,
was poised on a rise in the rough, double-track road, high
enough to give clear view of the cabin and approaching headlights from the distant highway. At this secreted location, however, there was slim chance of any trouble from the
environmental obstructionists who had done their best—and
failed—to deny the Mahak their heritage.

The Mahak Brotherhood was the local branch of ARM, the
AmerIndian Resistance Movement, a small but radical band of
angry young men. Jimmy's father, Jimmy knew, would have
approved, because his father had been a great chief.

His mother had been a red-haired, freckle-faced
Appalachian woman named Maggie McDowd from east Tennessee. She fell in love with his dad in a whirlwind romance in
Nashville. Her lover left town, never to be seen again, and she
turned up pregnant. She raised Jimmy in east Tennessee until
her death in a mountain flood twelve years later. After that, her
father, Jimmy's Grandpop, took Jimmy under his wing.
Jimmy's mother never revealed his dad's tribal affiliation or
even his name, referring to him only as the Chief.

Jimmy inherited his mother's light skin and gray eyes,
although his Grandpop thought he and Jimmy's mother had
Indian blood on their side, too. Jimmy inherited the Chief's
black hair and wanderlust, along with half an Indian head
penny, a gift to Jimmy's mother the night she and the Chief
met at a Nashville bluegrass bar. When Jimmy's mother
pressed the coin into Jimmy's hand on his tenth birthday, she
told him the Chief had found it walking the battlefield of the
Little Big Horn. "Never lose it, Jimmy, it will bring you luck."
Jimmy had worn the coin at his neck ever since.

Geographically, Jimmy's father might have been Eastern
Band Cherokee, but with only a nickname to go on, Jimmy had

been unable to link him to the Smoky Mountain reservation. The penny suggested Sioux or Cheyenne, the great warriors of the Plains, but Jimmy had traveled the West and come up with no leads.

At sixteen, he christened himself Jimmy Feather, said good-bye to his Grandpop and set out on a quest for identity. He had been among the most vocal of Native Americans picketing the white museums, calling for return of ancestral bones. After the Native American Grave Protection and Repatriation Act of 1990, when the issue of bones and burial artifacts became moot, Jimmy joined the fight for casino gambling on tribal lands. He jumped from one cause to another: Columbus Day celebrations, sports logos, cable reruns of cowboy and Indian movies, and, most recently, the Mahak protest. When his pockets ran empty or his spirits low, he headed back to Tennessee to see his Grandpop, recharged in the cool green hills, and again hit the warpath.

A month before, he linked with the Mahak Brotherhood after hearing about the Clarion Grampus on an ARM buddy's car radio in Medicine Bow, Wyoming.

Jimmy turned up his collar at the misting rain, glanced at the tank, and was greeted immediately with clicks and whistles. He hunched his shoulders and looked away from the glistening puppy-like eyes. He stared at the overcast sky. Though it would no doubt be obscured, the first sliver of the new moon would rise tonight behind those clouds. This, everyone agreed, was the night the ancestors would have chosen. The only uncertainty—the matter Jimmy's compadres debated at this moment—was how to dispatch their vocal prize, and what to do with it after.

Unfortunately, the most wizened of the tribal elders had no recollection of the ancestral Clarion Grampus hunt, no idea of the rituals surrounding the kill, no memory, in fact, of the miniature porpoise at all. Indeed, the elders had little interest in the Grampus, being more concerned with such mundane matters as the declining salmon catch, developing a website, and replacing the leaky roof on the tribal headquarters.

Jimmy had listened to (but had not joined) the Brotherhood's debate held over a dinner of cold pizza and brews. From the start, they agreed they would mount the tail on a high pole on the shore as testimony to the Mahak victory, but as to the form of sacrifice, there was no consensus. The favored options: spear the porpoise, cut out its heart and eat slices of the warm meat. Or, club and skin it, then dry strips of its flesh in the sun and make a ceremonial rattle from its hide. Or, simply shoot it and roast the carcass over an open fire. No one had tasted Grampus meat, but the Brotherhood agreed that everyone, Jimmy, too, would partake of at least a mouthful, cooked, or à la sushi.

Until the previous year, no one realized the Clarion Grampus was a distinct species. The small porpoises sighted occasionally in the remote, nearly landlocked and seldom-visited Thunder Bay were assumed to be merely oddly patterned juveniles of the common Bottlenose Dolphin and were ignored. Then, an oceanographer from Seattle routinely dissected a small female found dead on the shore, and discovered, to her considerable surprise, six near-term embryos, proving her subject was hardly a young Bottlenose, but the adult of a species entirely new to science. The researcher's conclusion was confirmed by DNA analysis, and she duly described the miniature porpoise and its restricted range, Thunder Bay, Washington, in a scientific journal.

As new marine mammals are worthy news, the Northwest media sent videographers in a chartered fishing boat to Thunder Bay, hoping for a sighting. They got more than that. To the delight of the cameramen, when their craft stopped to reconnoiter, two Clarions surfaced within minutes, poked their snouts from the water and began what was now known coast-to-coast as the "Clarion Call," an animated chatter that witnesses swore was an attempt at conversation. It wasn't long before zoolinguists and their computers attempted translations. Zodiacs chock full of the curious crowded the cold waters, leading to a booming tourist industry on the hitherto pristine shore, and environmentalists began protesting the commercialization of Thunder Bay. This led to a declaration of the Clarion Grampus as an endangered species.

The tiny Grampus made national news, but had there been more than passing mention of the nearby Mahak?

To rectify that omission, the Mahak Brotherhood proclaimed sovereignty over Thunder Bay and announced a Grampus hunt, endangered species be damned. Media cameras and microphones materialized as if by magic.

Environmentalists protested. Greenpeace, Fish and Wildlife, the Coast Guard, PETA, the Cousteau Society, and Friends of Animals sent boats to Thunder Bay to guard the Grampus. The Brotherhood and an aggressive young attorney turned to Congress. Though there was no tribal recollection of the Grampus, no myths recording hunts, no ceremonial objects constructed of Grampus skin, tooth, or bone, the Brotherhood found several worn rock carvings in nearby hills they believed proved the Grampus was integral to Mahak religion. The carvings consisted of several fishy forms, a circle, obviously a ritual drum, and a humanoid figure, no doubt a shaman. Environmentalists said "no way," but several influential Congressmen, sensing publicity and a cost-effective nod to ethnic sensibilities, pushed through a bill granting the Brotherhood the right to capture or kill one Clarion Grampus and do with it as they wished. One. Thereafter, the species would remain securely protected and on the endangered list.

So, ironically guarded by a Coast Guard ship under Congressional orders and in clear view of an armada of environmentalist and media vessels, the Mahak Brotherhood had motored into Thunder Bay in a fiberglass skiff to claim their prize. No sooner had they stopped, than a small Grampus greeted them with its Clarion Call. Harpoon and firearms were set aside for a simple net, since motoring away with a *live* Clarion Grampus to an uncertain fate would prolong both media attention and the anguish of the Save the Whalers.

Lost in deep thought, Jimmy nearly missed the cabin window lights go dark, followed by three on-off blinks of a flashlight to signal a decision had been reached.

"Looks like this is it, little fella," Jimmy said, his gaze vacant but still on the shadowed cabin. With a dry swallow, he stole a glance at the truck bed, hopeful the Clarion would be making its round at the far end of the tank.

Jimmy winced as the Clarion chirped, clicked, and whistled a foot below Jimmy's truck roof perch. Its head rose from the water, eyes locked on Jimmy's. It ducked under the surface, rose half out of the water, its tail sculling anxiously, chattering even louder.

Jimmy pressed his palms to his ears and jumped to the ground. A minute later he slid behind the wheel and, as previously agreed, flashed the headlights three times at the cabin in acknowledgement of the Brotherhood's signal. He started the engine, drove forward slowly in waning twilight, lights off as he had been directed so as not to alert potential enemies scanning the area.

Jimmy slowed to an idle. He looked over his shoulder at the darkened truck bed, to the left at the cabin, and turned the wheel hard right, toward the highway.

He left the light off until he reached asphalt, then drove thirty-one miles to the launching ramp at Thunder Bay. There, he dropped the tailgate and backed his truck slowly into the water until the galvanized tank shifted, briefly floated, and submerged.

With a single swish of its tail, the Clarion Grampus disappeared.

Jimmy stepped from the cab, reached inside to release the handbrake, sending the truck, too, into the cold murky depths of Thunder Bay. The old pickup would never have made it home anyway. He stood staring at the choppy black water until he heard the familiar Clarion Call, a chattering goodbye, fifty feet out.

Jimmy put two fingers in his mouth and whistled back. "Take care, little guy," he said, and walked to the highway to hitch a ride back to East Tennessee for a long talk with his Grandpop.

7

unior, Peaches, and Six-pack, with their nude captive, stopped before a steel-walled warehouse, "Great Smoky Foods—World's Best Beef Jerky," wedged between a mountain and the rear of a motel in downtown Gatlinburg. Junior pressed buttons on a pad. A truck-sized rolling door rose squeakily and closed after admitting them. The trio, with their captive, stopped short of Thadeus Trout's office to let Junior test the waters for turbulence, Mr. Trout being known for his tempestuous moods. They hovered by the door.

Trout, a principal supplier of fast if usurious loans to the East Tennessee financially needy, and orchestrator of truck hijackings throughout southern Appalachia, was on the phone with a militiaman, touting the shelf life of freeze-dried meat. Great Smoky Foods, purveyors to the restaurant industry, also supplied hikers, hunters, and survivalists with freeze-dried victuals suited equally for trail or bunker.

"Will it keep for ten years?" Trout was saying. "Shee-it, yes. You ever see those Egyptian mummies, how good they look? How old you think *they* are?" His dewlap and prodigious jowls flapped with the enthusiasm of a bloodhound on the prowl. Trout's normally pallid facial flesh, speckled with brown liver spots, flushed pink. "Too *high?* How much you think electricity for refrigeration would cost over ten years? As if there'll be any power after NATO invades . . ."

Junior backed away, awaiting a lull in the storm. Mr. Trout took this food business far too seriously for Junior. His father's other straight-Joe enterprises—Mr. T's Fudge Shoppe on the Gatlinburg strip, Moccasins! Moccasins! and the Truck-to-Trunk outlet store in Pigeon Forge, had been acquired to cleanse tainted loot from Mr. Trout's less public endeavors. Laundering made sense to Junior, but why did his father get so worked up over business like some nine-to-five asshole? And his daddy's favorite toy: the Bible Alive Museum, Gatlinburg's star attraction, a four-story, former mattress factory reconfigured as a Babylonian pyramid at the top of the hill, in front of the old armory. All the profits from Mr. Trout's other enterprises, legal or larcenous, were finding their way into that sinkhole. "This is the Biggie," Trout reminded Junior at least a hundred times a day, followed by, "Do you know what the most read book in the world is?" (Junior would always respond, "The phone book?" just to piss him off.) Trout pretended not to hear, would say, "Before you know it, they'll be calling me the Walt Disney of religion. There's gold in the Bible, boy, and I intend to mine it."

The only other thing that motivated Junior's father was bowling. Bowling! Junior shot a dirty look at the trophies. There must be a hundred. In what was once a supply room to the side of the office, Trout had installed a shrine. Photos of famous bowlers and old score cards papered the walls. The ball that garnered Trout a perfect game in the Hoinke Classic in Cincinnati thirty-one years before, sat on an altar. The sacred ball was flanked by two pins, which once formed a formidable 7-10 split, snake eyes. In another memorable tourney, Trout had picked off not only that split, but (back in the days of pin spotters) sent one of the holy pins flying into the pin boy's roost, knocking him down and out, too. That stunning spare-plus-spotter garnered Thadeus Trout immortality in the

International Museum of Bowling and Hall of Fame in St. Louis, Missouri.

Screw bowling. What gave Junior a hard-on was thrilling, high-profit criminal action involving hot women, guns, and the infliction of pain. That, alas, was seldom more than a dream. Even his father's hijackings were tame. Mr. Trout bribed the drivers to pull onto a back road pretending to be lost, allowing Junior's crew to tie them up. Junior and his men were no more than porters, hefting boxes from one truck to another. Rare was the pleasant task of punishing a deadbeat. When Mr. Trout wanted somebody gone, did he tap Junior? No. He phoned the Hammer.

Junior wanted to move to Vegas, run a string of hookers and contract killers like the Hammer, but Mr. Trout had steadfastly refused, maintaining that competition in Vegas was stiff, life in Gatlinburg, easy. In particular, Mr. Trout liked his bowling buddies and the clear mountain air, on account of his allergies. And the fly fishing. And—Junior felt his cheeks heat up—the goddamned straight-Joe, boring as dirt, *businesses*.

East Tennessee was painfully shy of Junior's dreams. Occasionally, he picked up some grass or coke down south, or local crank, and moved it at modest profit in Knoxville or Asheville. Recently, he bought a used bakery delivery van with high hopes of finding a hot female to work truck stops along I-75, but the women he had pitched so far lacked entrepreneurial spirit and either laughed at or slapped him. And the cathouse he had hoped to establish in Gatlinburg? Forget it. Besides the lack of employees, the male tourists were invariably chained to wives and kids, strolling the streets at night, watching fudge set up or chuckling at stupid-ass tee shirts in the crappy shops. Most of the straight-laced kids probably never smoked a joint, so forget that idea, too. Gatlinburg, Junior had concluded, had to be the cleanest, most boring, white-bread town in America.

Thadeus Trout slammed his hand on the desk, breaking Junior's bleak train of thought, and then went sotto voce, waxing friendly to the phone. "Let me check inventory, maybe

I can do you a little better." He punched the hold button and motioned Junior forward. "Big freeze-dried meat order here, enough to bind up twenty-three camo assholes for a decade. Gonna work 'em for enough nine millimeter ammo to wage another World War Two before I'm finished." He squinted into the darkened warehouse (ever thrifty, Trout was not one to waste electricity on light not needed). "You got Doone, fuck-up?"

Only three days before, on his father's orders, Junior and his crew had thrown a blanket over the head of the captain of an opposing bowling team in Mr. Trout's league. They snatched the man off the sidewalk like hawks on a bunny, fingering him by the bowling ball bag he was carrying, and threw him into the back seat of the old Buick. Peaches sat on his chest while Six-pack, the new man, broke their victim's middle finger with a summary explanation, "Bowl below your average in the finals." As a last insult, they kept his bowling ball, a purple and teal, El Niño Gold and presented it to Mr. Trout as proof of a mission completed.

Now, *that* was fun.

Unfortunately, the damaged digit belonged to the wrong man. Mr. Trout immediately recognized the initials on the El Niño Gold ball as belonging to the captain—woe!—of Mr. Trout's own team. Junior lost the keys of his Camaro and was assessed a twenty-five-hundred-dollar fine.

"We got Doone, all right," Junior said, and, with a victorious grin, waved to Six-pack and their victim in the shadows beyond the doorway. Six-pack moved forward. Spot-lit by Mr. Trout's desk lamp, he lifted their small hostage by the upper arms, swaying him side to side, puppet-like, so the boss could see they really had him.

Trout glanced up, squinting, not having the correct glasses perched on his ample nose. Apparently unfazed by Doone's nudity, he gave a grunt in acknowledgement.

"We're gonna start with the fudge torture," Junior was saying to their captive. "Make you eat till you go red in the face and puke—"

Trout shook his head and pointed to a glowing corridor in the dark recess of the warehouse. "No. I'm due at the Civic Center for league bowling in twenty minutes—for what that's worth, with our captain out with a broken finger.

"Throw Doone in the meat locker overnight to show him I mean business."

"Yes, sir." Junior back-stepped from the office. Six-pack had a muscled arm around Doone's chest, squelching his "wrong man" pleadings with python-like contractions.

"Hey guys!" Peaches called from the break room, a hundred feet away, glowing with a television's flickering blue light. "The game's on. I've got a case of beer and a sack of freeze-dried pork rinds. Hurry it up."

Junior moved to join him, relaying his father's instruction to the new man, Six-pack. "Throw Doone in the meat locker—down that long hall, runs along the loading bays, big ass door, can't miss it. Think you can handle that yourself?"

"No problem." Six-pack hoisted Doone over his shoulder and walked to the hallway, oblivious of the small bare feet furiously kicking his back, or of the, by now, boringly repetitious, "Let me go, goddammit. You've got the wrong man."

Six-pack saw the word FREEZE on the round, stainless steel door halfway down the corridor, sparsely lit by half-burnt-out fluorescent lights. The door was impressive, not unlike the entry to a bank vault, but with clusters of hoses, pipes, and gauges. He swung it open, pitched the little man inside, shouldered the door closed, spun the big wheel at the center to seat it, and pushed a big red button labeled ON to be sure Doone got his butt sufficiently chilled. A bright LED flashed INITIATE CYCLE.

Not being much on details or reading, Six-pack failed to notice the other words bracketing the "FREEZE" . . . ACME EVERLAST FREEZE DRIER.

Leaving the chugging, whirring, and kerthunking of relays and pumps behind, Six-pack trotted back to the break room, to his comrades, a case of Bud, and the game.

Inside the ten- by ten-foot steel-walled chamber, growing

chillier by the second, Doone scampered, looking for egress. He pounded on the door, tugged at copper pipes, brass valves, and steel ventilation grates, all disappointingly solid. "Holy shit!" he said, and jumped at the sight of a skunk, a pink-nosed possum, and a sitting-up, bandit-faced raccoon, dead still, secured with stiff wire harnesses. Once more, even louder, he shouted, "LET ME OUT . . . YOU'VE GOT THE WRONG MAN," but the cold metal walls flung the words back at him. He slapped at his bare goose-fleshed shoulders, chafed his chilling blue thighs, climbed from the icy floor onto a low wooden shelf lined with racks of meat to one side, baskets of strawberries to the other, and curled into a teeth-chattering, fetal crouch.

Even before the indicator on the dial at the center of the door shifted from FREEZE to DEEP FREEZE, the small man in the chamber had fallen into a comatose slumber. Long before it clicked to VACUUM/SUBLIMATION with a ding and a hiss, his shivering ended.

8

The next morning, at nine thirty-five, Mr. Trout raised his hand, ready to swat his son Junior because Six-pack had gone AWOL.

"It's Sunday, sir. I told him he could—"

Trout cocked the hand back another six inches. "Every day's a work day. You wanna stay up drinking or whoring, it's your business, but when I tell you to have your crew here at eight sharp. Do . . . Not . . . Disobey . . . Me."

Junior shied. "Six-pack'll be here real soon, sir. He said he had to take his mama to church."

The hand hovered by Junior's head as Mr. Trout pondered the relative merits of Six-pack's parental devotion and Junior's filial disobedience. He finally lowered the hand and gave his bowling bag a swat instead. "Doone," he said, and gave it another swat. "This is last time I'm Mr. Nice Guy."

"I don't get it," Junior said. "Why'd you give him that junket to Vegas? You said he's gambler. He probably lost—"

"Lost?" Trout said. "Of course he lost. That was the idea. He holds a long, cheap-as-dirt lease on the armory behind the Bible Alive Museum for that cult of his. I had my eye on that building for years. It stood empty, no takers. I was waiting for them to drop the price again, big time, and pick it up for nothing. Then Doone shows up, leases it right out from under my nose for a song. The song I wrote. Now I'm screwed. I *need* that armory to expand the Bible Alive, add a New Testament wing.

"When Doone collared me at the bowl a couple of weeks ago, wanted more money, I thought, sure, I'll add another straw to the load he was carrying. Stuffed his pockets with cash and gave him the junket for being such a good customer. He swore he'd return from Vegas and pay it all back yesterday. I figured I'd be generous, take what he had—if he had anything left—and let him sign over the armory lease for the balance. I could taste that lease. Taste it!

"But, did he come calling? No, he did not. You had to bag his ass and haul him in, didn't you? Did you hear him say, 'Here's some of the money and how about taking this armory lease in my jeans pocket for the rest of it?'"

"Doone wasn't wearing no jeans. He was naked."

Trout took a swat at his son, who darted out of the way. "All right. Did you hear him say, 'The money and the lease are in the clothes I left behind?'"

"Wasn't in his clothes, neither. I looked."

Trout shook his big head and sighed. "So here we are. He *will* sign over that lease today. To start, I'm thinking of having your man Six-pack bowling ball Doone's cold toes . . . assuming," he gave Junior a hard look, "that Six-pack remembers to come in this morning."

"He'll be here any minute." Junior hefted the bag. "Can I do it? Drop the ball on him?"

"With a hundred and seven average? You'd be lucky if the ball hit the floor." Trout turned to Peaches. "And you?—get that sucker out of your mouth. You wouldn't be able to get the ball over that fat gut of yours. The two of you—go get the little prick so we can get this show on the road."

Junior set the bag beside the column to which he planned to tie Doone. He set up a folding chair six feet away for his father's comfort during the inquisition, arranged a work light to shine in the inquisitee's eyes, and motioned for Peaches to follow him to the meat locker. There, at the heavy door, Junior said, "I'll haul him out. In case he gets around me, you block the door."

Peaches assumed a wide stance at the doorway, arms out, ready to grab Doone should he make a run for it. Junior cracked the door and leaned inside the cavernous meat locker. He cast a wary eye at crates stacked on wooden skids, at sides of beef hanging in rows from the ceiling, dimly illuminated by bare bulbs.

"Smells like old meat," Peaches said. "Kinda rank."

"Cold meat, not old meat. It's supposed to smell like that."

Peaches peered in. "Spooky. Kinda like that scene in *Alien*. You know, where the pods—"

"Shut up with that kind of talk." Junior spoke into the gloom. "Hey, Doone? Come out." Doone didn't answer, so Junior reluctantly edged inside, cat-stepping warily toward the rear, peering behind skids, kicking sides of beef in an attempt to flush out his quarry. "Won't do you no good to hide," he warned, but Doone refused to show himself.

"You ever see that movie, *The Thing*?" Peaches called from his post at the door. "Took place in the North Pole or somewhere real cold like this. This monster from outer space was hiding behind—"

"Enough of that already," Junior said, and, "*Yeow!*" as a side of beef he had kicked out of the way swung into his back, knocking him to his knees. He nearly bolted.

"What happened?"

"Nothing." Junior gave the half cow that attacked him an angry boot and dodged the rebound. He moved forward another ten feet, casting furtive looks over his shoulder with each step.

Doone had to be hiding behind a pallet near the far corner, stacked with cartons of lamb chops. A shiver ran down Junior's already chilling back as he sensed someone, some *thing*, behind it. "Doone? You there?"

Doone didn't answer. Junior extended his arms wide, ready to catch Doone, or whatever, if he—it—ran out.

He shouted, "Dammit, come outa there." It sounded more a plea than a threat.

Silence. "Okay, that's the way you want it? I'll drag your ass out." Junior warned Peaches to be ready in case Doone—it *had* to be Doone back there—scooted left when Junior rounded the pallet to the right.

Junior took three quick steps to the right and saw: nothing. He shouted to Peaches at the door, "Did he run out? Didja see him?"

"Didn't see nothing."

"Well, hell." Junior waved his arms in frustration. "Come in here and help me look. And don't forget to chock the door. There's no release inside."

The locker dimmed. The door clicked shut.

"Peaches?"

Peaches didn't answer.

"Sonofabitch, Peaches. If you let that door close behind you . . . *Peaches?*"

The door creaked open six inches, accompanied by high pitched giggles from the corridor.

"Dammit, that ain't funny. Chock the damn door and get in here. I can't find the bastard."

A long minute later, Junior and Peaches faced one another and shrugged.

"He's gone," Peaches said.

"You sure he didn't get by you?" Junior's voice was thick with accusation.

"I didn't see him, okay?"

"Great. Just great. Six-pack put him in here, Daddy sent us to get him, and now he's gone. The little bastard got away."

Heavy of foot, Junior and Peaches returned to Mr. Trout's office, reluctantly bearing the bad news.

"He *what?*" The liver spots on Mr. Trout's face darkened ominously.

"He wasn't there."

"No, he wasn't," confirmed Peaches.

"Bullshit. You let him escape."

"Did not."

"Did not," echoed Peaches.

"I swear," Junior added. "We looked good."

Mr. Trout led Junior to the interrogation stool reserved for Doone. "Sit," he said. "You," he motioned his puffy chin toward Peaches, "get me a chair, and stand right there. We'll wait for Six-pack."

Twenty eternal minutes later, Six-pack hurried in, whistling, his hair wet, pumped from a brutal workout with his steroid supplier. The music stopped when he saw the welcoming committee. A minute later he was swearing he had locked Doone in the freezer. Yes, he had shut the door. No, there was no way Doone could have gotten out. No way.

"I had that inside safety latch removed myself," Trout said. "It's impossible he got out without help from somebody or stupidity from one of you." Mr. Trout's complexion was waxing a high shade of red, bordering on purple, his liver spots growing black as flies. "One of you, or all three, screwed up again."

Without warning, he took Junior by the ear and dragged him, squealing, toward the meat locker. "C'mon, all of you. I want to see this for myself."

He released Junior's ear with a final twist when they reached the hallway leading to the locker, and waved a palm at the corridor. "Go on, show me."

Junior walked to the refrigerated room, demonstrating how the door was properly shut and locked. Mr. Trout lifted the bar and re-secured it. "Solid. You're sure it was like this when you got here?"

"I swear, Daddy." Junior sought confirmation from Peaches, who nodded vigorously.

Trout studied both their faces, anger rising, then huffed in disgust. "So. Somebody got in here and let him out."

Fortunately, neither Mr. Trout, nor Junior, nor Peaches looked too closely at Six-pack: fidgeting, sweating, profoundly worried. For, on their way to the meat locker, his companions had passed, to Six-pack's considerable surprise, right by the stout metal door marked ACME EVERLAST FREEZE DRIER, the one with the big red button at the center which Six-pack had mashed after opening and pitching Doone through.

On the way back, Six-pack took solemn note of the flashing LED: FREEZE DRY CYCLE COMPLETE. COMPLETE. COMPLETE.

9

I swear, Deacon Patch, Reverend Doone just *vanished*. I walked by his house on the hill admiring it from the road—like you would a movie star's?" Ginger Rodgers snatched a quick breath. "He came home and recognized me from the choir, and invited me in for a cup of chamomile tea, and to help him choose hymns for Sunday services."

Ginger had driven like a demon from Doone's home to the Temple of Light, stopping at her own apartment only long enough to change into more modest attire. The Temple of Light had been a National Guard Armory, empty for years until the Reverend Doone leased it for his ministry. An aesthetically uninspiring, square, blockish building occupying half a city block, it had thick, poured concrete walls thirty feet high, and a flat roof. Two thirds of the interior, the former assembly area, was open to the roof trusses, and now served as the sanctuary. It was presently half-filled with folding metal chairs. The floor was concrete painted gray and the interior walls were flaking gypsum board, once institutional green, but now the color of pale mold. The rear third of the structure had two floors comprised of offices, lavatories, storage areas, and two efficiency apartments. The Reverend's ambitious plans called for carpeting the assembly area, trompe l'oeil stained glass windows, and cherry pews facing a remodeled stage (formerly the reviewing stand for Guard officers). All that seemed moot today.

Ginger's voice echoed through the still spare, hard-surfaced sanctuary. "I was so excited—I never saw his house before—it's as fabulous as, like, Tiara in *Gone with the Wind* or maybe even Graceland. We were standing in the hallway, and for just a second I turned away, looking up at this painting of heaven on the ceiling and when I glanced back again—Poof!—the Prince was *gone*. Raptured."

"Good Lord." As if struck by a divine thunderbolt, Deacon Creely Patch rocked on his thick legs, dropped to his gnarly knees, and onto his ham hock haunches. "It has begun." Heart pounding, blinking, he sat on the concrete, legs splayed, lips moving, though no coherent sound emerged. Prone to excessive perspiration in the calmest of moments, Patch felt his skin liquefy. The armpits of his stiffly starched white shirt, as well as his hairy back and chest, were sodden, would soon meld to his moistening, shiny black suit. Moisture beaded in the steel-wooly tufts of brown hair over his ears and at the back of his head, and dripped down his neck. He removed his thick glasses and mopped his thick, bushy brows and bald bony dome with a checkered kerchief. He knelt, shut his eyes, and awaited the divine touch signaling his ascent to heaven. "I'm ready, Lord."

". . . his clothes were all that was left of him: shirt, pants, undies, lying in a heap on the floor on top of his shoes and socks. Kind of like the Wicked Witch of the West in the *Wizard of Oz* when Dorothy threw water on her—only, of course, it wasn't the same at all, because Reverend Doone, being the Prince of Light, went straight up to heaven—right through the ceiling I guess—instead of, you know—" Ginger pointed to the floor, left of the kneeling, sweating Patch.

Deacon Patch had, in fact, begun perspiring prior to Ginger's astounding news. Anticipating Reverend Doone's return from a proselytizing circuit through western Tennessee and Kentucky, during which the Reverend had been strangely incommunicado, Patch stopped by the Lighthouse to confer about the coming month's Bible study schedule, Bible study being Patch's specialty. He had knocked on Doone's office door, and, finding it ajar, peered inside. The Reverend had apparently not yet returned, so Patch entered briefly to jot a note on the Prince's desktop calendar.

He would not have remained, snooped, but the stacks of unpaid bills on the desk snagged his attention. Not only bills, but threatening letters from the bank, the bus company, the hymnbook people, the tract printer. How could it be? The Children of Light were a generous flock, accepted a tithe of twenty percent gladly, not a meager ten like the Baptists. The twenty-percent had been one of Doone's ideas since he came on board, and the coffers should have been flush.

Aware the Prince was more of a visionary than a detail man, Patch had wondered if, in Reverend Doone's enthusiasm, he had diverted too much of their resources to launch the blimp. Tethered to the roof, the angel-shaped, helium-filled balloon with the strobe lights for eyes could be seen, as the Prince proudly proclaimed, "from seven states, maybe even eight. A beacon to draw hungry souls to our ministry." Or, perhaps the Prince had been imprudent in acquiring such a large structure for the ministry. Granted, the Temple of Light's hilltop setting above Gatlinburg, with its flat-topped roof, was ideally suited for the mass ascension, as was the internal steel staircase linking the sanctuary with the rooftop. The building's thick, protective walls and steel doors would also serve the flock well during the post-Rapture Tribulation if some of the Children of Light were left behind after the first wave flew to heaven. But . . . the roof leaked, the walls lacked insulation, the wiring was aluminum, the ceiling concealed asbestos, and, worse, cooling and heating the big concrete barn had to be eating them alive.

Patch shut his lids even tighter, oblivious of the pools of perspiration collecting in pinched pockets of flesh as he knelt, for, he was certain, he must be right behind the Prince on Saint Peter's Rapture list.

"It's true!" Ginger was explaining to half a dozen of the faithful, standing in a loose circle around Patch on the floor, their mouths agape at the news. "Raptured. Right before my eyes. I came straight here and told Deacon Patch. No, he's okay, just shook up over the news. I think he's praying down there. . . ."

Oblivious of the conversation over his head, Patch felt a rivulet of sweat run down his shoulder, join another to form a virtual Nile at the small of his back. He tried to speak but stammered. Get your wits about you man, a small, but so far, ineffectual voice whispered in a distant corner of his skull, These people need to be told what to do or they'll panic.

"Just like in *Titanic*," Ginger was saying to the choirgirls in their Rapture robes, scurrying like frightened white mice. "Remember? When the first class passengers put on their life preservers and went to their lifeboat stations?

"But if everybody stays calm, we'll be okay. Form lines and proceed in an orderly fashion up the stairs to the roof. Betsy, start the telephone chain, have everyone who's not here already come to the Temple of Light, let them know the Rapture has begun."

Rapture! The shock of it jellied Patch's brain. He knelt slack-jawed, staring unfocused at a spot on the floor. A slamming door brought him half around, and he shook his head side-to-side to gather his wits. He blew out a sharp breath of astonishment and, yes, resentment. Patch had always assumed that when the Rapture began, he would lead the Worthy to heaven. He, after all, could cite circles of Scripture around the Prince. He, Patch, was devout, devoted to the Lord's plan, led a life of asperity, had preached the Word long before Shickleton Doone wandered into town. "Why did you take Doone first, Lord?" he asked aloud, eyes open and upraised.

"Because," Ginger answered, from somewhere over his left shoulder, "the Reverend Doone was the Prince of Light, the new Messiah, the Chosen One."

Patch kneaded his wet temples, throbbing with worry and realization. Yes, and like Thomas, I doubted. What if the Lord leaves me behind for my faithlessness? Alone, to face the Antichrist and the Time of Troubles?

No! That can't be. Patch thought it through. While the Lord moves in mysterious ways, He moves with purpose. So, what is His purpose in leaving me sprawled on the floor while Doone soars to heaven? I started this ministry, didn't I? I strode the streets, shouting the gospel to the sinners of Gatlinburg, tourists and locals alike, warning them of the anguished times to come, of hellfire, and the need for salvation. It wasn't my fault they were more interested in wild bears, saltwater taffy, lewd tee shirts, and outlet malls. Not my fault I was scorned by the local churches for my vehemence, warned by the Chamber of Commerce police lackeys to "tone it down."

Then I encounter Doone one day outside the Bible Alive Museum, searching, he says, for a "charitable enterprise." I enlighten him about Daniel and Ezekiel, the prophecies in Revelation, tell him of the hungry souls in need of salvation, the myriad tourists who visit this small town each year, throwing away millions on frivolous baubles. I tell him of my struggling ministry. And when he offers to help, I invite him to join me.

Join me? The man *took over*. Relegated me to Deacon. Me, a self-ordained minister of the Lord.

Ginger was tugging at his elbow. Patch pulled away, anxious to fathom the divine plan. He rocked on the floor, palms pressed to eyes.

Why Doone? Admittedly, Doone, had a way with words, Patch acknowledged. He was a master at sermonizing and recruiting. He did project a certain presence, though resembling more a peacock than a prophet of old. Despite his short stature and plain face, he had a tan like burnished bronze, and, unlike my own, his teeth were white as an angel's wings. He wore his thick hair long, like Jesus, though it was black and not fair like the Lord's. Yes, Doone could charm an asp into a lap pet. They followed him like the Pied Piper, hung on his every word.

Word? Ha! If Doone read the Good Book every spare moment like he said he did, how could he mangle Scripture so? Why, it was only last Sunday he told that elderly couple, confused by the intricacies of Old Testament genealogy, that Cain and Able had been raised in the wilderness by a she-wolf! Did the parishioners gasp with indignation? No. They merely nodded like happy, sleepy sheep.

The resentment that had eaten at Patch like hot acid for weeks seared his brain. Doone took over and I was relegated to his assistant. Why Doone and not me, Lord?

He felt a tap on his shoulder. "C'mon, Deacon Patch, we're going up now." He shut his ears to Ginger's words, thinking, Why? Why? Why?

To the raucous clanging of shoe leather on metal, the Children of Light trooped up the steel staircase to the roof where Ginger rang the Rapture Gong with its mysterious Chinese symbols, suspended by two thick poly-silk cords from a six-foot teakwood frame. The gong came from the Holy Land, the Prince had explained, legacy of a crusader knight, and had never before been rung. Now, it summoned the faithful to the Roof of the Ascension.

Patch interpreted the noise as the pealing of heavenly bells, a preamble to a message from God. God!—speaking at last in Patch's ear, explaining His divine logic: *I* sent Doone to Gatlinburg because *you* needed his help, Creely Patch. Doone was useful, was he not? He swelled the ranks, raised the money to acquire the armory and launch the blimp to attract the faithless. He wrote copy for the handouts, set up a choir, and whipped the congregation to a frenzy during his—if not wholly accurate, at least spirited—sermons. I raptured Doone as a promise and a warning to the multitude. To them I say: the End Times are nigh. Find salvation. Follow My new prophet Creely Patch, and you, too, shall rise to the kingdom of heaven.

God asked: Will you be My messenger? Take command of our ministry? Prepare My children for the Great Rapture?

"Yes!" Patch answered. He rose to his feet. "*Yes*, Lord, I shall." Electrified with this divine directive, Creely Patch raised his arms high, turned to address the Children of Light.

But the room was empty.

10

Junior held a palm to his cheek, smarting from his father's angry swat. Peaches rubbed the back of his head. Six-pack stood, arms dangling, oblivious of the sting at his shoulder from Trout's blow, his mind racing, sending a silent plea: Please don't look in the other freezer. He pictured Mr. Trout's damning phone call to the deadly Hammer, putting a fatal hex on him.

". . . only thing I can think of," Mr. Trout was saying, his face red as a cherry bomb, "is, whoever let him out of the freezer snuck in when you three opened the rolling door. There's no other way. You screw-ups were followed."

Junior shook his head emphatically. "No way!"

"No, sir," said Peaches. "I watched our backs good."

Six-pack heard opportunity knocking, said, "I'll bet that was it."

Junior and Peaches shot him Are you nuts? looks.

"I mean," Six-pack said, "it had to be like that, didn't it? Maybe it was the girl." Any*one*, any*thing*, he said to himself, but me and the freeze drier.

Mr. Trout's big head swiveled to fix an angry glare at him. "Girl?"

"Uh," Six-pack backed away. "There was this girl at Doone's house."

"She went in with Doone," Junior said. "We saw them from the car. They were gonna, you know . . ." He formed a donut with his curled left thumb and first finger, poked his right fore-finger through the hole, drawing it in and out with a leer. "We went up to the porch and watched them through the window by the door. That's why Doone was bucknaked. He stripped and stood there while she went upstairs. She was in the bed-room when we snatched him and split. The girl couldn't have seen us."

"What did she look like, this girl?" Trout asked. "You ever see her before? Maybe it was his wife. Doone's married, I hear."

Junior said, "I doubt it. Doone was too interested. She was a blonde. Good body."

"Real good," Peaches added.

"Sharp dresser," Junior said. "You know, high heels, short skirt barely covering her crotch, tight sweater. Had long legs, nice tight butt."

"Fine butt," said Peaches.

Mr. Trout waved the air. "I got that picture. What I wanna know is, would you recognize her if you saw her again?"

"It was dark outside," Junior said.

"You saw her in the hall . . . lights must have been on."

"Yeah . . ." Junior looked at Peaches, at Six-pack. "Guess I didn't get a real good look at her face though." Six-pack and Peaches shrugged in agreement. "But she was a looker, blonde like I said. I guess I'd recognize her if I saw her again. Had these long legs—"

"We've been over that ground." Mr. Trout's hands balled into fists. He kicked, angrily but ineffectually, at Junior, who jumped out of the way. "Listen. Word gets out I let somebody stiff me and thumb their noses, everyone'll lose respect." He began an agitated dance. "You understand? Lose respect!"

"Yes, sir."

"I haven't spent forty-one years building my businesses,

my contacts, putting the fear of crossing Thadeus Trout in—" Trout's face went blotchy, and then purple. He gasped like a beached carp. His eyes bulged, opened and closed in slow, unnatural blinks, and fluttered shut. He gripped his chest.

"Daddy!" Junior ran to his side, threw an arm around Trout's quivering shoulders. "Peaches, get him a chair." Junior removed a silver, bowling pin–shaped pillbox from his father's pocket, took a tiny white tablet and stuffed it under Trout's fat gray tongue.

Peaches slid a chair beneath his bulk. Six-pack picked up a *Bowling Times*, and fanned Trout's face, which changed slowly, chameleon-like, from spectral purple, through red, to pink.

His eyes opened. He lurched from the chair, stood, and took a deep breath. "Whew—that was a bad one. That sonof-abitch Doone almost *killed* me, getting me so riled up." He wheeled to confront his son. "I want that girl, hear?" He flailed his arms, growing blotchy again. "And I want Shickie Doone. Keep an eye on that church, his house. Snag 'em, bring 'em to me. Put the word out: warehouse workers, people at the fudge store, the museum, the moccasin joint, the outlet."

He slapped his palms together and a malevolent smile spread across his broad, speckled face. "Cross Thadeus Trout and see where it gets you."

ix-pack left with the others, but stopped to pick up a fifth of bourbon. He drank a third of the bottle in the cab of his pickup to calm his fears. Shaky from the booze and his still-ragged nerves, always jazzed from the steroidal cocktail juicing his body, he returned to the warehouse alone.

All he could think about was Mr. Trout's "final solution," the deadly Hammer. "He's a huge mother," Junior had said. "Doesn't just stomp or strangle or shoot 'em dead. They say he shoots off fingers, toes, noses, ears—their dicks—for fun. I shit you not. My old man told me about this guy he did in Lexington a couple months ago. The Hammer must have emptied two or three clips, chipping off pieces before he put a slug through his heart."

Even more ominously, Junior related how Mr. Trout had discovered Six-pack's predecessor stealing from the warehouse, his pickup backed up to a loading dock one night, its bed chock full of T-bones and aged prime rib. Junior overheard the fateful call. Two days later, the beef thief didn't report for work. Nor the next day, nor the next. No one mentioned his name again, but it was rumored the Hammer had ground him into hamburger and delivered it wrapped in white butcher's paper, a hundred and fifty-three packages in all, to Mr. Trout for distribution to fast food eateries in Gatlinburg, Pigeon Forge, and Knoxville.

Six-pack hadn't eaten a burger since.

Mr. Trout had made no mention of it, simply told Junior to add another man to the crew, Six-pack as it turned out. That had been less than three weeks ago. Already there had been the unfortunate misunderstanding about Mr. Trout's bowling team captain. Now this.

Six-pack skulked to the warehouse door. What was the alarm code? They hadn't entrusted him with it yet, but he had watched Junior push the buttons often enough. He punched a perfect bowling score times three: 3–0–0–3. The LED flickered and stayed red. Damn. Had he remembered the bowling stuff wrong or hit the wrong buttons? Maybe it was two hundred, 2–0–0–3. He tried it that way. Flicker . . . Red. 2–0–0–2? Three wrong sequences and the alarm would go off, so Junior had said.

Three hundred had to be the magic number. Maybe he had hit the wrong button. Six-pack concentrated, guided his right forefinger with his left: 3–0–0–3.

Yes! The light flashed green. Six-pack cracked the door and peered inside. The lights were still out. He called a cautious "Hello?" but heard only the echo of his own quivering voice from the dark interior. He entered, flicked on his flashlight and wobbled to the cooler corridor. Youthful fears of ghosts and bodies gave him a bad case of the jumps. His steroid-induced paranoia kicked into high gear. He stopped before the fateful freezer, played the beam across the heavy steel Acme Everlast Freeze Drier door, left and right, fearful the Hammer might be lying in wait. Six-pack muttered a short, garbled prayer, and spun the cold metal wheel. Cracked the door. Before shining the light into the room he whispered, "Doone?" hopeful Doone, and not some fanged creature of the night or giant rat, would run out.

Doone didn't answer. Half-ready to bolt should the beam

reveal something with yellow teeth and sharp claws, Six-pack crisscrossed the interior with the light. It reflected back from stainless steel, brass, and copper tubing. And, black and white fur. A skunk, a possum, and a raccoon. All frozen with fear. What else lurked in there?

Wait . . . curled up on a bench at the back between a tray of beef jerky and some kind of dried fruit . . . Yes! Doone. Was this good news or bad? If Doone had really escaped, it would have meant there was a chance of Mr. Trout getting his money back. If Doone was dead—a specter of the Hammer rose. No, don't even go there. Think positive. With Doone here and still kicking, Six-pack might yet be a hero for "recapturing" him.

"Hey, Doone. Wake up."

Doone didn't move. Nor did the wildlife.

Six-pack gripped the edge of the door. "C'mon, Doone. It's okay. I'm gonna let you out."

He swung the door wide, waited to be sure it wouldn't close on him, and entered. He fixed the beam on the small fetal figure and watched for breathing, but Doone lay still as a stone, on his side, arms crossed at his chest, knees drawn to his chin. Six-pack leaned closer and stared. He saw profound immobility, unnaturally dull, gray, puckered skin drawn tight over Doone's bones, eyes not merely shut, but sunken, like the animals.

"Oh, hell." Six-pack retreated two steps, felt his stomach flip-flop. He flicked off the flashlight, wiped his forehead with the back of an arm, and rocked into a shelf. The dark closed in and he again turned on the light. "Be sure." He moved closer.

It was Doone, all right. The same man, though, somehow, less of him.

"Oh, no." Six-pack staggered with realization: "He's a *mummy*."

As were the animals, trussed up in little wire harnesses.

He nudged Doone's small body with his flashlight. It rocked like a walnut. Adrenaline and fear—fear of what he had done, fear of Mr. Trout and the Hammer, fear of the mummy— surged. Six-pack ran from the room, suddenly claustrophobic.

He caromed off the far wall. What was that they said about mummies and curses? Shining the light up and down the corridor, he looked for a light switch, found it, flipped it on. The fluorescents blinked twice and bathed him in sickly green light.

"All right," slurring his words. "Now what?"

He answered himself. "Mexico?"

"Not yet. Get rid of the evidence. They think he escaped. Let him be escaped. Ditch him."

He got goose bumps at the thought of the little body on the shelf.

Six-pack had inflicted his share of pain over the years. Pinching, gouging, compressing, ripping living flesh. That was fun, hearing the punks plead and wheedle and whine. He had knocked out men in fights half a dozen times, but they always came back moaning, or crying, or coughing, or puking. But always *alive*. He had seen a woman unconscious once, too. His aunt flopped stone cold onto the parlor carpet when she found that dead chipmunk he put in her purse. They brought her around soon enough with the ammonia. Cursing. Alive.

Six-pack had seen bodies by the hundreds on television and in the movies, but he always knew in the back of his mind they were phony dead people. Despite his stories, he had never killed a man, never seen a real dead body. Except Uncle Benny.

When Six-pack was nine years old and still Randolf, his mother had led him to Uncle Benny's casket. He had gone willingly, curious. She asked him to kiss Uncle Benny good-bye. And that he had done just as willingly. He cringed now at the memory of the cold, rubbery flesh. The weird smell, a blend of formaldehyde and cheap perfume. After that kiss, Six-pack, little Randolf, fell to his knees at the base of the casket and threw up on his mother's shiny new Sears funeral pumps.

"Listen," he said aloud, outside the freezer, reassuring himself. "You don't have to touch or even look at him. Find gloves."

A glove search proved unproductive. He did, however, find a box of garbage bags. Big ones. He returned to the freezer, fumbled with the bag. His fingers weren't following directions. Which end was which? There. He shook it open with a snap, and bent over Doone, his gaze deliberately fixed at the wall. Watching peripherally, he slid the bag over Doone's head, cringing when his hands touched—through thin plastic, but close enough—flesh. Not rubbery and cold like Uncle Benny, but hard and brittle-feeling. Doone slid six inches along the bench at Six-pack's touch.

He tied a knot in the top of the bag, got a firm grip, and heaved, but with too much muscle. Whoa!—the bag zipped past his shoulder toward the ceiling like a runaway balloon. Six-pack regained control of the bag on its way down and lowered it gently to the floor. Doone, he realized, weighed no more than a twenty-five pound dumbbell.

"No wonder they call him the Prince of Light." The pun did little to relieve his jitters.

A man who could bench-press two-sixty, he had no difficulty toting Doone over his back, Santa Claus–like, from the warehouse, although with every step he imagined a squirm or a kick. At the exit, he held the bag at arm's length like a strangled turkey, staring at it for motion. He carried it extended, in front of him, to his pickup.

With Doone in the truck bed, he breathed easier. He took a deserving slug of bourbon, and another. The warm buzz took the edge off his fear of Mr. Trout and the Hammer. He continued drinking and, before long, forgot them entirely. Six-pack slumped in the seat, and snoozed.

A fly walking across his upper lip brought him around. "What the hell? Where am I?" He sat up, saw the parking lot, the warehouse and the sun peeking over the mountainous horizon. It came back in a rush. "Holy shit!" Mr. Trout always bragged how he got to work before everyone else. Six-pack swiveled his head to check the truck bed. The bulging black plastic bag was still there. "Oh, man. I've gotta get out of here. Fast. And ditch the evidence."

Nerves on fire, head aching, he accelerated from the lot and, several blocks later, turned onto the main drag, down the hill, past Mr. Trout's block-long pyramid, the Bible Alive Museum, past Ripley's Believe It or Not and the Guinness World of Records, along the candy and tee shirt shops and the motels hugging the Parkway. He nearly took out an early-rising family of tourists at a crosswalk near the Aquarium of the Smokies. He beeped the horn and shot by, past Hillbilly Golf and Dinosaur Golf, Cupid's Petals Wedding Chapel and Cracker Jack's Tattoos, and finally out of Gatlinburg, into a stretch of the Great Smoky Mountains National Park. He thought of pulling to the side of the road and pitching Doone into the woods, but even at this early hour there was a steady stream of traffic running between Gatlinburg and Pigeon Forge. What if a tourist got him on tape running into the woods with the bag, or some ranger stopped him for littering, or a bear followed him back onto the road with Doone in its jaws?

He drove five miles, out of the hills and woods and onto the six-lane divided highway of the flatlands through Pigeon Forge. Tourist sprawl hugged the side of the road like gaudy fungus. Too many people, too much traffic. He passed a cop shooting radar the other way, near the entrance to Dollywood, and touched the brakes. That's all he needed: "Have you been drinking, sir? Have a bottle in there, do you? What's that in the bed of your truck? Mind if I have a look?"

"Man, oh, man." Six-pack swiped his sweaty forehead with the back of his hand, took a short pull of the hair of the dog, and flipped the bottle into the median. "Got to get out of Pigeon Forge, fast." Reflexively, he turned onto Route 321 and left the commercial strip behind. Too wired to stop, he tore through placid Wears Valley and on to the sparse community of Townsend. He flew by a sign advertising Tuckaleechee Caverns and slapped the wheel with inspiration.

When he was a kid, he and his buddies had explored caves, thumbing their noses at parents' dire warnings. They put bats in crybabies' hair, left sissies inside without lights till they screamed like stuck pigs. The caves in the woods he could never find now, but he had a vivid recollection of a big sinkhole in a field near the base of a mountain. A farmer had fenced it in to keep cattle out. The sinkhole had no bottom, the kids said, calling it Hell. They dared one another to drop into it on a clothesline climbing rope, but no one took up the challenge.

Hell, Six-pack decided, was the perfect place for Shickie Doone.

Where was it? Up this road, down that one. No. He backtracked, drove more slowly, watched for once-familiar landmarks. He remembered the good times, mailboxes batted from posts with Louisville Sluggers swung from the back of pickups, the Friday night fights in town, adventures with sheep.

There—on the right, a familiar old church. A half-mile beyond, he saw the farmer's shack, smoke curling from a stone chimney. Hell would be in the next valley, just over the wooded ridge.

The field was nearly overgrown. At the center, he saw the circular fence. Though covered with brambles, it still rimmed the funnel-like depression.

Not a car on the road. Another cabin in view, but Six-pack detected no activity. He pulled over, hoisted the garbage bag, hopped the fence, and thrashed his way through brush to the sinkhole. The rusty barbed wire along one side trailed the ground, still attached to a fallen post. A shimmer of long-forgotten fear tickled his spine as he leaned forward and peered into the black mouth of Hell.

He set the bag down, scanned for farmers or hunters, but saw only a buzzard, circling high overhead. He looked again at the weeds clinging to the crumbling earth rimming the limestone aperture, a deep chimney dissolved by thousands of years of rainwater draining the valley, sinking into an underground cavern.

What if it was plugged up a few feet down and some nosy farmer's kid saw the bag and opened it? Six-pack found a football-sized stone, lifted it above his head and pitched it into the hole. It rebounded from the sides with scraping crashes accompanied by secondary thumps and skitters, dislodging mud and other detritus. He heard one more scrape far below, but no final crash. Bottomless.

He raised the bag—and snatched it back. Plastic. Fingerprints. Reluctantly, he pussyfooted to the very edge of the abyss, fearful the rim would give way. He untied the top, cantilevered the bag over the pit with extended arms, shut his eyes, and upended it. He felt Doone's dry fetal body slide out, heard it brush the rock once, knocking loose pebbles and earth.

And that was it. Six-pack opened his eyes. He held an empty bag.

To further assure no one would find the body, he worked a large flat rock across the opening, and pried loose gravel and stones to cover it.

He leaned against one of the fence-posts rimming the sinkhole and sighed. Six-pack was alone. Free of Doone. Safe from the Hammer.

12

*S*nagging rays in her bra and panties on the balcony of Orlando's Miami Beach condo, Rita Rae Deaver-Doone leaned forward in the plastic-webbed patio chair to add a final dab of paint to the last toenail on her right foot. She flicked her cigarette over the rail, blew gently on the polish and raised her heels from the glass table to admire her handiwork. The puffy twists of pale green tissue wedged between each toe, alternating with her scarlet nails, lent a Christmasy air to the ritual.

Rita Rae's mood, however, was less than festive. She leaned against the half-open sliding glass door, raised her voice over the street noise, three stories below. "I keep calling the house. No answer. Those loonies at his church won't tell me anything. They're up to something. Maybe hiding him. I'm flying up to Gatlinburg to find out what the little worm is up to."

Orlando, in a turquoise Speedo, was doing sit-ups on the carpet. "*. . . y cuatro, cincuenta y cinco*." He flopped back and cat-stretched. "I will come soon, *mi niña*. I have a big shipment of *antigüedades* coming in via Colombia tomorrow I must inspect for quality."

"Well, I hope the 'quality' hidden in your little treasures is what it's cracked up to be, because you're the sole breadwinner in this family since that little shit . . ."

"You will find him. And, if he is not generous, you will be collecting the life insurance."

Rita Rae's eyes glazed. "A million dollars." She touched a toenail to see if it had dried. "I'll stay at the house. You find a motel in Gatlinburg or Pigeon Forge. Call when you get in. And remember to bring your lucky flick-knife."

Orlando gave her a Cheshire grin.

Rita Rae let her eyes play over his dark, sweat-slick body. She wet her lips, unhooked her bra, and tossed it onto his chest. "If you promise not to muss my hair, baby, maybe we can have a little fun before I pack."

"Raul Orlando Sosa y Castro de Monteobeja," he said, already stripping off the Speedo, "does not know the meaning," he palmed his genitals and hefted them, "of the word 'little.'"

Jimmy Feather took a long swallow of cold beer. He was stretched out on the worn, sway-backed corduroy couch in his grandfather's cabin near Townsend, Tennessee, wearing shorts and flip-flops, his grandfather's border collie curled between his legs. ". . . and that's how the Navajo do it. Their rez is as big as West Virginia. What do you think of that?"

Grandpop made noises of admiration.

"They were real friendly, but . . . I'm not Navajo. You sure Mom never told you any more about my dad? The Chief?"

"Jimmy, we been through this a thousand times. She hooked up with him in Nashville. By the time she was swellin' up with you, he was long gone. Maggie was a romantic like you. Always looking for a hero, for the pot of gold over the next hill. For her, the hero was your daddy, the pot of gold was becoming a country-western star. Well, her hero left her, and her singing never went nowhere, but she brought you into the world, and you're a good kid, so somewhere up above, I'll bet she's smiling."

He gave Jimmy a long look. "I'm glad you come back, and

you're welcome long as you want, bed, food, beer—but I live close to the belt, you oughta think about a job, being as you're near broke. Young man like you needs some cash in his jeans to have fun, take out the ladies."

"No time for women, Grandpop, but I've been thinking. If I could find out who my dad's people were, or the Indians on your side of the family, maybe I could make a claim. Get some land, maybe."

"Good luck. My ma used to talk about Indians on her side way back, Cherokees, probably, but there's no record. Your father's long gone. Consider yourself Scots-Irish. Proud people, the McDowds, been over here for generations. Carved a living out of these mountains.

"This land will all go to you. Sixty God-blessed, lovely acres. What you want a quarter-acre on some reservation in the middle of a desert for? This is good land, with a pure water well. Right by the Park. We could work up some tourist angle—"

"Like what you do at the Moccasins! Moccasins! store, huh? Dress up in phony fringe buckskins, wear lipstick war paint and a turkey feather Plains headdress, moccasins made in Taiwan, Navajo concho belt stamped out in Hong Kong, wave them in off the highway. Jeezle!"

"It's a living, and the tourists don't know no better. I'm what they see on the TV. I have fun with 'em, too—shake my tomahawk at the kids and whoop, tell 'em my name's Thunder Cloud or Brave Eagle, make up all kinds of stories, like I was in some John Wayne movie—"

"Jeezle!"

"Jimmy . . . Mr. Trout, my boss, he's a bigwig hereabouts, owns half a dozen businesses. I heard they're looking for a security guard at the Bible Alive Museum. It's the biggest attraction in Gatlinburg and growing every day. Decent pay, benefits, though you'd have to take the odd shifts at first. I'll put in a word for you."

"I'll think about it." Jimmy untangled his legs from the dog and went to the kitchen for another beer. He twisted off the cap, walked to the bathroom, and stood before the full-length mirror bolted to the door. He took an appraising look at his Indian half, the dark arms, neck, and face, and his long, straight black hair, and, then, at the wrong half, his pale legs and torso, his gray eyes. "Some Indian," he said to his reflection. "I look like an Anglo construction worker. I'm gonna have to find me a tanning salon."

A day had passed since the mysterious disappearance of Shickie Doone. Junior's crew stood in papa Trout's office, staring at bowling trophies or stuffed fish, averting the boss's glowering gaze.

"No sign of him at all? Of the girl? You been watching the house?"

Peaches took a Slim Jim from his mouth to speak. "Yes, sir. Neither him nor the girl has been back. House is empty."

"No reports from anyone else? You put the word out?"

"Yes, sir," said Junior.

"And that cult of his? At the armory? If he shows up at all, it'll be there."

Six-pack cleared his throat. "Junior and me has been taking turns, sir. Lots of people wearing white robes up on the roof, but no Doone. Same as always, big searchlight shining on the blimp at night."

Trout thumped his fist on the desk. "The armory. Damn, I want that building." Red crept up his neck, past his chin to his forehead. "Stiffed me, still holds the lease, and skips out from under my nose." His eyes bulged like a Boston Terrier and he began to mutter. "Nobody does that to Thadeus Trout. Hell, what do I need him for, anyway? If I take Doone out of the picture, that cult will fall flatter than a cow pie. I'll pick up the lease for nothing." He scowled at the boys. "The three of you get back on the streets, keep looking. I'm gonna make a phone call."

The crew had an idea what that meant. They quick-stepped from the office.

"You think he's gonna call, you know," said Peaches, "The Ham—"

Junior cut him off. "Don't even say it."

"If he is," said Six-pack, "it's not for any of us, is it?"

Junior gave him a startled look. "Us? Why would you say that?" His voice went crackly at the edges. "We're not the ones let Doone out. Wasn't our fault. We're doing what he wants, aren't we? Well, aren't we?"

"Yeah, sure," said Six-pack.

B

Rita Rae detoured for cigarettes at the Knoxville airport. In line at the news shop, she glanced at the paper rack. An article caught her eye. She did a double take and shouted, "You bastard!"

Bent bodies studying magazines jerked upright. Faces snapped toward the noise. A student in a University of Tennessee tee shirt dropped a laptop with a disturbing *bonk* on the tile floor. The gangly woman in front of Rita Rae screamed contagiously, spun, and knocked over a chewing gum display. Attention settled on the man to Rita Rae's rear—under suspicion of goosing her, dressed as she was, in a tarty slit skirt, see-through blouse, and four-inch heels. The suspect, balding, in a Hawaiian shirt bloused over a round gut and khaki shorts, was a poker-playing, football-watching, cigar-smoking kind of middle-aged guy, the kind who might—but only if he could get away with it in a crowd—goose a looker like Rita Rae.

The gangly lady glared at him. "Apologize!"

"Shame on you," a young mother agreed. She had one hand on a stroller with a wailing baby, reached with the other for her seven-year-old, making a play for the spilled chewing gum.

Worried, uncertain, the clerk behind the register asked no one in particular, "Should I call security?"

The college girl, on hands and knees, scooping up fragments of her broken laptop, hurled a withering stare at the alleged gooser. "I hope you're happy. A whole semester, shot to hell."

The suspect raised his hands, said, "I didn't do nothing."

Unaware of the confusion, still staring at the headline, Rita Rae said one word: "Bullshit!" She snatched the paper from the rack, gripped it with white knuckles, and stomped out without paying, her gaze riveted to the article that had caught her eye:

Cult Leader Raptured, Followers Claim

Disciples of the Reverend Shickleton Doone, the charismatic leader of the Children of Light sect in Gatlinburg, claimed Reverend Doone was raptured (transported instantaneously to heaven) at nine P.M. Monday evening. A choir member, Miss Ginger Rodgers, allegedly witnessed the event.

"Raised to heaven on angels' wings," said the Reverend Creely Patch, who has assumed the ministry in Rev. Doone's absence. "He vanished in an instant, exactly as he prophesied, leaving his clothing and worldly possessions behind."

The parishioners, "Fireflies" as they are popularly known, believe that the biblical Rapture of worthy mortals will precede the beginning of the end of the world, a time of tribulation followed by appearance of the Antichrist and Armageddon, the final battle between good and evil.

Reverend Doone, called the Prince of Light, and second Messiah by his more ardent disciples, claimed he would lead the Rapture, to commence in Gatlinburg, and initiated by strange weather, trouble in the Middle East, and a shooting star. Awaiting the heavenly call, the Children of Light donned robes and, carrying flashlights to shine skyward, ascended the roof of their church, the Temple of Light (a former National Guard armory situated behind Gatlinburg's popular Bible Alive Museum).

"It has begun," said Rev. Patch. "Reverend Doone led the way as a warning and a promise. Before he left this earth, he placed the pastoral mantle on my shoulders, urging me to save more souls for the impending exodus from this sinful . . ."

"Hah!" Rita Rae flung the paper to the floor. Heels clacking angrily toward baggage claim, she assumed a stony glare. "You little worm," she said. "You can fool all of the bumpkins some of the time. And some of the bumpkins all of the time. But you will never, ever, put a con like this over on Rita Rae Deaver."

Maury Finkle raised a finger, signaling the waitress he was ready for his second Manhattan. He sat in the third, red leatherette banquette from the door, as he did every Tuesday and Thursday during happy hour at the Cincinnati piano bar, Cora's Cozy Cove. Maury was dressed impeccably in a navy blazer, starched blue and white pinstriped shirt with a maroon polka-dot bow tie, gray slacks, Cole Haan loafers, and pale blue silk socks. A tiny man, seventy-nine years old, bald, but with white side-hair and a neatly trimmed mustache, Maury was a regular. He nursed his Manhattans, exchanging greetings with the other patrons, dispensing avuncular advice to the waitresses, and flirting with the single, getting-up-in-years women who also made the Cove their home for a few companionable hours each week. The denizens of Cora's comprised the whole of Maury's social life.

The waitress passed the order to the bartender, who immediately stopped polishing glasses and set to work on Maury's Manhattan. Everyone at the Cove liked Maury, a friendly little guy and a generous tipper. Retired from the furniture business now for eleven years, Maury remained something of a personality from the old TV commercials. Anyone over thirty remembered the deep baritone voice and the smile: "Hi, folks! This is your Uncle Maury from M & N Furniture Bazaar. You come down and see me. Bring the husband, bring the kids, because today, and today *only*, we're gonna give you every stick of furniture in the store . . . every bed, every dresser, every dinette, every sofa, every recliner . . . yessir, each and every one of 'em . . . give them away for *one penny*. That's right, whatever you want: *one cent*." The camera would slow-zoom onto the smiling face, seconds would pass, and Maury would wink. "Just kidding about the one cent. What? You think old Maury's *cra–a–aazy?*" He winked again and grinned. "But I'll treat you like family, I promise."

Maury smiled at the waitress, patted her hand as she set the Manhattan on the table, remembering his wife, Rose, of thirty-one years, until that fateful night twelve years ago.

Rose had been an attractive woman and Maury loved her dearly, even though she began staying home while he went to the Cove. Fine. Maury wasn't demanding.

That last night, Rose brought Maury his third Manhattan of the evening and went to bed per their habit of recent years. He watched the late shows downstairs in the living room, lights out, sound turned low so as not to disturb her. Maury would fall asleep in his La-Z-Boy until somewhere around two-thirty, when he would nod awake, turn off the tube, and toddle up the stairs to bed in the dark, guided by a small flashlight. He would undress carefully, silently, so as not to awake Rose, slip into bed beside her, kiss her lightly on the forehead, and fall asleep, content.

Maybe not so content. The store's gross was sickly; the net, anemic. Had been for several years. Bringing in barely enough to feed one man, let alone two, and one with a wife, what with the chain stores muscling in, selling with practically no margin. Debt was rising like a hungry monster out of the swamp of business-gone-bad. Maury and his partner Nick Anarchos discussed it endlessly. Nick, a younger, impatient guy, said, "There could be a fire—I know a fella," but Maury loved the commercials too much to let it all go up in smoke. "Hold on, Nick," he'd say. "Things'll turn around like they always have, you'll see." But the furniture business fairy had turned her cold crinoline back on the M & N Furniture Bazaar.

So, that last night Maury had turned off the TV and remained in the La-Z-Boy in the dark, trying to think his way out of the bleak box constricting the two partners. Eventually, he dozed off. Somewhere around one A.M., the tinkling of broken glass, a loud *Bonk!* and an explosive grunt brought him to.

"Whazzit?" Maury worked the handle of the La-Z-Boy, tipped himself upright, grabbed his flashlight from the TV table, and played the light around the room. "Gevalt!" He saw a man lying on the carpet, his lower legs visible, his upper body hidden by Rose's high-backed easy chair.

Maury picked up a poker, a good, solid brass one from the fireplace, and tip-toed toward the still feet. He noticed broken glass in the window beside the front door and the prone figure, male, dressed entirely in black, except for Florsheim cordovan wing tips, facing the heavy chromed coffee table, and sprawled dead-still on the carpet, a tipped ottoman at his feet. Maury aimed the penlight at the head, saw a black bandana tied across the nose and mouth of the intruder, a bloody gash on his forehead and blood on the corner of the coffee table.

It didn't take a whiz kid to fathom what had happened. The prowler—the son of a bitch, in my house!—had broken the glass, reached in and unlocked the deadbolt, entered, tripped over the low ottoman in the dark, hit his head on the table, and . . . Maury felt the side of the man's neck. No pulse. Beside the burglar's hand, Maury saw a gun, an automatic with a thick cylinder at the nose end. A silencer. Maury recognized it from the movies. He felt for a pulse at the wrist, too, and again found none. Serves the schmuck right.

He heard the bed creak upstairs, Rose call down, frightened, "Nick? Is it over? Did you get him?"

Nick? Maury pulled the bandana from the face and confirmed it: his partner Nick Anarchos.

Quick of mind, if not of foot at his age, Maury put one and one together and came up with Nick and Rose, and Maury with a bullet in his brain. He visualized the scene as scripted: "The prowler must have entered through the front door, ma'am, unaware your husband was asleep down here in the La-Z-Boy. Your husband awoke, the prowler shot him and ran off before he could harm you."

Nick, the double-crossing cheater, would pitch the gun into the Ohio River off the Suspension Bridge, collect the sole-survivor insurance he and Nick carried on one another, and take over the Bazaar with Rose at his side.

Again, from above: "Nick? Is it okay?" Pause. "I don't want to see him. I'll wait up here, in bed."

Half dazed, Maury removed his monogrammed cotton handkerchief from his robe pocket, wrapped it around his own hand, lifted the gun, studied it for a moment to be sure he understood the mechanism—it was already cocked, ready to fire—and climbed the stairs, gripping the gun with the hanky. With "Nick? Is it over? Did you get him?" still burning in his brain, he put three slugs into Rose. He dropped the gun, fell to his knees, crawled to the bathroom, and threw up in the toilet. He sat on his haunches, sobbing for a long minute until the "Nick? Is it over?" overpowered his remorse. Nick schtuping Rose. The two of them planning this. For how long?

Maury took a deep breath and regained his composure. Downstairs, he replaced the bandito handkerchief over Nick's face and returned the gun to his hand. He worked Nick's finger over the trigger, lifted Nick's hand with his own hanky-wrapped one, and pulled the trigger, putting a slug into the wall through the top of his recliner.

Maury changed his clothes, took a quick but thorough shower downstairs, and called the police.

The new script read: "He must have killed poor Rose, Officer, then saw me asleep in the recliner. I woke up, lunged for him. He fired at me, tripped over the ottoman, hit his head on the table. I left him lying right there where he fell. He was after our insurance, murdered poor Rose so he'd get a hundred percent of the business. Nick, my partner and friend of all these years . . ."

Maury sold the store to one of the chains. Didn't get near what he wanted, but he didn't have to share with a partner, either, and they paid him a nice retainer for five years to continue the commercials.

During subsequent visits to the Cove, Maury thought about Nick's gun, how comfortable it felt in his hand, how easily he had dispatched his cheating wife, how righteous he had felt when it was over. It wasn't long after, following a lecture at the Senior Center on "Making Ends Meet: New Careers for the Retiree," he struck up a conversation with an octogenarian who told him about a friend of his son's who had been screwed out of his business by a cheating partner. Maury felt his anger rise, drew a line from Nick's gun, to the lecture, to opportunity. He made discreet inquiries, a connection, and completed his first contract. Efficiently. Effectively. So began Maury Finkle's one-man war on cheaters.

Maury took a sip of his Manhattan and smiled, basking in the solitary but warm glow of the superhero making the world a better place for decent folks to live. Yes indeed—

"Mr. Finkle? Maury?" It was the bartender. "You have a call. Somebody with busted furniture again, I guess. Asked for Mr. Hammer."

"You didn't mention my name?"

"Nossir. The repair business gives you a little extra money to pad the Social Security, huh? Cash, no names, no need for Uncle Sam to get involved, right?"

"That's the ticket. Thanks." Maury took the phone, watched the bartender thoughtfully walk to the end of the bar. "Hammer here," he said to the receiver. "A problem, you have?"

"This is T," said a voice. "Problem's got the name of Shi—"

"Are we talking furniture here, or do you have the wrong number?"

"Sure. Furniture. I've got this broken chair I got from, uh, my partner. Sold it to me for good."

Maury's hand tightened on the phone. "A cheating partner?"

"That's it. And I'm looking to make it right. This chair."

"Maybe I can help." Maury glanced at the bartender, pulling a draft on tap thirty feet away.

"What are we talking about, fee wise?"

"Fixing a chair? Same as last time unless I have to chase down—"

"I'm pretty sure you could do the repair right here in Gatlinburg. So . . . fifteen, uh, dollars?"

"Fifteen? You pulling my leg? The fee is still twenty. Plus expenses."

T sighed. "Afraid of that. Okay. I'll send you details, a photo of this chair, and the deposit to the P.O. Box. The balance, C.O.D. Dead or alive."

"I repair furniture," Maury reminded the caller. "Trees, I don't grow. I work with dead wood only. You follow?"

"Understood."

"I'll look for your package." Maury hung up.

14

Ginger set the cup of coffee on the desktop across from Creely Patch. "Is that how you like it, sir? Cream and sugar?"

"Fine. Close the door behind you, please." Patch, sitting behind the recently-departed Prince of Light's big desk, motioned for her to sit in a high-backed Gothic chair by the door. He leaned forward, elbows on the desktop. "Look at these articles." He waved a thick hairy hand over the papers.

Ginger brushed aside the Knoxville and Asheville newspapers to lift a tabloid. "Wow!" Her lips moved as she read to herself:

Raptured!

The Reverend Shickleton Doone of the Children of Light ministry in Gatlinburg, Tennessee, known as the Prince of Light to his disciples, was "lifted on angels' wings to heaven in an instant" Monday night, according to his successor, the Rev. Creely Patch, "exactly as prophesied by the Prince."

Choirmaster Ginger Rodgers watched the Rev. Doone disappear in a flash of light, leaving his clothes behind. "I guess it's warm in heaven," said Miss Rodgers, a former cheerleader and beauty pageant queen. "One second he was here, then 'Poof!' he was gone." Miss Rodgers said she was sure this "wasn't just an alien abduction. Two of our choir members were abducted last year from the Sevierville Wal-Mart parking lot and this wasn't at all like that. No aliens, no UFOs, just 'Poof!'"

Rev. Creely Patch, a leading Bible scholar, said the Rapture confirmed Rev. Doone was the second Messiah, "even though the Reverend Doone, unlike Jesus, was short and had dark hair. He was the first to be raptured," said Rev. Patch, "but more will follow, depart for heaven from the roof of our church, the Temple of Light. I was chosen to pave the highway to heaven for the next wave."

According to the Book of Revelation and the prophets Edward Cayce and Nostradamus . . .

Ginger wrinkled her nose. "I didn't tell them I was choir-master, Deacon—I mean Reverend—Patch, I swear. Or a beauty queen, either."

Patch waved that aside and sipped coffee.

"It couldn't have been an abduction. I'd of known if it was, I'm sure."

"Of course, Ginger."

She turned the tabloid for him to see. "Look at this picture. That's me in my high school graduation gown, not my Rapture robe, and I'm on the Temple of Light roof, not the school bleachers. It shows Reverend Doone skyrocketing up right past me. How did they do that? It wasn't like that at all. It wasn't even here, but at—"

"Forget the details, Ginger. Ginger?"

She was still studying the mysterious photograph. She glanced up and back at the photo.

Patch snapped his fingers. "Listen to me." When he was certain he had her attention, he said, "God spoke to me."

"No way!"

"He did. In a thundering voice. I put my hands to my ears in fear, but He said, 'Be not afraid,' so I opened my heart and my mind. He told me He raptured the Reverend Doone as a final warning to sinners.

"God wants *me* to show them the way before the real exodus begins. And . . ." Patch had her full attention now. "He wants *you* to help me."

"Me?" Worry lines creased Ginger's face. One hand began twirling a hank of wavy blond hair. Her eyes avoided Patch's.

"Yes, you. Why do you think He selected you to witness the first Rapture? My role in the divine plan is obvious. I am a man of faith, I know the meaning of Scripture as few men do. I have the strength and intellect to carry out the Lord's will. But we all have our cross to bear. I was not blessed with Samson's looks. I am a plain man."

Ginger nodded silently. Reverend Patch was plain all right. Well, so was the Prince, but the Prince had that smile, and sexy long hair, good teeth, and that sweet voice. If the Prince was plain, then Reverend Patch was . . . Ginger thought about Dr. Jekyll's alter ego, Mr. Hyde. Big bony ridges over hard beady eyes, magnified by bottle-thick glasses to the size of eight balls. Yellow horse's teeth, and the little hair he had at the sides he tried to comb over the top, but it only stood up like a clown's topknot because it was too frizzy, and he sweated a lot, and smelled sometimes, and—

"Ginger?" Patch snapped his fingers. "The point is, people today have been seduced by television and the movies. They are drawn to beauty, influenced by it. You, my dear, are a very attractive young woman. . . ."

Where was this going? Ginger edged back in her chair, glanced over her shoulder at the door.

"No need to be modest. The Lord selected you to welcome the converts. He selected me to minister to them. We are a team of complements: man and woman, doer and observer, substance and surface. I have the wisdom of age, you, the naivete of youth.

"These people coming by not only want to hear my message, but to see you—because of your photo in the papers, because you saw the first Rapture, and because you symbolize the angels they hope to meet when they, too, are raised to heaven."

He took a deep breath, another swallow of coffee, and concluded, "Henceforth, God has declared that I be known as His Messenger, and you, His Witness."

"*Me*?" Her mother's words, "Be a *star*, baby," until now, unfulfilled, rushed back at her. "Just think," she said, more to the memory of mom in Fred Astaire drag looming over little Ginger the klutz, than to her new mentor, Reverend Patch, "God's Witness."

"That's right." Patch slid his mug across the desk. "And, if you don't mind, dear, get me another cup of coffee. One sugar only—this is much too sweet."

15

Grandpop McDowd heard the cabin door slam, saw Jimmy walk quickly by in the hall, carrying a shoebox and a black dry cleaning bag on a hanger. He turned down the TV. "Jimmy? Heard you got the job at the Bible Museum. Everything okay?"

"I guess."

"That don't sound encouraging. They give you benefits?"

"Yeah. And free meals in the Garden of Eden café—fruit and salad bar, at least. I'll have to pay if I want the hot stuff. I gotta take whatever shift they need me on for awhile, but the pay's decent, considering I've never been a security guard. On the other hand," Jimmy stepped into the living room, lifted the bag from the hanger, "look at this."

"Some woman's skirt and blouse. Give you the wrong bag at the cleaner, huh?"

"No, this is my *uniform*. I'll get another one, too, just like it, different colors." He waggled the clothing. "Some uniform." A short, white kilt with gold trim was clipped to the hanger, a matching white and gold blouse hung over it. "They don't want anyone looking like a cop at the museum. I'm supposed to look like David. You know, the one who slew Goliath? I'm an attraction, too. Get more bang for their buck."

Grandpop stifled a laugh. "David," he said, by way of encouragement, "was a real hero."

"That's what they told me. Get a load of this." Jimmy opened the shoebox, held up a pair of leather sandals with long leather straps. "These things crisscross around my shins. And this," he held up a slingshot, "is my weapon." Jimmy managed a smile, but he was close to tears.

"Hell, Jimmy. You're built good. Trim. I'll bet the ladies'll get real turned on by that outfit. Think of all the movie stars, dressed like you in the old films: Victor Mature, Richard Burton, Tony Curtis, Kirk Douglas."

"Museum people liked my hair." Jimmy forced a crooked grin. "Not many jobs let a man keep his hair long. I guess it's better than wearing a polyester rent-a-cop outfit or a suit and tie. Maybe."

The old man walked to Jimmy's side, gave him an affectionate poke in the shoulder. "Lots of good-looking tourist girls come through Gatlinburg and that museum. They'll be drawn to you like flies to sugar. The David part fits: Jimmy-the-underdog, taking on giants with your protests." He made a fist, jabbed Jimmy's shoulder again. "C'mon, David, we'll celebrate. Baseball's on the TV and I got beers in the fridge."

As soon as Rita Rae Deaver twisted the key in the lock at the front door of the Doone/Deaver residence, a hard callused hand cupped her mouth from behind. A muscular forearm wrapped her waist, hoisting her off her feet and toward the sidewalk. She kicked, ineffectually. One high heel pump fell to the ground. She worked her mouth open to take a chunk out of the hand, but it shifted deftly and clamped her jaws together with a clack.

"I don't think so," Six-pack said at her back.

"That's her. That's the babe," Junior said. "We got her."

Rita Rae, pinioned, but far from helpless, honed in with the precision of sonar on the whiny "We got her." Her free arm lashed, raking Junior's face with scarlet talons.

"Ow!" Junior put a hand to his burning cheek, drew it away and saw blood. "You bitch! You see what she did?"

"That's gonna show for awhile, all right," Peaches acknowledged.

"Get her in the car, fast, before somebody sees us."

Six-pack tossed her in the back seat of the Buick and sat close enough to wedge her against the door. Before an emerging scream passed her throat, he made a fist at the tip her chin. "Yell and I break your jaw."

Rita Rae gritted her teeth and nodded.

Six-pack rooted through her purse, removed a Colt Pocket Nine. He handed it to Junior in the shotgun seat. Peaches, at the wheel, peeled away.

"Behave yourself," Junior said, "or I'll shoot you with your own gun."

"Bullshit," she spat back. "If you wanted me dead, you'd of shot me in the back when I was at the door. And if you plan on raping me, you oughta know I've got syphilis and crabs." She idly scratched her crotch.

Six-pack edged away.

"Somebody just wants to talk with you, okay?" Junior said. "Now shut up."

"Whoever you are," Rita Rae said, in a voice sharp enough to scratch glass, "you've got the wrong person. Let me go."

"Real cute," Junior said. "That's what your boyfriend said when we nabbed him."

"Orlando? How could you have Orlando? He's still in Miami."

"The one you was with the night before last. The one you was gonna do the hokeypokey with in your house there. We snatched him from the hall while you was up in the bedroom."

"Shickie? He's back? That little worm is two-timing me?" She let fly an impressive string of curses.

"Keep it down," Six-pack said, with an eye on the tourist-lined Gatlinburg strip rushing by the window.

"My ass, you muscle-bound turd, I'll—"

Six-pack grabbed her throat and pinched. Over the gagging sounds, he said, "You don't care about a broken jaw, puss, there's always strangling."

Peaches, thus far silent, removed his bowie knife and waved it over his shoulder. "Or I'll scalp you, mount that beehive hairdo on the dash."

Rita Rae rubbed her throat. "You know what they say about men who carry big knives, don't you doughboy?"

Peaches narrowed his eyes at the rearview mirror. "What's that?"

Junior explained: "They got little peckers. Guess the babe is on to you."

"Hell, Junior, who's side you on, anyway?"

Six-pack said, "You want me to deck her?"

"We bring her back unconscious, my old man'll skin us. But if she keeps it up with that mouth, find something to gag her with. If you'd hadn't-a left the duct tape in your Monte Carlo, Peaches, we wouldn't have to listen to her."

Peaches hunched over the wheel, sulking. Six-pack brushed Rita Rae's nose with his knuckles as another warning. Rita Rae made fists at her side and glared back.

Ten minutes later, Six-pack hustled her into the warehouse by her elbows. Junior rapped on the doorjamb of Mr. Trout's office. Six-pack pushed Rita Rae inside.

Mr. Trout looked up from a stack of invoices, gave her a quizzical stare. "Rita Rae?"

"Well, well. Thadeus Trout. How have you been all these years, sweetheart?"

Junior did a double take at his father. "You *know* her?"

"Oh, he knows me, don't you, Thaddie." She moved closer, sat on the corner of the desk and gently kitty-cat scratched Mr. Trout on the top of his bald head. Trout closed his eyes for a long second.

He scooted away and narrowed his eyes. *"You're* the one who let Doone escape?"

"That's her Daddy," Junior said.

Rita Rae shifted her gaze to him. "What a fine strapping son you have, Thadeus. And to think, I might have been his mommy." She rolled her eyes. "What a foolish girl I was to leave."

Junior snapped his eyes from Rita Rae to his father. "What's she talking about?"

Trout waved off the inquiry and frowned at Rita Rae. "What were you doing at Doone's house?"

"My house."

"Say again?"

"Shickie Doone, the son of a bitch, is my dear husband."

"Unbelievable. I heard he was married. But to you? What did you see in him? Did you get religion, Rita Rae?"

"I knew Shickie would be my next ex-husband the first time I met him. I figured he had a fine con going, and I expected heavy compensation when I divorced him. Truth is, the cheapskate barely supported me. Then, he split. Raptured? My sweet ass. I guess you saw the Knoxville paper?"

"No," said Trout, "but I heard. Doone supposedly poofed up to heaven. He's nuts if he thinks I'll buy that."

"Me neither." Rita Rae removed a pack of cigarettes from her purse, held one to her lips until Junior, at Mr. Trout's eye signal, gave her a light. She inhaled deeply, and returned Junior's favor by blowing an angry stream of smoke at his face. "Shickie double-mortgaged our house," she said to Trout. "They repoed the Mercedes. The bank account's cleaned out, and everyone and their illegitimate son," she winked at Junior, "is after him for money."

Junior looked confused, turned to his father for explanation.

Trout dismissed it with a flick of his fingers. "She's pimping you," he said, and to Rita Rae: "Why did you help him escape, then? He must have a fine nest egg stashed somewhere or you wouldn't have—"

Rita Rae stood, managed not to rock on her single high heel. She got a flinty look in her eye and jabbed a scarlet-nailed finger at Trout's chest. "Let's get something straight. *I* didn't help him escape. I was about to divorce his ass. And I *wasn't* in our house the other night like these jerk-offs claim. I was in Miami visiting my poor sick mother. Apparently the little worm was seeing some chickie." She reached into her shoulder bag, rummaged, and came up with a Delta ticket envelope. She flipped it onto Trout's desk. "Check the boarding stubs."

Trout put on his reading glasses, examined the contents. He shook his head wearily, sighed, and then glared at Junior, Peaches, and Six-pack. "You *sure* she's the woman you saw with him the other night?"

Sensing an unfortunate turn of events, the three held mute.

"Go ahead, take a good look."

"It's her, all right," Junior said. "We saw her from the back real good. How many babes got a build like that? Was dressed real classy like this, too, with the short skirt and the legs and high heels."

"One of which," she said, "you lost for me, pimple-face. Charles Jourdans. That's gonna cost you, to say nothing of the kidnapping."

"It could be," Peaches said, with a sideways glance at Junior, "that the babe the other night was younger."

Six-pack took a long look at Rita Rae. "A lot younger."

Rita Rae huffed. "So, the worm's been banging school girls."

"No," Peaches said. "The other night babe was near thirty."

Rita Rae swung at him but he dodged away. The swipe reminded Junior of his cheek. He turned it toward his father. "Look what she done to me."

Mr. Trout put his hands to his own cheeks and slumped forward, elbows on desk and muttered, "Screwed up again." He pursed his lips and exhaled like a walrus surfacing at a blowhole. He nodded for Rita Rae to take a seat in the chair across from his desk. "Your husband," he said, wincing at the word, "borrowed fifty thousand dollars from me for improvements at his church and to send up that angel blimp—the one they can see from seven states, maybe eight? He starts raking it in, but he's got expensive habits," he jabbed a thick forefinger at Rita Rae. "He's a gambler."

"He's got a hard-on for poker, all right."

"He talked me into giving him another fifteen grand last week, swore he'd make it all right.

"The due day came and went. With interest, we're now close to ninety gees." Trout dropped his hands to his desk, unlocked a desk drawer. "To make it clear I expect to be paid back," he rummaged through files and removed a sheet of paper, "I had him sign this: says he agrees to give me a pound of flesh for every thousand he's delinquent on. So, I own his ass. Literally.

"He didn't show up. I had the three musketeers haul him in to show I mean business. We gave him time to think in the meat locker. Apparently the woman of the house, the *other* woman, followed the boys here, snuck inside when they opened the door, and let Doone out. But if he thinks he pulled the wool over my eyes, he thunk wrong. People don't thumb their noses at Thadeus Trout. Your husband, my dear, is in deep doo-doo. And as far as I'm concerned, you inherited his debt, being his loving spouse."

Rita Rae flicked her cigarette onto the floor. "Bullshit. He stiffed me, too. Cleaned out our bank account, and, look—" She extended her ring finger.

Trout slipped his liver-spotted hand under her palm, smiled at first, preparing to remove the ring as partial payment. When he peered at the fat stone through his reading glasses, he dropped her hand. "Don't need a loupe to tell me that's bogus."

"Cubic zirconia. It *was* a beautiful five-carat diamond. He switched it the night he left for Vegas."

"Right, Vegas," Trout said. "But he did come back."

"To pick the bones of my marriage clean. I flew back to salvage what I could, and to get my ring. All that's left of value, far as I know, is that armory—which he leases, doesn't own—and our furniture, which I plan to sell."

Trout linked his fingers and rotated his thumbs one around the other. His thick-lidded eyes raised from the twirling thumb to Rita Rae. "Tell you what I'll do, for old time's sake. Junior," Trout swiveled his large head toward his son, "will buy you a new pair of shoes. You send me the bill and I'll deduct it from his next paycheck."

Junior squealed, "No way."

Rita Rae gave Junior an exaggerated grin, and said, "What about my gun?"

Mr. Trout arched an eyebrow at Junior, who removed the little Colt from his pocket, unloaded it, and tossed it back to her.

"Now," Mr. Trout continued, "Junior and his screw-up buddies are going take you back to the house and scour it. Any money turns up, my share comes off the top. Then they can haul away the furniture on their backs. I'll sell it for you in the outlet shop, put the proceeds against hubby's loan.

"I'll also give you a two grand finder's fee if you locate Doone for me, and I guarantee he'll be out of your life. How's that?"

Rita Rae chewed her lower lip in mock deliberation. Considering her Charles Jourdan pumps were scuffed anyway, the furniture would have been repossessed, and a dead Shickie Doone meant a fat insurance pay-off as well as the worm neatly disposed of, she shrugged. "What choice do I have?"

Creely Patch set his broom in the corner of his office. "Haunted by buzzards."

"No, sir." Ginger sat on the arm of the Gothic chair facing his desk. "I talked to a park ranger and he said they're not buzzards but vultures."

"Whatever. But why infest our roof?" He took a seat in the Prince of Light's swivel chair. "When I shoo them away they hiss at me. And, as soon as I leave, they fly right back."

"They really do like it here."

"Why now? The only birds up there when Doone was with us were those white doves he was always pulling from his robe. Buzzards haunting us like this doesn't speak well for the purity of my ministry. You've seen their droppings?"

"They sure poop a bunch, don't they? Do you know why they do it on their feet?"

"I'm sure you're going to tell me."

"It's to keep cool. It gets awfully hot with the sun beating on the tar paper."

"Demons like heat." Patch assumed his faraway look and spoke to the air. "Foul excrement . . . calling in raucous tongues . . . hellish heat . . . three beasts with scarlet heads, three hooked beaks, six black wings, twenty-four clawed toes . . ." He placed a hand on the leatherbound Bible at the center of his desk. "It's one of the signs of Revelation, if only I can fathom the meaning."

Boogers Tarbell and Teddie Keene nodded with the rest of the troop at Scoutmaster Brown's instructions: "As long as you stay on this side of the ridge you can't get lost—the mountain's on one side, creek's in the valley. Use your compasses and stay with your buddy at all times. Keep away from snakes, poison ivy, caves, and strangers offering you rides. If you get into trouble, use your whistle. Your mission is to identify fifteen trees. . . ."

As soon as they were out of sight of Scoutmaster Brown, following the woods parallel to the mountain, Boogers pushed Teddie into a poison ivy patch. Teddie pushed Boogers into the same patch. Before long they were flipping rocks and logs, looking for snakes. When nothing more than a scorpion turned up on dry land, they turned to a creek bed, working their way upstream. "I'll bet this place is full of water moccasins," Boogers said. All they found were salamanders. The salamanders, however, proved good fun, being fat, fast, and slippery.

Thirty minutes later, straining at a streamside boulder, Teddie glanced up. His mouth dropped open and he shouted, "Hey Boogers, look—the creek's comin' out of a cave."

"Cool. Let's explore."

Fulfilling the Scouts' motto, Be Prepared, they removed the flashlights clipped at their belts and flicked them on.

"Watch your head," Boogers said, "it gets real low."

Ten minutes into the hillside, and several cursing, head-bumps later, Boogers turned off his light and dared Teddie to do the same. No sooner had Teddie said, "I can't even see my hand," than he got the creeps and turned his light back on. "Maybe we oughta go back."

"Naw," said Boogers. "Let's see where it goes." He pitched a pigeon-egg-size pebble into the receding blackness and dislodged a bat.

"Shit! Shit! Shit!" Teddie ducked. The bat flew toward his face, dipping and bobbing with each silent flap of its leathery wings. Three feet away, it darted to the side, neatly bypassing him.

"I'll bet it was a vampire," said Boogers. "Would'a sucked your blood if you hadn't a dodged."

"Oh, man, let's go back. There could be a whole herd of them in there."

"Chicken! You're a chicken-shit, Teddie. Wait'll I tell the guys how you chickened out, you chicken." Boogers shone his light at Teddie's crotch to see if he'd wet his pants. What a story that would make, Teddie peeing his pants on account of one little bat. Unfortunately, Teddie's trousers were dry from the knees up, but Boogers was encouraged by Teddie's red, wrinkled-up face. The puss was ready to burst into tears like some wimpy girl. "Crybaby, crybaby, chicken-shit, crybaby." Boogers kept it up until Teddie swore he wasn't afraid, that he'd follow the stream to its source.

The source was only ten minutes further: water gushing from a channel fifteen feet up a mud-covered, nearly vertical, flowstone cliff. It was too steep and much too slippery for the boys to climb, though Boogers gave it a real Scout's effort.

"Guess that's it," said a relieved Teddie.

"Hold on," said Boogers. He stood on his toes, directing the flashlight's beam under a ledge slightly above his head. "There's a side passage."

"No way," said Teddie. "It ain't more than a foot tall, don't go nowhere."

"Wrong. I can't see the end of it. Maybe there's stalactites and stuff in a room big enough to drive a truck through right on the other side. Bet no one's ever been there before." So far, the cave had been no more than a low, meandering limestone tunnel with no more than a bump or two on the roof.

Before Teddie could protest, Boogers scrambled onto the ledge and was wriggling headfirst, belly-down like a lizard, into the cramped passage.

"I'll stay back here in case you get stuck," Teddie said, shining his light one way, then the other, wary of bats.

"Fine. You stay there, you chicken-shit chicken." Boogers's front half was entirely in the passage. His legs kicked air. "But if I find a super cave, I get to name it."

"Okay." Teddie didn't like the sound of the falling water—what if it flooded and rose to the roof? He also didn't like being alone. The soles of Boogers's sneakers had disappeared. But there was no way Teddie was going to crawl into that snake hole, either. He backed against the rock opposite the side passage in case more bats flew out of the hole with the flowing water. Or, what if there was a bear up there and they woke it up with their lights and shouting, and it came crashing out, wet and angry? Teddie went silent.

Five minutes later, he scrambled to the ledge and shone his light into the side cave that had eaten his buddy. He saw only scrabble-marks on the dusty floor. "Boogers?" he called softly. No answer. Teddie began to panic. What if Boogers had dislodged a big rock and it had squashed him? Or, he fell into a pit like in the movies where the heroes are trapped in a mine. Or, a wildcat got him, was gnawing off his leg right now—

"Hey, Teddie!" The shout echoed through the cavern. It didn't sound hurt, or terror-stricken, but excited. "I found stalactites and stalagmites and it goes forever. Hold on, I'm gonna explore."

Teddie took a deep breath and muttered an Okay. Minutes passed. Maybe hours.

Boogers called every so often, still excited, his voice growing more indistinct and ever more echoey. Then, he really shouted: "Oh, man! Oh, man! Wait'll you see this. C'mon in. This is so cool." Bouncing and rebounding off the rock, muffled by the *shusss* of falling water, the words were barely intelligible, but the intent was clear: Boogers had found something wonderful. Maybe treasure.

"I'm staying here." Teddie had made his mind up. But he

couldn't help cupping his hands to his mouth and calling out a "What is it?"

"It's a *mummy!*"

"—ummy,—ummmy" echoed through the passage.

"A what?" Teddie wasn't sure he heard right.

"I shit you not, Teddie—a mummy. A dead cave man or somebody who got stuck and—"

"No!" Teddie was really scared now. Somebody who got *stuck*. If somebody else had got stuck, then Boogers could, too, and Teddie would have to go for help, alone, and explain, and—

"I'm coming back." Boogers's voice was louder, more clear.

Minutes passed and Boogers's muddy head and one extended arm emerged, his hand grasping the flashlight. The passage was so narrow he had to squeeze through it with one arm forward, one arm back.

Boogers dropped to the entry cave floor with a splash. "A dead guy! All crouched like this." Boogers tucked his chin to his neck, crisscrossed his arms over his chest, and crouched so his knees touched his stomach. "All covered with dirt and dried out just like those mummies on TV."

"You aren't shitting me?" Teddie had been the butt of innumerable Boogers scams. One time Boogers had scrambled down to a stream running below a high bridge to look for turtles. He opened a water-soaked cardboard box on the bank, and yelled up to Teddie on the road above that he'd found a dead baby. Teddie followed, tearing himself to shreds on raspberry brambles on the way down, only to find it was a decomposing chicken. Maybe Boogers hadn't really found a cave on the other side at all, just a pocket big enough to stand up in, and had muffled his voice to make Teddie think—

"No way! No way! A dead guy. A *mummy*."

"Let's get out of here. Don't tell nobody. If Mr. Brown finds out we've been in a cave, he'll—"

Bats and bears forgotten, they argued on the way out. "We'll be famous," Boogers said.

"Nuh-uh. Mr. Brown'll be pissed, throw us out of the troop. Mom'll kill me."

"Famous," Boogers repeated. "We'll be on TV, in the newspapers."

As it turned out, the debate was moot. It was twilight when they emerged and one of the other scouts—everyone had been searching—saw their flashlight beams, heard their voices, and relayed the news via scout-to-scout shouts to the anxious Mr. Brown.

After a thorough grilling, during which Boogers stuck to his story, Mr. Brown called the police on his cell phone. The police, in turn, called a cave rescue team based in Knoxville. Though Boogers swore he had found a "dead guy, a mummy," the adults had doubts. If the boy had truly seen a human, perhaps he had run away, frightened, before determining the unfortunate's condition. It could have been a foolish tourist, entering the cave alone, now hurt, unconscious.

The scouts, including Teddie, trembling in anticipation of his mother's wrath, were bused home. Boogers, scared, but thrilled at being the center of attention, stayed at the cave entrance to direct the rescuers. The police sloshed through the underground stream to the side passage, called into it with a bullhorn without response, but went no further, fearful of dislodging loose rock and getting stuck themselves. A mobile TV unit arrived, and the entrance was dramatically lit by the time the three-man, one-woman cave rescue crew, dressed in coveralls and miners' helmets, bearing ropes and other gear, entered.

The rescue team returned empty-handed but confirmed to the growing crowd that not only had the boys discovered a significant new cave, but there was, indeed, a body inside—one they were reluctant to disturb. Long-dead, they suspected. Nude, desiccated, it was half-embedded in debris that had fallen from an overhead chimney leading to either a higher passage or, perhaps, eventually, to the surface. While the police discussed the likelihood of foul-play and contacted the medical examiner, the cavers raised the possibility the body was that of an ancient Indian, perhaps a ritual burial, and alerted an anthropologist affiliated with a historical museum in Pigeon Forge.

The reporters were in media heaven: a mysterious murder victim or an ancient Indian, naked as a jaybird, discovered a thousand feet back in a fantastic new cave, ten short miles from Dollywood and twenty-first century civilization.

17

Jimmy Feather, the new security guard at Gatlinburg's Bible Alive Museum, dropped the two-way radio in the box and punched out after his first eight hours on the job. Having roamed the American West for the better part of a year, Jimmy was suffering a fierce case of claustrophobia. Though the museum was massive, a seventy-foot high, ersatz Babylonian pyramid running a full block along the Gatlinburg strip, it was also confining: honeycombed with exhibits, packed with tourists, and, lacking windows, dim as a tomb.

Jimmy ran outside, took a lungful of clean mountain air, and took long strides of freedom downhill. Three blocks away, tourist stares and the breeze on his bare legs reminded him he was still in his David suit. His faded jeans with the concho belt, his western boots and shirt, and the Levi's jacket were still in his locker. Well, shoot.

The hell with it. Jimmy needed a beer. The Indian head penny still hung from his neck, his wallet was tucked in the costume girdle at his waist, so he kept walking, muttering about punching time clocks, ten-minute potty breaks, half an hour for lunch and the rest of it. Teenage girls wolf-whistling, giggling, asking what he wore under his "skirt." Old ladies asking questions about the Bible. Kids wanting to hear the David and Goliath story straight from David's mouth, and tourists of all stripes posing with him like he was one of those life-sized cardboard cutouts of Elvis or Marilyn Monroe or the President. An old maid schoolteacher from Atlanta scolded him for carrying a slingshot and not a "sling," whatever the hell that was. A Baptist preacher complained to the management that Jimmy said "you," not "thou," "has," not "hath," and no fewer than three yokels wanted to know if he was really a Jew like David and could they touch him.

Jimmy wanted to shout I'm a red-blooded Indian for crissakes! but he kept his cool. His grandfather had stuck his neck out to get him the job, and Jimmy promised to hang in for at least a week.

I need a beer, he thought. Or two or three. He saw a neon "Poncho the Pirate's" with the second P burned out. The place looked friendly, so he entered and took a stool at one of the high round-topped tables, kilt, vest, and lace-up sandals be damned.

He pressed a cool mug to his forehead, closed his eyes and silently cursed. I should have stayed on the Navajo rez, he concluded, taken a job bagging groceries at that truck stop in Shiprock. At least the Four Corners tourists would have mistaken me for a Navajo instead of . . . whatever I am.

The drive from Cincinnati to Gatlinburg in Maury's rented Lincoln Town Car took four hours and fifty-three minutes. Maury checked into Whispering Pines, the motel AAA had reserved for him in the frenetic heart of the Gatlinburg strip. He showered and donned a fresh, pink, oxford-cloth shirt, a bright blue paisley bow tie, and a navy blazer. A .22 Colt Woodsman semiautomatic pistol sat snugly in a holster below his left armpit in case he got lucky.

He left the motel and paused at the sidewalk to get the feel of the place. Tourists were returning from day trips to the Smoky Mountains, Dollywood, and the Pigeon Forge outlet stores. Some had begun their first of the evening trophy-quest, strolling through store after store of airbrushed tee shirts, hand-carved candles, log slices with decals of the Last Supper, ceramic gnomes, Indian feather headdresses, cornucopias of shop-brewed candies, myriad salt shakers, beaded moccasins, real oysters with real pearls, Olde Tyme portraits, and more. Too much more.

None of which interested Maury. His internal clock told him it was happy hour, time for a Manhattan, a chance to schmooz with the locals, and zero in on his quarry, Shickleton Doone. A few inquiries, a few blocks, and Maury reluctantly abandoned his initial hopes of finding a Cora's Cozy Cove. He settled on a bar named Poncho the Pirate's, notable for its ten-foot neon sign, a leering, handlebar mustachioed Mexican wearing a sombrero and eye patch. Poncho's good eye winked open and shut in time with a dancing parrot on his shoulder. Maury chuckled at the burned-out P in the name and the new read: Poncho the 'irates. The décor was pseudo-Mexican primitive with exposed brick walls, dusty palm trees, and phony parrots in cages hanging from the ceiling. Huge speakers, thankfully as yet silent, and a long bar and ample dance floor suggested the place might really hop on a weekend night.

In a passing bout of nostalgia, Maury recalled dancing with Rose in the good old days. Foxtrots, swing, and rumbas. He wondered if anyone in Gatlinburg cheek-to-cheeked or whether they just jiggled around.

Maury sat at the bar and nursed his first Manhattan, served over the rocks in an Old Fashioned glass the way he liked it. He held his right hand steady with his left as he lifted it to his lips. The years had been kind to Maury, but his hands weren't as steady as they once had been. He perused the clientele, mostly tourists, young and noisy, even at this early hour. The bartender, a perky youngster barely out of high school dressed in a sombrero, red satin running shorts, and a yellow tee shirt with a one-eyed Mexican leering from her chest, knew all about the Poof! of the Reverend Shickleton Doone. The whole town was buzzing about it, she said. No, she had never seen the Prince himself, but she told Maury he could recognize the Fireflies, Doone's followers, from their white robes and the flashlights they carried at night. She also drew a map on a napkin with an X marking their church, which she called the Temple of Light, and led him to the sidewalk to point out their soaring angel-shaped blimp with strobe light eyes. To Maury, it looked like a bloated, upside-down diver with fat swan's wings, its legs pressed together, toes pointing down, extended arms stretching heavenward.

"A searchlight lights it up at night," the bartender said. "They say you can see it from seven states, maybe even eight."

"Is that a fact?"

"If you want a closer look, go to the top of the space needle. One ticket's good for two visits, daytime and night."

Maury decided that wasn't a bad idea. From up there, he would have a bird's-eye view of Doone's church and his house. He drained the glass, popped the maraschino cherry into his mouth, and ordered another.

Halfway into Maury's second drink, three young men strolled in, sat two stools away, and ordered beers. Their hair was sweat-matted, their tee shirts moist. One wore a leather jacket over the wet tee shirt. Must be proud of it, Maury decided, to wear leather on a day like this. Working men, probably. He figured one for construction, or (he shut his eyes for a moment, awash in fond memories) a furniture mover. He was a big, hard-looking fellow, late-twenties, with a ponytail, piercings, tattoos, and bulging muscles—no doubt a free weight junky. His companion was chubby, freckle-faced and fair, a year or two younger, already gorging himself on bar peanuts. Maury pegged him for working in one of the fudge shops; probably ate as much as he sold. The third, a ferrety fellow, the one in the leather jacket, sported a sparse goatee, a shaved head, and a bad complexion. From the low whistles and hoots emanating from their mouths, they were no doubt foraging for young female tourists. Maury figured if these three didn't know about Doone, they would have at least taken notice of the young woman who supposedly witnessed his disappearance. She would be Maury's first link to cashing in on the contract.

He cleared his throat. Cleared it again, finally clacked his glass hard on the bar for attention. The three heads turned as one and scowled.

"Hey, boys, how's tricks?" Maury said, realizing as he spoke, how old, how alien, he must seem to these kids.

The three heads turned away, began snickering at some inside joke.

Maury spoke louder. "Just being friendly. Feeling a little lonely traveling by myself. Wife's been gone twelve years."

Sympathy didn't play. The trio turned their backs in a deliberate snub, so Maury took a different tack. "How about a round of beers on me?"

The chubby one, the skinny one, and then the muscle-bound one cocked their heads Maury's way. Maury motioned to the bartender for a round for the boys, and moved over one stool, beside the fat kid. "Maury, you can call me," he said, with his salesman's smile, and extended a hand.

The pudgy one, uncertain, gave Maury a limp, salty-handed shake. "Peaches."

Maury leaned toward the big one, extended his palm and immediately regretted it when he received a bone-crunching squeeze. The man held on, grinning at Maury's pain. "They call me Six-pack."

Maury merely waved to the third one who nodded and said, "Junior."

"Nice town, Gatlinburg," Maury said. He got no response. "Did you hear the one about . . ." No one cocked an ear. The beers arrived and the boys returned to their conversation.

The three beers didn't last long. Maury gave it another try: "Nice jacket," he said to the skinny one.

"Hard Rock Cafe," the kid answered, but said no more.

"Bet you work hard for your money. How about another round?"

That earned him a moment's more attention, so he plowed on, thinking, If this was the Cozy Cove, we'd be laughing at one another's jokes already. "Nothing like honest labor to work up a sweat, eh? Let me guess. Construction?"

"Worse," said Junior. "We been moving furniture."

"Furniture?" Maury felt a rush of nostalgia. "I used to be in the stick trade. Got into it right after the war."

"Nam?" Junior said it like he'd been there.

"No . . . W W Two. The big one. Europe."

Junior gave him an intent stare. "You kill people?"

Maury did a double take. Surely this kid couldn't— "Ah," he said, relieved, "the war. I imagine we killed our share. Army Air Corps, Fifteenth Air Force. Bombardier in a B-17. Did fifty missions out of Foggia, Italy. Hit Rumania, Poland, and Germany. Would've been no party down there. Nossir."

Peaches twisted his stool to face Maury. "Cool."

"Bombs away," Junior said, and made a whistling sound. He lifted an empty beer bottle and dropped it on the counter as a climax. "Goodbye Gooks, huh?"

Maury raised an eyebrow.

Six-pack waxed reflective. "You never had to look at them? Dead guys, bodies?"

"Not *then*," Maury said, and went silent. He recovered a beat later, and steered the subject to more productive ground: "Tell me, boychik," he said to Six-pack, "about this Shickie Doone. What's the real scoop?"

"Who? What? Nothing. I don't know nothing." Six-pack white-knuckled the neck of his beer bottle and stared at the label.

"You looking for Doone?" Peaches said. "Guess you and Mr. Trout been talking, huh?"

Maury look confused, worried. "Trout? How could you know—"

"None of us don't know nothing about nobody," Junior said, with finality and a hostile glare. "See? So drop it."

Maury's face blanched. "Of course. Sorry." He gulped the dregs of his Manhattan, tried to sort out the conversation. How could these kids, strangers, possibly—

"Holy shit! Would you look at that?" Junior tipped his head toward a new visitor to Poncho's, a slim, well-built young man with shoulder-length black hair, dressed in a gold-trimmed skirt and vest, wearing sandals with leather thongs crisscrossing to his knees. He took a seat at a high bar table and ordered a brew.

Six-pack thumped his fist on the bar. "Who do they think they are, coming in here like that?"

Maury, thankful to be discussing anything other than his profession and his supposedly anonymous employer, muttered, "Hoo-boy, a faygeleh."

"You *know* him?" Peaches jerked away so fast he nearly fell off the barstool. No wonder the old man was buying them drinks.

Maury said, "No, no. Faygeleh's not his name and I don't know him. It means, like they say it now, gay."

Junior expressed it more directly. "Fucking queer."

Hoping to lighten things up, so he could re-pose the Doone query from another angle, Maury said, "To each his own, I always say. I'll give them this: they have impeccable taste in furniture. Good color sense. Usually willing to spend more for quality as well. It does bother me about the words they stole." He noticed the quizzical looks and smiled. Maury, with his gift for gab, was back in command. "You know, those words that used to mean other things? For instance, my wife Rose, bless her, and I were a gay couple." He cast Peaches a corrective look. "Happy. Light hearted. That's what it meant, then, before the faygelehs stole the word. 'Queer?' That meant no more than 'odd.' During the war 'fags' were cigarettes. And 'queen?' An old lady with a crown on her head. 'Drag?' All together different, then. And 'dike?' That's what little Dutch boys stuck their fingers in."

Junior snorted. "Now, it's what little *girls* stick their fingers in."

Maury chuckled and slapped his thigh. This was the sort of barroom banter he was accustomed to.

Before he could rejoinder, Junior shot at wicked look at the young man across the floor. "Men touching men? Makes me wanna puke."

Junior put an arm around Six-pack's shoulders and drew

him close, motioned for Peaches to join the huddle. Their foreheads nearly touched. "I say," said Junior, "we beat his ass up."

"Cool," said Peaches.

"I'll throw a hammerlock on him and you can break his arm," said Six-pack.

"Here's how we'll do it." Junior lowered his voice. "Peaches? They're always licking their lips over you, what with that girly skin, curly hair, and your pudgy butt."

"Christ, Junior, don't say that."

"It's true. I've even seen Six-pack eye your ass when he's stoned."

Six-pack grabbed Junior's hand and squeezed. "You say that again, I'll bust your fingers, boss's son or not."

Junior writhed, trying to regain his hand. "Kidding. Just kidding."

"Boys?" Maury said, from outside the huddle.

They ignored him. Massaging his liberated hand, Junior said, "We'll send Peaches over, have him wink at the guy and walk outside—"

"No way!" said Peaches.

"I'll leave first," said Six-pack. "Twist his arm up behind him when he gets out. Throw him in the back seat and—"

"Boys?"

Junior glanced at Maury, annoyed. "What?"

"He's gone. The faygeleh. He dropped a bill on the table and left."

"Shit," Junior said. "Why didn't you say something?"

"Let's find him," said Six-pack.

The three rose, hurried to the door, and disappeared into the street.

Maury ordered another Manhattan. When it arrived, he toasted himself in the bar-side mirror. "And this one, you thought would be easy."

18

lato Scopes, a nervous young man clad in an over-starched lab coat two sizes too large for his gaunt frame, raised his hand for attention. The media, all five of them—a scruffy camera/sound-man, a perky second-string, female TV field reporter from Knoxville, two bored newspaper correspondents, one each from Knoxville and Asheville, and a novice stringer for AP—set down their complementary cans of pop and turned his way. With his flyaway hair, bulging dark-circled eyes, and bony body rattling in hospital whites, Scopes looked like an electroshock patient who had been juiced a few times too many. He squinted at the video light, blinked, and squeaked, "I have earth-shattering news—"

He cleared his throat and repeated the words more intelligibly, if not with the force he intended. The small cafeteria should have been packed. Where were the networks? *TIME*, *Newsweek*, *Scientific American*, the *Discovery Channel*, *National Geographic*? Although, what could he expect? Had any of them ever heard of the tiny Captain Hook Museum, barely funded by a slim endowment and meager attendance? Surely, they had never heard of him: Plato Scopes, Chief (and only) Scientist. Mrs. Trillip, the volunteer PR lady, had done her best, Scopes imagined, on such short notice.

Just as well, he decided, because the evidence was hardly conclusive—yet. But if his instincts were on the money, this would indeed be earth-shattering news, news that would finally propel Plato Scopes from dusty obscurity to scientific fame.

Obscurity was the word for it, all right. Though passionate about science, Scopes had always been cursed with bad luck. It began with an abortive attempt to harvest pheromones surreptitiously from the panties of his high school cheerleading squad. His intentions: misunderstood. As an anthropology grad student, his purely scientific investigation, "Trans-specific eroticism via visual stimuli between members of the Pongidae, in coitus, and *Homo sapiens*," nearly got him thrown out of the program when a myopic administration misinterpreted his observations of student couples cuddling on a cot while viewing videos of ape sex in his dimly-lit laboratory.

During a summer dig in New Mexico, Plato was nearly killed in a Gallup bar for his honesty, explaining to several burly Pueblo Indians how their Anasazi ancestors had been cannibals. He achieved notoriety, if not fame, when he took a vocal stand against NAGPRA, the Native American Grave Protection and Repatriation Act of 1990. Plato was incensed that NAGPRA was stripping museums—many of them receiving federal funding, and that was practically all of them—of their indigenous skeletal material and burial-associated artifacts. Giving it back to the Indians, literally, for reburial, destruction, sale to collectors, whatever they wanted to do with it. The thought of religion subduing science made Plato Scopes seethe. Ignorant hotheads.

Scopes had written letters, phoned talk-radio shows, appealed to Congress, despite the shushing of his lily-livered advisors. How many of his peers joined him? A handful. The rest? Though the sheep knew he was right, they were too damned timid to speak against the PC rhetoric. And look where it got them. Their collections looted. Invaluable skeletal material that could track origins, reveal ancient disease, morbidity, nutritional data, lost forever.

Where had it gotten Plato Scopes? Blacklisted from any meaningful anthropological research in the US of A, that's for damned sure. No institution dealing with Native Americans wanted the controversial Scopes on their staff.

So, as soon as he got his master's degree, he went to Mexico in search of monumental discoveries in Maya country before that, too, went to hell.

He had been working on a site called Chichixmal in Chiapas, unraveling amazing rituals of royal bloodletting, the lancing of penises and tongues with stingray barbs, when he discovered grave robbers stealing vital steles and invaluable hieroglyphic pottery from under the noses of the government guards. *Policía?* Hah! Graft mongers. Scopes lambasted the authorities but got nowhere. He greased a few palms, found where the thieves were hiding their loot. One night he arranged for easy women to visit the larcenous cache with drugged tequila. By stealth of night, to the sound of looters' snores, Scopes loaded the stolen artifacts into a truck and headed for Mexico City, intending to stack his cargo on the desk of the Director of the Museo Archeologico, with a sharp word about protecting the national patrimony.

He would have been a hero if the damned looters hadn't gotten wind of his plan and arranged for the *Federales* to intercept him. Plato Scopes, charged with looting national treasures. The indignity! There went research in Latin America, or employment in any institution doing south-of-the-border research. Goodbye PhD, as well as publishing in any but the most obscure academic journals.

Hello middle-of-nowhere, historical Captain Hook Museum, in the heart of Pigeon Forge, Tennessee, founded by Captain Horatio Hook, Spanish-American War hero, one of the world's great buttonhook collectors. Buttonhooks: tools from an inch to a foot long with a handle on one end, a hook on the other to pull buttons through buttonholes. Some were fancy, some plain, but ubiquitous in the mid-nineteenth century into the twentieth when shoes and gloves had well over twenty buttons, dresses might have had more than a hundred, and everything from spats to jackets to corsets were buttoned.

Buttonhooks—whoever heard of them now, let alone cared? The same might be said of Plato Scopes. When he wasn't cataloguing buttonhooks, Scopes spent most of his time excavating pioneer privies and compiling coprolite—petrified feces—analyses. Plato Scopes, shit specialist. Hardly the scintillating career in anthropology he once imagined.

Yesterday's phone call from the cave, however, would soon change that.

Scopes heard himself speaking to the reporters, ". . . examined by the police detective and myself *in situ*—that is, still in the cave. We concluded, pending analytical confirmation, that this was not a homicide. Not a recent one, anyway." He chuckled at his little joke, but realized from the blank stares that they didn't get it. "Our mummy appears to be *centuries* old. There are glyphs inscribed on the now dry, muddy walls of an adjacent chamber, suggesting a fertility sacrifice."

That perked them up.

"How was he killed? Was it some sex thing?" asked the TV reporter, her voice an octave higher than it had been earlier when she asked if they had Diet Sprite.

"We don't know that yet. However, the processing of the body is remarkable. It bests the work of the South American Shuar—with no shrinkage."

"Can we see it?"

"Not yet. Tomorrow, perhaps. We left it in place to allow analysis of the surrounding matrix. The mummy is half-covered by fallen detritus that may well provide clues to its origin."

The TV woman: "Can you take us there so we can get some footage?"

"Or stills?" said the stringer, sensing Big Story.

"Sorry. The chamber is difficult to reach and it is important no one disturbs the floor of the cave. The Park Service is guarding the entrance. Who knows? We may find the footprints of the people who left him. Imagine that! I hope to extract the mummy tomorrow and bring it to my laboratory. . . ."

Laboratory? Grade schools had better facilities. But Scopes wanted that mummy in his hands ASAP. Perhaps not the best scientific method, working so fast, but the cave might be on Smoky Mountains National Park land, no one was sure yet. If it was, the Park Service archaeologists would want dibs on the mummy. NAGPRA, the Native American Grave Protection and Repatriation Act, would rear its ugly head. Other researchers would swarm in.

". . . will you do with it?"

"Photograph, measure. X-ray it thoroughly, have a CT scan done. We'll date it with a C-14 analysis and AMS—accelerator mass spectrography. And trace the DNA to establish relationships."

"It's an Indian, right?"

They would ask that. "Could be, but from the look of it, I'd say, no."

"So it could be a pioneer? A lost miner?"

"Not likely. The body is flexed," Plato folded his arms over his chest, drew one knee up to demonstrate, "which is a common archaic burial position. More significantly, the mummy is nude," active scribbling by the reporters, "and, as I said, remarkably mummified. This is a limestone solution cavern, not a mine. There's nothing of value in there other than a little bat guano, and there's no sign of resource exploitation or repeated entry. Everything points to a ritual placement of the body."

Scopes raised both hands, warding off further questions. "I'll have more information for you tomorrow at two P.M. Thank you. Please, help yourselves to another can of pop."

The video lights winked out and the reporters exited.

Alone, Scopes took a deep breath, held it in, and exhaled audibly. This whole media thing was premature, he knew.

No, he said to himself. It is essential I stake out my turf. This could mean a scientific monograph in a legitimate journal.

Please, don't let me be wrong. There's no down from this sorry place. I know my instincts are good, the preliminary data—

Clapping interrupted his ruminations. Slow, sarcastic clapping. Scopes turned to the sound. Uh-oh. The museum director, Horace Duckhaus. Scopes had forgotten to mention the press conference. Failed to mention the mummy, in fact.

"Well, Scopes. Thanks for keeping me in the loop." Duckhaus was a humorless man near retirement, reminiscent of a Dickens countinghouse scribe, tall, bent, hairless, with a small pot belly and a perennial squint. All he wanted was to retire with the collection larger than when he started, the museum in the black, and his pension intact. Duckhaus rested his hands on his hips and arched his eyebrows. "Well?" he said to Plato Scopes's embarrassed silence.

"I'm so-oo sorry, sir. The police called me after closing last night. I was in the cave most of the night. Uh, some boys found this mummy in a cave, and—"

"I listened." Horace Duckhaus gave him a grudging smile. "Not bad publicity for the museum, but you should have spoken to me first. How much did you spend on those refreshments?"

"Just pop and a large bag of chips. I paid for them myself."

"A-hum. All this testing you mentioned? Sounds costly. You've nearly exhausted our research budget on your privy work. With all the competition from the outlets, the tourist traps, Dollywood, and the mountains, we're lucky to pay the electric bills and salaries."

"I'll find a way, sir. I can't overstate how significant—"

"Maybe we could put this thing on display. Lord knows, our wonderful buttonhooks don't pull them in anymore. You get some media play out of this, we could give Ripley's a run for their money. What do you think?"

"Oh, *no*, sir." Scopes ran his fingers though his perennially unkempt hair and did a little dance in place, too agitated to answer. He finally said, "We have an obligation to follow scientific protocols. We can't make a freak show out of it. Besides," Scopes's nemesis rose to his defense, "no one displays burials anymore. The Native American outcry would be—"

"We damn well can't afford bad press."

"No, sir."

Duckhaus shook his finger at the younger man. "Very well. Here's the bottom line: if this thing pays for itself, brings in visitors and cash, more power to you. But if it costs us money, or embarrasses us, out it goes." He spun on his heels and walked away.

Scopes, flushed with anger, fumed for half a minute. He lifted an opened pop can and pitched it at the wall. Cola geysered across the room. "Hah!" he said, pleased with the result. He shook a fist in the direction of the director's office. "That mummy is *mine*," he said to the empty cafeteria. "No one—not you, not the Indians, not the Feds. *No* one is going to take it away from me. *Mine*. You hear?"

19

Rita Rae greeted Orlando on the front porch with a chilly peck on the cheek. "Welcome to Gatlinburg and my home sweet home. I'd offer you a chair, but," she flung an arm toward the empty interior, "as you see, there aren't any. Hubby's loan-sharking goons took it all. Everything but the mattresses. They were too lazy to haul them off."

Orlando shrugged and slipped an arm around Rita Rae's waist. He reached up to stroke her hair with his free hand, but withdrew it at the brittle touch of her shellacked bubble do. He shook his fingers behind her back with a shiver, and pulled her close. "*¿Como se dice?* A bottle of wine, a mattress, *y nosotros.* What more do we need, *mi querida flaquita,* but the mighty *pinga* of Orlando?"

Rita Rae wriggled free. "My beautiful diamond for a start. Then, the money the little worm owes me for living with him for a year. 'Raptured?' If God took him up, he'd spit him out like a rancid peanut." She began an angry jitterbug, muttering curses. "Wait till I get hold of him."

Orlando snagged her again and pulled her inside. He kicked the door shut, placed one hand firmly behind her neck and gave her a rough kiss.

Rita Rae squirmed several seconds, and eased, getting into the feel of his mouth on hers, the tickle of his mustache against her upper lip. The embrace lasted a good minute. Soon, her hands were mussing Orlando's slicked-back hair and he had her short skirt hiked up, one hand working her crotch, the other melon-gripping her right flank. He nibbled her ear and whispered, "Orlando would like to see a bedroom."

Rita Rae's tongue flicked over her still-tingling lower lip. She curled a finger through the belt loop of Orlando's trousers and tugged him toward the stairway. "Upstairs. We'll do it on the worm's mattress."

Ginger screwed up her face. "Gee, Reverend Patch, I told the girls I'd go dancing tonight."

"Ginger, you have responsibilities. Divine responsibilities. Now that the good Lord has made me His Messenger, you His Witness, it would be untoward of you to be seen dancing in some common bar. As Paul tells Timothy: 'Flee youthful lusts, follow righteousness.'"

Ginger pouted, squirmed in the gilt throne Patch had hurriedly prepared for her—a kitchen chair, actually, spray-painted gold and sparkling with gold glitter. It had a lower back and seat than the Messenger's, but was showy, nonetheless. It would do until they could afford better. Both chairs were positioned at the center of a low wooden stage at one end of the cavernous room the Temple of Light euphemistically called the sanctuary. In the building's military incarnation, the National Guard made the room available for amateur theater productions, dog and cat shows, and an annual gun and knife extravaganza. Since the Rapture, supplicants—more often, merely curious tourists—formed a queue at one end of the room and, one by one as their number was called, climbed to the stage to speak with the Messenger and the Witness.

Ginger stuck out her lower lip, wouldn't look Patch in the eye. "I promised the girls."

"I promised the Lord." He leaned over, extended a hand toward her chest. "Close your robe."

Ginger shied away, tightened the sash of the pale lavender robe Mrs. Binkle had sewn on Patch's orders. His was royal purple, with the same gold-braid border and yellow embroidered flame over the heart. They had matching seat cusions.

"Ginger, in two short days, three hundred and sixty-one pilgrims have come to hear about the Rapture. Many, we will save from hellfire. Souls aside, we should not overlook their generosity. Despite his good intentions, the Prince's profligacy put us in dire financial straits. If we don't pay the helium bill soon, our angel will be dragging her wings on the ground. How would that look? Her strobe lights eyes have been falling out of phase. I called the repair people. Despite our good works, they expect to be paid."

"Hmmm." She still wouldn't look at him.

"I wouldn't want to constrain you. If singing the praises of the Lord isn't enough—"

"Choir practice is tomorrow night."

"Ahum." Patch drummed his fingers on the arm of his chair. "Let me put it this way: where would we be, if, when the angel of the assumption had informed Mary she was to receive the seed of the baby Jesus in her womb, Mary had said, 'No thanks, I have to go dancing?'"

Ginger kicked the rung of her throne. "I'm not Mary and I'm not about to get pregnant."

Patch flushed. "Of course not. But the Lord chose you to witness the Prince's Rapture. You are very special to Him."

Ginger cocked her head. "Like a saint?"

"Saints are for Catholics. The Children of Light need no intermediaries. We speak directly to God. God speaks to us. He has spoken to me, Ginger, and was very specific: I am to save souls for the Rapture, you are to assist."

Ginger stared at her shoes. "I wanted to be a nun, once."

"Fie on that Catholic talk. You are the Witness, far more important than any nun. Being my assistant puts you practically at the foot of God. In Catholicism, nuns have to kowtow to priests, priests to bishops, bishops to archbishops. There are cardinals, popes, saints, purgatory, rites—it's a theological quagmire."

"Yeah, but they always know what to do, kneeling and stuff. I feel weird when those people come in and stare at me. I don't know what to say."

"They want to see the young woman who stood beside the Prince when God took him up, maybe touch your hand, hear how he disappeared. I do the hard work, warning them of the End of Days, offering them salvation. Doesn't it gladden your heart to save souls?"

"Oh, sure." She glanced at the Messenger, and thought, Why couldn't this be the Prince like I planned, instead of Deacon Patch? Maybe God is punishing me. The Prince would have these new people laughing or wide-eyed with Bible stories and miracles.

She tippety-tapped the floor with her toes, bar dancing, beer, and hard-bodied, romantic men on her mind.

Patch was going on about salvation. ". . . fifty dollars from those elderly women from Charlotte. And that whole family from Memphis knelt down, got saved right at our feet. And what about that old Jew? What was his name? Manny? Ginger—converting a Jew counts double."

"Not 'Manny.' His name was Maury." She remembered him as lonely, missing his wife. A cute old guy like Groucho Marx. When he saw the loose arm on her chair, he offered to fix it. Did it, too. Just a little tap with the heel of his shoe. He knew funny stories like the Prince. A good thing Maury came by when Reverend Patch was in the little boys' room or Patch would have bored the old man away before he opened his mouth.

Patch was quoting Scripture. "We must be as wise as serpents, and harmless as doves . . ."

She felt a sudden need to deflate him. "We didn't come close to converting Maury. All he wanted was to hear how the Prince was raptured. You know—Poof! I'm not sure he even believed me. He kept asking over and over how it happened."

"Jews are hardheaded, Ginger. Remember the trouble Jesus had with the money changers? How he warned the apostles about being scourged in synagogues? But I think you're wrong about this one. Mrs. Binkle told me how interested he was. Manny will be back. We'll work on him together."

"Yeah, sure." Ginger had oonched in her throne long enough. The girls would be leaving without her. She looked up and saw Joline at the door, tapping her wristwatch. "Oh," Ginger said, and stood. "I promised mother I'd call." She slipped off the robe and tossed it over the back of the gilt chair. "I'll see you tomorrow, Reverend Patch. Right after work. We'll save a bunch more souls, okay?" She turned on her heels and ran for the door.

Patch lifted the small scepter that had belonged to the Prince, an aluminum shaft with a battery-illuminated yellow plastic flame at the end, and shook it at the closing door. "Ye have set at nought all my counsel, and would none of my reproof," he said through pinched lips. "Beware, young woman, lest you do not choose the fear of the Lord."

Following the advice of the bartender at Poncho the 'irate's, Maury Finkle had availed himself of the surveillance potential of the Gatlinburg Space Needle. The night before, he used the first half of his ticket to observe the Temple of Light from above. He watched white-robed church members scurrying over the roof, waving flashlights. High above, a hundred feet higher than the space needle observation deck, the angel blimp soared. The strobe lights set in its eyes winked crazily, one eye, then the other.

Now, the afternoon of the following day, Maury trained his binoculars on several hulking black creatures at one end of the armory roof. With no people in view, he had difficulty with the scale. They looked like Pterodactyls from one of the dinosaur movies. He refocused, wondering what bizarre creatures must come out of the wild mountains rimming the town.

He panned to the Temple of Light's entrance and an LED

marquee flashing OVER 223 SAVED. The three blinked and reformed as a four. High above the roof, he followed a daring repairman climbing a flexible ladder to set the blimp's eyes right.

Maury reflected on his conversation with Ginger Rodgers, a lovely young shiksa, definitely not the brightest bulb in the firmament, but bubbly, charming in a naïve sort of way. He couldn't imagine her making up the Rapture story, although she wasn't telling the whole truth, either. Maury couldn't see her conspiring with Doone to stage his disappearance. If Doone had half the smarts he apparently had to set up this cult, he wouldn't trust a ditzy kid like Ginger to keep his secret. More likely, the draykopf fooled her—threw his clothes on the floor while she was out of sight and beat a quick exit. Now, after telling the story so many times, Ginger couldn't admit the truth. Either Doone did the goodbye act to evade Trout, or it was a trick to draw converts. Maybe both.

"Rapture-schmapture." He drummed his fingers on the railing. "Converts mean gelt. No fool, this Doone. Once he lays his hands on the cash, he'll pay off Trout, who will call me off, and, then, Doone will reappear. All of this, soon, I'm thinking, because he can't trust that noodge Creely Patch to run the show for long.

"I should take a turn at this racket some day, show them what a real salesman can do. Yessir. That would be fun."

A sudden movement of the repairman on the cable ladder, swaying in the wind, brought Maury back to the problem at hand. He raised the binoculars and searched for Doone's house, tracing one road, then another to the chalet with the white columns. The old Caddy was still at the curb. An hour earlier Maury had watched the slick greaseball drive up, greet Doone's wife with the big hair at the door, fondle her tuchis, and steal inside. No doubt what they were up to. Fifteen minutes ago, sweat-slick and naked, they appeared on the upstairs rear porch—invisible from the ground—cigarettes in hand, the sleazer's arm around Doone's wife's waist, her high blond hair wrapped in a protective shell of toilet paper.

Doone wasn't at home; that was for sure. For a moment, Maury felt for him. Poor schlemiel's trying to make a buck, doing what he has to do, and the wife's doing the hokeypokey with some slimy greaseball in the man's own home while he's on the lam. On the other hand, Doone had been Trout's partner, hadn't he? Cheated him out of serious cash, Trout said.

Another look at Doone's wife with the paper-wrapped hair made Maury recall his Rose's kvetching toward the end, when he wanted a little spousal affection: "Don't muss my hair, Maury," or, "Do it if you have to, but no kisses, I just put on fresh lipstick." More often: "I'm too tired. Later," or the old headache or bad back ploy. And all the while schtuping his partner, Nick. Maury shuddered. Cheaters.

Ridding the earth of cheaters like them had become Maury's raison d'être. It put a spring in his step, a smile on his face, and a Manhattan in his ever-more-shaky hand at the end of a long and trying day.

20

Jimmy worked swing shift when he could, to avoid the tourists. He walked in the door and flung the morning paper on the table. "Read this, Grandpop. They still don't get it, do they? The damned scientists, stealing our ancestors, cutting them up, putting our bones in boxes to gather dust on museum shelves—"

"Calm down, Jimmy." His Grandpop was opening a tin of Spam. "Have some coffee."

"I will not." Jimmy walked to the window. "You can practically see it, the entrance to that cave in the woods over there. Park property. They have a guard posted. The mummy's somewhere below a sinkhole in that grown-over field." Jimmy pointed. "See? I'll bet that's on your property."

Grandpop slapped sliced Spam in a frying pan. "No, it's not. I did some phoning. A narrow stretch of Homer Delaney's property runs between our land and the park. The sinkhole's on his land, all right, and he gave permission to take the mummy to that historical museum in Pigeon Forge." He ignored Jimmy's cursing, lifted his coffee cup and waved it at the Mr. Coffee as a hint. "Like it says in the paper, some kids found it. Museum fella was in there most of yesterday and this morning. He's coming back this afternoon to take it out."

"Doesn't that *burn* you? Stealing an ancient Indian burial?"

"Could be that. Could also be some poor drunk wandered in there a year ago and got lost, starved to death."

"A year ago? Way back in a cave? Mummified? You read what the scientist said: *centuries* old, nude, flexed body. I've read about enough burials to know that's a ritual position. The paper didn't say anything about grave goods. They'll keep quiet about that. I already called ARM."

"What's that?"

"AmerIndian Resistance Movement. We'll invoke NAG-PRA, have pickets at that damned museum by this afternoon. We'll sue the bastards, get that mummy back, rebury it in holy ground—"

"Where would that be, Jimmy, this holy ground?" His Grandpop was smiling at him. "Some Christian cemetery?" He set a paper plate with a Spam-on-white-bread sandwich, and a mug of coffee, on the windowsill.

"Don't you give me a hard time, Grandpop." Jimmy shook a finger at him. "My people know places." He sat on the arm of the sofa, thinking. He took a bite of the sandwich and gave his grandfather a hard look. He swallowed, took a sip of coffee. "You know what I think? Feel in my bones?"

"I'll bet you're gonna tell me."

"This mummy is *my* ancestor, either on the Chief's side or your's. This land's been in your family for like forever, you said. I'll claim him, rebury him right here. What do you think of that?"

"I think you're gonna have a hard time with the claiming part. I got no records and your daddy is long gone. Lawyers are expensive. Thing like that can drag on forever."

Jimmy stood, looked around the room. "Where's your gun? That deer rifle?"

Grandpop put his hands on Jimmy's shoulders, forced him onto the sofa. "Listen to me. You're my only living kin. I don't want to die with you in prison for shooting some FBI or whoever. I don't want you losing your job, neither, by loud-mouthing yourself into trouble. I stuck my neck out to get that job from Mr. Trout at the Bible Alive for you. If you embarrass me, I could lose my job. A man my age doesn't find work so easy."

"Yeah, I know."

"Promise me you won't raise hell at that museum, carry signs and shout, get us both fired."

"I can't—"

"Jimmy, for me . . . if you got to, work it behind the scenes." He pulled a vinyl-padded kitchen chair to the sofa and sat, facing him. He leaned over, looked Jimmy in the eyes. "This means a lot to you, doesn't it?"

"Hell, yes. I traveled all over the country fighting for other people's rights, now here I am with a situation in my own backyard. The worst kind of disrespect, stealing an ancestral burial. I can't ignore—"

"That's what I figured. So . . . if you promise to keep your nose clean in public, I may know a way out of the woods, so to speak."

"Oh?"

"I kinda figured you'd get fired up over this. Look here." He removed a folded sheet of lined notebook paper from his back pocket and smoothed it on the coffee table, revealing a crude map. "Here's the cave entrance," he tapped a small circle with a wavy line running from it, "and the stream flowing out. The dashes mark the national park boundary. Here's the sinkhole, this X, about where they say the mummy is under Delaney's land, and here's our property line. This dotted line is about where the cave runs."

"How come your line goes on past his sinkhole?"

"To this X, right?"

"Our land." Jimmy leaned closer, sensing where his Grand-pop might be leading.

"That's the big-ass one on our property. Fence fell down thirteen years ago and a cow nearly fell in. Mooed bloody mur-der, front end out, ass end in that hole. I had to haul her out with a tractor. I fixed the fence, put sheet tin over the top for good measure, weighted it down good with rocks."

"Not just to keep the cows out," Jimmy added. "You threatened me with a willow switch if I ever went near it. When my buddies and I went caving, it was on the other side of the farm or in the park. I was always afraid you'd spot me from that rocking chair of yours by the window."

"I damned well would of." Grandpop McDowd slapped his thigh and chuckled. "Here's a little confession: when I was a kid, a friend and me climbed down that hole. You could bust your neck if you ain't careful. That's why I threatened you to stay out of it. Not far down, there's a low passage that don't go nowhere, then, maybe thirty feet deeper, a decent one. There's caves honeycombing this whole valley. We explored a bunch like you must have, though we was always scared our daddies would tan our asses, or bears or bats would get us. Whew-ee, we had fun! Used to shut our lights off on dares—kerosene lanterns. Scared the beejeezus out of us."

"We did the same thing with flashlights."

"Boys and caves. Some things never change, huh?" Grandpop chuckled again, remembering. "My buddies and me spent one whole night down in that cave, under our sinkhole, when my parents was away. We scratched dirty pictures and animals on the walls. Ate, slept, and pooped inside just like the cavemen must of."

"*Indians.*"

"Sure. Oh, we had a fine adventure. Look," he traced the X on his property to the mummy's X. "Delaney's sinkhole is about a thousand feet from ours. What I was thinking, is, if our cave runs all the way to Delaney's, and I recollect it does, I could lower you down our hole, you could make your way over there, pick up your mummy—the eggheads aren't supposed to retrieve it until this afternoon, and—"

Jimmy hugged him.

21

P lato Scopes, M.S., Chief Scientist at the Captain Hook
Museum, drew a deep breath. His stomach fluttered. His
palms felt cold and wet.

The magical words "mummy," "nude," "centuries
old," and "ritual sacrifice" uttered on TV and repeated in the
Knoxville and Asheville papers, snagged a plethora of media
types for this, his second press conference. Though they out-
numbered the complimentary soft drinks and donuts, no one
seemed to mind feeding the pop machine with their own quarters. Director Duckhaus, Scopes noticed, arrived early enough
to latch on to three of Scopes's cream-filled, chocolate long
johns and a Dr Pepper.

Scopes moved to the head of the cafeteria and glanced nervously at his watch: 2:00 P.M. He had barely lifted a hand for
attention when three sets of video lights bloomed like super-
novae. He staggered, grabbed the museum's aging microphone, and blurted out his name. Too loudly, too close to the
mike. Hands went to ears at the piercing feedback. Plato
noticed Mrs. Trillop's gesturing Hold the Mike Away, and managed to say "Welcome" without further consequence. He also
recalled her suggestion that he acknowledge Director Duck-

haus, did so, and was shocked to see the director hurrying to the front of the room.

Duckhaus, a smudge of chocolate at the corner of his mouth, a dab of white cream filling at the tip of his nose, smiled broadly, wrestled the microphone from Scopes, and began a windy pitch. "Welcome, members of the American free press, to this, the Captain Hook Museum, poised at the edge of the Great Smoky . . . third-largest collection of button-hooks east of the Mississippi and south of the Ohio rivers . . . school children and scholars alike . . . our mission, the increase and diffusion of knowledge of buttonhooks and the golden age of buttonhooks . . ."

The media people did focus and sound checks, fiddled with PCs, and jockeyed for better position when, if, the nerd in the lab coat with the mummy news ever regained the mike. Unaware of the inattention he was commanding, Duckhaus droned on, ". . . name of Pigeon Forge derives from a forge built . . ." A tedious five minutes later, he wound down, ". . . to introduce our resident mummyologist and Chief Scientist, Plato Scopes."

Scopes lifted the mike, but before he could speak, he was inundated with questions.

"Can we see it?"

"Are you surprised by the ARM pickets?"

"Exactly how old is . . ."

Scopes waved his arms to restore order. "Let me bring you up-to-date, and then I'll answer specific questions. First, the mummy is still in the cave, *in situ*, for conclusion of our microstratigraphic analysis." Left unsaid was that a proper excavation of the surrounding soil ought to take weeks, but Scopes was not about to let the Park Service, or the University of Tennessee forensic people, or anyone else move in on his specimen. An hour or two more of troweling and dirt sifting would have to suffice.

The "mummy still in the cave" news was met with a collective groan. "However," Scopes said, to quell the unrest, "immediately following this press conference, I will proceed to the

cave assisted by two gifted Pigeon Forge high school students."
He motioned to a nervous couple in lab coats—a pale, over-
weight young man and an anorexic young woman with hen-
naed hair and a double nose ring. "I shall then remove the
mummy and bring it here.

"Yes," he said, to the perky reporter who had attended his
first conference. "You may film the cave entrance when we
emerge with our ancient American. That should be around five
P.M. Now," he removed the white sheet cloaking a metal table
before him, "here is some fascinating news." He lifted a shiny,
apparently heavy, black-shot-with-beige, semi-opalized object
the size of a small loaf of bread, with rhythmic serrations
along one edge. "This," he held it high, "is a wooly mammoth
tooth."

The film crews moved in, reporters buzzed. Scopes cradled
the tooth at his chest. "There are at least two layers to the cavern in the area where the mummy lies, with numerous solution
channels leading up, down, and to the sides, most of which are
impassable. One of these vertical channels, referred to as a
chimney, wends its way to a sinkhole at the surface. There are
many of these funnel-shaped sinkholes in the valley. Geologists
call such terrain karst topography, after a region in . . ."

A reporter shouted, "What's that got to do with the
mummy?"

Scopes snapped: "I was getting to that. The point is, while
the sinkhole I mentioned is now closed at the top, this was not
always so. Over the centuries, surface material such as this
tooth fell or washed into the chambers below."

"A mammoth's a prehistoric elephant, right?"

"Yes, yes." Scopes pinched the bridge of his nose, wanting
to paint the full scientific picture for them, the Pleistocene
fauna, the geology, but realized all they wanted were simple-
minded summations they could regurgitate to an uneducated
public. "This tooth is in excess of ten thousand years old. We
cannot ascertain the mummy's age until analysis, but we have
reason to hope it is of equal antiquity."

"Ten *thousand* years old?"

"Yes. Maybe older."

More zooming onto the tooth. Frantic scribblings in note-pads, on handheld electronic devices.

"You mean to say, this mummy, this cave man may have ridden these mammoths like the Indians rode horses?"

"Don't put words in my mouth. My postulation as to age is supported by—" Scopes reached to the table, picked up a broken blade of flint with chipped edges, "—this. Though incomplete, the flaking on this blade tells me it was worked over ten centuries ago. Its thinness," he held it on edge so they could see, "is significant. Though the blade was found near the mummy, it may have fallen from the surface earlier or later. Unfortunately, that is a problem with all the associated material."

He scowled at that, but brightened. "Even more exciting," he lifted a sheet of cardboard, upon which were mounted several photographic prints, "are petroglyphs, rock carvings scratched on the cave walls, of strange fauna, apparently Pleistocene, Ice Age, creatures, long extinct, and of fertility rituals." The cameras zoomed onto the fertility ritual photos, crude stick figures with exaggerated genitalia in blatantly sexual poses. "Again, we cannot be sure these are coeval—dating from the same period—as the mummy, but added together—the tooth, the petroglyphs, the lithics—the evidence is highly suggestive."

"I'll say," said a wag. "Look at the schlong on the stickman the third print over."

Scopes frowned, pretended he didn't hear. "And this," he lifted a small polyethylene bag, "is a coprolite, one of several. Human, I would surmise, pending analysis."

"What's a coprolite?"

"Uhmm . . . ancient excrement."

"Yuck!" That was echoed by other sounds of disgust mixed with snickers, although the cameras honed on the coprolite as eagerly as they had the porno pix.

"Mummy shit," one reporter said to another.

"Please." Scopes held the bag close to his heart. "Coprolites are invaluable. They inform us of ancient diet, whether their originators harbored parasites, or suffered from . . ."

"Where are you going with this?"

Scopes blurted out his fond hope, something he had not planned to mention prior to analysis: "What if this coprolite shows our mummy or one of his companions partook of the very mammoth whose tooth you see before you? Or one of the creatures portrayed on the cave walls? What would you say to that?"

"I'd say they had one hell of a barbecue."

Scopes ignored the levity. "To validate this hypothesis, I plan to do a thorough analysis," he waved an arm across the table before him, "C-14 dating, microscopic examination, dissection, scanning—"

"So, bottom line, this mummy is really old."

"Old," Scopes repeated the word with a mysterious smile, "may not be the most significant issue, but, rather, Who."

"Who? You mean you know his name?"

"Of course not. But, if what I suspect is true, our vocal friends outside," he nodded to the window and the barely audible shouts of half a dozen ARM protestors, "will be less than pleased."

Aha! Controversy. Pens and typing fingers hovered, awaiting elaboration.

"I'm sure you recall that Mongoloid people, the ancestors of today's Indians, were believed to have walked across the Bering Strait Land Bridge—Beringia—at the end of the last ice age no earlier than thirteen thousand years ago, to populate the Americas. Gospel, yes?" He acknowledged the nods. "No longer. In recent years discoveries indicate non-Mongoloid groups may also have migrated to this hemisphere; subsequently, and earlier. An ancient skull, Kennewick Man, found in Washington State, has been reconstructed to suggest it is of non-Indian, Caucasoid origin. Another Caucasoid skull from Mexico has been dated to thirteen thousand years ago. Such discoveries are setting on end conventional thought about the peopling of the Americas."

He noted the raised eyebrows. "Indeed. There is evidence

of Caucasoid people migrating by boat from Asia along the southern rim of Beringia, Polynesian-types crossing the Pacific eastward, directly to South America, and Europeans sailing the North Atlantic. Some of them may have reached the New World many thousands of years prior to the Mongoloid influx."

Scopes let it sink in. "It's no wonder groups like those outside conspire to suppress anthropological investigations by claiming skeletal remains before scientists can explore their significance and determine affinities."

A timely shout from one of the protesters underscored his point.

A science writer raised her hand. "Aren't terms like Caucasoid and Mongoloid rather archaic? Isn't race usually considered—"

Scopes scowled. "I'm trying to make this easy for you and your readers to understand, okay? Now, if I may continue, DNA evidence suggests at least four unrelated groups colonized North America before the end of the last Ice Age. Some twenty percent of eastern North American Indians hold mitochondrial DNA haplogroup X—a rare *European* genetic marker that is lacking in East Asia or Western North America. The obvious inference is that they inherited it from mixing with older, European-derived populations. Thin flint blades of the Clovis type, like this one," he held up the mummy cave specimen, "resemble European Ice Age Solutrean artifacts."

Scopes realized from the confused faces he was losing them. "Refer to my handouts. To sum it up: our mummy appears to be of *Caucasoid*, not *Mongoloid* ancestry," underscoring the words for benefit of the upstart science writer.

He let that dangle, watched eyebrows rise expectantly. "And," he continued, "we need not resort to reconstructions as have been done with Kennewick man, because our mummy is remarkably preserved. It has a *European* face."

Scopes smiled with satisfaction at the response to his startling news.

"We'll be able to see it when you bring it out? Photograph it? Film it?"

"Absolutely."

"When?"

"Three, no more than five, hours from now. But . . . why wait till then?"

"Say again?"

"I don't follow . . ."

"I thought you said . . ."

Scopes crossed his arms, enjoying the suspense. Ten long seconds later, he reached to the table for an eight-and-a-half-by-eleven-inch box. "I photographed it yesterday. I'm sure you'll do better when we bring it into daylight, but I think these," he lifted a stack of eight-by-ten glossies, "will suffice for the present."

They shoved him aside in a mad scramble for the photos.

22

To the consternation of the two National Park Service Rangers, the unruly press corps was trampling vegetation and roiling the once clear waters of the stream flowing from the recently named Mummy Cave. "Mosses and perennial wildflowers are fragile," the female ranger was saying, "and an ecosystem like this must be— watch out! There's a spring by that mossy area. I spotted a *Pseudotriton* salamander—"

Splosh. Splat. A video man's boot hammered down the moss to secure footing for his tripod. A square of waxed paper from a reporter's submarine sandwich wafted into the stream. A still photographer broke off a sapling at waist height to get less obstructed view of the cave entrance.

"I see lights."

"Get back. Be careful," the senior ranger ordered, to no effect.

"They're coming," shouted a voice near the front of the pack.

"Did you see that? A *bat* flew out. There's another one."

"Look out!"

The perky Knoxville TV reporter covered her perfectly

coifed hair with outstretched fingers and screeched. Her sound-man swung at the bobbing mammal with his boom mike.

"Cut that out!" said the female ranger. "Bats are gentle creatures. That flying into hair nonsense is an old wives' tale. They—"

"Here they come."

"Do they have the mummy?"

"Can't see. Cave's real narrow. First one's all hunched over."

Camera lights flared and photographers' flashes blipped. The two high school assistants emerged first, wearing miners' helmets, mud-spattered coveralls, and sour looks on their faces. Scopes, the scientist, trailed, sloshing through the water, barely lifting his feet as he walked. He was even muddier, water-soaked, his face dripping with—perspiration? No: tears. Fat ones, racing down his cheeks, leaving long clean streaks on his dirt-stained face.

Heads craned, videos purred, still cameras snick-snick-snicked.

"He doesn't have it."

"Where is it?"

"Did you leave it inside?"

"I hope to hell we didn't come out here for nothing."

"Well?"

Scopes shielded his eyes from the lights with a hand. He sniffled, swallowed twice, searching for words, swiped his teary cheek with the back of one hand and, finally, said, barely audible: "It's gone. My mummy's gone. I saw tracks. A . . . a bear must have got it."

Orlando entered the Temple of Light parking lot in his 1972 Cadillac El Dorado. Rita Rae wanted to accompany him, but Orlando knew if she saw the young Ginger Rodgers, who, according to the newspaper, had witnessed Doone's "Rapture," there would be sparks. That temper of hers. *¡Carajo!* Never make that woman jealous and turn your back on her. So, he had handcuffed her to the refrigerator door handle. Left her

cursing and threatening. Not that Orlando was above witnessing a good catfight, but Doone's church wasn't the place for it.
Not now, not yet.

He made the sign of the cross at his gold-swagged chest.
Mother of God, he thought, my Rita Rae is a demon. *¡Ai, mi
madre, que fiera! ¡Que mujer más ardiente!* No wonder she is
such a fine lover. He groped his *cojones*. She has the fire of a
Gypsy and is fit as a jungle cat, except for the coughing from
the cigarettes and hair spray. And, she will do anything for the
con. Even sleep with this *gusano* for a year.

Orlando found himself frowning. Why had she become so
angry at mention of the *gusano*, her husband, *dando el palo* to
the young woman if the worm meant nothing to her? Perhaps
she was jealous of this Ginger? Yes, a slim woman like Rita,
with the crow's feet around her eyes and lips, and her little
inadequate behind. Perhaps Ginger is luscious and fat. With
plump *nalgas* and a soft, round belly that puts skinny Rita, *mi
querida guajira flaquita*, to shame. This Ginger is in her twenties. And Rita Rae? Not the thirty-one she says. Forty? Forty-
five? Older?

Apart from the age, why should she care if Doone had the
girl? Rita Rae was out of town and left him alone, no? Doone is
a man, the girl came willing to his bed. Orlando shrugged, trying to make sense of it. He finally said, "*¡Cuidado* Shickie
Doone! With the empty bank accounts and worthless diamond
ring . . . you are a dead man when Rita Rae finds you."

So, how do we find you? Through Ginger Rodgers, I think.

Entering the double, metal doors of the armory, lost in
internal dialogue, Orlando bounced off the broad spongy back
of a thickset woman with prodigious breasts, wearing a
cotton-print dress and mules on swollen feet. At least five or
six grimy children gripped her hands or the hem of her dress.
"*Permiso, señora*, Orlando said, flashing his fine white teeth.

For the first time he looked around. This was the first
Protestant church Orlando had been in. Some *catedral*, he
thought. These *norteamericanos*, they worship in barns.
Instead of a steeple with a cross on top and a grand bell, they

have a balloon in the shape of an angel. Bare walls, concrete floors. Where are the *santos*, the rich woods, the paintings, gold, candles, and relics? No confessionals? Not even a Madonna! To one side, he watched several people in white robes climb a steel staircase to the roof. When he had driven in, he saw at least thirty of them up there, staring at the clouds.

The thick woman and her brood were stopped by an elderly lady in a white robe, sitting behind a long folding table with a cash box and a roll of tickets. Behind her, a velvet rope, the kind theaters use to queue patrons, blocked access to the main room. Half a dozen people awaited entry.

"Ten dollars, please," said the robed woman, "and take a number. Half price for children under ten. The Messenger—Reverend Patch—and the Witness—Miss Rodgers—will see you in turn."

"Can we take pictures of her?" asked the thick woman's husband, a shadow of a man clutching a disposable camera.

"Of course. And of the Messenger, too."

"Who's he?"

"Messenger Patch is the successor to the Reverend Doone, the Prince of Light. He was appointed by God Himself and will answer your questions about the Rapture. Only the saved enter the kingdom of heaven when the Great Rapture comes, so if you wish to get saved—and time is running out—he will hear your proclamation of faith." The robed woman cast a harsh look at a seven-year-old, pulling the hair of a smaller one until it wailed. "Undeserving children," she added, "will be left behind, clutching the empty garments of their mothers." The twister ignored her, but the mother cuffed the offending hand.

"What's with those folks trooping up the stairs?" asked the husband.

"Those are the Children of Light climbing to the Roof of Ascension. The Prince foretold the Great Rapture will occur there."

"No kidding?" said a rotund man wearing denim overalls

and no shirt, a ticket pinched in one hand. "How long before it all starts?"

"The Prince prophesied it would begin following strange weather, a shooting star, and trouble in the Middle East. I suspect this unseasonable hot spell . . ."

Orlando picked up a three-and-a-half by five-inch religious tract, WILL YOU BE LEFT BEHIND? and began reading about the mark of the beast: *During the Tribulation, the Antichrist will implant smart cards coded with the mark 666 under the skin of* . . . He tossed it back on the table and regarded the far end of the room, a low wooden platform with two gold-painted but otherwise unimpressive armchairs holding what he imagined must be the Messenger, or whatever they called him, and Ginger Rodgers. He whistled to himself. From here, this Ginger appeared *muy guapa*.

Ten minutes later, Orlando watched the family before him approach the stage. The woman put one after another of her small progeny on the lap of Ginger Rodgers while the husband took snapshots. The Messenger, to Ginger's left, seemed to be speaking, but the family ignored him, devoting all their attention to Ginger.

It was then Orlando realized what was going on: this Messenger was supposed to be God, Ginger, the Madonna. And a fine Madonna she was. Golden hair, nice legs from what he could see of them below the robe. No wonder the *rústicos* ignored the old man, with his bald head rimmed with tufts of clown's hair, and wearing a cheap suit with no class. An unconvincing god. If he was running this, Orlando thought, his god would be someone on the order of . . . himself. Tall, fit, tanned, stylishly dressed.

"Sir? Sir?" The robed woman spoke to him. "Number four-seventy-eight. You're next." She unhooked the velvet rope and motioned him forward.

Orlando strode across the concrete floor, admiring Ginger Rodgers more with each step. Uncertain what was expected of him, he stopped two paces away, crossed himself, and dropped to his knees, genuflecting. "*Madre Maria,*" he began, eyes downcast.

"Stop that!" said the Messenger. "We'll have none of that popish rigmarole in the Temple of Light."

Orlando leapt to his feet, his right hand fingering the flick knife in his pocket. He gave the Messenger a heart-stopping glare. Then, in the blink of an eye, he relaxed, flashed his wide Latin smile, deciding sugar would serve better than the blade. "*Permiso,* God the father," he said, silkily. "I did not know."

"*I'm* not God," Patch said gruffly, "I'm His Messenger—though He speaks to me." Patch's eyes unfocused and he began to intone, ". . . we which are alive and remain shall be caught up together with them in the clouds—"

"Yes, yes," Orlando said, "of course. Look, Señor Messenger, I wish to speak with the virgin" he pronounced it *veerhen,* "alone for a moment or two."

"The what?" Patch said.

"Veerhen." Orlando said it loudly, as if Patch hadn't heard, then, "Oh," and re-articulated the awkward English, "Veergin."

Ginger giggled. Patch cleared his throat. "Impossible!" Then, embarrassed, he clarified to Ginger, "When I said 'impossible,' I meant seeing you alone, not—" He cleared his throat again and coughed, shifting his gaze to Orlando. "We, the Messenger and the Witness, bring the Lord's message as one. You may not—"

"*Alone,*" Orlando hissed. His hand was on the knife again. But instead of withdrawing it, the hand emerged with a crisp hundred-dollar bill. "I have *mucho respeto* for you, señor," he said with a slight bow, "but I wish to be alone when the young woman tells me of the miracle, *entendiste?*" With a friendly, teasing smile, he waved the bill. "I would be grateful."

"Hmmm." Patch reached for the bill.

Orlando held it back. "Alone, yes?"

Patch relieved Orlando of the C-note. "I suppose I could check with Mrs. Binkle about getting our robes back from the cleaners." He left the stage.

Orlando took a seat in Patch's chair, leaned close to Ginger. "Tell me of the miracle, *bonita*. How this Doone vanishes."

Ginger took a little breath and repeated the, by now, rote story. "I went to the Prince's house to talk about the hymns the choir would sing, about seven o'clock last Tuesday evening. We were in the hallway downstairs, with heaven painted on the ceiling above. I turned my back for a second, and when I looked back—Poof!—the Prince was gone. He left his clothes and shoes in a little heap on the floor. They're over there, now, under that plastic box." She pointed.

"Oh?" Orlando lifted an eyebrow at a Plexiglas cube with the vanished Doone's earthly vestments. So, at least they had relics.

Orlando wanted to hear more. "And perhaps you hear the door open, just after this 'Poof'?"

"No. He closed it when we came in. It stayed closed."

"The lights were out, yes?"

Apparently unaccustomed to such pointed questions, Ginger responded with an emphatic, "No! The lights were on the whole time."

"How far from Doone were you when you hear this 'Poof!'?"

"Umm," Ginger shifted uncomfortably in her chair. "I didn't *hear* it, okay? It just *happened*. I was only . . . a few feet from him."

"I see. And why did you turn your back? He asked you to do so, yes, and maybe to count to ten?"

"No. I, I was, like on the stairs, I guess, and that's when it happened."

"On the stairs? Not so close, then. Not in the hall with Doone?"

"Yes. I mean, no, not exactly." Ginger began to blush. "I, uh, had to go to the little girl's room, and was, like, upstairs. But I was just, uh, a few steps up when I turned around and he was gone. Poof! Vanished! *Raptured*." She said the last word with finality.

Orlando watched Ginger chewing her lip, staring into the open room, avoiding his gaze, her fingers white-knuckling the arms of her chair, and realized he would get no more from her by playing bad cop. So he dropped the flinty edge to his voice and said softly, "Pardon my questions. It is only that I find the miracle so, how you say—astonishing." For some seconds he said nothing, then, "Ginger Rodgers," he placed a hand gently on her knee, "*Tus ojos, tus labios, tu trasero bien gordo . . . que maravilla de la naturaleza erés tu. Ven, jovencita.* My beautiful *pinga* would enjoy the time alone with you. *Mira,* look how he rises to salute your *belleza.*" To Ginger's bewildered stare, he added, "You are the most beautiful Madonna I ever see."

Ginger lifted his hand by the wrist and dropped it off her leg, then cocked her head and gave him an inquiring look. "Madonna? Like the rock star?"

"*Claro.*"

Ginger looked him up and down, regarding his dusky, Latin good looks, his pomaded hair, the swarm of gold chains at his neck, his loose silk shirt and linen trousers, his sockless feet in white espadrilles. Orlando looked nothing like the rest of the visitors, or the Fireflies. "Are you a singer?" she asked.

Orlando replied without missing a beat. "A movie star."

"Wow! Like what movies have you been in?"

"Cuban movies, *jovencita*. They do not show here because of that *hijo de puta dictador comunista.*"

Ginger wrinkled her brow with uncertainty, but twisted in her chair to face him. She drew her feet onto the seat, knees up under her robe, something Patch never permitted. "But I'll bet you know real movie stars, don't you? Like, say, Antonio Banderas?"

"Tony? Of course. Tony and I play jai-alai every Thursday."

"Wow!" The brow wrinkled again. "What's hi-lye?"

"Jai alai is . . . like golf, only faster." Orlando touched the tip of Ginger's chin with a manicured forefinger. "Perhaps we could get together for a coffee? Away from this place, and speak of the films?"

Ginger pursed her lips, cast a wary eye at Patch, with his back to her at the other end of the room. "I don't know. Reverend Patch doesn't like me leaving or talking with visitors. He wants me to move in here, even, so I'll be around when people come asking about the Rapture."

"*¡Qué lástima!* I would enjoy telling you about my friends, the movie stars."

Ginger twisted a hank of hair over a finger, untwisted it, twisted it again. She squirmed in her seat. "I don't know," she said, and then, "Do you really know Antonio Banderas?"

23

Mere hours before Plato Scopes emerged from the cave empty-handed, Grandpop McDowd had belayed one end of the rope to a rusted-out Chevy and passed the other over his thigh, half around his back, down to Jimmy.

He felt a continuous pull and occasional sharp tug as his grandson, some forty feet down, negotiated the twists and turns of the sinkhole. No more than a second after Grandpop shouted, "Everything A-OK?" for the fifth time, he heard a dull thump and felt the rope go slack. Silence.

He yelled again. Nothing. Sensing something gone awry, his border collie began barking, circling Grandpop and the sinkhole entrance. "Oh, Lord," Grandpop said, "what have I done?" He yanked the rope, felt it rise freely. Another shout. More barking above, more silence below.

A minute passed. He thought he saw a movement of the rope at his feet. Merely gravity or was it Jimmy? It jiggled again, like the first tentative tugs on a float fish line. Grandpop gave a hand signal for the collie to stop barking and sit. She did, but kept up a soft, troubled whine.

Then, from below, he heard a muffled but audible, "Kinda fell," and the rope went taut as before.

"You okay?"

"Got thumped good, but, yeah, okay. Slippery down here. Slick stone, mud."

A minute later, his muffled voice called. "I'm at the bottom. Wow."

Jimmy had been stunned for half a minute. The fall knocked the wind from his lungs and wrenched his shoulder. He still felt needles of pain when he put weight on his left arm, and his ears continued to ring. The WWII helmet Grandpop had given him, did for Jimmy what it never had to do for Grandpop. It saved his life.

As the rush from the fall subsided, the thrill of discovery coursed through his veins. Grandpop had been right on. The cave under their sinkhole linked with the cavern on Delaney's land. Despite a compass, Jimmy probed three blind passages before he found the one leading to the mummy. In a deeper section heading off in another direction, he discovered fantastic rock formations: stalactites and stalagmites, rainbow-hued flowstone, sparkling calcite crystals—a fairyland rivaling the best commercial caves, but unsullied by electric lights and wires, signs with goofy names, pipe-railed trails, or noisy tourists. Virgin.

He knew he was on the right track when he found the very unvirgin drawings his grandfather as a thirteen-year-old and his childhood buddies had scratched on the walls. Jimmy didn't spend much time with the elephants and bears—or whatever the poorly drafted animals were supposed to be—but he couldn't help scrutinizing the sex stuff: stick men with big dicks doing it to stick women with watermelon breasts, stick men doing it to other stick men, diving between the stick legs of stick women, even doing it to animals. Who'd have guessed old Grandpop had such a raunchy imagination as a kid?

Not far beyond the drawings, as Grandpop had said,

Jimmy spotted the mummy. He shivered when he first saw it, and averted his eyes. He nearly cried at the thought of the ancients carrying it into the cave for what they hoped would be an eternal rest. They had drawn its knees to its chest, crossed the arms over the tucked legs and rested it on its side in a reverent fetal slumber. It had a dry gash on one shoulder, perhaps from a falling rock, but was otherwise perfectly intact.

Nearby, a breach in the floor led to what must be another cavern below. Above and slightly to one side, the ceiling rose into a wide crack and a zigzagging chimney that apparently led to the surface sinkhole on Delaney's land, quite a way up, as no light penetrated. The rubble below—loose rock, grit, and the occasional stick—told the story of material falling from the surface over the ages.

Jimmy swore softly at the scientist's stakes and string forming a grid, snaring the mummy like a squared-off spider-web, and an excavation that left the small body resting on an island of earth. To one side lay a large sieve, a shovel, trowels, brushes, tiny picks like dental instruments, and two crumpled Coke cans.

He saw no grave goods, no cache of flint points, favored pipe, or buckskin medicine pouch, and assumed the archaeologists had already stripped the body of those.

He had approached the mummy's back, and at first failed to see its face, but when he moved closer, playing his light over the head, he nearly fainted at how nearly alive, how un-movie-creepy, it looked. Though the lips were slightly parted, the eyes closed and sunken, it had thick, nearly shoulder-length black hair, remarkably preserved, and the face, though ashen, dry, and drawn like the rest of the skin, could almost have been that of a sleeping man. Jimmy squinted at the face, convincing himself it resembled him.

He hunkered beside it and muttered a short prayer previously rehearsed before the bathroom mirror. "Oh, Great Spirit of the universe, mother and father of the earth's creatures, man, animal, and plant—of the living earth herself—please forgive me for disturbing this, one of your children. But, if I do not, disrespectful scientists will take him away, take pictures of him, put him on display, cut him up, and store his bones in boxes. I must move your child, my ancestor, but I shall rebury him in safe ground, where white eyes will never find him."

He wiped a tear from his cheek and got to work. Ever so carefully, he rocked the mummy, working one of his grandfather's Pendleton blankets beneath, and around it. He placed that bundle in a second blanket, knotted two corners to form a sling, lifted it gently over his shoulder and carried it about twenty feet away. It was surprisingly light.

Jimmy wore moccasins out of respect. To minimize footprints, he walked on rock as much as possible, avoiding soft earth or dust. He returned to the excavated area, carefully obliterated the footprints he had left, and slashed the ground with his knife where the mummy had been. He replaced the knife and removed a buckskin bundle from his pack: the stuffed lower foot of a bear, a gift from an ARM comrade in Montana. Backtracking from the mummy in a low crouch, he obliterated impressions of his moccasins as he moved, replacing them with claw marks and paw prints.

Jimmy chuckled at his handiwork, hoisted the mummy to his shoulder and, keeping to hard ground, returned to the sinkhole. He cupped his hands at his mouth and gave a loud whoop to rouse his grandfather.

"Damn you, Jimmy," sounded from above. "I was nodding off, nearly peed my pants. Did you get it?"

"Went like clockwork. I'm tying it to the rope. You hoist while I climb. Pull. That's it—easy."

Fifteen minutes later, Jimmy, his Grandpop, and the blanket-wrapped mummy were on the surface. They rested in the funnel of the sinkhole. Jimmy motioned to the binoculars. "Any activity at the park?"

"I saw a little motion in the forest by the entrance, but it's too far to see good. There's still only the ranger's car there, so your scientist ain't got back yet."

"Good." Jimmy pointed to the bundle. "You want to see him?"

"I do not. I don't have many years left, and I'm not eager to see what I'll look like when I croak."

"Don't talk like that, Grandpop. Look—I want you to see him anyway. At least his face." Jimmy parted the blanket. "Tell me what he reminds you of."

His grandfather took a step back, but could not help looking. "Reminds me of what I see every time I look in a mirror—only this thing looks a dang sight better."

"Not what I meant." Jimmy turned his face to the same angle as the mummy's. "You see the resemblance to me?"

Grandpop McDowd narrowed his eyes, looked for long seconds at the mummy, then at Jimmy. "Light skin and long black hair—is that enough?"

"Never mind." Jimmy re-wrapped the mummy and lifted the sling to his shoulder.

"You're driving it to the other side of the farm, remember?"

"Don't worry, I scoped out a real pretty place on a little hill with a view of the valley."

Back at the house, Jimmy opened the door of the car he had bought with a loan from his Grandpop, a three-hundred-and-fifty-dollar, used Yugo, the cheapest car on the lot. The dealer had two. When he saw Jimmy's cash, he threw in the second one, free, "for parts."

Jimmy arranged the mummy on the front seat. Aware it would soon be out of his hands forever, he left the blanket open around the face so he could talk to it as he drove. "I wish I knew your history, little guy," he said as he left the driveway. "All the battles and adventures between when you bit the dust and I was born . . ."

At the highway leading to the prearranged, pre-dug plot on the other side of the McDowd land, Jimmy took a deep breath of fresh country air. He winced from his sore shoulder, but his earlier jitters were long gone. Conquest gave him a rush. He turned on the radio, loud country rock.

He sat upright, spine straight—had the mummy joined in on that last prolonged note? He looked down. Had its lips moved? The wail continued.

Oh, no–ooo! A siren. He glanced at the rearview mirror. Sure enough, a cop on his ass, roof lights flashing. The speedometer read twelve miles over the limit.

Jimmy swallowed hard, looked again at the cruiser, hoping he would pass, be on his way to some emergency, but no such luck. The cop pointed to the side of the road. Jimmy cast a worried look at the mummy. What now? He panicked, hit the gas pedal hard. The Yugo ignored him. A hundred feet later, the road took a slow rise and the car actually slowed. The cop was still motioning, now flashing headlights. He threw the siren into a *Whoop, Whoop*.

Oh, man. I . . . am . . . screwed. He shrugged in resignation, pulled onto the berm. He tugged at the blanket to cover the mummy's face, but the cloth was twisted below the head and wouldn't budge. Jimmy felt his throat go dry, his forehead bead with sweat. A glance at the mirror—the cop was stepping out.

Think. Keep him away from the front seat. Jimmy opened his door.

The cop's hand went to his waist, hovered by his holster. "Stay in the car, sir. Hands on the wheel, if you don't mind."

Jimmy complied. He died a thousand deaths as the cop walked to the window and leaned down to get a good look at a man who could speed in a Yugo.

"License and registration?" At Jimmy's rigid pose, the cop said, "Take it easy—no need to be nervous."

Jimmy reached for his wallet in the upper pocket of his coveralls. He removed it, flipped it open, trying to lean forward enough to keep his torso between the cop and the passenger on the seat beside him. He extended the wallet.

"Keep the billfold, sir. Documents only."

Jimmy fished them out, felt the life drain from him.

The cop took the papers, said, "Remain seated. I'm going back to—" Pause. "What's that on the seat?" Long pause, squinting past Jimmy to the shotgun seat. "Whoa mama!" The cop backed away, flipped the strap from his holster. "Get out of your car, nice and slow."

Jimmy felt his stomach flip-flop as he did so.

"Hands on your head. Ten paces forward. Don't turn around."

Jimmy counted off ten steps, shut his eyes, fighting back tears. Fifteen seconds passed. He heard the passenger door open. Several more beats passed, and the cop said, "This is the mummy from the National Park cave."

Jimmy sighed. "Yeah, that's right." So, they'd been tracking him with binoculars the same way his grandfather had been watching them, only the rangers had the benefit of the woods for cover. Once out of the sinkhole, he and the mummy were easy to spot. They put out a call to pick him up.

"I knew they were taking it out today," the cop continued. "C'mon back. Sorry about the mix-up, but you were acting kind of squirrelly there, plus the muddy clothes, exceeding the limit in—what kind of vee–hi–cal is this?"

Jimmy turned, mouth open, unsure what to say. The cop was still staring at the mummy on the seat. "Would've thought you guys'd transport it in an ambulance, or, maybe a hearse. Guess you figured driving alone the back way in this midget car, no one would notice you, huh? You don't mind my saying so, sir, with those angry pickets at the museum and all that publicity, I'd of called in some security, regardless. You the archaeologist?"

Feeling like the Governor had just called off the long walk to the gallows, Jimmy, said, "Uh-huh," took a deep breath and returned unsteadily to his car.

The cop handed him the license and registration. "On your way to the museum, are you?"

"Sure. The museum. Sorry about the speeding. I guess I was a little anxious." He was loosening up now, getting into the archaeologist role. "Like you say, with all those pickets and reporters hounding us."

The cop walked back to his patrol car, gave Jimmy a short salute, and said, "Watch that gas pedal, okay? Never can tell, you fly over one of these hills in a rust bucket like this, there could be a tourist camper creeping along at twenty miles an hour on the other side. You'd run right up his exhaust pipe, and . . ."

"Yes, sir." Jimmy opened his door, slid into the seat. He shut his eyes and pressed his forehead against the cool steering wheel. He cranked the engine, winked at the mummy to his right, and heard the cop add,

"Tell you what . . ."

Jimmy leaned out of the window, looked back.

"Just to be on the safe side, I'll run escort for you back to the museum. How's that?"

24

T
hadeus Trout tapped the keys of his calculator. Without warning, he slapped the ledger with a loud smack, scattering papers and toppling a brass bowling pin. He caught the pin before it rolled to the floor, and wheeled to face Junior's crew at the doorway. He shook the pin at them. "I *hate* losing money. You dunderheads have no idea what's involved to make ends meet. Wholesale food sales are flat. The outlet store's doing good, but inventory's down—I haven't been able to set up a hijack in two months. Fudge is off six points in town and my baby, the Bible Alive Museum, is sucking me dry. Oh, attendance is up, but the utility bills for heating and cooling Genesis Hall are eating me alive. Noah's flood tank needs shoring up, and the two-thousand-year-old man is threatening to retire again. The climate control in the lower level went blotto, and Lot's wife was melting from the humidity, so the idiots put her out in the sun to dry, and a deer licked her arm off. I got a deal on a sixteen-foot anaconda for the Garden of Eden exhibit, but the trainer can't get it to climb the tree of knowledge of good and evil, let alone hold an apple in its mouth.

"But that's not the worst. Word must have got out about

Doone skipping and everybody and their cousin are reneging. My loan business is in the crapper."

"Why don't we drop your bowling ball on a few of their feet?" Junior asked, seeing only the cloud's silver lining and not the tempest raging within.

"*You*—" Trout's face began to flush. "You let Doone get away!"

"No, sir, he escaped. . . ."

"He wouldn't have, if you screw-ups had been more careful." Trout's color heightened to a dangerous rose purple. He gasped three times, panted for half a minute, regained his breath, and wheezed to Junior, "Boy, why do you get me so worked up? Some day I'll have a stroke and my head'll blow right off my shoulders."

"I'm sorry, sir."

"Sorry don't cut it in the world of business." Trout cradled his fat cheeks in his palms, lay his forehead on the desk, and let out a lengthy sigh. Then, he raised his ponderous head, shook it side to side, jowls jiggling, as if to cast off his financial worries.

He regarded the boys, a bit more subdued from the head-shaking. "Hell, I blame myself, too. I encouraged Doone's gambling, knew he'd piss away most of the money I lent him. But, I was sure he'd show up wetting his pants with fear, offering the lease if I'd let him off the hook. Instead, he bolted.

"Oooh, that Doone pisses me off."

Another sigh. "Pissed me off enough that I may have acted rashly." He fell silent for a moment. "I called someone else in to look for him." A sidewise glance at the boys. "A professional. A real no-nonsense kind of fellow who tells me after I contract him he 'doesn't do alive.' You get my drift?"

Junior, Peaches, and Six-pack exchanged furtive looks. They knew exactly to whom he was referring.

"My dilemma is this," Trout continued. "If we find Doone, I know I can get him to sign over the lease. If something happens to him, dealing with that cult may not be as easy as I thought, because it looks like their business is going gang-busters since this Rapture crap.

"The professional I mentioned? I can't call him off. I don't know where he is, who he is, or what he looks like, and, if he eliminates Doone now, my odds of getting that lease go long. Plus, I'll have to pay this fella's fee—and he ain't cheap.

"So, I want you three to find Doone for me. There's a bonus in it if you do."

"Real good, Daddy. Do I get my Camaro back, too?"

Trout rooted through his desk drawer, removed a set of keys and tossed them to his son. "Incentive. Here."

Junior snagged them in mid-air. "Yes!" He elbowed Peaches and Six-pack. "No more lard-ass Buick."

"Pay attention," Trout said. "Our best lead is the broad he was diddling, the one in the paper. Ginger Rodgers. What's the word on her?"

"The babe has an apartment," Junior said, "but she spends most her time at the armory. We been keeping an eye on it as well as Doone's house. No Doone anywhere."

"I think," said Mr. Trout, "I'd better have a word with this broad myself. Find her and give her some story about me being a fan of Doone's, that I want to join their cult. Offer to bring her here to talk with me. Think you can handle that?"

"No problem."

Plato Scopes drove into the Captain Hook Museum parking lot, alone and red-eyed. "Stinking bears."

The press had abandoned him in disgust at the cave site. He tried to console himself that he had proof it existed, photo-graphs, and had given copies to the media. And he had the mammoth tooth, the flint point, several more chips of worked stone, organic material that could be dated, the coprolites, and, last but not least, the marvelous petroglyphs on the cave wall. Those alone were worth a scientific paper, despite his academic blacklisting. The cave drawings of wooly mam-moths, cave bears, and other Ice Age mega-mammals wouldn't make it to the bottom of the list of European cave art, but they weren't bad for the eastern U.S. And the fertility rituals? That was a *first*.

Still, no mummy. His wonderful, perfectly preserved, almost certainly European, not American Indian (how could he prove that, now?), ten-thousand-year-old-plus mummy was in the jaws of some stinking bear. Scopes tasted bile at the back of his throat, was close to wailing, when he noticed Director Duckhaus standing before the door to the museum, giving him a look to kill.

Great. Just what I need: salt in the wound.

"Well, Scopes," the director huffed. "I might have expected you to be more careful."

"I couldn't help it—"

"Horse feathers. You hang at the cave, basking in the glory of the press, while you send your assistant here with the mummy."

Scopes dabbed at a tear about to launch itself from the corner of his left eye. What was the man talking about? "Excuse me?"

"Sloppy science, if you ask me. I had him put it in the lab, on that folding table."

Scopes flew by him, nearly knocked over an elderly tourist admiring the "Buttonhooks of the Rich and Famous" exhibit. He bolted through the lab door, and, there on the table, wrapped in a Pendleton, Indian-design blanket, lay his precious mummy, no worse for wear.

Plato Scopes, devotee of science and reason, was beginning to believe in miracles.

With the cop three paces behind him and the old museum director leading the way inside, Jimmy had no choice but to leave the mummy at the museum. "I'll save you," he said over and over on the way back to his Grandpop's. "I swear I won't let them cut you up, or put you on display for gawking tourists to make fun of."

His Grandpop gave him a sympathetic hug and told him to let it go, reminding Jimmy how lucky he was not to have been pinched by the law, to have a good job, a full belly, and a roof over his head—and freedom.

Jimmy called his ARM coordinator for an update, but was too embarrassed to mention his near-rescue of the mummy. He took a long hot shower, drained a jelly glass of his Grandpop's bourbon, and fell into bed blissfully dazed. He slept fitfully, dreaming he was bound to a gurney with Nazi scientists hovering over him, wielding toothy saws and scythe-like steel knives, placidly discussing his imminent dissection.

The next morning he awoke to the smell of fresh-brewed coffee, bacon, and eggs. Grumbling, head still buzzing, he showered again, donned his David suit and joined his Grandpop at the breakfast table. His head hurt, his heart hurt, but he managed a weak smile for the old man before leaving for his job.

By the time he rolled into town, Jimmy's spirits had been buoyed by sunshine and clean mountain air. He was singing along with Roy Orbison. A block off Park, he heard a scream over the last chorus of *Pretty Woman*. He turned down the radio, pulled over, and cocked his head, heard another scream, this one muffled, in the parking lot between the old National Guard Armory and the Bible Alive Museum. He saw three men, two hundred feet away, wrestling a woman.

Jimmy was out the door running, threading through cars, passing an elderly couple, staring, frozen in place. He braked when he saw sun glinting off a long knife held high by a short, pudgy kid holding a car door open. His buddy, an evil Mr. Clean wearing a black tee shirt, had the girl around the waist, trying to force her into a red Camaro. The girl had a foot planted on each side of the door frame, her hands on the roof. The third assailant, a weasel in his early twenties, wearing a Hard Rock Cafe leather jacket, was directing the operation from six feet away, waving his arms like a rap star.

Jimmy shouted, "Let her go!" from forty feet away. The weasel flipped him off, shouted an unintelligible insult, and, apparently in reference to Jimmy's David outfit, held out one arm, the wrist limp. The pudgy one flashed his knife. The muscle man had his hands full.

Jimmy scanned the lot for a weapon. Dancing foot to foot, frustrated, he saw only asphalt. Then he remembered the sling shot at his waist. Despite the antiquing by the Bible Alive prop department and the Jewish stars on the handle, it was the real McCoy, made of oak with good rubber. As it was never intended for use, however, the museum failed to issue Jimmy ammo. He lusted for a handful of fat ball bearings. Scouring the ground, he found several pebbles, a rusty lug nut, and a big jawbreaker with ants on it. He loaded a marble-size pebble, the best one, and shot it at the kid with the knife. The stone rattled off the hood of the car. A smaller pebble dropped short, dribbled to the weasel's feet. The third sailed high, out of sight.

The weasel was holding both arms at shoulder height now, dangling limp wrists, making kissy-lips, prancing on tippy-toes. The pudgy kid was laughing so hard at the weasel he nearly dropped the knife. The girl had all of Mr. Clean's attention—he may as well have been trying to force a ten-foot ladder cross-wise through a three-foot doorway as get her into the Camaro.

The weasel unzipped his fly, spread it wide, dropped his jeans and Jockey shorts, turned around and bent over, ass-end to Jimmy. "Here you go, fruit-loop," he shouted, head upside down through spread legs. He waggled his bare hips side to side. "Give it your best shot."

Jimmy loaded the jawbreaker and let fly. It caught the weasel in the center of his right cheek. He went down like a shooting gallery target, writhed on the pavement with a hound-dog howl.

For an instant, the girl and the muscle man stopped struggling. The pudgy kid lowered his knife, staring at the downed weasel, then, worried, re-directed his gaze at Jimmy. Jimmy dropped the lug nut into the sling shot's leather pouch, stretched the rubber nearly to his chin, aimed at Mr. Clean's broad back and released. The nut missed his target by four feet, but caught Mr. Clean on the tendon an inch over the heel of his Nike running shoe. He screamed a high-octave obscenity, released the girl and fell onto his back. The girl landed hard on his chest.

Jimmy charged. The pudgy kid yelped and ran. The weasel was still howling, the muscle man huffing on his back, trying to regain his breath.

Jimmy scooped the girl from the big man's chest, boosted her to her feet, took an elbow, and said, "Let's get out of here."

25

immy hustled the girl into his Yugo and drove toward the
center of town, traffic, and people. Neither he nor she
spoke. He pulled into a motel lot, parked several rows
back from the road and, still white-knuckling the wheel,
took a deep breath.

"Wow!" the girl said as soon as the engine died. "You saved
me. Just like in the movies." She leaned toward him, set one
hand lightly on his knee for leverage and gave him a brief kiss
on the cheek. As she turned, her short denim skirt rose to the
top of her thighs.

Time slowed. As if he had taken a morphine hit, Jimmy felt
his bones go rubbery, a warm, dizzying glow suffuse his body.
His gaze hung on those long bare legs, jumped to her face, all
blue eyes and white teeth. Tousled, shoulder length blond hair
hung past her shoulders. This was one of those girls, Jimmy
realized, who, if he wasn't careful, could melt his righteous
anger and jelly his brain, have him wearing cologne and show-
off clothes, going to dinner at her place, candles on the table,
him bringing flowers, ARM no more than a memory—

"—a real hero."

"No dig beal," he said. "I mean, 'No big deal'."

"Sure it was. They could have beat you up, or the fat one could've stabbed you, or, maybe they had guns. You were really brave." She noticed Jimmy staring at her hand, still resting on his knee. She withdrew the hand, leaned chin to elbows against the dashboard, and scouted for the Camaro. Her pink tee shirt hiked up, exposing a bare midriff.

Jimmy dry-swallowed. "Who *were* those men?"

She wrinkled her nose. "Atheists, I'll bet."

"Atheists?"

The nose unwrinkled and she smiled. She had a tiny gap between her upper incisors, but her teeth were otherwise flawless. "I'll just bet they were," she said, "from the nasty names they were calling the Prince."

"Prince?" Whoever this Prince was, Jimmy despised him already. The girl sounded local. The son of a bitch had probably rolled into town in some fancy limo with a driver and bodyguards, met her at a town shop, invited her to go to, where? Monte Carlo or somewhere, and—

"My job's with the Children of Light," she was saying, "you know, the church on the hill over town, the old armory? With the angel blimp?" She scooped her ankles onto the small seat with her right hand, tucking them under her thighs, showing even more leg as the skirt gathered at her waist. "They call us Fireflies because of the flashlights we carry at night on the Roof of the Ascension. Well, it's not exactly my job." She tugged absently at the skirt, but it didn't lower more than an inch. "Or . . . yes, I guess it is my job, now, because I used to work in a fudge shop until I saw the Prince of Light raptured— you know, like, Poof!—up to heaven—and now the Messenger, that's Reverend Patch, he wants me full time at the church, so he's paying me the same as I made at the fudge shop plus a bonus for everybody who gets saved. What I mean, is, I do the Lord's work now, so I guess those men were sent by the devil to disrupt us. Atheists."

"Sure," Jimmy said, blinking. "This Prince is some kind of religious guru with a church and you work there."

"Not just work there . . . I'm the Witness now, and, yes, I

work there, but—weren't you listening? The Prince was rap-tured. He was the very first and—"

"'Rapture.' Sorry, I don't know the word. Means like 'bliss'?"

"It's in the Bible, and like the Prince himself pro–phe–sied," enunciating, "the Rapture will start with a shooting star, trou-ble in the Middle East, and weird weather. When you're *rap*–tured," drawing out the first syllable, "God takes you up to heaven, leaving your clothes and everything behind. The Prince was the first to go, probably to get heaven ready for the rest of us. We're all waiting for the Great Rapture to follow, see? Those who don't make it will be left behind to face the Tribulation, the rise of the Antichrist, and the End of Days. Do you understand now?"

She tugged at the skirt again, frowned at it, tilted her head to one side, and gave him a long look. "Why are you dressed like that? In that skirt and blouse?"

Jimmy fumbled for words. He felt his face burn and spun left, pretending he was still scouting for the three men.

Apparently misinterpreting the silence and blushing, the girl scooted beside him, put a hand on his shoulder, and squeezed gently. "I don't care what Reverend Patch says. I don't think you're going to burn in hell."

"What?" Jimmy's eyes snapped wide.

"On account of being gay. Everyone to their own, huh?" She watched the back of his ears turn red, and added, "You really have a nice tan. Tanning booth plus bronzer, huh?"

Jimmy spoke to the side mirror. "I'm . . . not . . . gay. This is a costume I wear for my *job*. At the Bible Alive Museum. I'm *David*." He wished himself a thousand miles away.

"Pleased to meet you, David." She held her palm out for a handshake, but as Jimmy couldn't see the hand, she jabbed him in the ribs with extended fingertips to get his attention. "I'm Ginger. Ginger Rodgers. That's Rodgers with a D in the middle."

Jimmy rubbed his face, willing away the absurdities. "My

name isn't David," he said, finally looking at her. "It's Jimmy. People call me Jimmy Feather."

"Jimmy. Okay. I'm Ginger." She extended her hand again.

Jimmy shook it. The hand was soft, warm, weighed no more than a sparrow. He felt his cheeks flush again and released her hand, changing the subject. "I guess we ought to call the cops."

"No way. Reverend Patch would get pissed—I mean, angry. Next thing you know he'll have me chained to the stage. No. God watches over me. He sent you to save me, and He will punish those men, too."

Unsure of the 'stage' reference—actress in some pageant?—or the likelihood of divine retribution, but relieved at not having to confront the law again, Jimmy said, "Maybe," then, "Hold on . . . I saw your picture in the paper. I remember . . . about the guy that disappeared."

"Well, du–uhhh. What did I just tell you? The Prince of Light. I guess I'm, like, famous now. You wouldn't believe the bizarro people who come by to see me. That's my job—letting these people stare at me up on the stage while Reverend Patch tells them how they'll be raptured, too, if they let him save their souls.

"I'll tell you something, though," Ginger stared into the distance. "Being a star isn't all it's cracked up to be. Half the time I feel like Santa Claus, all these creepy people plopping sticky kids on my lap while they take snaps, saying, 'Smile! Smile!' My face is frozen—you know, like the Joker." She gave him a cheesy grin. "At least at the fudge shop, you could really talk to people and smile because you were happy." She took a deep breath, gave him a questioning look. "What's your job like? You have to smile, too?"

"Sometimes. I'm supposed to be a security guard, but they want me to pose, too. I'm David. Remember? Like David in the Bible, who slew the giant?"

"Way to go. A Bible character. And you slew a giant to save me. Three of them—or one giant and two helpers. Shame on all those people who don't believe in Bible stories. This is so–oh cool. Wait till I tell the girls back at the Temple of Light—you know, where the atheists attacked me?" She checked her watch. "I'd better be going."

"I'll give you a lift."

Ginger asked him if he would mind stopping at a fast food drive-through for a Coke fix, "because the Messenger makes me drink chamomile tea at work." Jimmy ordered a shake. They sipped them in the lot. Jimmy loosened up when Ginger asked what it felt like to be an Indian. He segued into his travels, confessed how he had released the Clarion Grampus.

"Well, I hope so. I'd hate to think I was saved by a man who'd hurt a little Flipper." She told him about the vultures on the roof, how she was feeding them, how the big one, the one she called Creely, was taking french fries from her hand already, and how much Reverend Patch hated them because they pooped on their feet and hissed at him. Jimmy told Ginger about his Grandpop's border collie, how she ran and stopped and barked at his Grandpop's whistles.

"Oh-oh," Ginger said, noticing her watch. She held the face for Jimmy to see. "We've been here for fifty minutes— would you believe it? I'm late."

"Oh, man. I was supposed to punch in half an hour ago."

"What did we talk about for nearly an hour?"

"Buzzards, I think," Jimmy said. "Pooping buzzards."

"Pooping *vultures*." Ginger said. "You weren't listening."

Jimmy began to apologize until he saw her laughing. He opened his mouth, but found he was again at a loss for words, so he cranked up the Yugo.

Conversation ran thin on the drive back. Jimmy wondered what he had done wrong or should have said or—

"Right here," Ginger said. She opened the door, leaned over and gave him another quick kiss. "Thanks," she said. "You're all right, Jimmy Feather. I want to see you again. Why don't you stop by the Mad Mexican's tonight? The girls and I will be there if I can get away from Reverend Patch." She squeezed his hand, and backed out of the car. "Bye!"

"Wait—the Mad Mexican's?"

"You know, Poncho the 'irate's."

Jimmy nodded, recalling the burnt-out letter P. But before he could tell her he had an ARM meeting this evening, Ginger was out the car and up the stairs.

"I gave one of the *chicas* in the white robes a note for this Ginger," Orlando explained to Rita Rae, "telling I wish to speak with her of the movie stars. The girl phones, tells me Ginger will be at a café tonight, Poncho the Pirate's."

"A tourist dive," Rita Rae said. "Noisy college kids. Beer and barfing in the bushes. Count me out." She gave him a hard look. "You don't have a personal interest in this girl, do you? Not letting me see her? I swear, if you ever handcuff me outside the bedroom again, I'll scratch your eyes out."

Orlando waved away the threat. "Not to worry, *mi vida*. As I explain, you have too much sophistication for this Ginger. She is a simple peasant, yes? Like the schoolgirl at the foot of the movie queen, she would lose her voice in your presence."

"A mute schoolgirl who spreads her legs with no back talk. No wonder Shickie fell for her. I can just hear her, 'Beam me up, Shickie, oh wondrous Prince of light.'"

She jabbed Orlando in the chest with a pointy fingernail. "If you value your balls, mister, you had better keep your hands to yourself."

"*Mi amor*, this Ginger is *muy religiosa*. Very conservative. I speak to her as I would a sister of the Church. But when I ask her of Doone? The answers she gives are not right. She knows more, *por cierto*. Tonight, I buy her drinks, she will tell Orlando what she knows."

"She damned well better. We need to find Shickie before Trout or we'll never see our money and my ring. Odds are, if Trout does the worm in, he'll ditch his body, and I'll be gray before I see that life insurance money.

"Where is he? I've exhausted every lead." She ticked points off her fingers. "The bank hasn't seen him. Nor have the cleaners or the stores he used to shop. He hasn't tried to use our credit cards, not that it would do him any good with them maxed out. The car's been repoed, and it's not in his character to thumb or take a bus. His clothes are upstairs. I swear, if he's still around, the worm went underground."

At five till nine, nearly time to open the doors of the Temple of Light to the public, Ginger was bouncing on the cushy seat of her new throne, encrusted with gilt rococo filigree and padded with red velvet over thick foam rubber. It was nearly as impressive as the Messenger's. Patch had special-ordered them from the prop master at Dollywood. He paid for them in cash, as he had for the plush, royal purple carpet gracing the previously bare plywood dais. The runner extended from the dais to the ticket table, and to a roped-off square of carpet under the Plexiglas box containing the Prince's last vestments. Business was booming. Membership had grown from a hundred and three to a hundred and sixty-one, and the take-a-number curious queued up patiently at the entrance each morning, willing to bear the harangues of the Messenger for the opportunity to see, speak with, touch, or photograph the Witness.

Ginger said nothing about the attack by the atheists, fearing Patch would ground her. She knew she had become the golden goose of the Temple of Light, and the Messenger would do anything he thought necessary to protect his prime asset.

It was nearly show time. Patch, at Ginger's left, was calmly sipping hot water with lemon and a dash of vinegar, reading the paper. Without warning, his back straightened and he blurted out, "Lord, what's this?"

Ginger jumped, edgy at his recent outbursts of shouting, the conversations with unseen companions. She nearly spilled her chamomile tea.

Patch shook the front page of the Knoxville paper and dropped it in her lap.

"Wow!" she said. "Trouble in the Middle East. Where's the weather report?"

"No, no," Patch said. "Over to the right. There." He pointed.

Ginger read, "Ten-thousand-year-old mummy discovered in—"

"The *picture*. Look at the photograph. Do you see the resemblance?"

Ginger gasped, gave Patch a wide-eyed stare, and did a double take at the photo, a portrait of the mummy's face. "It's *him*. Reverend Doone, the Prince of Light. I know it is . . . I think."

She gave Patch a quizzical look and gazed again at the photograph. "His skin's kind of tight-like, and his eyes are closed, but look—" She tapped the center of the head shot. "The Prince had this wart on the side of his nose and one in his right eyebrow, just like this. I remember noticing them before he was raptured. That big nose, the wide forehead, the black eyebrows and long hair? It's got to be him."

"They say this is a mummy, ten thousand years old. Dried up, weighs no more than thirty pounds, naked. They found it in a cave south of here and took it to a museum in Pigeon Forge."

"It's *him*. Don't you remember the warts?"

Patch scowled. "I never looked at his face that close. Warts? I have thirteen of them on my hands, see?" He held his hands out. "No one ever notices. How can you be—"

Ginger averted her eyes from Patch's warty hands. "I saw them, okay? The night he was raptured. It's him, all right. And of course he's nude—his clothes are right over there." She pointed to the Plexiglas shrine.

"Nonsense. How could his body still be on earth?"

Ginger screwed up her face, thinking. "Maybe God only wanted the Prince's soul. If this was His first Rapture, maybe He took too much and sent the body part back."

"Ginger, God doesn't make mistakes. Although, frankly, it never made any sense to me why He would want human flesh polluting heaven. You'd think souls would be enough . . ." Patch's voice trailed off as he pondered the imponderable.

Ginger brought him out of his reverie. "You said it yourself: the angel Gabriel is the one who does the rapturing. So it wasn't God who screwed up, but Gabriel. God told him to return the Prince's body and—"

"Ten miles from where Doone was raptured?"

"As big as heaven must be, ten miles on earth is practically nothing. God probably didn't even notice from way up there."

"Foolishness. It says here the mummy weighs only twenty-seven pounds. The Prince had to weigh, what, a hundred and sixty?"

Ginger pursed her lips, and gave him a bright-eyed answer: "A soul has to weigh something."

Patch scratched his chin. "I suppose it does. But they found this mummy in a cave."

Her eyes grew large. "A *cave*, Reverend Patch. Just like—"

"Hmmm."

"It's *him*. I know it."

"This *is* vexing." Patch leaned back in his throne, eyes closed, hands clasped, and began to mumble. A half minute later, he nodded, and opened his eyes. "Perhaps," he said to Ginger, "we should see this mummy in the flesh. What's the name of that museum?"

26

Mrs. Binkle, the Temple of Light Greeter, looked uneasy. "Excuse me, sir," she said to the Messenger. "There are some . . . people here to see you."

Reverend Patch set down the phone book. "Send them up. We're always ready to save souls, aren't we Ginger?"

Ginger was curled in her throne, still staring at the front page of the Knoxville paper. She nodded.

Two minutes later, twelve very large men with long, scraggly beards and matted hair hanging past their shoulders, wearing overalls and hiking boots, approached the stage. They were followed by ten burly women, their hair tucked into bonnets, and at least four dozen children of every age, also big-boned, with similar unkempt hair. All had a congenital shoulder-slump and protruding eyes.

"I'm Goliath Jones," the largest, evidently dominant, male said. He clutched a Mail Pouch cap at his waist. His head was nearly at eye level with Ginger and Patch, seated four feet higher, on the armory stage.

Ginger scooted from her throne and stood behind it, gripping the back.

Patch tensed. He took an awkward breath, glanced skyward for courage, and said, "Welcome, Mr. Jones. I am the Reverend Creely Patch, the one God has anointed as His Messenger, and this—come out from behind your throne young woman—is Ginger Rodgers, His Witness."

"We heard," Jones said. He gave a quick nod over his right shoulder. "This is Levi Jones and his wife, Bethalee Jones, and their kids, Samuel, Randy Ray, Ginny Lou, and Mark Jones. This is Luke Jones and his wife, Ruth Jones, and their kids, Mathew, Ezra, and Bonnie Jones. This is Ephraim Jones and his . . ."

Patch and Ginger exchanged glances. Their eyes glazed as the introductions played out.

"We," Goliath Jones waved an arm, encompassing the others, "the Jones clan, all of us, read about the Rapture and come up from Texas. Jonestown—that's where we lived. When we heard about this Prince of yours going up, we sold everything, lock, stock, and barrel, bought a used school bus, and . . . here we are."

"Good for you," said Patch. "Are you prepared to be saved?"

"Oh, we been saved already. Lots of times. All of us. Kids, too. What we want is the Rapture. We'll stay till then."

"I'll have Mrs. Binkle recommend some motels in town."

"We'd druther stay here if it's all right."

Patch jolted upright. "Here? In the sanctuary?"

"We was thinking out there," Jones waved his cap, "at the side of the building. We brought tents and all what we need. Us men can hunt for meat and the women'll forage. We keep the kids in line, so none of them'll be no trouble."

"I suppose," Patch said, "that would be all right. You can use the facilities inside."

"The what?"

"The bathrooms."

"Oh." Goliath turned to the rest of the clan. "He said we can stay and use the johns inside here." Half a dozen small hands shot high over wriggling bodies, suggesting the offer of the facilities came none too soon. Ginger pointed to the back hallway and Jones shooed the kids toward it. "How soon?" he said to Patch.

"Excuse me?"

"How soon is the Great Rapture?"

"Uh, soon," Patch said.

That netted a scowl. "How long is soon?"

Ginger replied for the Messenger: "God just started talking to him, so he's not sure yet."

"That's okay. We'll wait."

After the Jones clan, nearly every one of them, had used the facilities and retired to the side yard to pitch their tents, the Messenger sent Ginger to the kitchen to brew more tea. He strode to the Prince's old office and dialed the number of the Captain Hook Museum. A woman answered. Patch said he wanted information about the mummy. She forwarded him first to the chief scientist, Plato Scopes, who did not answer, and then to the museum director, Horace Duckhaus.

"This is the Reverend Creely Patch of the Temple of Light." Patch ignored the "Sorry, I don't know you," and continued, "Mr. Duckhaus, this mummy you have interests me. I wonder if it might be possible for me and my assistant to see it?"

"You'd have to talk to our scientist, Plato Scopes, about that. He's out picking up pop and donuts, renting folding chairs for a press conference this afternoon. However, I'm sure his answer would be No. Eventually, I suppose, it will be put on display. Why don't you call back in a week or two?"

Patch huffed with impatience. "Perhaps you didn't catch my name: Creely Patch? You may know me better as the Messenger since the Prince of Light, Shickleton Doone, was raptured last—"

Duckhaus huffed back. "Never heard of any of you. Perhaps you didn't hear *me*. Our mummy is *not* for public view."

Patch huffed more audibly. "Look . . ." He covered the receiver with one hand and spoke aloud to the side, "Yes, I know. Patience. What's that, Lord? Ah—as David with the

Philistines, strategy will conquer." Back to the phone: "Director Duckhaus, perhaps I did not fully explain. Our ministry has been blessed by a generous congregation. When I read about your mummy, I said to myself, 'Creely, this is a small museum. Perhaps they are in need of financial assistance. I'll bet a generous grant would be helpful. Why don't you call them up and offer to—'"

"Ahum," Duckhaus cleared his throat. "Reverend *Patch*? Of *course*. I'm a great admirer. We get so many calls from cranks, I fear I misunderstood. I'm sure a viewing of our mummy could be arranged. . . ."

"We can be there in twenty minutes."

"No problem. Scopes won't be back by then and just as well. Ask for me at the entry desk and I'll take personal care of you."

Nineteen minutes later, Patch and Ginger were being led by a smiling Horace Duckhaus to the museum lab. Duckhaus opened a door, motioned them in. "There it is, on that table, in the big enamel tray. Scopes hasn't moved it to the cafeteria for the press conference yet. Oh," He cast an embarrassed glance at Ginger. "I forgot, it's naked."

"Avert your eyes!" Patch said, and to Duckhaus, "Get something to cover its privates."

"That's all right," Ginger said. "I took CPR and was a candy striper in junior high." She was already walking toward the table.

"Well, don't look down *there*," Patch said. "Keep your eyes on its face."

Ginger had already seen the face. The warts. Had already made up her mind. Ignoring Patch's warning, her gaze dropped to the mummy's privates, remembering the Prince waving his thing twelve inches from her face the night he had been raptured. It was definitely larger then. Quite a bit larger. Ginger had dreamt about it, after. And, yes, uncircumcised. It was all shrunk up now. Poor little peanut, she said to herself, and felt tears welling. She tried to tell herself the Prince's soul was up in heaven, consorting with angels, and that this was only his mortal shell, but her heart ached. The Prince made people feel so good: joyful hymns, upbeat sermons, no devil threats or ranting. What fun she would have had as the Prince's wife.

She knew she should be grateful. After all, she was somebody now, the Witness, a star just like her mommy had wanted. Sitting beside the Messenger, however, was a pale reward compared to the could-have-been glory of being the Princess of Light. She swiped her eyes with the back of a hand, said a silent prayer for her fallen—No, she told herself, *risen*—Prince.

With trembling lips, she looked longingly at the lifeless husk. Could this really be him? She leaned closer, nose twitching, on the trail of a familiar, lingering scent: Doone's Old Spice. No question, this was her Prince, all right.

"What are you *doing?*" Patch watched Ginger bend close to the mummy's face. "Don't *kiss* it, for God's sake. You don't know where it's been."

Ginger faced him, set her jaw. "I wasn't *kissing* him. I was sniffing."

Patch's lip curled with revulsion. Duckhaus clapped a hand over his nose and mouth.

Ginger cast a regretful look at the Messenger. "It's him, all right," she said with finality, and dabbed at a fresh tear rolling down her nose.

Patch moved closer, studied the face. "Does look like him, but . . ."

"What are you two talking about—'*him?*'" said Duckhaus. "That mummy is thousands of years old."

"It's *him*," Ginger spoke to the wall, sick of these two old men, sad at seeing her Prince so still, so gray, so dead. "It's *his* face. *His* warts. *His* Old Spice. *His*—" She thought better of the last part. Her voice trailed off.

Patch dropped to his knees, addressed the empty air. "What do You think?"

Ginger and Duckhaus exchanged uneasy glances.

"Yes," Patch said to neither Ginger, Duckhaus, nor the

mummy, but to a higher presence. "I do, too. And, he's by Your side now, his spirit? I agree. A sacrilege. He belongs in the Temple of Light, suitably enshrined. Of course, this very minute."

Patch's eyes opened and fixed on Duckhaus. "This," he said, pointing to the mummy, "is the mortal remains of Shickleton Doone, the Prince of Light, whose soul ascended to heaven, raptured by the angel Gabriel, and who now sits by the right hand of God. I have been instructed to remove the Prince to the Temple of Light." He took a step toward the table. "We'll take him with us."

"Like hell you will." Duckhaus's jaw dropped, he sputtered, jumped between Patch and the mummy, arms windmilling, blocking Patch's advance. Duckhaus shouted for a guard.

Patch continued, "Do you have a big box?"

27

*S*ix-pack leaned against the wall by Mr. Trout's office, knee bent, foot six inches off the floor. Peaches stood behind him. Junior sat in the chair across from his father's desk, on a donut-shaped, plastic-sheathed pillow.

"Let me get this straight," Trout said. "You asked this Ginger Rodgers real polite to come here and talk, and she attacked you?"

Junior nodded. "Went crazy. Six-pack tried to get her off me and—"

Trout finished the sentence. "And some sissy in a skirt came by and knocked Mr. Steroids on his butt with a slingshot? And shot you in the ass."

"That's right." Junior kept his eyes on his lap, adjusting and readjusting the foam support. He had one hand under the donut, running his fingers over his wound, a painful contusion the size of a strawberry.

Mr. Trout rotated the chair to face Peaches. "Let me guess. You watched."

"No sir, I tried to get hold of her, but she was really strong, and—"

Trout shook his big, bloodhound head. "It's a shame the fourth of July is so far away. The three of you could march at the head of the Independence Day parade like in that painting: one on crutches, one with his ass in a sling thumping a drum, the other blowing on a flute. Bah!" He exhaled a disgruntled huff of air. "Maybe I oughta fire the three of you and hire this sissy and the girl."

"We'll get the babe. And we'll pay back the guy in the dress."

"Stay away from both of them—they can ID you. If the cops haven't been here by now, they probably didn't get your license number. If they do show up, I'll tell them you've been unloading sides of beef all day in Bay Three."

"Way to go, Daddy."

"Why you would drive your own car instead of the no-one-would-notice beater out back with the muddy plates mystifies me." Trout held his thick palm out to Junior. "Keys, please."

"Not my Camaro. I hardly got to—"

"You'll drive the Buick till this quiets down." Trout gave his son a questioning look. "You wouldn't want to make a liar of me, would you?"

Junior looked confused, but shook his head.

"I thought not. So get your butts back to Bay Three. There's a full day's work ahead unloading that beef."

Creely Patch's hands gripped the steering wheel. "Imagine that Duckhaus fool asking if we were still making a contribution. I'll have twenty demonstrators there within the hour. How's that for a 'contribution'?"

Ginger squirmed. "I don't think I can make it, Reverend Patch. I, uh . . ."

"What's that?" Patch addressed not Ginger but the car's sun visor. "Of course. A shrine beside Doone's Rapture clothes."

Ginger screamed as the car drifted left of center.

Patch swerved. A pickup spouting gravel along the far

shoulder continued honking for another three hundred feet. "Pardon the interruption, Lord," Patch said. "Oh, yes. We'll have the Prince in the cradle of the faithful by nightfall."

It was all Ginger could do to restrain herself from nibbling her nails again. Besides the Messenger's doomsday driving, she was fighting back tears from seeing the poor Prince all dried up. Absolutely, positively, somehow, she would escape the Lighthouse to go dancing and down a few beers with the girls at the Mad Mexican's tonight.

Without explanation, Patch shouted, "The Book of Daniel!"

Ginger rechecked her seatbelt. She had to get *away*. The Cuban movie star, Orlando, would be there. And maybe Jimmy Feather, her good-looking Bible hero. She was sick of herbal tea, sick of sitting on her throne, smiling, endlessly repeating the Poof! story. And Patch's weirdness was getting . . . really weird.

God would get the Prince back, just as he had sent Jimmy Feather to rescue her from the atheists. And God, she had faith, would get her to the Mad Mexican's.

"Right hand, honey," the manicurist said. "Leave the left one soak."

Maury placed his right hand in her palm.

"You poor dear," she cooed. "You're all shaky, aren't you?"

"Too much coffee," Maury said, but he knew that wasn't it. The shakes were definitely getting worse. He passed his last physical, no problem: blood pressure, heart, fine; but Maury hadn't mentioned the palsy. He corrected himself: not palsy, little case of the jitters is all. Right. You're nearly eighty. He recalled his last contract, a conniving appliance store manager who not only had been frying the books, but stealing merchandise from his employer for a year. It took two whole clips to finish him off. Maury put more slugs in the plywood behind the cheater than in him. And those that hit him? Fingers, toes, an ear . . . messy. And hardly because the guy was a tricky target. He had a clubfoot, a thirty-six-inch flat screen Panasonic TV in his arms, and was trapped in the back of a semi.

Twelve years ago, it had taken only three rounds to send Ruth to cheaters' hell—and that was the first time Maury had fired a pistol. For a pro, it shouldn't take more than one pop in the head, with a backup for security. Maury was slipping, all right.

"Ohh . . . look," the manicurist squealed. "A bambi and her family."

Maury glanced through plate glass at the rear of the shop, to the grassy slope beyond. No more than fifty feet away a young buck stood at attention while a doe and a spotted fawn grazed, content as milk cows.

What a place, this Gatlinburg, Maury thought. Bears and deer yet, in your backyard. More outlet stores than retail, and not a Cora's Cozy Cove in fifty miles. Although Maury had, in desperation, become a happy hour regular at Poncho the 'irate's.

Familiarizing himself with Doone's turf, Maury had toured Ripley's Believe It or Not, the Elvis Museum, Dollywood, the Bible Alive Museum, and nearly every other tourist trap. He had played miniature Hillbilly Golf beside rosy-cheeked teenagers, and schmoozed with plaid-panted salesmen playing hooky at the real course. He listened to every time share pitch, read every goofy tee shirt, watched taffy drawn and quartered and fudge go stiff on cold marble slabs in the candy shops. He figured he must have spoken at least twice to every man, woman, and child who called Gatlinburg home. A surprising number knew Doone and they all seemed to like him. "Stopped by every morning to play dollar bill poker—you know, with the serial numbers?" "Made you laugh, that guy, pulling quarters out of your ears or nose." "Wasn't no fanatic despite the rigmarole at the armory."

Maury Finkle had a way with people, too. No one held back. Doone had been here, all right, until, as young Ginger put it, Poof!

Had Doone, the cheat, blown town? Somehow, Maury doubted it.

Despite the blind alleys, Maury still had an ace or two up his seersucker coat sleeve. Ginger seemed to believe the screwy Rapture exit, but went squirrelly when pressed. Then there was the wife, Rita Rae, whom Maury had been following all day. She went outlet shopping, and was now in a roomful of yentas at Laurel Lynne's House of Beauty, three feet to Maury's right. If anyone knew the real poop, it was her.

Maury regarded her: red nails drying, toes too, feet propped up on little pillows, her hair, under the ministrations of Laurel Lynne herself, rising above Rita Rae's head like radioactive yeast was brewing in it, looking like one of those beaver hats the English royal guards wear, only bushier, and yellow. She wore a monster diamond on her finger, although it looked a bit too sparkly to Maury's eye.

Maury coughed as Rita Rae lit a third cigarette from the smouldering stub of her second.

Laurel Lynne passed her a hand mirror.

Rita Rae considered. "Hmmm."

Laurel Lynne gushed. "I think the bubble cut becomes you, sweetheart. Tray boo-font, as they say in Pair-ee. Much more ow-cow-rant than that old beehive. Your man's gonna be all over you when he sees this do."

"Spray it firm," Rita Rae said. "I don't want him squishing it."

Maury noted the "him." Was it Doone she was making pretty for, or the greaseball lover?

Laurel Lynne lifted a professional-size spray can, cautioning Rita Rae to snub out the cigarette first, lest they both go up in flames. Rita Rae flipped the butt onto the floor.

Maury decided to drop his little bomb, see the reaction.

"A fine fellow, I came across today," he said to the manicurist but loud enough to be heard in the chair to his right. "Shickie Doone, I think he said his name was."

"*What?*" Rita Rae dropped the mirror. Shards of glass skittered across the floor. She spun toward Maury so fast she nearly fell from the chair. Laurel Lynne sprayed thin air. Rita Rae's bare feet rose and sank teeter-totter-like from under the styling cape. She gripped the chair arm to regain her balance and leaned closer. "Where'd you see him?"

Maury said, "Don't believe we've met. Folks call me Maury."

"Maury. Fine. Shickie Doone. Where'd you see him?"

"Let's see," Maury said. "On the main drag, I think. Parkway, they call it. I gather you know the gentleman?"

"*Know* him? I *married* him. The worm ran out on me. Stole my beautiful diamond ring." She waved her left hand at him. "Left me with *this*: cubic zirconia. And more debt that you want in a lifetime."

"You poor dear," Laurel Lynne said. "Men are such snakes."

The manicurist signaled the cashier for a broom for the mirror and a pitcher of water for a stinky brush fire Rita Rae's cigarette butt had ignited among the snippets of hair littering the floor. Oblivious of the smoke and broken glass, patrons focused on the dirt playing out between the blonde and the old man.

Maury studied Rita Rae's face, deciding, alas, her reaction was bona fide. She didn't know where Doone was either.

Rita Rae hadn't entirely recovered her equilibrium. The drape slid half off her body, revealing, Maury could not help but notice, a fine set of gams descending to her bare, red toe-nailed feet. Rita Rae gripped Maury's wrist, jerked it from the manicurist's hand, and pumped it to extract more information. "Tell me *exactly* where and when you saw him. Are you sure it was him? Shickie Doone?"

"Well," Maury said. "I think that's what he said his name was. Smallish Chinese gentleman. Let's see . . . Doone . . . no, Poon, I believe it was, now that I recall. Rikki Poon. Runs a chop suey place in Knoxville."

"Balls!" Rita Rae dropped Maury's wrist and slumped in the chair. "Balls, balls, balls."

*   *   *

Ginger and Betsy, a plump nineteen-year-old with doe eyes behind owlish glasses, sat on the washstand counter in the Temple of Light's ladies' room.

"I can't believe you got out of it," Betsy said. "Reverend Patch has almost a full busload to march at that museum. He wanted you to lead us."

"No way. I had my fill of shouting and hopping when I was a Hare Krishna."

Betsy scowled. "They're not Christians, are they?"

"It's a big world out there, Betsy. Anyway, that was before I found the Prince and the Children of Light."

"I was a Nazarene, before." Betsy lowered her voice. "I can't believe the Messenger's going to let you go to the Mad Mexican's tonight. Since he moved into the Prince's room at the Temple of Light and set up a place for you, too, I'd be surprised if you ever get out again." She jumped from the counter and peered under the stall doors. "Truth is," she continued in a whisper, "Reverend Patch knows it's you who draws them in. That's why he wants you here all the time."

"I really miss the Prince," Ginger said. "I had a dream— just between us?"

Betsy crossed her heart.

"I never got to talk with the Prince before that night, but I dreamt he was going to fall in love with me. After he got the divorce from that bitch of a wife."

"You shouldn't say 'bitch.'"

"That's what she is, a bitch. Everyone knows it, and that's why I went to see him. An angel came to me in my sleep and told me to do it. And it would have worked out that way, too, if he hadn't been raptured first."

"An angel! That's like a miracle."

"Of course it was. The angel didn't explain, but God must have sent me to his house to be the Witness, like Reverend Patch says."

"Ginger . . . you're like a saint."

"Reverend Patch says saints are for Catholics."

"Then, God's angel on earth."

"But that doesn't mean God wants me to spend every minute here, either. All the sitting, holding those squealing babies, putting up with Reverend Patch." Her lips curled into a devious smile. "You know what I've been doing?"

"What?"

"Feeding the vultures. They eat anything: french fries, pizza crusts, banana peels, chicken bones. They're not very pretty with that crinkly red skin on their heads, and pooping all over their feet, and they're stinky, but they're kind of cute. I call the big one Creely."

"Oh, that's evil."

"Yeah, a little. It makes me feel good to see them fly back as soon as Reverend Patch or one of the Joneses chases them away. But that's not enough. I need to get away. Tonight. To the Mad Mexican's."

Betsy stared at her hands. "Maybe I'll go, too. If you do. Did Reverend Patch say you could?"

"Sort of . . . I told him my Aunt Rose was visiting me."

Betsy touched her forearm. "Poor baby. Cramps?"

"I won't start for two weeks. Listen to this. I saw Reverend Patch's face Wednesday when Cindy told Suzanne she was having a rough time of the month. His face got all pinched up and red, and he left the room. Yesterday I kind of let 'tampon' and 'period' drop in a conversation with Joline while he was on the throne beside me, reading his Bible. He got all flustery, said, 'Don't talk like that.' 'Like what?' I said. 'You know—those inciteful words.' 'What words?' I asked, 'Period and tampon?'"

"You said that to Reverend Patch?"

"Sure. Here's the best part: when I mentioned Aunt Rose, he asked if I was bringing her by to get *saved*. I looked at him like he was crazy. 'I'm on my *period*, Reverend Patch,' I said, 'so I won't be able to go to the demonstration, or come back here tonight.' He coughed and sputtered, wouldn't look me in the eyes. Finally he said, 'Yes, of course,' and slunk away."

Ginger gripped her abdomen and groaned. "I don't think he knows anything about women. I figure telling him I'm on my period will get me out of here at least a couple times a week."

28

orace Duckhaus stared through his office window at the disaster unfolding outside the buttonhook museum. Eight ARM demonstrators carried signs with ARCHAEOLOGY = DESECRATION, or RETURN OUR ANCESTOR! some bearing a raised red fist. They marched counterclockwise in a long line to the beat of a tom-tom, trying to out-shout twenty-two Children of Light in white robes, singing hymns, marching clockwise, bearing hastily-constructed signs reading ARCHAEOLOGY = ATHEISM, or, on a long banner, RETURN OUR PRINCE! Harried cops were doing their best to keep the protestors separated, a growing crowd of onlookers back, and traffic flowing in and out of the outlet malls and Dollywood, while two news vans with extended antennae in the glutted parking lot attracted even more of the curious.

Duckhaus wrung his hands. "Damn Scopes. Damn his mummy. All these people, none interested in buttonhooks, police threatening to charge us for the crowd control—Hey!" He knocked on the glass, with no effect, as a photographer climbed onto the roof of Duckhaus's automobile for a better view of the debacle. The new shrubbery lining the lot had long ago been trampled, litter was everywhere, and Scopes's press conference had yet to begin.

Duckhaus checked his watch. Ten minutes to the hour. He rushed from his office, and was immediately engulfed by reporters and cameramen hurrying toward the overcrowded cafeteria. He caught snatches of conversation:

". . . hell of a story if the Indians and the Bible thumpers light into one another—maybe we could rile 'em up. You know, throw a bottle or something."

"Never heard of this place before today."

"That's right—porno cave drawings . . ."

". . . buck naked."

"Get a good crotch shot—this is science, so the FCC won't . . ."

"A prehistoric turd?"

"Damn Scopes," Duckhaus said again, and elbowed aside a grungy kid carrying a digicam. He worked his way into the rear of the cafeteria—standing room only—mere seconds before Scopes began his pitch.

He saw Scopes standing behind a roped-off area containing a three- by six-foot table with the sheet-covered mummy at center. The sole museum guard was waving his arms to keep the press contained. Blow-ups of the cave drawings, and photographs of the mammoth tooth, the flints, and the coprolite were mounted on easels. Some of the audience perused press kits containing the same glossies. Duckhaus calculated the cost of it all and muttered yet another "Damn Scopes."

Plato Scopes's stomach churned, the collar of his new white shirt chafed his neck, his lab coat already had a ketchup stain on the lapel, his off-the-rack outlet shoes pinched his toes, but his soul soared. Who would have guessed the world would be at his feet like this? He anticipated telling, impressing, the media how "I spoke with the National Geographic Society this afternoon and they are very interested. . . ." The NGS response was, in fact, no more than polite, but these people didn't need to know that.

He had also neatly sidestepped the offers of assistance from the Department of Forensic Anthropology at the University of Tennessee, the kingpins of forensic research, with their famous "body farm" and their out-the-whazoo resources. Oh, they would have his mummy sliced, diced, and quantified to the last iota in no time flat, but where would Plato Scopes be? In the cold, that's where. And what if the National Park Service people with their coast-to-coast network of specialists and the facilities of the National Museum in Washington to back them up, got hold of it? Wham, bam, and thank you ma'am, Plato Scopes.

How fortunate that Scopes's brother-in-law was one of the cops responding to the Boy Scouts' discovery, that he had called him first, that his wife's uncle was county medical examiner and smart enough to realize a twenty-seven-pound, nude, flexed mummy in a cave was no contemporary murder victim. Lucky, too, the mummy had been on private land, and the owner readily signed a release.

What of the disappearance of the mummy from the cave and its mysterious reappearance at the museum? All Scopes could imagine was that the bear that got hold of it came out another entrance with the mummy in its jaws and some hunter had shot or frightened it, recovered the body, remarkably undamaged, and had the brains to bring it to the museum. Special delivery. Scopes doubted there was a God in heaven, but if there was, He smiled on Plato Scopes.

Everything was proceeding as planned. Scopes imagined a feature in *National Geographic*, the illustrations of a white-skinned clan dressed in fur kilts and boots, grazing mammoths behind them silhouetted against a mile-high glacier, the women bare-breasted, the men carrying torches, guiding a drugged warrior to the mouth of the cave for ritual sacrifice. The story would open with a photograph of the scientist-discoverer Plato Scopes pointing to the cave art, the mammoth tooth cradled in his arms.

Scopes wrinkled his nose as a maggot of doubt wormed its way into his grandiloquent visions. What about those damned Indians and religious cultists? Surely the media would dismiss them as irrelevant troublemakers. Wouldn't they?

"Hell–oh–o, it's time to begin," someone called, followed by, "Take the sheet off. Let's see this thing, Dr. Scopes." Plato beamed at the "Dr." What the press assumed today would become reality soon enough.

He raised his hand for order, swallowed several times to lubricate his dry throat, and began with his rehearsed script. "You are about to regard the most amazingly preserved mummy the world has seen. Nothing in North America compares with it. The Egyptian pharaohs are dross beside it. All the gold of the Incas could not duplicate . . ."

"What about the Indians? They say you should return it—"

"Yeah," a tweedy reporter broke in. "Doesn't NAGPRA—"

Another voice: "What's NAGPRA?"

"Native American Grave Protection and Repatriation Act," replied the man in tweed. "Says mummies like this or bones and grave goods should be return—"

Scopes cut them off. "None of that applies here, and if my hypothesis is borne out, we will learn this is *not* an ancestor of modern Indians, but a descendant of ancient Europeans, crossing the Atlantic over ten thousand . . ."

"How can you tell it's not an Indian? Those people outside think it is."

"Wishful thinking," Scopes said, irritation rising. "A scientist relies on fact, such as mitochondrial DNA analysis, CT scans to reveal dentition—"

"What if it's got a mouthful of gold inlays?"

Scopes glared. "Then I'll formulate a new hypothesis. As a scientist I am on a fact-finding mission and shall proceed accordingly." He raised his eyebrows. "May I continue? People of Mongoloid ancestry have shovel-shaped incisors, a definitive trait—check the handout, page three. I shall take a number of anthropometric measurements of the skull and long bones to further clarify the mummy's identity.

"Why do I suspect great antiquity and European ancestry?" He lifted the mammoth tooth, explained the affinity of the worked flint with European blades. "There is snowballing evidence elsewhere in the Americas to support multiple migrations from Asia, from Europe, even Africa. When you see the face of our mummy, I think you will agree it looks European, not—"

"So let's see it."

Another voice raised another question: "The Fireflies claim it's the body of their leader, Shickleton Doone, who was raptured to heaven five days ago."

"Get real," Scopes said. "As a scientist—"

"They say that's why it's so perfectly preserved, that God took this Doone's soul and left his mortal remains and clothing behind. They have an eyewitness and the clothing, too, as proof—shirt, trousers, socks, shoes, underwear." The reporter winked at his colleagues.

Another newsman, enjoying Scopes's distress, added, "If they're right, of course your mummy looks European, since this Doone was Scots-Irish. In fact, they've been passing out photographs of him." He waved a church newsletter with a full-length photo of the Prince of Light, not nearly as detailed as Scopes's glossy of the mummy, but adequate to make a comparison.

"Preposterous." Scopes began an agitated dance behind the mummy table. "So, a thunderbolt zapped down," his hand airplaned the air, "and instantly," he snapped his fingers toward the cloth-covered mummy, "Zap! Desiccated the body? Transported it to a cave miles away? While the soul," his fingers fluttered ceilingward, "rose to heaven. Is that what you're telling me?"

"Yes."

"Believe me, it would take a century or more to mummify a human in that cave—and desiccation like that would result in a shriveled-up body the color of shoe leather. And don't suggest some hapless miner or caver. Whoever heard of one of them wandering around naked?

"I suggest our mummy was a ritual sacrifice associated with the fertility rituals portrayed on the cave walls. Thus its nudity. And I believe this ancient culture possessed remarkable processes of mummification that have been lost through the ages. When you see our specimen, it's going to knock your socks off."

Someone called out, "Start knocking."

"Sure," Scopes said, followed by a pregnant pause. "Why not?"

Video lights sparked in anticipation. Cameras were lifted high overhead for unobstructed views. The audience pressed forward.

Scopes waved an arm in warning. "Stay behind the rope." He took a deep breath and lifted his arms high, wiggled his fingers and dropped them to pinch two corners of the white sheet. He lifted it slowly and with a dramatic swish, revealed the mummy, curled on its side, facing the crowd, nude (except for a hanky covering its privates, per Duckhaus's insistence).

Motor drives zip-zip-zipped, videos purred, necks craned, reporters shoved and jostled for the best views.

Thirty seconds later, Scopes re-covered the mummy as he had planned.

"Hey—I barely got to see it."

"Take off that sheet."

"That's enough," Scopes said, adding a rehearsed line he hoped would be quoted in their stories: "I don't want to be disrespectful of the dead."

When the groans died, someone said, "So tiny. I wonder if it was a kid."

"No," Scopes said. "I estimate his height to have been around five foot six or seven. Early humans were smaller than people today."

"How much does it weigh?"

"Twenty-seven pounds."

"No kidding? What did he weigh before he got dried out?"

"Perhaps a hundred and sixty."

"So . . ." the needler who brought up the Fireflies concluded, loud enough for all to hear, "his *soul* weighed a hundred and thirty-three pounds."

"*What?*" Scopes gave him a withering look. "We're talking science here, evaporation of H_2O, not—"

"The face and body really are well preserved," said a helpful voice in the news pack. "I've seen Egyptian mummies and they look like prunes compared to—"

"I told you," Scopes said. "Didn't I?" He lifted one corner of the sheet again to reveal the face, "Did you notice how European it looks?"

"It looks a lot like this Reverend Doone," a troublemaker remarked, holding up the Temple of Light newsletter.

"Sure does," said a reporter up front. Others consulted their own copies.

Scopes dropped the cloth. "That's *it*. This press conference is over."

Walking to the exit amid growing shouts of the Fireflies and ARM protestors outside, one reporter said to another: "I'd say there's three ways to play this."

"And those would be?"

"One: 'Scientist hot over discovery in Bumfuck, Tennessee.' Two: 'Indians throw fit over dug-up ancestor.' And three . . ."

"Yeah?"

"'World's first Rapture: God keeps soul in heaven, sends body back to earth.'"

"Not bad. Cut the length and that's a page-one headline."

29

It was Oldies and Classic Rock night at Poncho the 'irates. Ginger Rodgers and sister Firefly, Joline, threaded through a growing crowd. They wore jeans, cowboy boots, and extra large tee shirts, sleeves rolled up, with silk-screened angel blimps and "Show Me the Light" blazoned across the front. Ginger wore her hair in a ponytail tied with a blue ribbon. Joline's glossy black hair fell straight to her shoulders. Male patrons hooted or lit Zippos in answer to the tee shirt message.

They took an empty booth. Joline signaled to a waitress for two beers, and raised a flat palm to slap high fives with Ginger. "How'd you get out of the demonstration? I'd have died if I'd gotten roped into that."

Ginger didn't return the slap. "It would have been awful to be so close to the Prince, all dried up inside that museum. Even though I know his soul is in heaven, it makes me sad."

"Cheer up, Ginger. You're the Witness. Who'd have guessed?" Joline cast a quick look around the bar, as if Creely Patch might be lurking in a nearby booth. "Tell me the truth, what do you really think of him? All the time you spend together . . . I think he likes you."

"Reverend Patch? Get real. But, you know what? I'm afraid

he's going to cut the choir. He thinks music is sinful. Like dancing."

"He does that, I'm outa here. We have the best choir in Gatlinburg. It's the only reason I joined."

"He doesn't like the 'so many saved' sign over the door, either, or the blimp. I'm getting tired of hearing how he's saved twice as many souls as the Prince. I think visitors say they're saved just to get away from him."

"The only reason they come is to see you, because you were with the Prince when he was raptured."

Ginger grew pensive. "Maybe God is testing me. Reverend Patch is such a grumbler. The Prince was always happy. He got his Bible sayings crossed up sometimes—"

"Like his miracles? Remember the time he sent the goat to the Holy Land? I swear I saw the curtains at the back of the stage wiggle after the flash."

"Hold on to your faith, Joline." Ginger leaned close, spoke in a low voice. "As much as I wanted to believe in the Rapture, I always had this black smidgen of doubt at the bottom of my heart." She stared at her hands clasped tightly on the table. "Then it happened—Poof!—and my life was changed. So, watch what you don't believe, 'cause it might just be true."

The waitress set two bottles on the table.

Joline said, "What's with him yelling stuff out?"

"Talking with God. It is kind of creepy. Sometimes he sounds like that little girl in *The Exorcist*." Ginger lifted the bottle of Miller Lite to her lips, filled her cheeks with beer, lolled her head left to right with bug eyes, stuck her tongue out, and let foam gurgle from her mouth with a throaty growl.

"Gross!"

Ginger snagged a handful of napkins from the dispenser to blot her neck.

"Those new converts are creepy, too," Joline added.

"The Jones clan. They don't shave or cut their hair because, 'If God wanted it short, He wouldn't make it grow.' Get this. A family came by this afternoon. Five kids: two teenagers and three little ones. The father was eating up Reverend Patch's Tribulation talk about the floods and bug plagues and the Antichrist numbering everybody with implanted six-sixty-six chips—"

"Fast forward, Ginger. I've heard his sermon before."

"Right. So the man's wife kind of yelps and brushes a grasshopper off her shoulder—you know how they're always buzzing around from that weed patch by the Jones's tents with their kids running around out there. Reverend Patch sees it, gets that faraway look in his eyes, and mumbles, 'Locusts shall plague the earth.' Then, in a blink, he's back on planet earth, ruffling the young ones' hair. He asks their ages. 'Six, sir,' says one. 'They're triplets,' says the mother, real proud. Reverend Patch does a double take, says to the father, 'Three children age six? Six, six, and six?'

"The father pretends he didn't hear him and starts talking about the weapons and freeze-dried food they've stockpiled, when the teenage boy back-talks him: 'Like we're gonna live in a hole and eat bugs?'

"Reverend Patch, with his faraway look, says, 'And children will rise against their parents.' He gets stony-eyed when he notices the kid has braces. 'Lo,' he says. 'The beast with teeth of iron.'"

"He didn't!"

"There's more. One of the little ones is playing with this rubber vampire bat. Reverend Patch swats it out of his hand and says, 'The first beast was like a lion with eagle's wings.' He turns to the sister—girl has a mean case of acne. The Messenger squints at her zits and shouts, 'Good Lord, look at her forehead—the mark of the beast!' The girl goes all red, tries to cover her face, and cries."

"Poor kid."

"Yeah. The parents don't know what to say, they're backing up, looking over their shoulders at the door, tugging the kids. Patch is a wild man. He leaps from his throne and yells 'Wormwood!' whatever that means, and, "Armageddon is upon us. Drive the devils out.'

"That big Jones, Goliath, was on the roof chasing the buzzards. He heard him, came running, swinging a broom. The kids scattered like chickens, but Jones connected with the father, sent him into a rolling somersault. He got up on the fly, outran his wife to their van. Let me tell you, that family aced it out of there, fast."

Joline held a palm up for Ginger to slap high fives. "Go, Messenger."

"Remember," Ginger spoke in a low, radio announcer voice, "you heard it first from the Witness."

"What's so funny?" Firefly Betsy slid into the booth beside Joline.

Joline shook her head in a "Don't tell" motion. "What happened at the Buttonhook Museum, Betsy? Are we getting the Prince back?"

"I prayed we would. But . . . everyone says they're going to cut him up."

Ginger exhaled a sharp "No."

Betsy touched Ginger on the hand. "The Lord will come through, you'll see."

"I hope He comes through for me tonight," Joline said. "I'm dying to meet someone hot," adding, "How about a beer, Betsy? Loosen up, maybe you'll get lucky."

Betsy blushed. "You know I don't drink. And I doubt you'd find a good Christian man in a place like this."

"Hey." Ginger shifted her gaze to the door. "There's Jimmy Feather. The one who saved me from the atheists."

30

If Jimmy Feather's that cute guy in the Levis with the big silver buckle and his hair in a pony tail," Joline said, "I'd say he's one fine-looking cowboy."

"He's a professional Bible hero." Ginger caught Jimmy's eye, motioned him over. With a side-glance to Joline, she said, "He's here to see me."

Ginger patted the seat beside her, scooted to make room, and introduced her friends.

Joline repeated her name, squeezed Jimmy's fingers, and held onto them.

Jimmy pulled his hand away and dropped it in his lap. "I've never been to this place at night."

"It's safe," Betsy said, followed by, "Are you a Christian?"

Jimmy nodded. "I guess."

"Are you secure in the knowledge that if you died tonight, your soul would go to—"

"Give it a rest." Joline extended her legs under the booth, brushing a calf against Jimmy's boot. Above the table, she said, "Betsy proposes to criminals. Lifers."

"I write to them to help them find the Lord," Betsy said. "I only asked one to marry me, and he isn't a criminal because he's innocent."

"That would be the taxidermist," Joline said. "Tell Jimmy what he did with his mother."

Ginger gave Joline a look. "Lay off her." She turned to Jimmy. "We were talking about that museum in Pigeon Forge. Betsy was one of the demonstrators."

Jimmy raised an admiring eyebrow. "You're with ARM?" He took Betsy's hand with both of his and gave it an odd grip. "I couldn't be there, had to work. The mummy is my ancestor."

Betsy stared at her hand in his. "You're related to Reverend Doone?"

Jimmy shook his head. "Who?"

"The Prince of Light," Ginger said. "The mummy is what's left of Reverend Doone, the Prince of Light, after he was raptured. Remember? I told you I was with him when God took him up."

"Sort of."

Joline bumped her hip against Betsy to signal she wanted out. She took Jimmy's wrist. "C'mon, cowboy, let's dance."

"I'm not a cowboy. I'm an Indian."

"No problem. So, how about a dance, Tonto?"

Betsy made bug eyes. "Jo-*leen!*"

Ginger removed Joline's hand from Jimmy's wrist, set it lightly on the tabletop. She turned to Jimmy. "How about dancing with me?"

Jimmy took a sudden interest in one of the beer labels. "I'm not much of a dancer."

Ginger tipped her head to the dance floor, some twenty people bopping solo. "It's only free-dancing. Like, move to the music. C'mon, *Grapevine's* playing."

Jimmy's face flushed red through his tan. "Maybe later."

"Then Joline and I will dance." Ginger scooted from the booth. "Won't we, Joline?"

Joline gave Jimmy a shrug and followed. On the dance floor, she spoke over the music, looking not at Ginger, but somewhere into space like everyone else. "You're hot for the guy, aren't you?"

"He saved my life."

Joline shuffled to the left. "That's not what I asked."

Ginger shuffled right. "He's nice."

They reversed direction. Joline spoke as they crossed paths. "That's it? Nice? I'm surprised you left him alone with Betsy. How do you know she isn't playing footsie with him right now?"

Ginger backstepped. "He's not Betsy's type. Jimmy's not in prison."

Joline skip-hopped toward her. "So, are you going to see him again?"

Ginger stopped, planted her feet flat on the floor. "He's just a friend, so drop it, okay?" She pivoted, turned, and danced away.

Joline spoke to her back. "A friend. Whatever you say."

Two songs later, they returned to the booth.

"Jimmy lived with the Navajos," Betsy said. "He told me about their curing ceremonies. What a great place to do missionary work, fighting superstition like that."

"You missed the point," Jimmy said. "They're not—"

Joline poked Ginger. "That old guy's waving to you, Miss Popular." She motioned to the entrance and a dapper white-haired gent in a blue blazer, pink shirt, and maroon bow tie.

Jimmy looked at the old man, at Ginger. "Excuse me," he said. "I don't think that beer's ever going to get here. I'll get it myself."

Ginger said, "Oh, it's Maury," then, "Wait," to Jimmy, but Jimmy quick-stepped into the crowd.

Maury threaded toward them. He bowed, tipped an imaginary hat, lifted each girl's wrist, and kissed the backs of their hands. "My favorite prophetess," he said in his resonant, M & N Furniture Bazaar TV voice. "Miss Ginger Rodgers."

Ginger explained how Maury had come by the Temple of Light.

"Good for you, sir," Betsy said, and, gravely, "Get your affairs on earth in order, because you never know when the Lord will take you. If you died tonight—"

Maury winked, assured her he had no intention of dying for quite a few years. He declined Ginger's invitation to join them. "Wouldn't want to intrude. No, I would not. But a turn on the dance floor with Miss Rodgers? That, I would enjoy." Before Ginger could protest, he was leading her away.

When they stepped onto the hardwood, Ginger raised her arms in the air and began rocking.

"What I had in mind . . ." Maury took her left hand in his, "was real dancing. A foxtrot, what do you say? Though a bit loud, and hardly Benny Goodman, this tune should do fine."

Ginger shook loose, recalling in a flashback her mother in Fred Astaire drag with the slicked-back hair, Ginger in her confirmation dress, wobbling on little girl pumps. Her mother's rebuke rose with a sting: "For chrissakes, don't be such a *klutz*."

"I can't close dance."

"Nonsense." Maury pulled her toward him, lifted her right hand to shoulder height, and cupped her back. With firm pressure, he steered her around the floor. "All you need is a good lead."

She tried to wriggle loose, but Maury, though half a head shorter and barely her weight, had her in a firm ballroom grip. Before she knew it, they were foxtrotting.

"Relax, already. Follow my lead. See?" They circled the floor. "You're a natural, I should say." He guided her into a left cross turn, neatly avoiding a collision with a heavy-set woman in a Steelers sweatshirt. He long-stepped, wove, glided, whirled. "Why, you're a regular Ginger Rogers."

Ginger giggled.

Several smooth-stepping minutes later, Maury said, "How about we swing?" He pushed Ginger lightly away and spun her beneath outstretched fingers. In a slick inside-out move, he turned one way beneath their arched arms, Ginger the other. She yo-yoed out, this time top-spinning while Maury stayed in place.

Initial snickers at the old man with the built young blonde

turned to curious, and, soon, admiring looks as Maury expanded his repertoire. Dancers parted, backed to the perimeter. A few bystanders clapped. The dance floor cleared, people rose from tables to see who was doing what out there.

Maury finished the second number with a deep dip. Ginger laughed, arched till her ponytail brushed the floor.

Maury gave Ginger, and then the audience, a theatrical bow. They hooted for more, but Maury led Ginger to the bar instead, motioned to two empty stools. He sat beside her, removed a cotton handkerchief from his blazer pocket and wiped his forehead. He asked the bartender for a Manhattan. "Rocks. Old Fashioned glass. And, what can I get you, dear?"

"A beer, I guess."

Maury small-talked until the beer and his Manhattan arrived. He lifted his glass to Ginger's bottle. "To Ginger Rodgers," he said. "Were but I your Fred Astaire."

Ginger clinked a toast, but her brow knitted at Maury's quaking hand. The amber liquid in his glass spilled over the rim, down his fingers.

Maury swung his knees to the side to avoid a drenching. "It's nothing," he said. "Coffee jitters is all. I should know better than to have a third cup after dinner." He set the glass down and gave her a soothing smile, lowering his voice. "Dear, I wanted to continue our discussion about this Shickleton Doone fellow. I was wondering, has he returned yet?" He leaned forward expectantly.

"He's back all right. I saw him this morning."

"Really?" Maury was all smiles. He stroked his chin with one hand. The other, wrapped around the glass on the bar, began to shake. Maury seemed not to notice. "And where might I find him? I'd dearly love to meet Doone, perhaps speak with him about saving me, eh?"

"Maybe they would let you see him," she said. "You're so persuasive. More than Reverend Patch, that's for sure. The Prince is at the Captain Hook Museum in Pigeon Forge. They brought him there when they found him in that cave. He's in a back room under a sheet."

"Under a sheet, you say?" Maury's rattling glass was attracting the attention of other patrons. "He's hurt?"

"You can't talk to him."

"Why not? Hurt bad, is he?" Booze sloshed onto the bar.

"He's dead."

"Oy!" Maury released the nearly empty glass, wrung his hands, and began to mutter. "All this way, I came. I can't believe he died before—"

"Well, not dead exactly. You know how I told you how he went up to heaven? Poof?"

Maury belayed the hand wringing, made hurry-up motions.

"God kept his soul, but sent his body back. They found it in a cave—"

"Hiding in a cave? Must have got wind that I was—"

"Not hiding. Gabriel put him there. Some Boy Scouts found him and they took him to that museum. That's where he is now. Where I saw him." Ginger stuck out her lower lip in a growing pout. "And they won't give him back."

"They have his body? How do you know it's him?"

"I saw him real good before he was raptured." Failing to mention how much she had seen. "He's kind of dried out with his soul gone, but it's him, all right. He smells just like he did, before. And he had this little wart on his eyebrow. It's still there, and that thick black hair, and—"

Maury reached for his Manhattan and lifted the glass to his lips. He sipped air, glanced at bare ice cubes and set the glass down hard.

"Oy!" he said again, and "Dead." Then a sly smile crept over his lips and he muttered to himself, "'Dead or alive,' as I remember Trout telling me. So, who's to know whether it was the hand of God or the hand of the Hammer that fulfilled the contract?"

31

Maury slapped a ten on the bar and, with a tip of his imaginary hat to Ginger, bowed deeply, and breezed away.

When Ginger returned to the booth, she found Joline beside Jimmy. Betsy had moved, or had been moved, to the other side of the table. "Dammit, Joline, leave for a minute and—"

"Ginger Rodgers," a syrupy, accented voice said to her back. Ginger turned. "Orlando!"

"*A sus ordenes*, Ginger." The Ginger came out *Jeen–jairrrr*. The gold chains at Orlando's neck tinkled, and his blousy, pale green silk shirt ballooned as he dipped in a bow. "I come especial to see you."

"Uh, these are my friends—"

"Of course. Hello to you, Ginger's friends." He bowed again, took her wrist. "Come, *jovencita*, *vamos a bailar*. I hear salsa."

"That's 'La Bamba.'"

"As I say."

Ginger cast a brief look over her shoulder at Joline and Jimmy as Orlando cleared a path through standing drinkers. In a sea of jeans, shorts, and running shoes, Orlando wore white linen trousers over low-cut lime green loafers with no socks.

He clasped Ginger's right hand in his left, snugged the small of her back in a more intimate approximation of Maury's ballroom stance, and pulled her in a silk-snaky grip against his lean, cologne-scented body.

Ginger struggled. "I can't dance close."

"Not to worry, Jeen-jairrrr. Orlando *es el maestro*. You follow me, you going to dance good, *chica*."

Within seconds she was turning as easily under his dark, manicured hands as she had beneath Maury's deft if more bony and shaky ones. Again, patrons backed off to watch.

The music changed. "Merengue," Orlando said. "See, in my arms you dance like a princess." To show his tender feelings for her, he moved skin close and delicately humped her leg.

As Ginger struggled to disengage Orlando from her thigh, the disc jockey switched to skull-rattling rock. Orlando put his palms over his ears. "*¡Qué feo!* This noise! And *mira los norteamericanos* bouncing like *marionetas*." Under his breath, he muttered, "*Maricónes*." To Ginger, he said, "*Ven, mi amor*. I want to buy you a drink."

All the stools were taken, so he made room by clacking his flick knife, unopened, against the bar wood, out of Ginger's view. "Look," he said. "Two stools open. A small miracle, yes?" He waved a twenty at the bartender. "Two Cuba Libres, *por favor*." To Ginger: "Guess what? Tony calls today. I tell him about you and the grand miracle. Your 'Poof!'"

"Antonio Banderas?"

"Is there any other? Of course, Tony." The drinks arrived. Orlando motioned for the bartender to keep the change. "Tony and I are friends ever since he films *Zorro*, and I teach him the sword work." He traced a quick Z across Ginger's upper chest lightly with a fingertip. The finger lingered.

Ginger returned the finger to Orlando's space. "You've been in movies with Antonio Banderas?"

"Ah, no. I am, how you say, a *gran estrella*, a big star of *el cine Cubano*. A national treasure of *la patria*. But *el hijo de puta tirano Castro* say that if he ever see me in a film from the Hollywood, from *el imperialismo*, he will deport my beloved mother to work in the cane fields of Bayamo. *¡Coño!* What can I do? Tony, he could put me in the Hollywood films like . . . that," Orlando snapped his fingers, "but my *madre*, she is old. And sick. *¡Cojones! Mi querida madre*." He assumed a downcast, faraway look, side-glanced to Ginger to be sure she was watching. The sad face vanished, replaced by a toothy smile. "Is no matter. I am happy now. Happy for the friendship of *amigos* like Tony, and now you, Ginger Rodgers."

Orlando leaned close to kiss her cheek, but Ginger turned and Orlando kissed ponytail. "I don't know how often Tony comes to Gatlinburg," he said, "but next time, I promise, I introduce you. We will all drink here at the *pirata's*, *bailamos toda la noche*, and eat the trout fish for breakfast, *oiste?*" He ordered another round of drinks and told more Tony stories, ones of camel races and marathon ocean swims. ". . . and then I see Tony waving his arms on the deck, pointing. I look over my shoulder and see a fin. A big one, like a tall black sail, swimming at me. I reach side of boat, and Tony, he lift me from water with one hand just as big jaws snap-snap my behind. Tony laughs, tells me never to wear the chains at my neck in ocean again because the she-sharks, they are like the women, no?" Orlando lifted the glittering metallic mass and rustled it suggestively below Ginger's chin. "They love the gold, *sabes?*"

He swung his barstool toward her, spread his legs and closed them to encompass Ginger's knees. "Ginger," a shift in inflection suggested a change of topic. "Since I see you at your beautiful cathedral, I am thinking, Orlando, I bet Ginger Rodgers, she has seen this Shickie Doone again." He leaned forward, gave her a soul-searching look. "Yes?" he patted her knee. "You tell me now."

"You must be psychic," Ginger said, "like the hotlines, because I did see him. This morning."

"Ai! I knew it. Tell me. Where is he?"

"You won't like it."

"*Da le*. Speak."

"He's dead."

"*¡Carajo!* How did this happen? Where is he?"

"Like I said, God took him up, but kept his soul and sent his body back. They found it in a cave and took it to the Captain Hook Museum in Pigeon Forge. It's so sad. Reverend Patch and I saw him, but they wouldn't give him to us. He's all dried out with his soul gone, but it's him." She made a face. "That damn museum."

"I wonder if he had keys? A—how you say?—briefcase."

"He wasn't wearing a stitch. I *told* you that at the Lighthouse. All of his clothes were left behind when he was raptured."

"Ai!" Orlando pressed his palms to his eyes, muttering. "Gone. Unless it's in this cave—"

"There's nothing in the cave but an elephant tooth, stones, and an old turd. The scientists searched it good after they took the Prince out. That was in the papers."

Orlando fingered his mustache, muttered to himself. "He try to hide from Trout and Rita, goes into this cave, makes himself lost, and dies in the dark."

"The Prince didn't die."

"No?" Orlando leaned close.

"He was raptured. Only his body is in that awful museum."

"His body," Orlando repeated. He tilted his head to the side, like the RCA dog, tuning into a satisfying insight. "Dead . . . but all is not lost . . . we get the body, make identification, and then . . . *bienvenido*, Señor Life Insurance Man!"

Orlando sprung to his feet, grinning at Ginger's confusion. He palmed her chin with his left hand and gave her a lingering kiss on the forehead as his right hand snaked to her rear to pinch a buttock. Before she could protest, he pinched, gave her a conspiratorial wink, backed quickly away, and disappeared into the barroom crowd.

Ginger returned to the booth to find Betsy alone, sipping a Diet Coke.

Jimmy had gone with Joline.

PART TWO

Resurrection

.

32

hickie Doone emerged from nothingness to the Light. Dazzling, scintillating, overwhelming, it suffused his being. He had no sensation of self, of body. No feeling. Only the Light.

It was the alpha and the omega of his existence. A super-nova. Glorious, yet simultaneously painful. Radiating heat like a blast furnace.

Doone's first coherent thought: he was in hell.

Though dimly conscious, he summoned comprehension, and from the brilliant mist made out a shape. A shadow. An angel. Heaven?

Hovering, haloed by the Light, the angel bent close and whispered, "I knew you would make it."

His vision blurred. Doone felt himself slipping away.

"Don't leave us," the angel pleaded.

Though he longed to speak, to grasp her outstretched hand, he felt himself falling. Away from the Light. Down.

Down, down, down.

33

Maury dabbed a napkin to his lips, assured the waitress the breakfast had been to his liking, and asked for directions to a pay phone.

He punched numbers, watching his fingers jitterbug drunkenly over the keys, hitting a four instead of a five, a three instead of a six. Gripping his right hand firmly in his left, he redialed with a sigh, recalling that fateful debacle of a contract six months ago—the snippets of ears, toes, and assorted pieces of cheater flying around the interior of the semi.

It brought little consolation that the word on the street ran, not that the Hammer couldn't shoot straight, but that he was one sadistic son of a bitch. Maury did his best to make the subsequent assignment efficient, but damn his shaky hands—more flying flesh, extra clips to get the job done. Sooner or later, he would miss altogether and cheaters would rule the world.

The contract business supplemented Maury's social security, paid the tabs at Cora's and the haberdasher's (Maury was a bit of a clotheshorse), and gave purpose to life. Alas, nothing lasts forever: the furniture business had gone sour, his loving wife of thirty-one years, and his loyal business partner of twenty-three had betrayed him, the TV commercials for the chain petered out, and now his own fingers were letting him down.

Time to move on. To what? Maury couldn't see himself slinging fun meals at McDonalds.

The call connected. "Trout here."

"Hammer," Maury said in his deep baritone. At least he hadn't lost the voice. "Shickie Doone is dead. I'll take payment today, if you please."

"Hold on. You did in Doone?"

"I said I did, did I not?" Maury felt a tiny flutter in his stomach at the accusatory edge to Trout's voice. All did not feel right. Had Ginger Rodgers been mistaken?

"You saw the paper this morning?" Trout asked, "The news last night?"

Maury had not. Unsure how to respond, he swallowed hard and said nothing, discretion being more desirable than a foot in the mouth.

"Exactly when did you do him in?" Trout was asking. Maury failed to respond, so Trout filled the silence: "Boy Scouts found him three days ago—if it's really him. In a cave. Buck naked. Weighing twenty-seven pounds. A friggin' mummy. He's in some museum now. That sound like your work?"

"Certainly," Maury responded, with a decided lack of conviction. Ginger Rodgers had said nothing about three days ago or Doone weighing twenty-seven pounds. A mummy? What, like in Egypt?

"I was wondering," Trout said, "why you didn't call right after you did the job. I'm also wondering if this mummy really is Doone. Museum egghead says it's a prehistoric caveman. Indians are calling it their ancient ancestor. Police are mum—not a word about foul play."

Ginger Rodgers seemed so certain. Maury watched his fingers chattering against the pay phone wall, over the "For a hot lay, call Flora."

"I'll admit," Trout was saying, "the picture in the paper does look a lot like him, despite the shriveling."

Maury breathed a touch easier.

"His followers," Trout continued, "claim it is him, saying he was raptured by God Almighty then spit back from heaven, all dried up. How do you explain that? What the hell did you do to him—if it *is* him and if *you* are the one what did him in?"

Salesman's first rule, Maury reminded himself: a good offense is the best defense. "I did him all right," Maury said affirmatively. "How, is my concern."

Trout voiced a long "Hmmmm," then, "What I'm wondering, is, what if I call the cops, see what they have to say here? I'm not paying for a hit if Doone wandered off and got himself lost in a cave." A trace of temerity softened his voice. This was the infamous Hammer he was speaking to, after all. "You see my position, don't you? I'm entitled to assurances."

Assurances. Maury recalled Trout's initial call to Cora's Cozy Cove, Trout's phrasing. "Look here," Maury said, lacing his response with threat, "our deal was this: twenty grand. Advance, with balance, C.O.D. Dead or alive. Those were *your* words."

"I suppose, but—"

"How I did him is a trade secret. You think all I know is bang-bang? Better to make it look like an accident for both our sakes." He snarled into the phone. "You're pissing me off, you cheap k'nocker—"

"Look, all I—"

"Dead or alive. C.O.D. Doone's dead. You want him, I'll pick him up, dump him on your doorstep, special delivery. Contract fulfilled. You have the balance of the twenty G's ready or Doone's not the only one who will have breathed his last breath before I depart this burg."

Maury hung up, thinking, I guess I'd better get a morning paper and find out where this museum is and what is what. C.O.D. yet. What am I? UPS?

"Caveman? Indian? Messiah?" muttered an angry Plato Scopes. "Ignoramuses don't know the difference between Pleistocene mammals and dinosaurs. Try sixty-five million years, you idiots!" He tossed the newspaper on Director Duckhaus's desk. "Talk about misinforming the public."

Duckhaus spread the paper and read:

Mysterious Mummy: Caveman, Indian, or Messiah?
Pigeon Forge. Traffic along Route 66 ground to a halt yesterday as onlookers slowed to view a noisy demonstration at the normally sleepy Captain Hook Museum. Controversy raged following the discovery of a mysteriously well-preserved mummy (photo above) by Boy Scouts in a cave bordering the Great Smoky Mountains National Park. The mummy, a naked, middle-aged male with shoulder-length black hair, was taken to the museum for analysis.

Plato Scopes, Chief Scientist at the museum, announced at a press conference that, based upon cave drawings of dinosaurs and a fossil mammoth tooth found nearby, the mummy appeared to be that of a prehistoric warrior sacrificed over ten thousand years ago in a fertility ritual. Mr. Scopes further believes the caveman may be of European ancestry, which he expects to confirm through X-ray and DNA analysis. He also announced that *National Geographic* plans a story on the caveman and "his remarkable mummification."

Angry members of the AmerIndian Resistance Movement picketed the museum, claiming the remains were those of a Native American and should be turned over to ARM for reburial, while the Children of Light, a Gatlinburg religious sect, counter-demonstrated.

The Reverend Creely Patch, leader of the apocalyptic sect, identified the mummy as Children of Light founder, Shickleton Doone (see photo), a.k.a. the Prince of Light, called Messiah by some. The Rev. Doone allegedly ascended to heaven from his home, leaving the clothing he was wearing in a heap on the hallway floor.

Rev. Patch declared, "God kept the Prince's soul and returned his mortal remains to earth to become a holy relic in our sanctuary. The mummy is ours."

"That mummy belongs to science," said museum Chief Scientist, Plato Scopes. "Rationality must prevail."

"That was a sacred Indian burial," said an unidentified ARM spokesman, "and should be returned to mother earth."

"Possession is nine-tenths of the law," added Mr. Scopes.

Duckhaus crumpled the paper and wagged a bony finger at his chief scientist. "Bad publicity. This whole business is bad. I warned you about controversy, young man." He read it again. "'Normally sleepy,' it calls us. That'll pull them in, won't it? Not a mention of our buttonhooks. I see they spelled your name correctly, but there's no mention of me at all."

"I'm sorry, sir. I had no control over—"

"Although," Duckhaus said, mellowing, "*National Geographic* magazine, doing a story on us? That true?"

"They, uh, expressed interest." Scopes lowered his eyes and stared at the paper, shifting nervously from one foot to the other. He glanced back at the director with renewed enthusiasm, and said, "Think what color photos of our buttonhooks in *National Geographic* would do for museum attendance."

Duckhaus drummed his fingers on his desk, imagining.

"We'll need another guard, sir."

Duckhaus blinked, gave Scopes a quizzical look. "Nonsense. The kind of people who appreciate buttonhooks never cause trouble—not like that rabble you stirred up. Haven't had one buttonhook stolen in all the years I've been here."

"Not for the buttonhooks, sir. To protect the mummy. From the crackpots."

The director shook his head emphatically. "No money in the budget for another guard."

Plato Scopes kicked at the floor absently, repeated the seductive words, "*National Geographic*."

"Hmmm," said Horace Duckhaus, picturing a color spread of Buttonhook Hall with himself at center, leaning on a display case, facing the camera, smiling with professional pride, the famous Queen Victoria's Chambermaid buttonhook in his palm. "I'll take it under advisement."

"All I know is, they left together," Betsy said.

Ginger huffed. "What a nerve that Joline has. He's *my* friend."

"You had a *bunch* of friends last night."

"Don't you start in. What with the Prince in that museum, the scientists wanting to cut him up, put him in a jar or something—"

"They won't," Betsy said.

"And how do you know that?"

Betsy's chin lifted in defiance. "Because I saw a vision this morning. In my pancakes."

"In your pancakes."

"Don't mock me, Ginger Rodgers. That's what the doubters did to you, isn't it?" Betsy accepted Ginger's acknowledging nod. "It was like this: the very instant I started squeezing Mrs. Butterworth I saw the face of the Prince in the fry marks on the top pancake." Betsy caught Ginger's raised eyebrow. "I swear. It had that big nose of his and he was smiling like he always did. Then the syrup sloshed over his face and he was gone. But the moment he appeared, I knew in my heart that God was going to make the Prince whole and send him back to us."

"That's sweet," Ginger said. "I hope you're right."

"In fact, his mummy may be back sooner than you think."

Ginger motioned for her to continue.

"I overheard Reverend Patch talking with Goliath Jones. He said God told him not to fool around with pleading and demonstrations and lawyers. To take what belonged to him."

*   *   *

Rita Rae slammed her cell phone on the counter. "I asked that scientist sugar pie sweet to return my dear departed husband. He hung up—are you listening to me?"

Orlando, doing push ups on the kitchen floor, grunted. "Yes, yes."

"And, according to you, according to the paper, who identified him? Me? The woman who married him, who lived with that worm for twelve long months? No—that teenage tart he was fooling around with, that's who."

"Ginger is no teenager," Orlando said. "She must be at least twenty-five."

The cell phone caught him in the rib cage.

He rolled onto his side, rubbed his ribs, and then, at sight of his lovely *fiera* on a rampage, rubbed his crotch. "Ai, I love it when you have the anger. Come, we make love."

"Make love, my ass. Did you hear what I said? They refuse to return him to me. No Shickie. No insurance."

Orlando's hand moved from his genitals into an open-palmed shrug. "Not to worry. We will get him back. That is what they have *la policía* for. Attorneys, also. Judges. This La United Estates! Land of law and order, *sabes?*"

"Cops?" Rita Rae said. "Attorneys? Judges? Did you forget they're still looking for us in Kentucky? All we need is publicity." She frowned and then pursed her lips in thought. "Although, you know, with Trout's connections, he could get the worm back for me to cash in on that insurance." More lip pursing. "On the other hand, if Thadeus thinks I'm too eager, he'll put two and two together and want a cut. Big problem."

Orlando had returned to his push-ups. "Yes. Many problems. Many."

Rita Rae's lips curled into a sly smile. "Then again, maybe not. I have a plan. First thing is to file a missing persons report."

"Listen up, boys. What if," Trout cackled, "the Hammer burgles this museum to get Doone's body back so he can deliver it to me like he promised . . . and there's nobody there?"

*   *   *

"Shoot, Grandpop, why are the pretty ones always trouble?"

"She sounds like a nice enough girl."

"She's got boyfriends coming out of the woodwork, and I don't have time for games."

"You're afraid of her."

"I am *not*. It's . . . like her friend I gave a ride home. They have expectations, and you never know what they are. I don't need some female complicating my life while my ancestor is lying on a dissecting table waiting to be cut up."

"Why don't you get the Cherokees involved? They'll—"

"Want him for their own. Bury him over there. He's my ancestor. I want to bury him on our land. And the only way to do that is—"

"Son . . ." Grandpop rose from his rocker, put a hand on Jimmy's arm. "Please don't do anything you'll regret."

"Oh," Jimmy said, "I won't regret it. Don't you worry about that."

34

hickie Doone writhed from the heat. And the stinging light. He had no sensation of body, but a stab of fear informed him he was in hell.

He squeezed his lids tight to shut it all out. The light and heat persisted.

The field of his sensation darkened. A presence hovered over him, eclipsing the light. He wanted to plead, Let me go back to the in-between-place: no feeling, no light, no heat. But he couldn't speak.

"Welcome back," said the presence. "We've been rooting for you."

It sounded like the angel, but Shickie feared a demon was taunting him.

"Poor baby, the sunlight's too bright, isn't it? Let me close the shades."

The light and heat diminished. A moment later Shickie felt something cold and damp on his forehead. He opened his eyes and beheld a blurry vision. An angel, cloaked in white, her hair backlit a radiant gold. She ran a hand over his scalp, brushed away his hair, and sponged his face with a cool cloth.

"Where am I?" Shickie was unsure whether he actually

spoke or merely thought the question. "Did I make it? Am I really in heaven, or—"

He felt the cool cloth again.

"Hold on, baby," the angel said, "I'll get the doctor. There are some other folks who want to see you, too."

35

ey!" Jimmy Feather's supervisor waved a clipboard at him.

"Sir?" Jimmy had been daydreaming in the shadows of the Noah's Ark tank, speculating how he might retrieve his mummified ancestor from the Captain Hook Museum while stuck at the Bible Alive, nine-to-five plus overtime.

The Noah's Ark exhibit had semi-opened, though the flood tank still had two-by-fours shoring up the sides and the signage was incomplete. Though well shy of every creature on earth times-two, the Bible Alive Ark did hold an impressive array of manger livestock, game fish, local woodland mammals, birds, and bugs. And exotic beasts as well: two humongous black rats with amputated tails billed as "rare Amazonian coypu," a pair of autoerotic Barbary apes, a corpulent boa constrictor grown fat in captivity, a couple of furtive Mexican coatimundi, and a single, smelly aardvark occupying a pen on the poop deck with a darkened retreat box implying a reclusive mate. A pair of motorized giraffe necks protruded from a starboard porthole, and the below decks resounded with recorded elephant trumpeting admixed with kookaburra laughter, insect chirruping, howler monkey howls, and assorted grunts and growls.

Jimmy forced a smile, awaiting rebuke, but instead, the supervisor said, "I know it's not in your job description, but our van driver hung one on again last night and didn't show up. We got three busloads of tourists from Charlotte on a Graceland tour arriving here in an hour and a half, and we're down to a dozen Lot's Wife salt shakers, one set of Grail mugs, and half a run of fig leaf bikinis. My ass will be in hot water with Mr. Trout if he gets wind of tourist dollars leaving the museum unspent. How about you drive down to Pigeon Forge to the supplier's warehouse? No need to change from the David costume. It'll only take you an hour or so. What say?"

"Pigeon Forge? Sure." Jimmy muttered a thank you. He could at least buzz the buttonhook museum. Maybe proximity would lead to inspiration.

Mr. Trout summoned Junior's crew to his office. "Get your butts to that historical museum in Pigeon Forge and scope out where they're keeping the mummy. If it's Doone, and I can get hold of him before the Hammer, I'll save a bundle."

Junior reminded him, "You've still got the keys to my Camar—"

"Take the Buick."

"That dog-shit ugly—"

Peaches put away the last bite of a Bluebird apple pie. "I just got my Monte Carlo Super Sport back from the pinstriper."

"Cool," Junior said. "Can I drive?"

"Dream on."

"Listen up," Trout said. "You boys be careful. All you're doing is scouting. And don't mess with the Hammer. He's after Doone, too."

Junior snorted. "How could we mess with the Hammer if we never seen him?"

Trout gave him a What-a-dumb-ass look. "You think a palooka like the Hammer won't stand out in a buttonhook museum like a sumo wrestler at a tea party? And if you spot him, keep in mind he won't think twice about rubbing you out if he thinks he's being cheated."

Six-pack felt his stomach bottom-out at recollection of the small matter of confusing the freeze-drier with the meat locker, and the prospect of again meeting, worse, touching, the small, gray, very dead body that was once Shickie Doone. Six-pack's stomach did another flip-flop with the knowledge that if Trout discovered his role in the sorry affair of the mummification of Doone, he would be next on the Hammer's list.

Trout jabbed a ballpoint pen in the shape of an elongated bowling pin at them. "Don't fuck up."

"No, sir," the three said as one.

Maury read the newspapers. He stopped by the Temple of Light to speak again with Ginger Rodgers. Creely Patch was all oily smiles, hopeful of Maury's conversion. Maury assured him he "was thinking about it" but needed the counsel of Miss Rodgers. Alone. Patch took him directly to her, promised no interruptions. Before Patch left them, he patted Ginger on the hand with a cryptic, "Remember, they count double."

Following another twenty questions with the Witness, Maury decided, however improbable, it must truly be Shickie Doone at the Captain Hook Museum. Doone must have gotten wise to the Hammer on his trail, hid out in the cave, and, then what? Got lost, went meshuggah, got naked, got thirsty—real thirsty—and dried up. Maury rationalized that if that was the case, he had been the agent of Doone's destruction, if a bit indirectly, and had thus fulfilled his contract.

He telephoned the museum and asked for the scientist mentioned in the papers, Plato Scopes. Brains and education had never been obstacles to Maury's furniture pitches, nor would they now. Einstein or Dumbo, make him a friend, tumble him into love with the goods, convince him you're giving him the deal of a lifetime, and—*KA-CHING!*

The receptionist told Maury that Mister—not Doctor— Scopes would be with him shortly, so, when Scopes came on the line, Maury addressed him as "Dr. Plato Scopes?"

"Yes." Scopes failed to correct him.

K-A—

"Brilliant work. Simply brilliant."

"Uh, thank you."

"The powers that be at *National Geographic* are impressed. Yes, indeedy. I was on a field call investigating some rare woodpecker behavior north of here, a flicker drilling for Japanese beetle grubs in the dash of a Lexus convertible— excuse me, I failed to introduce myself. I'm Dr. Maurice Finklestein, features scout for the National Geographic Society. HQ called in an A-1-A priority, told me the woodpecker investigation, I should drop, and buzz right down to see this mummy. Associations with Ice Age mammals? European ancestry? Cave drawings? Fertility rituals? I don't mind telling you, if my report is positive, not only an article in *National Geographic* I see in your future, but a toothsome research grant. But, perhaps I put the cart before the horse . . . would it be possible for me to observe the specimen? I'm in Gatlinburg at the moment."

Maury heard rapid breathing followed by, "Oh, *yes* sir!"

—C-H-I-N-G!

Scopes had been working on the exhibit he planned for the mummy: a twenty-foot, glass-fronted diorama across the rear of the cafeteria, better, across the front of Buttonhook Hall if Director Duckhaus would allow it. Now that *National Geographic* was coming on board, that appeared a certainty. Following the scans and DNA analysis, he planned to place the body on a rock altar (its privates virtuously covered by a fox skin) within a cross section of a mock cave, replete with stalactites, stalagmites, the mammoth tooth, flints, and edited-for-youth wall paintings. Visible through the cave entrance, at exhibit right, would be a Pleistocene landscape: a looming blue glacier in the distance, a band of happy European hunters spearing a wooly mammoth.

Unfortunately, there was no budget for any of it. Yet. So, for Scopes, it was a do-it-yourself project. While time-consuming, the cave itself would be the easiest: air-blown Sacrete and air-brush. A little varnish on the cave formations to simulate moisture, a stuffed bat here, a cave cricket carcass there, real limestone slabs comprising the altar. The exterior, however, posed a greater problem. Painting the background sky, coniferous forest, and glacial wall would require a real artist. Perhaps a volunteer from the Dollywood staff? Perspective would require miniaturization of the hunters and mammoth.

Scopes had been shopping for props already. With some modification, the plastic wrestling stars he had purchased, with their bulging muscles and shoulder-length hair, would suffice as hunters. A "Barbie goes to Camp" figure, redressed in a fur sarong, would pass for a warrior's woman, simultaneously injecting sex appeal for the masses and communicating the band's European ancestry. He had gotten lucky with the mammoth, too. One of the Pigeon Forge tourist shops had a three-foot, plush pink elephant on sale, thirty percent off, which he bought on the spot. The scale of the wrestling stars to the Barbie was perfect. Spray glue, hair clippings from a Pigeon Forge dog groomer, shoe dye, a back hump, and two long, up-curving tusks would complete the transformation from toy elephant to exhibition mammoth. He stood now before the stuffed elephant. The silly grin on its face would have to go, it being speared and all.

Scopes paced, and finally gave it up, unable to concentrate with the representative from *National Geographic* on the way. Why, with NGS money, he could buy the best, hire a real exhibition preparator. He retired the elephant to a metal shelf at the side of the room and plumped the sheet around the mummy, unfolded several more sheets to artfully drape the metal table supporting the dried body, and hurried to give Director Duckhaus the good news.

Rita Rae was getting a tune-up at Laurel Lynne's House of Beauty: a bikini wax and her do re-shellacked. She had sent Orlando to case the Captain Hook Museum with instructions to call when he located the remains of her dear departed Shickie.

Orlando was, at this moment, sitting on the edge of the museum entry desk, reading the chubby young receptionist's palm.

"Are you really a Gypsy?" She giggled as he traced his manicured forefinger along what he identified as her love line.

"Yes, of course. My grandfather was Rudolf Valentino, the famous Gypsy psychic." He lifted her palm to his lips, blowing softly on her Mount of Venus. "I see much romance in your life. You will win a TV quiz show and run away with a movie star to his palace on a tall mountain in Rio. Yes, I fear this *museo* soon loses its beautiful hostess."

Over renewed giggles, he watched an employee enter the far end of the hallway from the rearmost room, "the laboratory" as the receptionist referred to it, home of the mummy. The employee, a scrawny young man with wild hair, wearing an ill-fitting suit, tested the knob before walking forward. The door was metal-clad, self-locking, and in plain sight of the receptionist's desk and of anyone using the busy central passage. An external reconnaissance of the seventy- by a hundred-foot, one-story cinderblock building had revealed the laboratory possessed four tiny barred windows and one solid exit door, also locked. Securing Rita Rae's husband, Orlando concluded, would require either burglary or guile.

Orlando knew whatever he reported, Rita Rae would insist on coming to the museum for confirmation. That meant more waiting. He grew pale at the thought of staring at more buttonhooks. He decided he would repay Rita Rae for this oppressive assignment with a meal in the cafeteria. The special of the day was a boiled wiener with a side of shredded, carrot-infused, green Jell-O.

While he was here, however, he may as well make the most of his time and talent. He grew excited at the thought of bringing joy into the life of the receptionist, with her clammy nail-bitten hands, her tentative smile, and her wide, provocative hips. He scooted closer along the edge of the desk, allowing his elbow to familiarize itself with the young woman's ample breast as he explored the geography of her palm.

Contrary to Peaches's warnings not to touch the paint of his newly customized and pinstriped Monte Carlo SuperSport, Six-pack and Junior sat on the hood in the buttonhook museum parking lot, "making plans." Junior intended to not merely scout, but snatch the mummy for his father. Wary of museums on principle, and fearful of a potential brush with the Hammer, Junior had sent Peaches inside to spy, keeping Six-pack at his side for protection.

Fearful of bodies in general and of one in particular, Six-pack fidgeted, wondering how he could avoid looking at the mummy if, indeed, they were able to kidnap it.

The more their plans failed to materialize, the more Junior and Six-pack did nothing. They sat, ogled tourist daughters worthy of ogling, and waited.

36

Maury pulled into the crowded parking lot of the Captain Hook Museum, "Home of the third-largest collection of buttonhooks south of the Ohio and east of the Mississippi rivers," so the sign outside the lackluster block building proclaimed. He docked his Town Car between an SUV with Michigan plates and a conversion van bearing airbrushed script announcing "The Carter Family: Big Joe, Betty, Little Joe, Johnny, and Baby Liz, from New Madrid, Missouri, home of the Great Quake of 1812. We're shakin' up the world!"

Maury crossed the lot, tipped his hat to half a dozen protestors, apparently of two minds as to the disposition of the mummy, nodded to a slender Latin-looking fellow in what he regarded as pimp attire sneaking a smoke in the entryway, and moved inside to the ticket desk. Maury swept his hat across his chest with a courtly bow to the receptionist, an amply-endowed, freckle-faced, corn-fed young woman of the sort he might have made a pass at in his youth, pre-Rose-the-betrayer.

"Where's your mummy, miss?" Maury wiggled the hat for a long beat, and added with a twinkling smile, "That is to say, not your mama, but the dried-up fellow everybody's talking about?"

She gave him a blank stare. Several seconds later her face crinkled. "Mummy . . . mama . . . I get it! Oh, it's in the laboratory. Back there." She poked a thumb over her shoulder toward the end of a long hallway. "But it's off-limits to visitors. You can see a whole bunch of old stuff, though, in Buttonhook Hall, that big room to the right. The gift shop's over there, and the cafeteria at the left. Special today's a hot dog, Jell-O, and small Coke for three-seventy-five. Admission," she nibbled her lip, seemingly embarrassed, "is two dollars." She raised her eyebrows hopefully. "Seniors get in for a dollar-fifty."

"My, my. Haute cuisine and time alone with the world's largest collection of buttonhooks for a half a sawbuck and a quarter. It's my lucky day."

"Third-biggest," the receptionist corrected, "south of the Ohio River and east of the Mississippi."

"But yours, I'll bet, are the prettiest." Maury fished five quarters from a coin purse stashed in his seersucker sport coat pocket and placed them on the desk. He made note of the interior geography, windows and doorways in particular, saw nothing of interest in the gift shop, wrinkled his nose at the smell of boiled wieners in the cafeteria, changed course, and strolled into Buttonhook Hall toward the first exhibit: THE NOBLE BUTTONHOOK. KEEPING OUR FOREMOTHERS AND FOREFATHERS IN THEIR SHOES AND ON THEIR FEET. Regarding a collection of tiny, high-topped shoes with buttons instead of laces, he wondered if in some other small burg there might be a Temple of the Shoelace or perhaps a Wonderful World of Velcro Museum.

He tuned into the conversations of the dozen and a half tourists:

"What a screw. Thought we'd at least get a peek at the mummy."

"Where's Peter Pan, Mommy? Where's Tinkerbell? Will I be able to pet Nana?"

"Lunch is a great deal here, a lot cheaper than Dollywood."

"Let's cut our losses and hit that moccasin shop, other side of the road with the old Indian out front with the feather head-dress and hatchet."

"Motherrr! I gotta pee-pee."

The latter comment reminded Maury that he, too, had to visit the little boys' room. The receptionist directed him halfway down the self-same hallway that led to the mummy room. After completing his more immediate business, he walked quickly to the end of the passage, tried the knob surreptitiously, and found the door locked.

National Geographic would get him inside, but then what? He doubted he could waltz the goods right out the front door.

Back door? Had to be one as an emergency exit. He glided up the hallway, past the receptionist, and outside. He circled the building, comparing windows with his recollection of the interior. Of course: a doorway at the center of the back wall. As a sole exit, it couldn't be key-locked on the inside, although it might have a throw-bar-alarm. He saw no bell housing on the exterior—not that that guaranteed anything—and no security cameras. If he talked the staff into leaving him alone back there and he didn't trip an alarm, maybe he could boost Doone out that door to his automobile. What did the mummy weigh? Twenty-some pounds? He could manage that. Toss it in the trunk and be gone before they were any the wiser. Although, Maury sighed, he wasn't exactly a sprinter anymore. And it would be risky to carry it in the open. Cover it with his sport coat? Maybe it was in a case—but that might be heavy. "Such an alter kocker, I am," Maury said aloud in frustration, "I couldn't carry my suitcase from the Lincoln to my motel room, without help. Serve me right to get hold of Doone and not be able to—"

"Hey, old guy!"

Maury spun toward the shouted words, nearly stumbling. Were they on to him already? He looked around, saw some kid in a black leather jacket waving from the hood of a car. Another kid, a big one in a muscle shirt, beside him. Well, what do you know? The lads from Poncho's the other night. Big grins on their faces.

Maury returned the wave, his mind racing. Perhaps the Fates *were* smiling on him. If he needed help, maybe . . . He strolled toward them. "Hi, fellows. What brings you to a museum parking lot on a fine day like this?"

The skinny one said, "Just hanging out."

"To each his own, I always say. And are you apt to hang out a bit longer?"

"I guess." They looked at one another and shrugged.

"I'm a scientist, fellows, and have some business with the folks inside. A little help, I'm going to need with a package. How'd you like to make twenty-five bucks apiece just to carry it to my car?"

"Sure."

"Why not?"

Maury fished two tens and a five from his coin purse, handed it to the skinny, feral-looking one with the shaved head and see-through goatee. "The balance, I'll give you after. I'll move my car near the back of the building, meet with the folks inside, and come out that rear door. Say, half an hour? Put the package in my trunk and you boychicks will be fifty George Washingtons richer."

"Super cool."

Maury moved his Town Car within forty feet of the door, waved to the boys, and returned to the entrance.

"*National Geographic*? A grant, you say? And Dr. Finklestein's coming here? Today?" Director Duckhaus rubbed his hands in anticipation.

Plato Scopes rocked nervously, foot to foot. "He should be here any minute."

"We'll buy him lunch."

"They have wieners again today, sir."

"No, no. Not *here*. Take him somewhere special. Surf and turf, wine, banana split, whatever he wants." Duckhaus directed a sour look out the window. "I wish those dratted pickets weren't here."

"Sir, Dr. Finklestein is a scientist. I'm sure he understands the challenge of advancing knowledge in the face of ignorance and superstition."

"You've alerted Flora up front that he's expected? I took the 'Contributions Welcome' sign down. News of that mummy of yours has been drawing them like flies, so I told her to start charging admission. I hope she has enough sense not to hit up Finklestein. Do you think we should close off Buttonhook Hall? I don't want him to hear any disparaging remarks from yokels looking for pirates or crocodiles or fairies."

"Sir, all he wants is to see the mummy."

"Of course, although we must make clear our prime mission—"

The telephone rang.

Scopes answered, nodded, said, "Tell him I'll be right there, Flora. Be sure you don't charge him—Oh." He looked at a scowling Duckhaus, and said to the phone, "Give it back to him, okay? Yes, the whole dollar and a half. Be friendly. He's a very important visitor." To Duckhaus, he said, "I'll go meet him."

"We'll both go."

Peaches, half a wiener squeezed in his fist, mustard dripping from his fingers, ran from the front of the building. Junior and Six-pack slid off the hood, leaned nonchalantly against the side. Breathless, Peaches informed them, "He's here . . . inside . . . the Hammer. I seen him, got as close as this."

"No shit," Junior said. "What's he look like?"

"Like your old man said, he stands out like a third tittie. He's some kind of spic, wearing like purple pants and a pink shirt hanging loose. Real silk, I bet. Lots of gold chains. Sandals on his feet, no socks. I think I saw a bulge under the shirt from his gun. He's got a skinny mustache, black hair all oiled up. Dark tan. Wears a ton of smell-good. Oh, he's a hit man, all right. Not big like we thought, but the kind of guy takes people from Vegas into the desert on a one-way trip. Mafia type."

"Did you talk to him?"

"Hell, no. But I heard him ask the babe at the front desk where they kept the mummy."

"Uh-oh."

Peaches noticed mustard oozing through his fingers and crammed the rest of the wiener in his mouth. "Whadaeeon-nadoonow?" He gulped, licked his hand. "Huh, Junior? What?"

"If he comes out with it," Junior said, "maybe Six-pack can—"

Six-pack said, "Not me. Guys like that have, like, reflexes. You make a wrong move they'll shoot you before you know it. Maybe blow off a kneecap, then put one in your head to put an end to your screaming."

"Nuh-uh," Junior said, "he'll have his hands full of mummy."

"Your old man didn't want us to tangle with him," Peaches pointed out. "Just find out about the mummy."

"How we gonna do that?"

"I came through," Peaches said. "It's in the back room." He pointed to the rear of the building. "Other side of that door."

"Behind that door, huh?" Junior gave Six-pack a smug look. "You thinking what I am?"

"The old guy."

"Bingo." Junior explained to Peaches. "Remember the old fart in the bow tie, bought us beers at Ponchos? He's a scientist and he's here. Going to pick up a package inside, said he'd come to that door with it inside half an hour, wants us to carry it to his car, that big Lincoln. What I say is, when he opens the door, one of us keeps it from shutting all the way. We help him with his package, he leaves, we sneak back inside and snatch the mummy."

"Cool." Peaches wiped mustard on his jeans. "With all the people inside, the Hammer's probably waiting till closing to make his move. He'll pop the guard or take somebody hostage—but by then that mummy and us will be long gone."

"Meanwhile," Junior said, "you keep an eye on him. If he starts to make his move, beat it out here and tell me." He held out his hand. "Give me your car keys."

"No way."

"Look, when we get the mummy, the Hammer's gonna be pissed good. He'll be right on your fat ass. I'd better have the car running."

Peaches handed him the keys. "Just to start it up, okay?"

"Sure." Junior flashed a victorious grin. "My old man," he said, "is going to be so damned proud."

37

hickie Doone felt the cool hand of the angel stroking his face. He muttered, "Houdini?"

"Mr. Moses?"

He had been tumbling in and out of consciousness; a moment earlier dreaming of running through tall grass with Houdini at his side.

"Mr. Moses?"

The angel. So, he must be back in heaven. Shickie opened his eyes. She was cloaked in white, her golden hair haloed by light. He closed his eyes, heard himself say, "Sponge bath."

"Naughty boy." She gave him a gentle pat on the chin. "Who would guess an unconscious man could—"

"Nurse? Is he with us?"

Shickie started at the deep male voice. God. Come to punish him no doubt for . . . what? Something he had done or failed to do. "I'm sorry, God," he said, eyes still shut, but willfully so at the moment, reluctant to look God in the face.

God snapped his fingers. Shickie opened his eyes. God was wearing a camel blazer, a baby blue, oxford cloth, button-down shirt, and a bright blue tie with Tweetie Birds on it. He carried a clipboard.

Shickie mistook the Tweeties, with their huge eyes, for demons. He closed his eyes and lurched to the side, inducing a tug and a sharp pain at the back of his hand. Eyes open again, he saw a thin plastic hose running from beneath a strip of tape on his hand to a clear plastic bag of fluid hanging from a stainless steel hook. Instead of his Rolex, a cheap strip-of-plastic bracelet with a handwritten label banded his wrist. He tried to raise his head for a better look but it was too heavy. The angel placed a cool hand under his neck, plumped the pillow, and reached out of his line of vision. He heard a *whirr-rrr*, felt his head and back crook up from the waist. He discovered he was wearing a flimsy cotton, pale green nightie, and lying in a bent bed. His feet bare. Wires running from his chest to somewhere behind his head.

What the hell?

God sat on the edge of the bed and lifted Shickie's leg from beneath his knee. He tapped below his kneecap with a small, rubber-tipped mallet. Shickie watched his lower leg kick.

"Reflexes normal," God said. He lifted the nightie and pricked the skin over Shickie's thigh with something sharp.

"Ouch!"

"You feel that? Good. How are we doing otherwise, Mr. Moses? Try lifting your arm."

Moses? God had them confused. No wonder he'd made it to heaven.

Shickie watched his arm rise at God's command, his fingers flex. He lifted his other arm, wriggled his toes.

"Good for you. Do you know where you are?"

"Heaven?"

God chuckled. The angel stroked Shickie's forehead, leaned close and whispered, "You're in a hospital."

"Hospital? Back on earth?"

"That's right," she said. "If you call this earth. You're in Las Vegas."

"Vegas."

"Is it coming back to you?" God asked.

"Uhh . . . no."

"Do you remember your name?"

"Uhh . . . nuh-uh . . . wait . . . yes . . . Doone.   Schickie. Schickleton Doone. The Reverend Shickleton Doone."

Too late, he realized he should have kept his mouth shut.

"So, you're not Moses. You spell that D–O–O–N–E?" God made a notation on the clipboard, but instead of snapping his fingers again and sending Shickie south, he said, "That's a fine start. And you live in . . ."

"Um . . . Tennessee. Gatlinburg."

God continued playing twenty questions. ". . . a minister, eh? And whom may we contact to let them know how well you're doing?"

"Wife. No, wait—mother. No—I'll call myself. Why am I here? What happened?"

"That was going to be my next question. I can tell you this, Reverend Doone, you are a lucky man."

"Me? Lucky?"

"Indeed. You have been in a coma. Have you ever heard of Rohypnol?"

Shickie mumbled a No.

"It's a drug. Flunitrazepam, a benzodiazepine. Roofies, the kids call it. It's often referred to as the date rape drug. Someone gave you a dangerously strong dose of it, enough to—"

"*Rape?*" Shickie bobbed upright, rolled to one side, ran a hand along the crack of his posterior, exploring.

God gripped his forearm, eased him onto his back. "No, no. You were thoroughly examined. There's no indication you were violated. It appears—"

There was an insistent knocking at the door. "They're here," said the angel.

God tapped his pen against the clipboard. "I guess he's well enough to talk with them, although I think their visit is premature. I'll stand by to be sure they keep it short."

He spoke again to Shickie. "You have visitors. They have a few questions, want to find out what happened to you. They no doubt have information that will help you remember. Are you up to it?"

"I guess."

The nurse opened the door and three men entered, none smiling. The first had a buzz cut and a hard paunch protruding from a well-worn, plaid sport jacket. His knit tie, loosened, hung askew, the ends pinned together by a gold tie tack: a pair of miniature handcuffs. The second, perhaps an ex-Marine, his hair dyed too black and close-cropped, wore a yellow sport jacket snug over muscular shoulders. The jacket pocket bore an embroidered crest containing a curved scimitar cleaving the stem of a four-leaf clover and green script: Kabul Wonderland. The third, in his sixties, was tall and slender with an expensive haircut and steely gray temples. He wore a thousand-dollar-plus, gray linen Canali suit over a mauve silk tee shirt.

The doctor opened the conversation, addressing the visitors. "Our patient is awake. He is in good physical condition, although his memory is understandably spotty. He is from Gatlinburg, Tennessee. And we now know his correct name," he consulted the clipboard, "Shickleton Doone. He is a minister. That's as far as we got. Reverend Doone is up to answering questions, but go easy gentlemen."

"A minister," said the man in the yellow blazer. "That explains the phony moniker." He grinned at his associate in the plaid jacket. "He registered under the name of Moses."

The man in plaid chuckled. "I wonder why he didn't stay at the Luxor?"

"That's a good one, Crip," replied the gold jacket. The man in the suit merely nodded.

"You came in on a pre-paid junket from Knoxville," the man in plaid continued. "Since your arrival there's been no more plagues than usual and no reports of a Moses gone missing in the desert." Another chuckle. "Junket people didn't know anything about you. No ID when we found you."

The man in the suit added with a placating smile, "Not that we have a problem with disguising your identity, sir. Understandable, you being a man of the cloth. Many of our patrons prefer to travel incognito." He turned to the man in the gold jacket. "Right, Tommy?"

Tommy, in the gold jacket, nodded.

"I'm Detective Crippen, Las Vegas PD," said the man in plaid.

"What did I do?" asked a worried Shickie Doone.

The suit waved the air. "Why, nothing, sir—Reverend."

Detective Crippen added, "We ran your prints—trying to ID you. Nada. And, like I said, no missing Moseses."

"What we're trying to find out," said the man in the suit, "is who did this *to* you. And why." He added, "I'm Mr. Lassiter from the Kabul Wonderland." Leaning over the bed, he clasped Shickie's free hand briefly in both of his. He let it drop to the sheet. "My associate in the yellow blazer is Tommy Romano, our chief of security. Let me say, we are delighted to see you so fit. We were worried, weren't we, gentlemen?"

"That's right," said Romano, the security chief.

"Yeah, sure," said Detective Crippen, followed by, "Why don't you tell us what you remember before, you know, before you got this way?"

"Nothing. I don't remember anything. Except . . . Vegas. I sort of remember being—shoot, it's gone. Wait—Kabul Wonderland? Yeah, big room, hot tub, view of the Strip. Comped. Umm . . . sorry. That's about it."

Embers of memory re-ignited. Shickie recalled cigar smoke, a poker game. High stakes. A Roman centurion speaking into a spear. A sharp pain in his big toe. And shoes. Shoes? He stared at his bare feet.

"Tommy," said the Wonderland's Mr. Lassiter, "Fill Mr. Doone in on what we know."

The security chief kicked at the floor, apparently reluctant. "Everything?"

"Sure. I want this thing wrapped up as soon as possible. Today. Now." Lassiter glanced at his watch, a diamond-studded Piaget with a lapis lazuli face. "I'm sure that would please Reverend Doone as well."

Shickie noticed the wrist-glance and recalled his own

Rolex, the watch he had splurged on following the first—only—time, he won big in Vegas. "Was I wearing a watch when you brought me here?"

The nurse shook her head.

"Or a ring?" The star sapphire ring: a gift from his sleight-of-hand mentor, Denzel the Magnificent.

"No sign of a watch or ring," confirmed the security chief. "Let me see . . ." He consulted a hand-held computer. "The day maid found you out cold in your room at nine-forty-five in the A.M. Wearing a pair of black trousers, no shirt, soles of your socks dirty like you'd been walking outside, no shoes on your feet. Underwear, a couple of shirts, Dopp Kit and toiletries in your room. That's it. No valuables, no suitcase, no wallet. Zip.

"We pieced some of it together. . . ." He glanced at Mr. Lassiter, who nodded. "Security cameras show you got back to the hotel at seven-forty-seven the evening before, half-dressed like I said. Maybe doing some partying, huh? Got on the elevator. However . . ." Another look at Lassiter, another nod. "The turn-down maid says you approached her in the hallway an hour *before* that, fully dressed—in jeans and a big cowboy hat this time—told her you forgot your key card and would she let you in? She swears she recognized you, but she's still damp behind the ears from the trip north and I doubt—"

"Tommy? Stick with the facts, right?"

"Yessir. The maid didn't follow procedure, should have called us. The cameras didn't pick you up before seven-forty-seven, so it looks like somebody impersonated you, scammed or bribed her—"

Lassiter interrupted. "She's being dealt with, Mr. Doone. We run a tight ship. This sort of thing does *not* happen at the Kabul Wonderland."

Shickie said, "Of course not."

Tommy Romano, the security chief, continued. "We're still investigating. If this guy did look like you, we can't tell from the eye-in-the-sky tapes on account of the hat. He could have been on the hot prowl, mistook you for a high roller at high tide instead of a—uh, no disrespect. Or maybe he marked you because you looked alike and—see?—could flummox the maid. Whatever, he got into your room and waited."

More memories surfaced. Shickie recalled losing big at the Wonderland, at Harrah's, the Mirage, Caesar's, the second class joints . . . all over town. He recalled the disastrous, marathon poker game at Caesar's, the players laughing at him, taking his shoes and shirt. His ring and Rolex. His right hand moved to his left wrist, bare except for the plastic bracelet. But . . . he had recovered the watch with his fainting bit, and a fair share of the pot, too, he was sure. An image of champagne and chocolate rose before him. . . .

"He doped a bottle of champagne," the cop was saying, reading from a small spiral notebook, "Laced with Ro–hip–nal. Fluni . . . uh, Fluni-taz . . ."

The doctor finished it: "Flunitrazepam. I've already explained that part to Mr. Doone. The date-rape drug."

"But you weren't . . . you know," the cop said.

"Raped," Shickie said. "Damn good thing."

"You got that right." Romano rubbed his own rear end. "Yeeouch! Although, at your age, we didn't really think . . ."

"Never can be sure in Vegas," the cop added. "I'll tell you, we see it all. If there's an orifice and an opportunity . . ." He shook his head dolefully. "And not just people. Remember that—what the hell was it, Tommy—an anteater? Broad led it around in this jeweled harness like, could hardly tell the front from the back of it—"

Lassiter raised a hand. "Enough, gentlemen. Let's get back to Reverend Doone's unfortunate experience."

The security chief summarized: "It wasn't a sex crime."

"The Kabul Wonderland is a family resort," Mr. Lassiter added.

The cop finally moved it along: "You drank the champagne. The bottle and glass were still in the room. Only your prints on them. The bubbly wasn't from the Wonderland. Whoever this guy was . . ."

Rita Rae? Could she have set him up? Maybe she figured she'd take his stake, too, before she hung him up to dry in divorce court. Although, somehow, that didn't sound right. Rita Rae couldn't show her face in Vegas. Shickie learned that a month ago. Counterfeiting casino chips. A con. His sweet "oil widow." It hadn't come as much of a surprise. A babe like Rita Rae being so hot over him, agreeing to live in Gatlinburg. He grunted inwardly at her "allowance," the skyrocketing credit card bills, the mansion she had to live in. That diamond. And when she really turned against him—his nose stung and his eyes began tearing up as he remembered her selling his dog. Poor little baby.

If Rita Rae had somebody following him, why wouldn't they have moved in sooner? Before he went bust?

In a frightening insight, Shickie blew out his breath. Sheesh! What if the whole point was to do him in? Poison him, make it look like robbery. She didn't know about the mortgages, the debt to Trout yet. She would expect to inherit it all. Plus that fat life insurance policy she made him buy. Oh, yes. Do away with him in Vegas while she set up a solid alibi with her sick mother in Miami Beach.

Did she hate him that much?

Shickie felt a stab of regret. But . . . no. While he told her he was going to Vegas, he had been careful to hide the details, including the moniker Moses. Trout had given him the junket in a rare burst of generosity.

Trout? Would Trout off him for being a little late? Didn't seem to add up.

Romano in the gold jacket was speaking. "So, like I was saying, he cleaned you out—took everything but the shirt on your back and your shoes—and he couldn't get *those* because you lost them somewhere else." Haw, haw, haw.

Lasssiter, the suit, said, "Enough of that, Tommy."

The cop asked, "Can you remember what else you had in the room? If any of it turns up, we may be able to tie it to the perp."

Feeling more or less his old self except for the fur in his brain, Shickie added it up and heard opportunity tap-tap.

"Let's see . . . I had my suitcase. Plane ticket. A Rolex. And . . . over twenty-five thousand in cash. I was on a streak—"

The sympathetic, yet somehow ominous, Mr. Lassiter interrupted. "Doctor? Nurse? I wonder if we might have a few moments alone with the Reverend here?"

The doctor nodded to the nurse and they left the room.

"All right, Reverend," Lassiter said, his agreeable demeanor evaporating like a rare rain on hot Vegas asphalt. "Let's get back to planet earth. You deposited fifteen grand with us in a house account when you arrived. You pissed away nearly all of that on craps and poker the first night. Right, Tommy?"

The security man smiled. "And he wasn't winning anywhere else."

Shickie sputtered. "I got into a private game. I—"

Lassiter waived aside Shickie's protests. "Not to contradict a man of God, but . . . how about I make a proposal? Your room was comped at the Wonderland. The rest of your tab? Zap! It is no more. We'll cover your medical expenses—how's that? Enjoy the cuisine." He toyed with the IV tube, let it drop. "Make a play for the nurse, whatever." He gave Shickie a lascivious wink. "When you're ready to check out, Tommy here will pack your belongings in . . . how about a Louis Vuitton bag? Buy him a nice one, Tommy. The man will need clothes and some shoes, too. Tell Andre at Chez Ali Baba to fix him up. Top of the line.

"When you're back on your feet—doc says you should be fine—Tommy will have you picked up in a limo, driven to the airport. We'll buy you a ticket home, first class, and tuck five grand in your pocket. How's that sit with you?"

"Five? I was taken for twenty-five. Plus a Rolex watch."

"So you say. But I'm thinking if, like the doc says, this date rape drug makes your memory spotty, maybe you're remembering too big, huh?

"However, we want to do right by you. If you want us to walk out of here right now, just say so. You can file a report with detective Crippen here and stick around Vegas on your own ticket. Maybe you'll remember who your intruder was, and maybe the cops will nab him, and maybe this guy will still have your money—all that cash—on him when they pick him up, and maybe you can convince a judge it belonged to you or find a trusting attorney, and maybe—"

Shickie blinked. "Uh . . . I guess what you said sounds pretty fair."

"More than fair. All I need from you," Lassiter crooked a finger at the security man, who lifted four, tri-folded sheets of paper from the side pocket of his gold jacket, "is to sign a quit claim against the Wonderland. And, whadayaknow? Tommy has one right here. Tommy, fill in the Reverend's real name where it's needed and X the lines where he needs to sign. The detective here can witness."

Lassiter snapped his fingers. Romano made the requisite notations on all four copies and set them on Shickie's chest. Lassiter removed a chubby Montblanc fountain pen from his jacket pocket and put it in Shickie's right hand.

Shickie, lacking his reading glasses, pretended to scrutinie the document.

"It's all there," Lassiter said. "Including certain penalties should you discuss this unfortunate incident with anyone." He gave Shickie a too-broad smile. "It's a good deal, my friend. Take it. Believe me, it would be foolish not to. And if you should remember anything useful about your visitor and pass it along to Tommy here, there could be a nice bonus in it for you. We'd like to lay our hands on this perp, wouldn't we, Tommy?"

Tommy nodded.

Shickie lifted the pen and signed at the X's.

"That's my boy." Lassiter gave Shickie a pat on the shoulder, retrieved the papers, and turned to his associates. "Gentlemen?" He motioned to the door and followed them out.

Shickie slumped, perspiring, exhausted. Sheesh! And sat bolt upright as he remembered—identified—the voice at his back the moment before he blacked out that fateful evening. "Dear brother *Fenster*." he said aloud, and slapped the mattress, nearly ripping the IV needle from the back of his hand. Oblivious of the pain, he slapped again, cursing. "You thieving bastard."

38

As the Bible Alive van idled at a Gatlinburg stoplight, Jimmy's mind raced. The out-of-the-blue errand to Pigeon Forge was the opportunity he had been waiting for. Unfortunately, he had no idea how to capitalize on it.

ARM had embarrassed the Captain Hook Museum, but the institution had as yet to give up Jimmy's ancestor. Anticipating victory, some of the ARM members had nearly come to blows the preceding night arguing over who would claim the mummy when the museum capitulated. Jimmy held his tongue. There was no question in his mind: it was on his ancestral property, he had his hand on it once, and he wouldn't let it slip through his fingers again.

Though two of the pickets dropped out over the dispute, word had spread. Native American groups were calling his Grandpop, leaving messages. Jimmy hadn't returned any of them. This was the attention he had long wanted—but not exactly, either, because Jimmy could imagine the Cherokee, Shawnee, Creek, Yuchi, if any remained, all staking claims on the mummy. In which case, who would listen to Jimmy

Feather, last of the Mohicans, pure of heart, but son of a no-name chief?

He glanced at the traffic light and saw Ginger Rodgers, blond curls bouncing on her shoulders, long legs moving out with purpose. Adrenaline hot-wired him as he remembered the old man in the bow tie and the slick gangsterish dude holding Ginger in their arms. While she had smiled, enjoying every minute of it, Jimmy, non-dancer, sat on the sidelines.

He recalled Ginger's friend, Joline, telling him how Ginger flirted with every man she saw. The curse of pretty women: they could never get enough attention. "Blondes," Joline had said, with a toss of her dark hair, as if that explained it all.

Maybe it did. Down-to-earth, brown-haired Betsy said she would pray for him. And, when Joline saw how uncomfortable Jimmy had been at being ignored by Ginger, she gave him a ride to his car, as well as a sympathetic smooch and her phone number. Jimmy didn't need more complications in his life, so he hadn't called. Yet.

He slunk in the seat, hopeful Ginger wouldn't see him. But, of course, she did—turned for no particular reason, looked him square in the eyes, and flashed a smile.

"Hey—Jimmy!" She thumped the hood.

The light was about to change. Jimmy raised his hand in casual greeting and shifted into first. His foot moved to the accelerator. Before the red light turned to green, Ginger was at the shotgun door, opening it, jumping in.

"Made it!" she said, as traffic began to move. "Hey, Jimmy Feather," she said again, and punched him in the shoulder. "Where are you headed?"

"Uh, Pigeon Forge. Got to pick up some stuff, bring it back to Bible Alive."

"Mind if I ride along?"

He shrugged.

Ginger took it as encouragement. "I just had to get out of the armory. Reverend Patch fixed up this apartment for me in the back, is gonna make me move in. The Joneses brought my stuff over already. I was lucky to get out at all."

"What do you mean 'make you' move in? How can he do that?"

"He's God's Messenger." Ginger was the one to shrug now. "The Rapture of the Prince changed my life. I suppose it's like Reverend Patch says: God selected me to witness the first one and now I'm part of His plan—you know, saving souls before the big wave starts." She scowled. "God could have taken the Prince anytime, but He waited until I was with him. Me." She gave Jimmy a questioning look. "How can I turn my back on God?"

"I guess you won't be going to Poncho's so often now."

"Maybe not. Maybe you'll see more of Joline now. Did you have a good time, you two?"

"Not as good as you were having with all those men."

"*All?* Maury? He's like my grandfather. And Orlando? Get real. He's, like, this movie star. He only wanted to hear about the Prince. He is a good dancer, though."

"I noticed."

They rode in silence for several minutes, avoiding eye contact. Finally, Ginger said, "Do you still think the mummy is your ancestor?"

"He is."

"No, he isn't. He's the Prince of Light and . . . after tomorrow he'll be out of that museum so you won't have to worry about him."

Jimmy hit the brake and pulled to the curb. "Where did you hear that? Where are they taking him?"

"The buttonhook museum doesn't know he's leaving yet. Reverend Patch is planning to bus the whole congregation down there tomorrow morning to take him. They only have one guard and the cops are gone. They won't stop us this time. We'll give him sanctuary in the Temple of Light—like the Hunchback of Notre Dame—which means no one, not the cops, not anyone else, will be able to get him back."

She gave Jimmy a 'So-there' glare, opened the door, stepped out, and disappeared into a candle shop.

Jimmy thumped the wheel. "Double damn!"

"Dr. Finklestein?" Scopes extended his hand. "I'm Plato Scopes, Chief Scientist."

Duckhaus seized Maury's small hand before Scopes could get to it. "Horace Duckhaus. Welcome to the Captain Hook Museum, home of the third-largest collection of buttonhooks east of the Mississippi and south of the Ohio rivers."

"Buttonhooks," Maury replied, with a salesman's enthusiasm. "Rank right up there with the coat hanger and the internal combustion engine."

"They surely do," said a smiling Duckhaus. "Without buttonhooks in years gone by would we have had buttons? And without buttons, can you imagine the licentiousness? Civilization? Right down the drain. Come with me, sir, I'll give you a quick tour. Once you grasp the pivotal role of the buttonhook in American history, I'm sure *National Geographic* will—"

"Excuse me," Scopes said. "Dr. Finklestein is here to see my mummy."

"Of course, but—"

"Mr. Scopes?" the receptionist said from behind. "You told me to hold your calls, but I have more messages here from," she regarded a series of Post-it notes, "the Smithsonian Institution, UCLA, the University of Tennessee, the University of Michigan—"

"You see?" Scopes's face brightened. "They're all after it. But I've put them off because I wanted you to have first crack at him."

The real reason, of course, had been that if the big-time anthropologists, no more than curious at this point, got their mitts on the mummy, Plato Scopes, small town, not-even-PhD, chief-but-sole scientist at the who-ever-heard-of-the-place Captain Hook Museum would be cast aside like chaff in the wind.

Maury grinned. "Thank you so much. First crack at the little fellow is exactly what I want."

Maury's neck was sore from nodding, his cheek muscles ached from smiling at the requisite Buttonhook Hall tour, the longest half hour in history. He stole a glance at Horace Duckhaus, prattling on about mother of pearl and tortoise shell and agate and bone and rubber and leather handles and something about the frailty of nickel plating. In an overstated gesture, Maury lifted his pocket watch and studied it, hoping the museum director would get the point.

He did not, but Scopes did. "The mummy," Scopes blurted out. "Dr. Finklestein is here for the mummy."

"Indeed," said Maury. "I've seen enough buttonhooks." He wanted to shout *for ten lifetimes*.

"Oh," Duckhaus said. "I do get carried away. Well, uh, Scopes here can take you to the lab. It's significant, I suppose, this mummy, although the body is all dried up, it hasn't a stitch of clothing on, and—"

"Sir!"

Duckhaus cleared his throat and fluttered his fingers toward the back of the building. "Go ahead. Show Dr. Finklestein your mummy. Then bring him—Dr. Finklelstein, not the mummy," he chuckled, "to my office, and we'll all have lunch. On the museum. We'll go to that Poncho's place in Gatlinburg, have a big steak, one of those monster deep-fried exploded onion things. Perhaps a carafe of wine. How's that sound, Dr. Finklestein?"

When he heard the word "lunch," Maury had feared Duckhaus was going to propose boiled wieners and lime Jell-O. "Sure. Fine," he said, and looked again at his watch. He had told the boys half an hour, but kids, having minds like sieves, who knew how long they would wait?

Scopes wasted no time getting him to the mummy room. The body lay shrouded under a white bedsheet on a sheet-draped table, with bones and stones and a monstrous molar displayed on more sheets on adjacent tables. Two standing easels held photographs of crude drawings of stick figures and childish monsters.

Maury decided the whole affair looked like a grade school science project.

Scopes lifted a pointer and tapped a photo, one of the cave drawings. "I've identified this as *Smilodon*, and this, a *Glyptodon*, although the rendering of the feet suggests *Glossotherium*. Of course, even if you didn't recognize this as *Mammuthus*, since we have the tooth . . ."

Maury nodded, feigning interest as Scopes droned on about crude mud glyphs discovered in another Tennessee cave. ". . . in comparison, the renderings in Mummy Cave," he tapped another easel, "are so remarkably realistic, we . . ."

For the first time, Maury actually looked at one of the photos of the stick figures. "My God!" he said without thinking. "They're *fucking*! And that one's giving the standing one a bl—"

Scopes broke in: "Fertility rituals, sir. As I said, the Mummy Cave petroglyphs are unusually graphic windows into the behavior of—"

"Sorry for the outburst," Maury said immediately, reddening. "It kind of took me by surprise." His eyes moved to the hump under the sheet. "Is this it? Our mummy?"

Scopes rested a hand on the corner of the sheet, did sort of a half bow, "May I present . . ." he shot upright, unfurling the sheet with a dramatic flourish, "the Scopes Mummy."

"So real, he looks," Maury said, taken aback. Despite the newspaper photographs and Ginger Rodgers' descriptions, he had half expected it to look like a big raisin with shrunken arms and legs. He rested his hands on the table, studying the gray, parched, but quite human-looking face, comparing it to his memory of the photograph of Shickie Doone.

Could be, he thought. Indeed. I believe young Ginger Rodgers is correct. He clapped. "Excellent. And it weighs, how much did you say?"

"Twenty-seven pounds."

"Perfect. I mean . . . extraordinary."

"That's only one of several features that sets it apart. Clearly, his people developed embalming secrets the Egyptians merely dreamt of. Go ahead, smell it."

"The mummy?" Maury backed away, lest he might.

"You can still detect the scent of the embalming oils. Go ahead, sniff."

Apprehensive, Maury moved closer and took a whiff. "Not half bad. Why, it smells a bit like Old Spice, I'd say."

"I suspect frankincense or myrrh." Scopes pointed at the head. "Look at the facial structure. See how European?"

"Almost Scots-Irish, like some of the locals," Maury said, with an impish grin.

"Astute. European haplotype DNA has been detected in several locations around Eastern North America. A maritime migration from Ireland . . ."

Time, time, time, Maury repeated to himself, as Scopes moved to the mammoth tooth. He eyed the rear door, glanced about the room, making plans.

Maury had the uneasy feeling the mummy was watching him, anticipating its imminent kidnapping, so he casually re-draped it. "Respect for the dead," he said by way of explanation, and then, "You know . . ." He put a hand to his forehead and closed his eyes. "I'm feeling a tad faint. Low blood sugar. Not to worry, but could you get me a glass of fruit juice?"

"Oh, my. I'm sure the cafeteria must have some. Have a seat and I'll see what I can rustle up." Scopes motioned to a folding chair and trotted toward the front of the building.

As soon as the door closed, Maury tied square knots across the top of the sheet to create a secure bundle. He hefted it— even at twenty-seven pounds it felt a burden in his frail arms. He set it on the floor and walked quickly to a storage shelf he had observed at the side of the room containing a large, plush, pink elephant. He set that on the table, wrapped several of the sheets on the table around it for bulk, pushing and plumping to approximate the previously draped mummy, and covered it with another sheet.

He dragged the mummy bundle to the exit, opened the door, and looked for his movers. The skinny one—still there—waved from the hood of his shiny Chevrolet, and both he and the big one trotted to Maury's side.

"Here," Maury said, "put this in the trunk of my Town Car. Lid's unlocked. Slam it before you leave."

The big one lifted the bundle by the gathered knots and hustled to Maury's automobile while the skinny one remained at the door. Maury removed the twenty-five dollars he had placed in his jacket pocket and handed it to his young accomplice. For a moment, he considered leaving, there and then, but he heard voices approaching in the hallway, beyond the metal door. Fearful of discovery and a losing chase, he opted to play the heist out inside. "Thank you," he said to the young man. "You can go now."

"Umm . . ." The skinny kid lingered, hand on the door.

"You have your money," Maury said. "Go."

The kid pursed his lips with indecision, dropped his hand, and retreated, almost reluctantly it seemed. Maury, pulse racing, pulled the door shut, took three quick strides into the room and dropped to a seated position on the speckled linoleum floor just as the interior knob twisted.

Scopes and Duckhaus rushed inside.

"Dear me," Duckhaus said of Maury, sitting spread-legged on the floor. "Quick, give him the juice."

Scopes handed him an opened bottle of orange juice. "Are you all right, sir?"

Maury sipped, mumbled a "Thanks, I'll be fine," although he was practically panting. Three more seconds and he would have been caught in the act.

Scopes helped him to his feet, kept a hand on his elbow.

"That lunch?" Maury said quickly, side-glancing at the sheet-draped stuffed elephant. "Sounds like just the ticket. I had pancakes for breakfast. Too much syrup . . . blood sugar drops. Look . . ." He showed them a trembling hand.

"You finish that juice," Duckhaus said, "and we'll get you right into town. Big meal will fix you up, you'll see."

Neither man took notice of the plumped sheet. "Yes," Maury agreed. "Soon as I'm out of here, I'll be breathing a good bit easier."

39

*S*ix-pack had Maury's trunk lid halfway closed when he noticed Junior trotting toward him. Confused, he released the lid and it flew open. He called to Junior, "Did you shim the door?"

"Umm," Junior kicked at the asphalt. "Not exactly."

"Not exactly?"

"The old guy closed it before I could do it. It's locked again."

"Oh, man."

"I know."

"What now?"

Junior shrugged and kicked at the pavement.

Six-pack tipped his head toward the still-open trunk. "What if we hold on to whatever the old scientist guy gave us, like keep it hostage for, you know, the . . . uh, what we're after?"

"Could work, if it's worth something and not just history crap. Check it out. I'll keep a lookout."

Six-pack leaned into the trunk, untied the knots in the white sheet. As the cloth fell away, he eyed, not history crap, but: a *body*. *The* body. Doone. Haunting him like a crypt creature out of a Stephen King novel. "Oh, ma–annn!" He did an about-face. Stomach roiling, he gripped the big chrome bumper of the Town Car for support.

"What is it?" Junior moved around him, peered in. "What do you know? Bet the old guy was going to cut it up or something." He noticed Six-pack dry heaving. "What's wrong, man?"

Six-pack forced a swallow. "I'm not into bodies—I *told* you that. Ever since I was a kid and mom made me kiss Uncle Benny." He rubbed his lips with the back of his hand and sucked air, his gaze directed at the horizon. "When Uncle Benny was a dead guy. At his funeral. You swore I wouldn't have to look at this . . . body. I think I'm gonna puke."

"Puke later. The old guy could come out any second." Junior gave him a conciliatory punch. "Get it together. I'll carry it myself. You open Peaches's trunk."

Still limping from his encounter with the slingshot wielder in the skirt, Six-pack hobbled to the Monte Carlo.

Junior lifted the small bundle from the unfurled sheet. "Cool," he said to Six-pack's back, "It weighs like nothing. Hey—I got an idea. How's about we wrap something else in the sheet so the old guy won't know it's switched till he gets home. Car's got Ohio plates. It'll take him two days to get there the way old farts drive, and by then he won't remember us or whether somebody else snatched it while he was taking a leak or—"

"All right, already." Six-pack scanned the grounds, saw nothing of mummy size. "Gimme the keys, I'll check Peaches's trunk. Maybe he's got a moving mat, or a dozen bags of potato chips, or—" He unlocked the lid of the Monte Carlo, popped it up, said, "Peaches, you sick horn-dog."

"What's he got in there?" Junior lowered the mummy to the asphalt.

"It's an inflatable babe. In a blond wig."

Junior peered in, poked at the pink pneumatic body. It had the form of a puffed-out stick figure, arms stretched wide, legs in a Y with an infolded recess at the crotch, and a few embellishments: impressive conical breasts with red nipples, a protruding belly button, swollen red lips forming a deeply hollowed O, a crude nose, and silk-screened, wide-open Betty Boop eyes with long lashes.

"And I thought Peaches never got any," Junior said, grinning. "I wonder—"

"I don't want to think about it. Look . . ." Six-pack stuck a finger in the inflatable's recessed mouth, frozen in a pucker. "Babe like this couldn't say no."

Junior made a face. "Man, I wouldn't put my finger in there." He patted her on the cheek. "She does have a pretty mouth though—much too big for Peaches."

Six-pack said, "I wonder if she squeaks 'I love you,' like those kid's dolls if you feel her up?"

Junior cupped a pointy breast and squeezed. The doll's lips bulged but she remained mute. "My kind of babe," Junior said. "No back talk." He spread her legs wide, investigating inflatable anatomy, and then remembered their mission. "See that duct tape? Let some air out of her. We'll tape her arms and legs to her body so she's the same size as the mummy and wrap her in the sheet in the old man's trunk."

"Slick." Six-pack stripped off a length of silver tape and rotated the plastic doll by the ankle. "Where do you think the valve is?"

Junior pointed to her belly button. He tugged the umbilicus and a plastic hose sprang out. He popped the plug at the end and compressed her torso. The doll went from buxom to anorexic in six seconds.

Half a minute later, Junior had taped her ankles to her shoulders, her wrists to her thighs. "I always wanted to do that to a babe." He moved to the front of the car. "I'll stash the mummy in Peaches's trunk, you take care of this."

Six-pack stowed the pink inflatable in Maury's trunk, retied the sheets, slammed the lid, and joined Junior at the Monte Carlo. They slapped high-fives.

"Peaches made me swear not to drive his wheels," Junior said, "but, what the hell, we're in a hurry." He drove to the museum entrance and gave the horn a long blast, returning the dirty looks of protesters and patrons with a raised finger. He hit the horn again.

"Where the hell is he?"

Six-pack shrugged.

Junior honked again, finally told Six-pack to find him.

Five minutes passed without trace of Peaches or Six-pack. Junior fidgeted. The Hammer was in there. What if he got wise to the double-cross, recognized Peaches and Six-pack as part of Junior's—Thadeus Trout's—crew? Discovered they had stolen the mummy out from under his nose? He listened for gunshots, heard nothing unusual. But the Hammer would use a silencer, wouldn't he?

"Damned if *I'm* going in," he said to the steering wheel. "Daddy pays them good. They knew what they were getting into."

Six-pack and Peaches appeared at the front door, Six-pack hustling Peaches along by an elbow. Peaches held one wrist, evidently hurt, to his side.

Six-pack shouted, "Got him."

"Geez, what did the Hammer do to him? Shoot something off? Huh? What?"

"Wasn't the Hammer," Six-pack said. "Peaches got his arm stuck in a candy machine. I had to kick the shit out of it to get him free."

"It got hold of my hand," Peaches said. "Sometimes you can—"

"You dipshit, we're on a mission."

"I got hungry in there with nothing to do—what's the difference? Six-pack said you got the mummy."

"Just like I planned, no thanks to you."

Peaches shook loose from Six-pack's grip. "What are you doing in my Monte Carlo?"

"Thought we oughta be ready for a quick getaway if the Hammer was on to you."

"Well, he's not, so move over." Peaches peered into the back window. "Where is it?"

Junior grinned. "Getting it on with your babe in the trunk."

A look of terror gripped Peaches's face. He flushed scarlet.

"Actually," Junior said, "the mummy *is* in the trunk, but your inflata-babe left you for an old fossil in a Lincoln."

"You bastard!"

"Cut your griping," Junior said. "I'll buy you another babe." He gave Peaches a serious look. "Is the Hammer still in there?"

"Yeah. But he ain't doing nothing but trying to pick up the girl who sells the tickets. Some hit man."

"That hit man shoots pieces off for fun. With your lard ass, you'd of kept him busy for—" Junior's cell phone rang. He fumbled at his waist, lifted the phone to his ear. "Yessir. Guess what? I got the mummy."

Junior smiled at the response. "Wasn't no problem. We saw him, but he don't know who we are. He's one of them Mafia greasers. Right away. No shit? Thanks, Daddy."

Junior pressed the End button, grinned at Six-pack, and then at Peaches, who, face still red, avoided his gaze. "Tell you what, guys . . . beers are on me at the Mad Mexican's to celebrate. Daddy's giving us a five hundred buck bonus."

Jimmy Feather drove from the souvenir supplier in Pigeon Forge to the buttonhook museum. Lest his ARM compadres recognize him, he slouched in the seat as he entered the lot. He mouthed a silent prayer for return of his ancestor, lifted the Indian penny talisman hanging at his neck, and rubbed it for luck.

The back door opened and an old man appeared, waved to two young men sitting on the hood of a souped-up Chevrolet, and engaged them in conversation. Jimmy's hand tightened on the metal as he recognized the two as Ginger's atheists. The skinny one sat leaning to one side, apparently favoring his thumped rear cheek.

Jimmy watched the old man return inside. The atheists— the big one still limped—did a curious switching act between the cars with—the *mummy* and what Jimmy took to be a crumpled beach ball. Jimmy's ancestor now resided in the Chevy's trunk.

The third atheist joined the first two and they drove away. Jimmy followed at an innocuous distance, from Pigeon Forge to Gatlinburg, and into Poncho the 'irate's parking lot. The trio went inside. Ten minutes later, Jimmy maneuvered the Bible Alive van between the Chevy and the restaurant, lifted a tire iron from the back, cast a wary glance left and right for witnesses, and quick-stepped to the Chevy's trunk. One hefty pry under the lid and he stood face-to-face with the mummy, lying knees to chin in the bed of the trunk like a Vegas hit bound for a shallow grave in the Nevada desert.

"Welcome home," Jimmy said, as he rescued his ancestor from a bed of fast food wrappers, greasy orange shop-rags, yellowing newspaper, and half a dozen page-worn issues of porn pubs. He placed the tiny body gently in an empty corrugated carton at the rear of the van, sat behind the wheel and sighed with righteous satisfaction.

Maury, suffering a tedious lunch at Poncho the 'irate's with the buttonhook people, recognized his recent allies, the two kids from the parking lot, plus their fat companion, enter and go to the bar. Improvident youth, he said to himself. Can't wait to spend the fifty bucks I gave them.

The skinny fellow with the bad skin noticed Maury and nudged his companions who turned, stared for a moment, and broke into goofy grins. The skinny one raised a beer bottle in a toast across the restaurant, no doubt in appreciation of Maury's largess.

Maury lifted his empty Manhattan glass in acknowledgment. That seemed to give them the giggles. The three toasted him back. Maury raised the glass again, inducing more hilarity.

What's with these meshuggeners? Are they drunk, already? Maury turned away, pointedly.

"Dessert?" Duckhaus asked, oblivious of the antics of the young men.

"No thank you," Maury said, and, more emphatically, "It's getting late, nearly four. I'll have to be on my way soon back to—" he nearly forgot "—Washington. A memorable meal, this. Very filling."

Duckhaus persisted. "How about we have them wrap up some apple pie for the road? Poncho's is famous for their pie. With a slice of cheese on top? I'll bet Washington has nothing to match it."

Maury faked a burp. "Such a fine thought, but I'm positively stuffed." He lifted a wrist and regarded his watch. The boys, he noticed, were still cutting up at the bar. He needed to leave the mummy on Trout's doorstep like an orphaned baby before Trout called it a day. If Trout left at five, that gave him less than an hour.

"The sooner Dr. Finklestein gets on the road," Plato Scopes was saying, "the sooner we'll get the *Geographic* article under way—isn't that right, Dr. Finklestein?"

"Exactly," Maury said. "Get this business wrapped up."

Duckhaus sighed. "I suppose."

Maury gave the boys a small wave on the way out, inciting a final round of laughter.

Scopes and Duckhaus watched the *Geographic* scout speed from the lot on a "beeline back to Washington" as the good doctor had put it.

Irritated that the man had shown so little interest in buttonhooks, Duckhaus retired to his office to ponder the museum's seemingly unavoidable shortfall for the coming quarter. That new guard for Scopes's mummy was definitely out.

Scopes found himself fidgeting at the computer, too excited to concentrate. Dr. Finklestein had agreed to everything he had asked for: a grant for tests on the mummy, a *National Geographic* artist to paint the background for the diorama, a cartographer to thoroughly chart Mummy Cave, a photographer to properly record the cave drawings. And more. All Scopes had to do was ask. And, with *National Geographic* supporting his research, his nagging worries about the county opening an inquest, or the Park Service or the big institutions moving in on him, or the religious crazies making trouble, all faded. The Native Americans might still be a thorn in his side, but if he could fend them off long enough to . . .

Scopes pressed his palms to his temples and willed himself to relax.

Impossible. He grabbed his car keys and dashed from the museum, on a shopping expedition in search of tusks for his plush elephant toy, destined to star in the diorama. What Scopes had in mind was a miniature Texas longhorn hat rack he had seen in one of the Gatlinburg souvenir shops, designed, no doubt for some young future cowboy's bedroom. Detached from the central plaque, the matched, curving, plastic horns would do nicely. If only he could remember in which of the look-alike shops he had seen it.

40

*S*hickie planned to wave goodbye to the Kabul Wonderland limo transporting him from the hospital to the airport, catch a cab back to the Strip, and run up the five grand fast, winning enough to pay off Thadeus Trout and then some.

As luck would have it, however, Tommy Romano, the Kabul Wonderland security chief, arranged for a cop to dog him through security, through the departure lounge, all the way to his first class seat before handing over the magic envelope with the hundred Ben Franklins. As promised, the casino had dressed him in a twelve-hundred-dollar suit and packed his remaining, meager, belongings in a new Louis Vuitton suitcase. The limo driver checked it for him upon arrival at the Vegas airport.

Shickie touched the lucky charm in his pocket with a silent prayer all his toiletries had been packed. He wasn't worried about the Kabul Wonderland amenity shampoo, French-milled soaps, or shower caps, his toothbrush, dental floss, toothpaste, razor, or shaving cream, his aging hair brush, Preparation H, or aspirin, but, rather, the five-carat diamond ring embedded in a jar of vitamin E skin cream. Rita Rae's ring. The ring he had bought out of that first fateful loan from Thadeus Trout. The ring he switched for a masterful cubic zirconia reproduction before leaving for Vegas. Payback for Rita Rae's selling Shickie's best friend in the world, little Houdini, his four-pound Yorkie, to a stranger on the streets of Gatlinburg.

Houdini: a far better friend than Fenster, the date-rape drugging little prick. Barely out of prison, Fenster had phoned Shickie in Gatlinburg the day before Shickie left for Vegas. Shickie reluctantly agreed to listen to the "once in a lifetime" scam Fenster had set up in L.A.: marketing phantom cemetery plots to illegal aliens. The pitch would run, "See, the way it works is," waving a plot deed gray with small-print legalese, "if you're buried in U.S. soil, you become a citizen automatically."

"Stop by Vegas on the way out," Shickie had said, flush with Thadeus Trout's refresher loan. "We'll have drinks at the Mirage, catch the white tiger act, and if I can stake you, I will."

By the time Shickie and Fenster were exchanging brotherly hugs at the Mirage bar, Shickie's own stake, as well as his optimism, had become badly eroded. Over the first round, Fenster suggested they forget the cat show and phone two first class call girls. He proposed they meet the ladies somewhere other than Shickie's hotel, have a few drinks, and invite them to Shickie's room. The crux of the plan was that Fenster had some "really good shit"—good enough that they could entertain the ladies, ditch them later, and they "wouldn't remember their mamas' names," let alone whom they had been with, where they had been, or whether they had been paid.

"Count me out," Shickie said, as he always did to Fenster's schemes, unaware that Fenster's "really good shit" would wind up in the French champagne on the side table of Shickie's Kabul Wonderland comped suite.

Shickie planned to give his brother the slip in time to make the private poker game at Caesar's, his final shot at financial redemption. After a few drinks, however, he found himself bragging about his free lodging, his good luck, and the profitability of his church in Tennessee. When he saw the greed in Fenster's eyes and his outstretched palm, Shickie backpedaled, pled poverty, and, finally, gave his brother five hundred dollars. Fenster thanked him by bouncing a bowl of bar peanuts off Shickie's skull, leaving him with a knot on his forehead and the tickets to Siegfried and Roy in his shirt pocket.

The last Shickie saw of his little brother was that fateful moment before passing out on the plush pile carpet of his Wonderland suite.

Shickie watched McCarran International Airport recede into the desert haze. When the all clear for electronic devices sounded, he pried the Airfone from the seatback to call his Ma.

He phoned his Ma on her birthday and every Christmas without fail. The birthday had been two days ago. Ma Doone could be a difficult woman, as unforgiving about missed deadlines as Thadeus Trout, so Shickie did not look forward to her rasping voice and one of her lectures. Still, the call had to be made. Not only for the birthday wishes, but because Shickie needed a line on Fenster, the little prick who had date-rape drugged and robbed him of his wallet, his Rolex, his star sapphire ring, his remaining cash, plane ticket, and most of his clothing.

Lacking a credit card, Shickie called collect.

The first word out his Ma's mouth was, "Collect?"

"Sorry," Shickie said, and, before the operator could cut him off, "Happy birthday, Ma."

She hung up.

The flight rolled into Atlanta half an hour late. Shickie barely made the connection to Knoxville. When they landed in Tennessee, he hustled to baggage claim, anxious to probe the jar of skin cream packed, he hoped, in his posh suitcase.

He opened the bag on a baby-changing tray in the first restroom he found, and fumbled through the contents.

The Kabul Wonderland had indeed packed the jar. The ring was safe. Shickie said a short prayer for the traveler's saint, the hotel housekeeper, and hauled his suitcase from the men's room to a news shop for change, and then a pay phone to see if he could buy more time with Thadeus Trout. He asked the operator for Great Smoky Foods. As he awaited the connection, he rehearsed his "I don't have it all yet, but how about a partial payment?"

A whiney voice answered. Some kid.

Shickie cleared his throat. "Let me speak to Trout."

"Maybe I will, maybe I won't. Who is this?"

"Shickie Doone."

"Sure it is." Apparently, the kid put his hand over the receiver, because Shickie next heard a muffled, "Daddy, it's someone calling about Doone," and then, a faint but clearly recognizable response from Thadeus Trout: "Is it the Hammer?"

Shickie's breath caught in his throat. The Hammer. The hit man Trout had warned him about when he fattened the loan. The big toad had already put out a contract.

"How would I know?" the kid said to his father. "You want me to ask him?"

Trout responded: "No, no. Give me the phone."

Shickie heard a clearer, if hesitant, "Hammer?" from Trout.

Shickie croaked, "No."

"Who is it then? Someone at the museum?"

Shickie stuttered, "Uh, uh, I . . ."

"Speak up. If you got Doone's body, I'll give you five grand for it."

Shickie hung up and slumped against the phone stanchion, kneading his face. What now? A quick dash to the Lighthouse to recover the modest stash he had secreted, a goodbye hug to a few of his favorite Fireflies, and then . . . Mexico? He thought of his miserable luck, and remembered the woman who started the black ball rolling. His Ma. Her birthday. Two days ago.

He fed the phone more coins. "Ma?"

"At least you pay for the call this time."

Before he could respond, the icy edge to her voice melted and she said, "Thank God you're still alive."

"He didn't get me yet," Shickie said, meaning the Hammer. Although, how could she know about that? Had Trout tried to shake her down? His Ma? The rat.

"'He' who?" she said.

This was getting confusing, so Shickie said nothing. In point of fact, Rita Rae was the only one in Gatlinburg who knew he had a mother, and Shickie couldn't imagine Rita Rae telling Trout, even if he leaned on her to make good the loan.

". . . I was worried to death," his Ma was saying, "what, with the papers and the TV saying you were ruptured and then dead in a cave—how *dare* you put me through that. I called, couldn't get hold of you. You didn't call back. I swear you'll put me in my grave—"

"Me? Ruptured? Dead?"

"Those Fireflies of yours, saying the mummy was you."

"Mummy?"

"I saw the picture, and it looks more like you than that Glamour Shots portrait you use for the publicity. Thank God, they were wr—"

"When was this, Ma?"

"Yesterday. Don't you read the papers? Watch the TV? Where are you, anyway? That conniving, fortune-hunting wife of yours called looking for you, too. Probably wanted money for more jewelry. If you'd listened to me—"

"Enough, Ma."

"Rita Rae Deaver. Hah! Didn't I tell you she was no oil widow?"

"Ma? Have you heard from Fenster in the last few days?"

"Some brother, you are. How could you forget Fenster is in the can again? He calls the first of every month—not like my other son, who, though he's scot free, forgets even my birth—"

"Fenster's out, Ma."

"Out? Already? And he didn't call, either? Lord God above, what have I done to be cursed with *two* ungrateful sons?"

Shickie thought he heard the gnashing of teeth, and then, "Fenster always calls when he gets out. He had three months to go. Are you sure—"

Fenster. Shickie remembered bragging about his Gatlinburg income, his fancy house. Fenster had stolen the plane ticket along with the rest of it. If Fenster had gone to Tennessee . . . Shickie recalled Trout's reference to "the body," his ma's speaking of a "mummy," how much it looked like him. Uh-oh.

His ma apparently came to the same conclusion. "Jesus, Mary, and Joseph!" she wailed. "If it wasn't you, it was him. My little baby. They made a mummy out of him. You no good . . . how could you let them—"

"Ma, Fenster was alive and kicking the last time I saw him."

Kicking me in the balls, he added to himself, at the same time wondering if—or how—it was possible Fenster had gotten himself turned into a . . . mummy? Maybe it was a scam. Sure. Some scam to—

His ma broke that train of thought. "Good God in heaven. My baby. And you, his big brother, letting them—"

"Ma. Fenster's okay. It's one of his cons."

"If you ever want to hear my voice again, you'll find my baby and—"

"I'll find him, Ma. I swear."

Shickie heard her sniffling like she always did when she got wrought up. Probably pulling at her hair, too.

Ma Doone regained her breath and her voice went to cold steel. "You damn well better," she said, and hung up.

Rita Rae pinched her nostrils. "What is that *stink*?"

"The boiled weiner special," Orlando said. "Time to close and still it poisons the air. A shame you miss the *almuerzo*. American hot dogs put some nice fat on your *culo, guajira*," he said, giving her rump a playful slap. "Ai, *Dios mío*, I am here at this boring *museo* for," he glanced at his thin gold wristwatch, ". . . forever."

"Beauty takes time, sweetie. I changed the color of my toenails while they were finishing my new do. What do you think?" A mass of stiff blond hair, defying gravity, swept upward like a cresting wave from the back of her head, culminating in a cascade of frozen curls suspended ten inches above her forehead.

"*Muy bonita, como siempre*," Orlando said. "Did you hear what I say? They lock all the doors soon."

"Give me the rundown."

Orlando explained about the locked door, the mummy—as the receptionist had informed him—lying under a white sheet on a steel table in the laboratory. "Two people have keys besides a guard, who leaves when they close—" another glance at his watch, "in ten minutes. A scientist, who goes away hours ago, and the director, who works now in his office, halfway down the hallway. There." He pointed. "All others will leave soon."

"So, all we have to do is get into this laboratory, snatch dear dried-up Shickie, leave by the back door, and drop him off anonymously at the police station. The cops have my missing person report, will ID him like they should have done the day those Boy Scouts found him. A proper death certificate will convince the insurance company to pay me, the poor grieving wife, what I so justly deserve. Easy."

"Always easy, you think. But how do we get into the back, alone, in ten minutes?"

Rita Rae tippy-tapped her fingertips on her chin. "You hide out in the john until everyone leaves. I'll sweet talk this director out of a key, keep him busy past closing, pass the key to you, and you take my Shickie out the back to our car."

"Perhaps."

"No perhaps about it. What's he like, this director?"

"Knows only the buttonhooks. Baggy suit, many years out of style. Yellow teeth. Probably has breath like rotting meat. Ancient and ugly, like the *vampiros* who come out at night and suck blood from virgins."

Rita Rae made a face. "Yuck." She straightened her short leather skirt, ran a hand over her tall, shellacked hair, and checked her lipstick in a compact mirror. "What do you think?"

"I think you are safe, at least from the virgin blood sucking."

"Very cute. Get your ass in the john. Come to his office at five forty-five, sharp." She held her watch up for him to synchronize with his. "I'll hold his attention, toss you the keys. You unlock and shim the door to the laboratory, return the keys to me, and leave through the back with my poor husband in your arms. Shouldn't take more than two or three minutes. I'll say my goodbyes and go out the front, meet you at the car. How's that?"

"If that does not work, I have a plan B, *oiste?*" A long switchblade materialized in Orlando's hand.

"No. This has to be clean. My Shickie disappears, turns up at the police station. Period."

Orlando shrugged and pocketed the knife. At the "ten minutes to closing" speaker announcement, he retired to a stall in the men's room. Rita Rae remained in the cafeteria, checked the corridor, and, seeing no one, walked quickly to the office of Horace Duckhaus. Before entering, she unfastened the top button of her silk blouse and studied her reflection in the glass of a framed shadowbox of French enameled buttonhooks. She winked at her looking-glass double, opened the office door and stepped inside.

At sight of Duckhaus, bent over a ledger like a ghoul over a graveyard snack, Rita Rae put a hand to her mouth and bit her thumb. Insurance, she said to herself. One million bucks. Margaritas in the sunshine. Orlando giving me foot rubs on the beach.

The director's desk was situated such that he faced not the doorway, but a window overlooking the parking lot. Without lifting his eyes from his figures, Duckhaus waved the air. "Private office. Museum's closing. Please leave by the front door."

Rita Rae took a deep breath for courage and moved to his side of the room. She sat on a corner of the desk and crossed her legs, exposing long tanned thighs. "I so–o–oh enjoyed your buttonhooks. And, I'll bet you're the man in charge of all this."

Duckhaus cleared his throat, rolled his chair back a foot, and raised his chin. He focused on Rita Rae's face, trying not to stare at the bare legs, the bobbing calf, the cut-away red pumps. "May I . . . uh . . . help you?"

"I do hope so. I'm a high school teacher—history. What a won–der–ful collection."

"Yes, we do try to—"

"The director himself. Like some big corporate CEO or the President, huh? How does it feel to have all that power? To hire and fire people, sign paychecks, have them call you Sir?"

"I really don't think about—"

A burly guard appeared at the opened door. "Closing, sir. Ginnie's the last and she's about to go. One last check of the cafeteria and the restrooms, and I'll lock the front door on the way out. Mr. Scopes went into town, may not be back. You'll turn on the alarm?"

Rita Rae stiffened at the reference to the restrooms. Several puffy scars above the guard's eyebrows and the trace of a black eye suggested, while not so swift, he might be a brawler. He carried a metal nightstick.

Duckhaus swiveled to see the guard. "Yes, of course, Clarence. This young woman was just leaving."

Rita Rae rubbed the locket at her neck, raised it to her lips and gave it the tiniest of smooches. She batted her eyelashes. "Oh, pul–eeze?" With her back to the guard, she leaned far enough forward to reveal a braless cleavage. She rocked her shoulders rhythmically, letting gravity do its work. "I so hoped to ask you a few questions about buttonhooks."

Duckhaus blinked at the orbs of flesh swaying two feet from his face. "Well, I suppose. Uh-hum." he cleared his throat again, quite audibly. "I'll show her out, Clarence. We'll see you tomorrow. Enjoy your evening."

"You, too, sir." The guard put enough emphasis on the "too" to make Duckhaus blush. He backed out of the doorway.

Rita Rae listened to the receding footsteps, hoping the guard and Orlando would not have the misfortune of meeting.

She scanned the desk for keys, maintaining dialogue. "He called you 'Sir' twice." She lowered a hand to the director's arm, scratched idly with long red nails at his rumpled suit coat sleeve, and said, "I'm Maria. Power makes me go squishy."

Duckhaus stared at his arm as if it had gone to stone. "I . . . uh . . . what exactly is it you wanted?"

"Buttonhooks, huh?" She undid another button, the one over her solar plexus. "Like, why would you need a hook on a handle to do what fingers can do themselves?" She scooted from the corner of the desk, brushed aside Duckhaus's ledger and took its place. Ever so lightly, she lifted the director's wrist, positioned it so his fingertips brushed a mother of pearl button.

Duckhaus's forefinger twitched but didn't move. He stammered, "Um, you see, in the nineteenth century, shoes and, uh—"

"Go ahead," she said, "see if fingers don't have more fun in person."

He craned his head toward the hallway to listen, no doubt, for the receding steps of the guard.

Rita Rae fanned her face. "My, it's warm in here. What's a girl got to do to cool off?"

Duckhaus's mouth opened, his pale tongue swiped his upper lip. He swallowed and blinked three times, fast. At first slowly, and then in a rush, his thumb and first two fingers loosened the button.

Rita Rae undid the last button herself. She lifted a gold locket dangling in her cleavage, slung it behind her neck, free of the action to come, and guided Duckhaus's hand to her bare right breast. His fingers closed spasmodically. Rita Rae put a hand on his shoulder, leaned toward him, and moaned.

Duckhaus's other hand moved on its own to her left breast. He nudged open the draped silk with an outward extension of his forearms and stared.

"They won't break, honey," she said, keeping a watch over the director's bald head at the empty doorway.

Duckhaus first fondled and then kneaded her breasts like cookie dough.

Rita Rae's spine went pole straight at a distance-muffled *thump* somewhere toward the front of the museum. The cartilage in her ears stiffened, but the single thump was all she heard.

Duckhaus apparently missed the noise, but froze at her movement. "Did I hurt you?"

"Oh, no, baby. You've got the magic touch."

After another thirty seconds of melon squeezing with no sign of either the guard or Orlando, Rita Rae tapped Duckhaus on the top of his head. "Boy, oh, boy," she said, "that sure got me hot. Turnabout's fair play."

She slipped from the desk to the floor, scooted under the desk, watching the doorway from between the director's legs—

where the hell was Orlando? She ran a hand up Duckhaus's thigh and loosened his belt.

Duckhaus leaned back, chin raised, eyes shut. His knees parted.

Rita Rae undid his trouser button. While her left hand unzipped his fly, her more active right explored his left suit coat and pants pockets for keys.

She found nothing in his left-side pockets, so her hands switched roles: the left patted clothing, the right slipped into the open fly of his boxers, closed over a weak erection, and squeezed.

"Oh, you are a big one."

Duckaus shuddered. His breathing went ragged. He tried to push his shorts and trousers down but Rita Rae slapped his hand away. Obediently, his arms dropped to his side. His hips rolled in time with Rita Rae's now stroking half fist. "That's it, Mr. Big," she said as her left hand, at last, felt the elusive keys through fabric at his bony thigh. The angle, however, foiled repeated attempts to access the pocket. She shifted position, muttered a frustrated "Damn!"

"Damn!" Duckhaus echoed. "Damn! Damn! Damn!" His hips bucked with each stroke of Rita Rae's hand, jangling keys marking tempo.

"What the hell's that noise?" she said from between his legs.

Duckhaus's eyes opened. "Huh? What? Oh . . . keys. Coins. In my pocket—nothing."

Her hand went still.

"Don't stop."

"It sounds like the goddamned Salvation Army shaking a tambourine over my head. Take them out."

Duckhaus retrieved two paper clips, a key ring with five keys, and seventy-six cents in change. He slapped it all on the desk. Coins rolled onto the floor. "There. Do it . . . faster."

At the sound of extricated metal banging mahogany somewhere over her head, Rita Rae shifted position to move topside. She lost balance on the way up, lurched, and the crest of her bouffant do crunched against the underside of the desk. "Oh, screw!" she said.

"Yes, that's it—*screw* me!" Duckhaus said.

She answered without thinking. "Go screw yourself."

She caught herself, said, "What kind of a girl do you think I am?" and wriggled out from under the desk.

She stood at his side, said, "Pull your pants up and zip your zipper."

"Up? Please . . . I'm sorry. I didn't mean to—" Blushing furiously, he avoided her gaze.

"You wouldn't want me to get pregnant, would you?"

"Good God, no." Duckhaus fumbled with his trousers. "I'm sorry. I don't have a, uh, prophylactic."

"I'm a virgin," Rita Rae explained. "I took an oath with my students. Abstinence till marriage. It's the only way to go."

"I didn't know. . . ."

"I hope you can respect that."

"Of course." Duckhaus complied, tucked his waning semi-erection into his shorts, and re-zipped his fly.

"Good," Rita Rae said. "But that doesn't mean I can't enjoy myself." She hiked her skirt to her waist. Panties still in place, she straddled him in the armless chair, wrapped her arms around his neck, and began a slow bump and grind lap dance, cotton to polyester.

Duckhaus groaned. "Yes. Yes. Yes."

She arched her back, stretched her arms, one palm on the desk, the other crab-skittering across the top, searching. Leaning backward, she said to the ceiling tile, "Lord, forgive me, I can't resist powerful men."

At last, her fingers caressed keys.

The light in the hallway flickered as an approaching shadow lengthened along the far wall. Rita Rae leaned forward and waggled her breasts to occupy Duckhaus while keeping a watch over his hairless, bobbing head. The director had become quite vocal. "Ugh, Ugh, Ugh . . ."

The shadow looked too massive for Orlando. Rita Rae

blew a strand of hair from her face. "If it's that damned guard and I did this for noth—"

Orlando peered around the corner.

Rita Rae said, "Thank God!" aloud.

Duckhaus eyes opened. "Did you . . . you know?"

"That was the fourth time, baby. Let's go for five."

"Ohhhhh, yesss. Although, I'm, uh . . . not there yet . . . my age . . . but . . . I'm sure with just a little more . . ."

Orlando stood in the doorway. At the sight of Rita Rae's pelvic jitterbug, he slapped a hand over his eyes. A moment later, his fingers spread for a better look. He made bug-eyes.

She winged the keys at him.

He snatched them inches from his face and disappeared.

A minute, Rita Rae decided, should be enough for him to unlock the hallway door, find the mummy, shim the door, and return the keys. Another minute to exit with the goods: a hundred and twenty more seconds of hard labor. She checked her watch, but without her glasses, couldn't read the thin second hand. So she counted: a thousand and one, a thousand and two . . . grinding her hips against the director's bony groin in time with the count.

At forty-five, she moaned. "Oh, baby, don't stop. Don't stop."

Eyes closed, Duckhaus nodded, got a firmer grip on her thighs to increase friction, and began a more expressive chant, "Pussy! Pussy! Pussy!"

Rolling her eyes, Rita Rae answered, "MEE–OW."

Twenty seconds later Orlando reappeared with a thumbs-up. He slipped into the office, slid the keys across the desk to Rita Rae, and left to complete his mission.

Orlando moved directly to the sheet-shrouded bundle on the steel table at the center of the room, exactly where the receptionist had described it. He found a roll of Scotch tape, criss-crossed the fabric to keep it in place, scooped the bound package in his arms, and, noting how light it was, hurried to the exit.

Following a quick survey of the lot outside—no observers—he bounded across the asphalt to Rita Rae's car. Before the museum's steel door slammed shut, however, he heard the director's voice rise to a shout: "Yes! Yes! YES!" followed by a feral scream and consummate silence.

42

hickie passed a newsstand when he landed in Knoxville and saw—Ohmigosh—his name, on a tabloid. He nearly toppled as he spun for a better view. He read, "Prince of Light lifted to heaven, returns as mummy. The Reverend Shickleton Doone . . ."

He slapped coins on the counter, noticed the cashier giving him a long, Aren't you somebody? look. He placed his hand over the article and scuttled away, head down, feigning nonchalance. At a secluded bench he held the article at arm's length—damned eyesight wasn't what it used to be—and stared incredulously at the text, at a small reproduction of his publicity portrait, and at another photo: the mummy his ma had referred to. He couldn't read the fine print or make out details, but the resemblance, though fuzzy, was striking. The long hair, the nose. If this isn't me—Shickie slapped his face to be sure—and if it isn't a colossal joke—it could be Fenster. Curled up. Eyes closed, kind of puckery. Not a stitch on him. No wonder Ma was so wrought-up.

Shickie patted his pocket for his reading glasses for a magnified view, and realized Fenster must have stolen those, too. Another clandestine trip to the newsstand for over-the-counter specs, more stares by patrons, a more secluded bench, and he studied the photo.

He noticed the warts on the mummy's eyebrow and nose. "Sheesh. It *is* Fenster." His stomach bottomed out. What had the little peckerwood done to get himself dried out like that?

He regarded a second photo of a pile of clothing and recognized his own belt with the silver horseshoe buckle. He read, "'His clothes dropped to the floor when God took him,' said Miss Ginger Rodgers, one of the Children of Light, who witnessed the Rapture." There was a photo of her, too. Fine looking girl, a blonde, built, lots of hair blowing in the wind. Wholesome, like some rosy-cheeked Swiss milkmaid on a chocolate label. She'd look right at home standing in a flowered meadow, black and white spotted cows on steep hillsides behind her, the Matterhorn in the distance.

Ginger Rodgers? Familiar . . . Sure. Choir member, joined a couple of weeks ago. He had noticed all right—how could a man miss something like that?—but he hadn't had an opportunity to speak with her. According to the article this Ginger *saw* him raptured: "Poof! Gone to heaven, just like the Prince promised." What the hell was going on?

He picked up more pubs. The Rapture story had even made *People*. He learned how Creely Patch—that tight-assed fool—had taken over his Fireflies already, how he was demanding the return of the mummy from a museum for a shrine at the Temple of Light, how the Indians had staked a claim, too. Shickie chuckled. The closest Fenster had ever been to the Indians was Aunt Lou's house in Cleveland. The historical museum in Pigeon Forge claimed the mummy was of European descent. Well, if it was Fenster, they were right-on about that.

Was it possible? Naked in a cave? The more Shickie read, the more he concluded if this was one of Fenster's scams, it had gone horribly wrong. More likely, either Thadeus Trout, mistaking him for Shickie, had the Hammer do him in. Or, Rita Rae had it done for the life insurance. Or, because she had discovered the phony ring. Ouch!

What a temper. That gold, heart-shaped locket hanging

over the broken heart tattoo at the base of her neck? More than once she told him it contained the dried up tip of an ex-lover's penis. "The bastard did me wrong," was all she would say, smiling wickedly, lifting the locket to her lips. Shickie shivered.

He considered the words: *dried up*. Poor Fenster.

How had they done it? Staked him out in the sun? Baked him in a pizza oven? Hog-tied him under a haystack of those "Don't eat" silica gel packets they put in electronics boxes?

Shickie concluded he had best sneak into Gatlinburg, pick up his stash, and split.

"When, Lord? When will you take me, your Messenger?" Creely Patch, on his knees in the Prince's office, perspiring furiously, clasped his hands tightly below his chin. "Surely I deserved the Rapture more than—what Lord?" He cocked his head, listening. "What about miracles? That would do it, wouldn't it? Give me the power, like you gave Doone." Listening. "I see . . . recover the sacred relic You dropped to earth to draw the multitudes. And, then . . . miracles!

"I delight to do thy will."

A knock on the door ended the conversation. Patch mumbled an apology to God for the interruption and set a hand on the edge of the desk to leverage himself up. He wheeled to the noise. "Who is it?"

"You all right in there, sir?" It was Goliath Jones. "I heard talking."

"Not merely all right, but inspired," Patch said. "Come in, Goliath." He motioned for him to take a seat in a high-backed Gothic chair with a red cushioned seat, spoils, unbeknownst to Patch, from one of the Prince's poker games with a Knoxville antiques dealer.

"Is it time? Should I get my people ready? Take them to the roof?"

"Umm . . . not yet. Goliath, the Lord sent you and your clan to be my strong right arm. It is time to exercise that strength, recover the sacred relic of the Prince."

"Get him back, huh? And then, the Rapture?"

"Yes. Soon. I want every available member of the congregation on the bus by eight A.M. We shall shake the foundations of that heathen museum as Joshua smote Jericho, storm the doors the moment they unlock them."

Goliath slammed a fist into his open palm. "We'll be ready. And, sir?"

"Yes? You have a suggestion?"

"Little Billie Mike plays the bugle."

"Excellent. He can lead the charge."

Rita Rae twisted the rearview mirror to check her face. "Yucky." She rubbed streaked makeup with a wad of Kleenex, speaking to Orlando from the side of her mouth. "What took you so damned long to get to the office?"

He squealed onto the highway. "You think I wait on purpose? I am counting tiles, reading the walls of the *baño* while the guard he is looking for—*¿Como se dice?*—*huérfanos.* Orphanos."

"Orphans?"

"*Sí,* the *turistas* left behind at the close. Finally, he enters the *baño,* taps on one door and then another with his nightstick. I am standing on seat, waiting with my knife—perhaps breathing too big, because my gold chains make a slight music at my chest—like this." He demonstrated. "The guard stops, pushes the door open slowly and looks in. Somehow the door, it closes fast—bang!—into his forehead. When he wakes, I think this guard is more careful next time he has business in that *baño.*"

"While you were banging doors, I was—"

"Banging *el viejo maricón,*" Orlando said, and shuddered. "*¡Qué feo! Mi pobrecita guajira,* how you suffer for me. But, *no te preocupas, mi vida.* Tonight you will be with a real man, *oiste?* You will dance a little mambo with the handsome *pinga* of Orlando."

"My panties were ruined—I left them in that potted plant

by the front door." Rita Rae flipped the Kleenex out the window and cocked an eyebrow at him. "It's not like I kissed him on the mouth, you know." She re-buttoned her blouse, tucked it into her skirt. "Rats—look at this. A big wet spot on my leather mini. So much for a dry hump."

"Not so dry from what I see."

"It wasn't *me*."

"If you say so, but, please, take a long shower when we get home."

"Listen . . ." She forgot what she was about to say, suddenly pivoted to look at the back seat. "Where is he? My Shickie? In the trunk?"

"Wrapped in a white sheet. I find him waiting for me wrapped like *un regalo*—a gift."

"Perfect. We'll dump him at the police station as soon as it gets dark, read about it in the papers tomorrow if I don't get a 'Better sit down, ma'am,' house call first."

She dabbed at the corner of an eye. "I'd better practice my sad face." The sad face went happy. "Oh, baby, we are going to lead such a life. The Caribbean, the Riviera. A million dollars!"

Junior grinned as the boys left Poncho's. "I told Daddy how we snatched Doone out from under the nose of the Hammer. He said he was really proud of me. You guys, too. Shee–it, that must be one pissed off greaser about now."

"To say nothing of how confused the old guy will be when he finds Peaches's blow-up lady in his trunk," Six-pack added.

"Her name's Angelina," Peaches muttered. "I wonder what he'll do to her?"

Six-pack sniggered. "Hose her down before he slips it to her, if he's got any brains."

"Listen," Peaches said, "you don't get a girl like her knocked up, and you don't get crabs or the clap or none of that other stuff neither. You never seen me scratching my balls like you do."

"I do not scratch my balls," said Six-pack.

"Do so."

"Do not."

Junior settled it: "All men scratch their balls." He gave Peaches a questioning squint. "You sure the Hammer didn't see us?"

"No way. He was making moves on the girl at the desk the whole time. Didn't get nowhere, neither. Held her hand is all. That Hammer is a total screw-up."

They wove through parked cars, approached Peaches's Monte Carlo. Six-pack stopped in his tracks and pointed to the sprung trunk. "Oh, nooo!"

Peaches ran to the rear end. "My trunk!"

Junior shouldered him aside, lifted the lid. "Gone."

Six-pack shook his fist at Peaches. "So much for the Hammer being a screw-up. He let us do all the work, followed us, and got what he wanted, no sweat."

Junior slammed the lid. With the broken catch, it flew open, nearly taking his chin off. He gave it a withering look and kicked the bumper.

"What'll I tell Daddy, now?"

43

Jimmy whistled as he drove the van from Poncho's to the Bible Alive Museum. He planned to deliver the souvenirs to the gift shop and stow the mummy in one of the empty, under-construction exhibit rooms until his shift ended. Before the sun set, the mummy would rest forever in ancestral ground. The inquiring phone messages his Grandpop had fielded from mainstream Native American groups would go unanswered, Ginger's Fireflies could raise all the hell they wanted, and the scientists could gnash their teeth till they ground them to nubs.

Maury stopped at a gas station in Gatlinburg to refuel before dropping off Doone's dried-up body at Thadeus Trout's. He decided to spend one more night in Tennessee—he didn't like to drive at night—and return to Cincinnati the next day. He would be sipping Manhattans at Cora's Cozy Cove by happy hour.

"Life is grand," he said to a puzzled man in Bermuda shorts and argyle socks at the adjoining pump, and then, "Oops!" to himself as his shaking hand misaligned the nozzle. He barely missed spritzing gasoline on his shiny loafers.

Two minutes later, he cranked the ignition—and shut it off, deciding he had better check out the mummy. In case skeptical Thadeus Trout had any pointed questions about it, he should be able to answer. He backed between a tow truck and a rusty Dodge at the side of the garage and released the trunk lid.

He tugged gently at the unyielding tape binding the sheet-wrapped bundle. "Distasteful business," he muttered. Making corpses was one thing, having to look at them, entirely another. He yanked harder, ripping loose a fold of the sheet, exposing—

"Oy! What's this?"

It looked like a breast. Maury pulled the tape. "Gevalt!" he said at the sight of what was clearly not mummified flesh, but air-filled plastic.

A beach ball with breasts?

Those no-goodnik boys. Their idea of a prank. No wonder, with all the smirking at the bar. To think, I gave money to that pisher and the big golem that follows him like a shadow. My mummy, I'll bet, they left on some park bench to rile the tourists.

Furious, Maury gripped the pornographic beach ball by what he thought might be an ankle, and flung it over the top of his Town Car toward the street. It bounced off the sunburned back of a fat woman with a fuchsia tank top. She screamed. Without hesitation, her husband swatted the head of the tallest of their four children, warning him never, *ever* to do that to his mother again. The plastic ball rolled into traffic, under the wheels of a lavender van with *Bible Alive Museum: You read it, now live it!* in gold script across the side.

The van's brakes squealed. Too late. The sphere exploded beneath its wheels.

Maury ignored the hubbub in the street and slid behind the wheel of his Lincoln, still seething. He checked the clip in the Colt under his armpit and returned to Poncho the 'irates. As he feared, the three boys were gone. There would be no furtive drive-by at Thadeus Trout's today, no payoff, no Manhattans at Cora's tomorrow.

Maury took a seat at the bar to dull his anger with a drink. Or two, or three.

Jimmy saw it—whatever it was—out of the corner of his eye: fat and pink, running straight for his right front wheel. He hit the brakes, hard. The van skidded six feet.

KWOP!

He flew out and dropped on hands and knees to see the remains of the unfortunate creature he had hit.

The flattened mass of plastic brought a smile to his face. All he needed was an accident and another nosy cop like the one who had escorted him and his liberated ancestor to that damned museum five days ago. He rubbed the lucky penny hanging at his chest and climbed back into the van.

He heard an angry curse on the sidewalk and watched a rangy man beside a corpulent woman shake an adolescent boy by the arm: the kid, no doubt, who had thrown—whatever it was—into Jimmy's path. "Serves you right!" Jimmy shouted at the kid.

Back at the wheel, he noticed the dash clock. His supervisor would be spouting steam over how long he had taken. Jimmy wove through traffic, found the museum lot crowded with cars and three large buses, the Charlotte Graceland tours. He parked the van between the first and second buses, as close as he could get to the museum's rear door, flicked on the hazard flashers, and rushed to the gift shop with the boxes of souvenirs.

His supervisor was dancing behind the counter, taking money, bagging purchases. "What took you so long?" he said without looking up. "Help Sally unpack those boxes."

"Yessir."

"When you're finished, I want to you drive to our ware-house in town—here in Gatlinburg—you know it?"

"Yessir."

"We're running low on forbidden fruit. This tour's loading up on it like it's going out of style. Warehouse guy has half a dozen crates ready for you."

"Yessir."

"Shouldn't take—"

The radio at the super's waist crackled. He snatched it from his belt, put it to his ear. "Oh, crap! Jimmy?"

"Yessir?"

"Boys from that Lambs of God youth group are throwing pennies at the aardvark. Get your butt over to Noah's Ark pronto. All's I need is some kid's pecker bit off."

"I'll need to move the van first, it's—"

The supervisor's cell phone buzzed. "Just great. Yes, dear. Right away, dear." He holstered the phone, gave Jimmy an anxious look tinged with anger.

"Little bastard threw a firecracker down the toilet. My car's still in the shop. Gimme the van keys. I'll pick up the fruit on the way back. If we run out, we run out." He extended his palm.

"I left my slingshot in the van," Jimmy said. "Let me grab it first and—"

"Later. Ark. ASAP. Keys, mister. I've got a flooded house, and we're leaving tonight on vacation. You can get your slingshot later."

Jimmy handed them to him, cast a worried eye at the van outside, and withdrew from the gift shop to save the aardvark from the Lambs of God.

On the way to the Ark, he said a silent prayer of thanks that he had had the foresight to hide the mummy safely in a tarp-covered corrugated box at the back of the van. The only problem now was, he would have to wait for the supervisor to return. He would be lucky to get his ancestor home by dark, let alone in the ground.

The airport rent-a-car people refused to rent Shickie wheels without a driver's license or credit card, so he took a cab into Knoxville. Five hundred of his five thousand casino dollars bought him an on-its-last-legs Chevy pickup from a seedy lot on the seamy side of town, no questions asked.

After walking his fingers through the Yellow Pages, he

drove to a costume shop for a disguise. "Little joke—want to fool some friends at the office," he explained. "No, not a clown," he said to the first suggestion.

"The chicken suit is always fun. Check out the feet."

"Nuh-uh."

"Everyone loves this one. Look, when I put the teeth in."

"Real scary. Nice cape, too, but Dracula's not right, either."

No Clark Gable, no Bill Clinton, no Goofy, no Billy Graham. "No one famous. No masks. Want to look like somebody different, see?"

He finally settled on an Amish farmer. The chin-rimming blond beard and wire-rimmed, amber-tinted glasses came from a display case, the costume from the used clothing bin: worn and baggy, black gabardine trousers with a button fly, suspenders, no belt, a faded blue work shirt, and laced-to-the-ankles, black brogans, topped off with a round-top straw hat. He added a few more shirts and a pair of overalls, concluding the latter might not be regulation garb, but who in Gatlinburg would know the difference? He topped it off, literally, with a blond, Dutch-boy wig. "Real hair," the clerk said. "Been gathering dust for a year, give you a deal on it."

Before leaving Knoxville, he stopped at a magic store and replenished the bag of tricks that had served him so well in the past. A man with a bounty on his head might have use for a miracle or two. On the drive to Gatlinburg, he practiced raising his voice half an octave and speaking with the German accent he had used as The Amazing Schwartz in his old magic act. It would never pass muster with the Amish, but Shickie didn't expect to run into many Amish in East Tennessee.

His first stop was the town watering hole, Poncho the 'irate's, to see who knew what about a certain mummy.

44

Horace Duckhaus, alone in the museum, sat head back, staring at the ceiling, whispering "Maria, Maria." Had it been a dream? The incredibly bold high school teacher in the high blond hair who had stormed into his office unannounced and . . . jumped on him like a wildcat in heat.

He summoned dim memories of sex with his wife Ruth—how long had it been, now, eight years? But relations—they never said the word "sex"—with Ruth had always been shrouded in darkness and embarrassment. Furtive, silent, infrequent.

Duckhaus lay a file folder over the face-down framed photo of Ruth. "I know I'm no movie star," he said to the ceiling, "but . . ."

"Power," was the word Maria had used. Yes, that was it: the biological imperative, the female of the species drawn to the dominant male. After all, he concluded, I do hold the lives of six employees in my hand, as well as the safety of the third largest collection of buttonhooks south of the Ohio and east of the Mississippi rivers.

I'll bet she's a collector. And I don't know her last name. Will she return? Is she smitten or was this just a groupie conquest?

He jolted upright at a rap on his office window, nearly tumbled from his chair. Someone was outside, mouthing words muffled by the heavy, wire-laced glass. One of those damnable protestors? No, a man in a suit and tie, with neatly trimmed hair. Looked sane enough.

Duckhaus rose. He nodded, indicated the windows wouldn't open, that he would meet the man up front. He hurried to the entrance and peered though the thick glass doors. The man in the suit was alone. Duckhaus unlocked the door, opened it six inches, put his foot at the bottom to keep it that way, and said, "Yes? What is it?"

The man said, "I found a mummy in a box. I was wondering if it might belong to you."

Maury entered Poncho's and took a seat two stools down from an odd-looking farmer in an old-fashioned, chin-rimming beard, wire-rimmed sunglasses, a round top straw hat. Blond hair cut straight across the bottom hung to within two inches of his shoulders. Determined not to let the no-goodnik boys' costly prank get him down, Maury nodded and said, "Such a hot spell we're having, hmmm?" Maybe conversation would take his mind off the unfulfilled contract.

"Hotter zan you know, frent," the farmer said, with an accent Maury couldn't quite place. Dutch?

"I'll bet you're a long way from home. Holland?"

"Indiana," said the farmer. "I'm Amish."

"Really? What brings you to Gatlinburg? Not the alpine cable ride, I'll bet." Despite his funk, Maury chuckled at his little joke.

"Wife and kids. We come to see the Great Smoky Mountains." The man said it: "Vife undt kids. Ve kom to zee dee Great Schmoky Montans."

"You drove? Machines, I thought were forboten for you folks."

"Uh . . . we have a driver. Small school bus. It's a vacation, see?"

Maury imagined their school bus backing up traffic for miles on the curvy one-lane roads of the national park, nineteen whining children deserving to be thrown to the bears. Mention of a wife made him think of Rose, the betrayer. He scowled, quickly forced that thought from his mind and extended a hand. "Me, they call Maury. And you are?"

"Enos Schwartz."

They shook hands. The farmer, Maury noted, had surprisingly soft skin for a man driving mules or shucking corn, the sort of things farmers did.

The Amish fellow said to the bartender, "I'll have a beer."

"They allow you to drink?" Maury asked. "In bars?"

"Uh, sure. We pray more when we're on vacation, balances out the transgressions."

"That makes sense. You fish, too? They have some fine trout here, I'm told."

The bartender wearing a broad, horizontally striped tee shirt, a red bandana around his head, and a phony green parrot perched on top, slid a cold one to the farmer. "Trout?" he said. He tugged at a thick gold earring and glanced both ways. "If you talking about our Mr. Trout, I'd suggest you watch your step."

The farmer shifted uncomfortably on his barstool. "Mr. Trout?"

Maury repeated it, "Mr. Trout?"

"Local bigwig." The bartender cupped air to draw Maury and the farmer close. "Owns the Bible Alive Museum up the hill—that big pyramid, runs for a block?—Mr. T's Fudge Shoppe across the road, a food processing plant, lots of stuff. He's also known to make loans to people—you know, the no collateral, high interest, on the sly kind." He glanced left and right. "This guy was here yesterday, had a smashed hand, all bandaged up, in a lot of pain. My buddy said he was late with his payments and this Mr. Trout had his men hold the guy's hand over a cement block and he dropped a *bowling ball* on it. I shit you not."

The farmer took a gulp of beer.

"Tough customer, this Trout, I should say," Maury said.

The bartender lowered his voice, said, "Rumor has it, he's, you know . . ." he made a gun with thumb and forefinger, "had people shot. Has this hit man who shoots pieces off of 'em for the fun of it before he gives them the coop dee grass."

The Amish farmer toppled his beer bottle. It rolled three feet along the mahogany, spouting foam. The bartender righted it, held it to the light, saw no more than two inches of beer remaining. He sopped up the spilled liquid with a bar rag and set the bottle behind the bar. "I'll get you another one, sir," he said. "Sorry. I oughta keep my mouth shut about stuff like that. You Quakers are, like, pacifists, right? No TV or movies, probably never heard of that kind of thing." He gave the farmer a mollifying smile. "Don't worry—Gatlinburg is as safe a place as you'll find."

The farmer took a deep draught of his new beer, looking not at all relieved.

"Fine little town," Maury added. He cocked his head at the bartender. "This Bible museum you mentioned. That's in front of that church with the angel blimp, run by, what's his name, that Doone fellow?"

The farmer's new bottle bonked the bar top. He had nearly tipped that one, as well. Apparently, the man was unaccustomed to alcohol. "Zorry," he muttered.

A new patron entered, a trim young man of about thirty with shoulder-length black hair and a golden tan. He took a stool on the other side of the Amish farmer. Heads turned, as he was wearing only a loose, pink rayon blouse with purple piping along the edge, a kilt of the same fabric, and sandals with crisscrossed leather laces up his calves. To the bartender, he said, "Beer, Carlos. I need one bad."

Maury raised an eyebrow. It was the same faygeleh he had seen when he met those damned boys. Still wearing the same sissy outfit. Maury blew out a disgusted breath—not because of the young man in the skirt, but at the thought of the no-goodnik trio. And I bought them drinks, struck up a conversation. Such a fool I am.

"Here you go, Jimmy." The bartender set a Bud before the newcomer.

The bartender and the faygeleh are friends, Maury observed. Other than the skin-tight tee shirt, the ring in his ear, and the Carmen Miranda headgear, the bartender looks straight enough, but . . . he glanced around the establishment, wondering for a moment whether Poncho's might be a gay bar on off-hours. The Amish chap certainly wouldn't know the difference. For an even briefer moment, Maury wondered whether those no-goodnik boys—he met them, here, after all—might be light in their boots, too. The big one, the golem, was all pumped up, wore a see-though fishnet muscle shirt, the pudgy one had a baby doll-like quality about him. The skinny one in his leather. And, all that hugging.

No. Maury concluded the unequivocally uncouth boys were well outside the parameters of gayhood, and the young man in the skirt, considering the other folks in Poncho's, was the odd man out, so-to-speak.

"Doone?" the bartender was saying. "They say Doone got raptured—you know, God took him up, kept his soul, and then dropped him back to earth all dried up. A mummy, like. This museum in Pigeon Forge has him."

"It's not Doone," said the faygeleh.

"Oh?" said Maury.

"Oh?" said the Amish farmer.

"And, the museum doesn't have him any more."

"No," Maury said, with a sigh.

"No?" said the Amish farmer.

"The mummy is an Indian," said the faygeleh. "An ancient burial."

"Jimmy's an Indian, too," the bartender interjected.

A faygeleh Indian, Maury said to himself. Like one of the Village People.

"Where is he, this mummy, whatever he is?" the Amish farmer asked.

"Come to think of it," Maury said to Jimmy, the faygeleh Indian, "how do you know the museum doesn't have him? Do those boys have him? The big muscle-bound one, the skinny one with the little head, and the fat one?"

"The atheists?" Jimmy said.

"They're atheists? You know them? You're buddies?"

"Who?" the Amish farmer was asking. "Who?"

"We're not buddies, and I don't see how they could have him," Jimmy said. "They attacked Ginger and I saved her. That's all I know about them."

"Ginger? Ginger *Rodgers?*" Maury said. "You know Ginger Rodgers?"

"Ginger Rodgers," the Amish farmer repeated. "The Firefly?"

Jimmy nodded. "That's right, Ginger Rodgers. You two know her, too?"

"Ginger is Jimmy's girlfriend," said the bartender.

"She's just a friend," Jimmy said.

Just a friend. That, I can believe, Maury said to himself. To the faygeleh Indian he said, "Let an old man offer advice. If you are considering bringing a woman into your life . . . beware. She will betray you. Give one your heart and, sooner or later, hamburger she will make out of it. It goes back to the caveman days, I am guessing. The man provides. The woman roasts and chops. It's their nature."

"I'll toast to that," said the Amish farmer.

"Thank you for the counsel, sir," Jimmy said. "I'll bear that in mind."

"Wait a minute," the Amish farmer was saying, "A minute ago, you were talking about Doone. The mummy. Where is he?"

Jimmy shrugged and downed a third of his beer. "He appears and he disappears," he said, sounding like a man who had lost his best friend. "Poof!" He took another long slug. "My boss dropped the van off and left for three days in the mountains. The box is empty." He drained the last of it and stared at the empty bottle. "I have no idea where he is now. None at all."

Meshuggah Indians, Maury muttered. A pity what alcohol does to them.

45

Horace Duckhaus's fond recollection of the night before was broken by footsteps coming from the laboratory. He quickly pushed the fresh, dozen-count box of prophylactics with reservoir ends to the back of his pencil drawer, and checked his wristwatch: 8:20 A.M. The doors would not open until ten, the regular staff never arrived before nine, so it must be Plato Scopes, no doubt disgruntled again from the speed of his pace.

The chief scientist burst into the office, no hellos: "My elephant! Somebody stole my elephant. It's that squirrelly janitor, cleaning here at night. He brings his kids with him. One of those shifty little—"

"Whoa. Elephant?"

Scopes paced, clearly upset. "A stuffed pink elephant about," he held his hands apart, "this big. For the mummy diorama. I found just the right shade of brown shoe dye in town and a perfect set of tusks and—"

For a mere moment, the irritating and physically uninspiring Plato Scopes was supplanted in the director's mind by an apparition of bare-breasted Maria.

He blinked, saw not Maria, but Scopes, ranting about a toy elephant.

The thought of Plato Scopes in even fleeting sexual proximity to the torrid Maria was highly disconcerting. "Sit down, for God's sake," Duckhaus said, "you're making me nervous."

Scopes sat. "One of that janitor's thieving kids—"

"Otis," Duckhaus spoke with deliberate calm, "has been with the museum for seventeen years. His family assists him. We pay nothing for the rest of his tribe and Otis works cheap. We have never had so much as a brass buttonhook disappear because of him. You probably misplaced your elephant. Instead of worrying about some worthless toy, you ought to show more concern for your precious mummy."

"My mummy? What about my mummy?"

"Your mummy walked out of here last night."

"WHAT?" Scopes ran from the office. Duckhaus heard the steel door to the laboratory open and clank shut.

Thirty seconds later the door sounded again, and Scopes came puffing back to the office. "The mummy is where I left it, but those damned kids fooled with the sheets."

Duckhaus corrected him: "The mummy is *back* where you left it, and I'm sure it wasn't Otis's kids who fooled with it. As usual, I was the last to leave yesterday. I trust the mummy was on that table when you left for town after Dr. Finklestein departed at—when was it—three-thirty?" At Scopes nod, he continued, "The guard checked the facilities and closed up at five-thirty. I remained—" Again, that discombobulating image of Maria and her jiggling breasts intruded. "Um, uh . . . until after six. Last evening, someone knocked at this window. It turned out to be the assistant manager of the Bible Alive Museum. *He* had your mummy and was kind enough to return it."

"What? How did he get it? Impossible."

"Nonetheless true. He found it in the rear of their museum van. Apparently it got there through a mixed-up delivery from either that souvenir warehouse on River Road, or from their produce supplier in Gatlinburg. We use both of them as well, so somehow, it got from here to one of those companies, and from there to the Bible Alive van—don't shake your head at me like that, young man. I carried the thing from his truck myself, re-wrapped it in one of your sheets, and put it back on that steel table in your lab."

"Impossible."

"But true. The laboratory doors were locked. No tampering, nothing else disturbed. This is the second time that mummy vanished and returned, almost miraculously, one might say—akin to the claims of those religious fanatics that this Doone fellow was raptured from the earth and—"

"You are a man of reason, please don't talk like that."

"Spooky, you must admit. Remember how it disappeared from that cave, from under your nose and the park service guards? Now, it's done it again. Poof! Gone, and come back.

"Scopes," Duckhaus jabbed a long bony finger at him, "I am feeling increasingly uneasy about this mummy. It has caused us nothing but trouble. These vanishing acts, the Indians, the religious fanatics, the medical examiner and the police inquiring about DNA testing, the newspaper and TV ghouls. I wonder if we wouldn't be wise to get rid of it."

"What? The scientific find of the century? This is our chance to put this miserable museum—"

"Miserable museum?"

"Poor choice of words—under-recognized museum—on the lips of the nation, of the scientific community, on TV . . . in *National Geographic*."

"Yes, and that worries me, too. Our mandate from Captain Horatio Hook, lest you forget, is the increase and diffusion of knowledge of the buttonhook and the golden age of buttonhooks. Not mummies."

"Sir, you can't possibly—"

Duckhaus rested his elbows on the desk and leaned forward, fingers steepled at the point of his chin. He gave Scopes a long icy stare. "No more mummy trouble. Do I make myself clear?"

"We'll hire another guard, install video cameras."

"We cannot afford another guard or cameras. Chain your mummy down, sleep by its side. Do what you will. I want . . . no . . . more . . . *mummy trouble* in the Captain Hook Museum." Duckhaus slammed both hands on the desktop for emphasis, crossed his arms, and glared.

Red of face, pinched of lip, Plato Scopes ground his teeth, dug his fingernails into the arms of the chair, exhaled the sour air in his lungs with a hiss, and forced himself to say, "Yes, sir. No more mummy trouble."

"Want some bran flakes?" Rita Rae held out the box.

Orlando curled his lip. "Bran flakes are for *maricónes*."

They were seated on the kitchen floor, since the dinette set, along with most of the furniture in the Doone house, save three mattresses, had been carted off and sold by Thadeus Trout.

"It keeps you regular."

"If you drink enough coffee, you do not have such problems." Orlando rose to his feet and clacked his cup on the counter. Frowning, he ran a hand down one pant leg and then the other in a futile attempt to smooth the fabric. "If this floor sitting continues, I will have to ship my linen trousers to Miami and wear polyester or denim like the locals."

"I'm trying to be civil, dammit." Rita Rae jumped up, threw the bowl of bran flakes against the wall. Milk spattered, a sodden brown mass slid toward the baseboard. She faced Orlando, hands on hips. "*When* are the cops going to call? You did drop him off didn't you? With the note?"

Orlando stepped forward, feeling charged by her display of temper. "*Sí*. When the night came, at the front door of the *policía*." He absently caressed Rita Rae's neck and shoulders, his mind wandering from the matter at hand. "The note I pin to the sheet, it say, 'This is the body of Shickie Doone.' Then I sign it, '*¡Abajo comunismo! ¡Libertad!*' They are *estúpidos* if they don't understand that."

Rita Rae shook off his advances. "If the note said 'Shickie Doone,' then why haven't they called or come by? They have the missing person report. They have my name and address and phone number. How can they be so *cruel?*"

The cereal bowl had come to rest near her right foot. She gave it an evil eye and booted it across the floor. The motion threw her off balance. Her left three-inch heel slid eight inches on the slick floor. She shrieked on the way down, landing with a thump and a *splaaat* in the spilt milk.

Orlando helped her up by the elbows, gripping them firmly enough to prevent her from throwing a punch. He leaned to kiss her neck, but she twisted away, hurling curses.

When she calmed down, Rita Rae backed away, jabbing the air with a finger as a warning for Orlando to keep his distance. She stripped off her mini, blotted it with towels on the counter, filled the sink with Woolite, and submerged the skirt to soak. "If the cops won't play fair," she said, "I'll call *them*. I can't stand the suspense."

"I am having the difficult time, also. Yes. Please call."

When she had dialed the number, Rita Rae held her breath and screwed up her face to force a mood. "Yes . . . police? I'm so worried . . ."

"Calm down, ma'am. What's the problem?"

"This is Mrs. Shickleton Doone." Sniff. Sniff. "My husband, the Reverend, went missing . . ." Sniffle. "I filed a report, but I haven't heard anything. Those Fireflies people claim the mummy at that museum in Pigeon Forge—"

"Sure. Read all about it. Raptured, they say. Dropped back to earth. Doone—that's your husband?"

"Yes, the Reverend Doone. I got an anonymous call. This muffled voice said, 'We dumped your husband's body at the police station last night.'"

"His body? Here? Last night?"

A dollop of anger warmed her response: "You *are* the cops, aren't you?"

"Ohhh . . . wait a minute." Apparently, a hand went over

the phone, as the background noise diminished. Rita Rae heard muffled voices, and then, "Your husband have a small build?"

"He's a little man. Yes."

"Has a long nose?"

"A long nose? I suppose he does."

"Pink complexion?"

"What's that supposed to mean? Caucasian? Yes, he was a white man. Do you have him?"

The hand went over the phone again and she heard several men laughing. The voice returned, tried to speak, barely got out, "Dry skin?" before sputtering and snorting.

Rita Rae put the phone to her chest, and spoke to Orlando, "They definitely have him, but something's not right."

With the phone at her ear, she next heard, barely audible, "Willis—Give me that phone. Poor woman's lost her husband. This isn't funny to her. Ma'am?" Louder, the phone in the new man's hand. "You're calling about the missing man, Shickleton Doone?"

"Yes. What the hell's going on there? Do you have my Shickie or not?"

"Ma'am, sometimes people wander away for their own reasons. Whatever's bothering them, they usually work it out and return. As far as the rumors about this mummy, the medical examiner is aware of it and I understand *National Geographic* will be doing tests to find out its age and so forth."

"But you have it, right?"

"Us?"

"You. This caller told me you had my Shickie, said he dropped him off there last night, wrapped in a sheet."

"Ma'am, the world's full of crackpots preying on the worries of family. What your caller dropped off here last night was . . . a stuffed pink elephant. A kid's toy. It's on the desk in front of me."

"*Elephant?*" Rita Rae slammed down the phone.

Orlando began to speak, "What is this elephant? *Qué pasa?* Do they—" but was interrupted by the bran flakes box flying into the refrigerator. He barely ducked the coffee cup before it exploded on the wall over his head. *"¡Oye! ¡Mi fiera!"* He fled the kitchen before the rest of the china took flight.

46

Thadeus Trout, in technicolor anger, jabbed a fleshy finger at Junior. "Get my bowling ball."

Junior, Six-pack, and Peaches each took a step back, as if choreographed.

"Please, sir," Junior said. "Don't . . ."

"We did our best," said Six-pack.

Peaches stopped chewing whatever was in his mouth, something orange from the stain on his lips, and whimpered.

"If you need to teach us a lesson, do it to him," Junior said, pushing Peaches in front of him. "It was his fault."

"No!" Peaches scuttled behind Six-pack. In his haste, his fist opened and half a dozen Cheetos dropped to the warehouse floor.

"Do it?" Trout said to Junior. "Do what?"

"You know . . . aren't you going to, uh . . ."

Trout huffed. "I'm going bowling. If I hang around you incompetents any longer my arteries will burst."

He pressed his fingertips to his temples, shut his eyes, and rubbed. "I should blame myself for sending the three of you on a real mission."

With a sigh deep enough to set his reddened jowls fluttering, he added, "It's probably just as well. If you'd of snatched the mummy and the Hammer had found out about it—the man hates cheaters—he'd be shooting pieces off one or all of us soon enough."

The boys exchanged nervous glances.

Trout's heavy lids opened and he sat upright. His rubbery skin, like that of a moody squid, flashed through the hotter bands of the spectrum and faded to a flat gray pallor. His liver spots, hidden by the previous flush, reappeared. His thick lips sputtered. "Wait a minute . . . wait a minute . . ."

Fearing the Big One, Junior ran to his side. "Daddy . . . are you all right?"

Trout waved him away. "If you *had* glommed this mummy without the Hammer knowing about it, I'd of had to destroy it, right? No mummy: no pay off. That would be good, but, then, the mummy would be gone forever. As it is, if the Hammer brings it to me, I pay the contract—"

"It's about honor," Junior explained to his companions.

"Screw honor," Trout said.

Peaches proposed, "Advertising?"

Trout grinned. "A strike for the young man with the orange lips."

"I get it," Junior said. "We'll keep it here to show the deadbeats."

"A boon," Trout acknowledged, "but I had something more grand in mind. What do you think those television people get for one thirty-second commercial on prime time news? Multiply that by—how often have they talked about Doone on the TV since the Hammer mummified him and that egghead found him? On radio? How many articles have been in the papers? And the more hell these protestors raise, the bigger the buzz. Tell me why those tourists flock to that pissant Captain Hook Museum . . . to see a dried-up carcass?"

"Hell, yes," Junior said.

"That nets you a seven-ten split. Museums are as full of

mummies as they are empty of visitors. These rubes want to see Shickleton Doone, the Prince of Light, the first man lifted to heaven by the good Lord above and returned to earth, less his hundred-and-fifty-pound soul. *That's* why. It's a miracle, see? Like that robe or the bleeding eyes or the water cure in Europe.

"Now, tell me, what business are we in? See if you can pick up that split."

"Loan sharking."

"You got the ten pin, seven's still sitting there."

Peaches said, "Hijacking?"

"Pin's wobbling, but didn't fall down."

Six-pack finally spoke, "Freeze-dried meat?"

"Wobbling, wobbling . . . but no spare. Guess again."

Reluctantly, Junior said, "The Bible Alive Museum?"

"Bingo! As an exhibit, Doone will outdraw Noah's Ark and Jonah's whale combined. Our two-thousand-year-old man has been threatening for years to retire. Who needs him now? We'll stay open till midnight so the tourists can watch the Fireflies waving their flashlights at the clouds—won't cost us a penny. We'll stage Rapture reenactments, sell glow-in-the-dark mummy key chains and Rapture Robes, End Times survival kits—unload some freeze-dried meat while we're at it. We'll put in a spooky-mummy cave ride, have them zip up instead of down like your roller coasters. Maybe we'll snip little pieces off Doone and sell them as relics to fundamentalist churches. Why, boys, the possibilities are endless."

"So," Junior said, eager to garner credit for his father's good will, "you're happy we didn't get the mummy?"

"When the Hammer drops off the goods," said his father, "then, I'll be happy."

Rita Rae stood beside the mattress, scraping peanut butter and Hershey's chocolate syrup from her skin with a wet bath towel. Her probing fingers recovered an errant nugget, flung it into the waste can with a *ping*, and resumed searching. "So much for our Reese's Cup adventure. I should have known better than to send you shopping."

Lying on his back, frowning at a wilting erection, Orlando said, "You did not *send* me. I go because I needed *cigarrillos*."

She flung the towel at his head. "I can't believe you bought chunky. Didn't you read the label?"

Orlando lifted the towel from his face and tossed it on the carpet. "You say Jif, I buy Jif. You think I read labels like some *maricón*?" He swung his legs over the edge of the mattress and stood. "Take a shower. I know other games."

Rita Rae sighed. "I'm not in the mood now. I can't get Shickie out of my mind." She gave Orlando a long squint, adding, "Shickie would have known better than to buy chunky."

Orlando shrugged. "So? Your husband was a *maricón*."

Rita Rae picked up the towel, dabbed at a chocolaty smudge on her thigh, and snorted. "All that work for a toy *elephant*." She wadded the chocolate and peanut-butter-stained towel and pitched it at him again. "Why didn't you check it out?"

Orlando caught the towel and hunkered on the edge of the mattress. "I say all this before. The *recepcionista*, she tells me where this mummy is: in a white sheet, center of the room, on a steel table. I go in *laboratorio* while you entertain that weak old fool the director." He jumped up, pantomimed humping. "I see this white cloth," he draped Rita Rae's towel over his right fist, "and what I think is the mummy, exactly where she tells me. There is nothing else near. *Nada*. I lift it—it is light as one of the *ceramica*s with the snow-white centers I import from Colombia—" his left hand hefted his towel-covered right "and carry it to the car." He held the bunched up towel at stomach height and walked in a small circle. "Somehow, they trick us." He threw the towel at the wall. "I swear your husband is in that *museo, oiste?*"

Rita Rae lit an almost-post-coital cigarette and drew the smoke deeply into her lungs. She blew it toward the window, toward Pigeon Forge, in a long thin stream. "And we're going to get him. Soon as they open tomorrow, I'll have another chat with that horny old man."

47

immy might have slept in on his day off, or skulked around the house to nurse his hangover. He might have resorted to the proverbial hair of the pooch to quell his depression over once again letting his ancestor slip from his grasp. The thought of his ARM cohorts protesting without him at the—now mummy-less, thanks to him—Captain Hook Museum, however, weighed heavily on his conscience. Jimmy decided to join them, consequences be damned.

As soon as his Grandpop donned his ersatz Plains Indian costume with the turkey feather headdress and left for a day of flagging motorists from the highway into Thadeus Trout's Moccasins! Moccasins! tourist trap in Pigeon Forge, Jimmy dragged himself from bed and into a needle shower. He toweled off and, for the first time since his return to Tennessee, got out his Indian wear. He donned black gabardine trousers, a blousy, turquoise Navajo shirt, a fringed Cheyenne vest with a red beaded Thunderbird motif, a Zuni silver-buckled belt, calf-high Sioux buckskin boots, a Huron beaded shoulder bag, and a beaded Kiowa headband. From a hard cardboard tie box, he removed a single majestic, if illegal, golden eagle feather, a gift from a Navajo buddy, and tucked it into his headband.

The irony of the amalgam—reflecting the uncertainty of his origins, the unknown affinity of his father, the Chief—was not lost on him. Despite his promise to his Grandpop to stay clear of the demonstrators, lest he get him in trouble with Mr. Trout, Jimmy would spend one day as an ARM warrior, manning the picket line.

He cursed the fate of his ancestor, imagined him on a cold slab at the morgue, cops all around. If the Indian nations and their attorneys get involved, he speculated, there'll be a long court battle, and even if the good guys win, there's no way I'll get him. He'll probably go to the Cherokees. If the scientists win, they'll cut him up and print pictures of him in their books. If Ginger's Fireflies get hold of him, they'll put him on display in a glass coffin. And if none of them gets him, the county will probably bury him in a pauper's grave. In any event, the poor old warrior will never rest in ancestral ground.

Looking like an extra in a John Wayne western, Jimmy mounted his faithful Yugo, sans his eagle feather so it wouldn't break on the headliner, and rode to town for a day of battle at the Captain Hook Museum.

Courtesy of their employer, Junior's crew stuffed themselves at a Gatlinburg breakfast buffet: fruit, toast, jelly, eggs, grits, hash browns, and—not without a fair amount of rib-poking—the Gatlinburg special, fried trout. Their assignment was to rile the protestors at the buttonhook museum. An anonymous tip had already been phoned to the TV people. Mr. Trout wanted publicity. "Stir 'em up, but don't get caught, hear?"

Barely a block down the hill of Gatlinburg's main drag, Peaches punched the brake pedal. His sprung trunk lid flew open as the Monte Carlo skidded to a stop. The Camry behind nearly rammed them and was rear-ended in turn by a pickup.

Junior, never a seatbelt fan, bounced off the dash. Six-pack, in the backseat, also beltless, collided with Junior on the rebound.

Oblivious of the cursing inside and honking without,

Peaches flew from the car, ran past the interlocked Camry and pickup. Ten seconds later, he returned carrying a three-foot pancake of crushed pink plastic. Eyes smarting, he shook it at the Monte Carlo windows. "Look what that old man did to Angelina."

"Jeezle, Peaches," Junior said, still rubbing his cranium. "Peel out of here, you can pump her up later. We get into trouble with the cops, Daddy'll bowling ball all three of us."

The Children of Light church bus pulled into the Captain Hook Museum lot at quarter till ten. As rehearsed, the Fireflies de-bused and queued up. Creely Patch clasped his leather-bound Bible to his chest, and, flanked by the two largest Jones clan males wielding impressive Return the Prince signs nailed to one-by-threes, took the lead. Two burly Jones females followed Patch, one to each side of Ginger Rodgers, the Witness. A mass of white-robed Fireflies and gnarly Joneses trooped behind, three abreast.

At ten o'clock, Patch blew a whistle and the formation marched toward the museum entrance.

Director Horace Duckhaus happened to be staring out his office window, dreaming of his recent, sole, love interest, Maria.

The trill of a whistle drew his attention to the Children of Light phalanx. The sledge hammers in the hands of the two Paul Bunyans at the lead made their intent clear. He punched a number on the phone, got the guard on the line. "Clarence, trouble in the parking lot. Get to the front door. Lock it if it's already open. I'll call the police."

Jimmy Feather, in full colors, led the ARM protesters, four young men and a woman, marching in a circle near the front door with "Return Our Ancestor" placards. They chanted a repetitive, "Te-yeh-yeh-ah, Te-yeh-yeh-ah" to the beat of a sixth member beating a tom-tom.

Orlando Sosa y Castro and Rita Rae Deaver, several couples with children, and three hefty University of Tennessee football players, milled nearby, awaiting the unlocking of the museum doors.

A little girl tugged at her mother's shift, pointed to the female ARM protester dressed in buckskins, "Mommy, is that Tiger Lily? Will we see the crocodile? Do they keep Tinkerbell in a cage?"

One of the college men handed his buddy a disposable camera. "When they're not looking, I'm gonna get hold of that mummy and plant a kiss on its butt. Take my picture, like fast, before they notice."

Rita Rae overheard. "Keep an eye on the jocks," she whispered to Orlando. "If they find Shickie, I'll slip them a twenty to bring him out to the lot for us."

Maury sat in his Town Car at the far edge of the lot, tapping his arrhythmic fingers on the wheel, hoping for a return to the scene of the crime by the no-goodnik boys.

At the opposite corner of the lot, Shickie Doone, in his Amish disguise, sipped coffee in his rusty pickup, casing the museum. In a fit of alcohol-induced conscience the night before, he concluded that before he recovered his stash at the Temple of Light and departed for the nether regions of the planet, he ought to at least say a proper goodbye to brother Fenster, the little shit who had date-rape drugged and robbed him.

48

When he caught sight of Ginger Rodgers, looking pale and none too eager, Jimmy tripped, lost balance, and bumped into the ARM protestor at his side. Ginger walked lockstep between two big-boned, bonneted women near the front of the troop. Two hulking men with bushy beards and long tangled hair flanked Creely Patch. Jimmy saw more of the hairy men and big-boned women, all sharing the familial bulging eyes and stooped gait, all radiating fierce determination. The more numerous Fireflies, were it not for their robes, would have been indistinguishable from the tourists awaiting the opening of the front doors.

A young boy, nearly hidden by several bearded men, blew on a bugle, but what may have been intended as a cavalry charge petered out in an off-key toot. It was apparently enough for Patch, who raised his arm as a sign to his flock to begin chanting, "Give us the Prince, Give us the Prince. . . ."

The tightly packed line was on an intersecting course with the six ARM protestors.

When Ginger saw Jimmy, she gave him a doe-in-the-headlights look and struggled. With a firm grasp on her elbows, the bonneted women hustled her forward. One scowled and whispered something in her ear and, though Ginger's lips moved in synch with the mass chant, she shook her head at Jimmy, apparently urging him away.

Jimmy's ARM cohorts exchanged worried looks at the approaching phalanx, but closed ranks.

The door of the museum opened and a blocky, uniformed guard stepped out brandishing a nightstick, accompanied by the wizened director, Horace Duckhaus. Duckhaus raised both arms and shouted, "Stop! You're on private property. If you can't—" It was drowned out by conflicting chants of "Give us the Prince" and "Return our ancestor."

Seconds later, the Children of Light collided with the ARM line. The Jones at point brushed aside the single ARM woman and straight-armed one of her male companions in the chest, knocking him to his knees.

In an instant, the ARM woman was on the back of her assailant, pummeling his ear. Her fallen ARM comrade rose to his knees and head-butted the man's stomach. The big Jones doubled over but was carried forward by the momentum of the advance. Pushes and shoves gave way to punches and kicks. Combatants paired, scuffled on the ground.

At the first contact, Creely Patch dematerialized and scurried to the rear in a crouching retreat. The bonneted women held Ginger in place. The phalanx shifted composition as plump Betsy and most of the original Fireflies hesitated and fell out of step, while the Joneses broke ranks and swarmed forward. Three Jones males charged the museum steps.

Bystanders hustled their children to safety, but stopped thirty feet away to witness the unfolding drama. Cars on the highway slowed, pulled onto the berm.

The three football players in numbered jerseys slapped high-fives, yelled "Fight!" and joined the melee.

Horace Duckhaus clapped a hand to his mouth and backed against the door. He noticed Rita Rae, smiled uncertainly, and screeched, "Maria, run!"

Orlando bent into a martial crouch. He brushed Rita Rae

behind him with his left arm and flicked open his knife. "Maria, eh?" he said over his shoulder. "Well, Maria, you stay close to me. We follow *los locos*. If they discover your husband, I'll cut one or two to make the confusion, and we take him out the back door."

"Cool," Junior said from the back seat of Peaches's Monte Carlo. "The religious nuts and the redskins are mixing it up."

"Guess what?" Peaches said, "The Indian in the buckskins and feather who just slugged that big guy in the sheet? He's the twinkie who attacked us in that parking lot."

"Payback," said Six-pack.

They bolted from the car toward the museum, although Peaches slowed to a trot, and then, barely a walk as the shouting grew louder.

Shickie Doone, the Amish farmer, sat in his pickup a hundred feet away. "Patch, you bastard, where did you recruit those Huns?" He recognized the gay Indian in the opposing camp, the one in Poncho's the day before, and, then, Rita Rae. "You bitch."

He watched her snuggle up to a slim tango dancer with slicked-back hair, dressed in pastels and holding a switchblade close to his belt. One of Rita Rae's hands ran up the tango dancer's arm and she spoke to his ear.

Shickie slammed the steering wheel. "Cuckolded. And I'll bet that greaseball's the one she put up to doing in little Fenster, mistaking him for me."

It didn't take long to conclude, from the placards and shouting, that Fenster must be inside the museum. Shickie hunched low in the seat, afraid to show himself, despite his disguise, with Rita Rae and, no doubt, the Hammer lurking. He kept a close watch on the unfolding riot through the spokes of the steering wheel.

*　　*　　*

From the other side of the lot, Maury, in his Town Car, had binoculars to his eyes. "Such a crowd you're keeping company with," he said of Ginger Rodgers as the Children of Light advanced.

"Whoa, what's this? Doone's wife and her slippery friend." He shifted the glasses to the faygeleh who had just stomped one of the big Lighters on the foot. "Who said you fellows were nonviolent? Why, it's a regular war. Better than wrestling on the tube at Cora's." He saw a jock in a football jersey take a Return Our Ancestor sign to the mouth. "Ouch," he said. "That'll put some dentist's kid through college," and, "Take that," as the jock swiped his bloody mouth, made a fist, and took out the sign wielder with a roundhouse punch.

"Wa–a–ait a minute. . . ." he refocused. "It's those no-goodnik boys." Righteous anger rose from Maury's dyspeptic gut to burn his sunken cheeks. He dropped the binoculars to his lap and removed the pistol from the holster beneath his sports coat. He screwed in the silencer and set it at the ready across his spindly thighs.

He saw the fat one hang back—"You shmaltzik coward"—making quite a show of waving a huge bowie knife while going nowhere. His two friends, however—"Look at the pisher and his golem go"—kept running, dodging everyone in their paths, intent on attacking—no doubt of that—the faygeleh Indian near the museum steps. "Watch out, boychik!"

The skinny cheater with the too-small head, Maury's pisher, stopped to chase a skittering beer bottle across the asphalt. He ducked a blow from one of the protesters and ran the bottle down, grabbed it by the neck, and wended his way through the combatants, his gaze fixed on the faygeleh.

A broad-backed, bonneted Jones female tripped the muscle-bound golem as he ran past. He rolled onto the asphalt, but bounded to his feet, thumped one of her allies, and ran toward the faygeleh Indian. He grabbed him from behind, pinned his arms to his side as the skinny cheater neared with the raised beer bottle.

"I think not," Maury said. "I kind of like that lad. Furthermore, it's time for a lesson: cheating doesn't pay." He rested the barrel of his pistol on the edge of the partially opened driver's side window for support and took a bead.

The barrel chattered against the glass as the skinny cheater waved the bottle and mouthed insults at the pinioned faygeleh. Maury shifted to a double-handed grip. The gun continued to shake. He sighed. "I'd be lucky to hit the building, let alone the cheaters from here."

"Sorry," he said to the hapless faygeleh and dropped the gun to his lap, none too happy with his impotence.

The pudgy cheater, waving the knife and cursing sixty feet away, caught Maury's attention. Maury took note of the car the cheating three had arrived in: a pristine, nosed and decked, pinstriped, vintage Chevy Monte Carlo Supersport.

Hmmm. When I was a kid, Maury recalled, the most important thing in my life next to my dick was my car, and, since I can't shoot their dicks off at the moment . . .

He turned the key and gunned the engine of his 220 horsepower, 4.6 liter, fifteen-hundred-pound Lincoln Town Car, quite certain that, unlike the slugs from his Colt, the big Lincoln would go where he aimed it.

Director Duckhaus retreated at the first hint of violence, but Clarence, the museum guard, held his ground. When the first Jones swung at him, Clarence dropped to his knees and whacked the man across a shin with his nightstick, sending him into a one-legged jig. Another Jones rushed the steps and knocked the stick from Clarence's hands with a powerful swipe of his Return the Prince sign. Another swing caught Clarence on the bridge of the nose. Clarence staggered, blood streaming over his mouth and chin, but managed to open the museum door and run inside.

Duckhaus threw the bolt and stared in shock at the raging battle. A dozen Lighters clamored up the steps to the door, half of them tugging on the handle, the other half pushing, nullifying the effort. One raised a Return the Prince sign and rammed the glass with the butt end. A spider-web fracture blossomed. Two cracks radiated to the edges. Another whack and the outer pane of the double-glazed glass gave way.

The man with the sign raised it over his head, but paused in mid-swing at a painful screech of metal on metal some seventy feet away. The shouting outside subsided and the battle moved to slow-mo as heads craned to see the source of the crash.

A long Lincoln, driven by an elderly, no doubt distracted tourist, had collided with—destroyed—the front end of a parked Chevrolet. The Lincoln backed up, unscathed, and returned to plow a deep furrow along the entire side of the Chevy. Apparently confused and frightened, the old gentleman in the Town Car then sped from the lot.

A roundish young man, waving a knife, screamed and chased the Lincoln for five long strides before tripping and rolling.

In the lull, sirens sounded. By twos and threes, the antagonists paused, cocked heads at the wailing, dropped signs, unballed fists, and scattered. Some limped, others ran as panic set in. One of the ARM protestors, held by a big fellow in a muscle shirt, wriggled free during the distraction, just as a skinny civilian swung a beer bottle at his head. The bottle connected with the muscle-shirted civilian's shoulder instead, knocking him to his knees.

At the trill of a whistle, the white-robed Children of Light broke off the assault. For a tense moment they glared at Horace Duckhaus, Clarence, and the other frightened museum employees through the door's single intact pane of glass before backing down the stairs and quick-timing it to the church bus.

The ARM protesters sped away in two pickups and a beatup Yugo. The three battle-psyched University of Tennessee football players revved their Jeep, sounded Dixie on the horn, and hooted rebel yells as they four-wheeled it across weedy ground to an adjacent outlet mall.

A mere three combatants remained: a chubby one holding

a large knife, a thin young man in a see-through goatee grasping a beer bottle by the neck, and a muscular man rubbing his shoulder. Four police cars, roof lights blazing, sirens bansheeing, jetted off the highway and surrounded the trio beside their incapacitated Monte Carlo.

49

told you to stir up publicity," Mr. Trout lectured his recently sprung crew, "not *be* the publicity."

"If that old fart hadn't of run into Peaches's car, we'd of tooled out of there with the rest of them when the trouble started. We were just watching those idiots with their signs, when—"

Peaches stared at the floor. "My car," he repeated for the hundredth time. "My beautiful car."

"The hell with your car," said Six-pack. "I won't be able to do curls or presses for a week with this busted shoulder."

"I'm not sure I got this straight," Trout said. "Tell me again why this Indian attacked you with the beer bottle."

Junior side-glanced at Six-pack. "He must have been drunk. You know how they—"

The phone rang. Trout answered. "Oh?"

"Hammer here," said the baritone caller. "Listen, I'm running into a little problem getting hold of Doone. I had him, was going to bring him to you when these kids—"

"Kids?"

"Cheaters. Never mind. I'll deal with them. The point is,"

the Hammer cleared his throat, paused, finally said, "it's going to take me a while longer to get Doone to you."

Trout cursed silently. Junior and his incompetent associates had failed to recover Doone. Doone's cult had gotten nowhere. Ditto the Indians. Now the Hammer, the hardest case Trout knew, had failed as well. This historical museum, he concluded, must be a veritable Fort Knox of security.

The Hammer was saying something about punishing cheating kids. "Sure," Trout said, "you do that," and hung up. If he wanted the Doone mummy in the Bible Alive Museum, it was looking like he would have to do the job himself.

He did want Doone. More than ever. When Doone, the welsher, escaped the warehouse, Thadeus had let his temper get the better of him. Then, he wanted Doone dead and gone for perfectly logical reasons: vengeance, as an example to other deadbeats, and as an opportunity to pick up the armory lease from Doone's simpleton successor for a song. Now, however, he knew, more than ever, Doone, the mummy, had star potential for the Bible Alive Museum. P. T. Barnum class.

Trout discharged Junior and his crew and ruminated before his bowling shrine.

The hijackings and loan sharking had been profitable, enjoyable, but ultimately risky. Lest he spend his declining years in the pokey, Thadeus Trout began a segue several years ago from criminal enterprise into legitimate business: Great Smoky Foods, Mr. T's Fudge Shoppe, Moccasins!, Moccasins! the Truck-to-Trunk outlet store, and, most significantly, the Bible Alive Museum.

He ran across the fledgling Bible Alive when it was not much more than a storefront sideshow, a manger with mangy animals run by a proprietor who dressed in togas and did one-man Biblical reenactments—until he was discovered in flagrante delicto with one of his donkeys by a busload of Sunday schoolers.

Hopeful some heavenly scribe would count it against his more nefarious activities on the fateful day he arrived at heaven's gate and needed handicapping, Trout paid the back rent and kept the doors open.

That very night, he had what the psych people would call a Big Dream. His short legs were churning, his heart pounding, lungs aching, as he ran in the dead of night over a long slippery log bridging a festering swamp, pursued by a monstrous bowling ball. In the dark waters below, a lone shark, a real leviathan, thrashed and snapped.

Trout dared not look back, but when he heard a resounding crash, he knew it for a strike from the sound of crashing pins. The shark was no more. The log became a path, the path, a yellow gold-brick road running through what had become a fragrant pine forest. Ahead, the stygian darkness paled, and through the trees Mr. Trout saw the light of a new day, a scintillating sun rising over the towers of Fantasyland.

As he neared the high-turreted castle, the drawbridge lowered, the portcullis lifted, and Walt Disney himself strode toward him, smiling his beatific Walt Disney smile, carrying a massive, leather-bound, hubbed-spine Bible. The Bluebird of Happiness sang from one of Walt's shoulders. Mickey Mouse clung to the other, grinning, one white-gloved mousy paw gripping Walt's ear for support, the other waving a strapped bundle of hundred dollar bills. From the forest, the magnificent stag from Bambi stepped forth and struck a heroic pose, antlered head held high.

Humbled, Trout dropped to his knees. Walt bid him rise and opened the Bible. As he did so, a golden halo encircled the noble stag's head.

Trout's gaze fell onto a single line of illuminated script: "Seek ye not the almighty buck, but the Almighty Buck." At that moment, the divine stag bounded into the clouds and disappeared.

Trout awoke with a smile on his face, certain his future lay with the Bible Alive Museum. It would become the Disneyworld of Gatlinburg and Thadeus Trout, the Walt Disney of religion.

From that moment, all other Trout enterprises became subsidiary.

Initially, Trout grew the museum with proceeds from his more nefarious activities, acquiring a lot here, a lot there, eventually accumulating a city block of frontage. As his ambition and impatience rose, however, he had, perhaps unwisely, borrowed heavily from the boys up north to construct the present imposing edifice: a former mattress factory reconfigured as an elongated pyramid with stepped-back floors, a Disneyesque Hanging Gardens of Babylon.

Thematically, Trout started with the Book of Genesis, and moved forward. Exhibits were costly. The Heaven and Hell rides, for example, were immensely popular, but the payroll for the angels and demons was daunting—to say nothing of the soaring cost of propane to fuel the basement hellfire. Even details were dear: locusts for the Exodus plagues were FedXed in every Thursday from Brigham City, Utah. The Six Days of Creation Sound and Light Show employed state of the art technology, and, while Trout had gotten a deal on the animal stars of Noah's Ark from a roadside zoo gone bust in Chattanooga, the Ark itself—constructed entirely of wood, not an inch of plastic—had grossly exceeded budget. Now the building inspector was calling for costly structural reinforcements to the Forty Days and Forty Nights flood tank, one of the largest indoor bodies of water in the South.

The museum had barely scratched the New Testament. Trout dearly wanted to encompass everything from Genesis to Revelation, making him the first man in history to bring the Bible to life. *In toto.*

Situated beyond the museum's rear parking lot sat the perfect structure for such expansion: the old National Guard Armory, presently occupied by the Children of Light.

Trout stroked his Hoinke Classic bowling ball on the altar before him. "Money," he said, and repeated it: "Money, money, money. I need that mummy. With Doone's dried-up carcass on exhibit, I'll have the tourists lined up in the streets, be able to pay off the boys up north in no time. I'll pick up that lease from Doone's simpleton successor and have my New Testament wing going within the year."

He kissed the ball reverently and gave it a lively slap on the flank.

"My son failed me, the Hammer failed me. Now it's time for Thadeus Trout to take care of business himself."

50

Creely Patch knelt before his predecessor's desk, sweating as usual during his ever more frequent dialogues with God. He paid no mind to the wet shirt clinging to his back, nor to the rivulets of perspiration streaking his cheeks, running down his forehead and blurring the lenses of his thick eyeglasses. No matter, Patch needed no optical enhancement to see God, at this moment hovering between the desktop and the ceiling tiles, wearing a wrathful look that said He was in one of His Old Testament piques.

"I'm sorry, Lord," Patch said. "We tried to recover him, but Satanic forces thwarted us—Indians, hooligans, the museum guard, police. Eight more Joneses arrive from Texas tonight. Be assured, we shall recover the Prince with our next crusade.

"Ah . . . the angel blimp. I considered cutting that monstrosity loose, but the sinners seem drawn to it. The choir? Disbanded as you directed. No more sinful wailing. Now, all they do is grumble. Some good news—the tour buses running from the Cherokee reservation to Dollywood are stopping by, although not for inspiration, I fear. They take snapshots of the

Witness and the blimp, snicker when I admonish them, and run next door to that crass Bible Alive Museum.

"I regret to report that Ginger Rodgers is shamefully inappreciative of the role You cast for her as Your Witness and my future mate. Despite the lodging I arranged for her here in the Temple of Light, she insists on miring herself in the sins of this corrupting city."

The Messenger took several deep breaths, steeling himself for the big question. "Uh, Lord? When will it come? These Joneses don't know the meaning of patience. I lack the Prince's silver tongue, and the congregation begs for a sign, a miracle like the Prince performed."

Patch's back stiffened. "I see." He swallowed several times. "Take one more as a final sign? Yes! I will see she is ready."

Frustrated by the day's events, Shickie stopped by Poncho the 'irates for a beer. He wore a set of bib overalls today over a pale blue shirt, with—what the heck—red socks under his lace-up brogans. The socks no doubt violated the Amish dress code as much as the overalls, but looking down at the flash at his ankles buoyed his sinking spirits. He left the straw hat perched on his blond Dutch boy wig.

He recognized the young man sitting three stools down, dressed today like an Indian: no skirt, blouse, or lace-up sandals. Two empties rested on the bar before him, and he was working through his third.

"Name's Jimmy, if I remember right," Shickie said. "You and the old man and I were talking yesterday. Didn't I see you at the riot at the Captain Hook Museum?"

"You were there, too?"

"Buttonhooks are big with us. The family was looking forward to it, but that ruckus broke out before we went in."

"Ginger's Fireflies seem to be good at stirring up ruckuses."

"Ginger Rodgers. Your 'just a friend,' right?"

Blushing through his tan, the young man averted his eyes and stared at his beer. "We met and kind of, you know, liked one another. I thought. But now that her people and mine are fighting over my ancestor—"

"Shickie Doone, the Prince of Light, eh?"

Jimmy shot him an irritated glare. "No. That mummy is an ancient Indian."

Shickie motioned for him to explain, nodding agreeably as the boy did so, but concluding he was on the wrong track, as were the scientists.

Ginger Rodgers's explanation of meeting Shickie—Fenster—at Shickie's house made sense. The house would have been Fenster's first stop, all right—he had Shickie's keys and no doubt planned to loot the place. No wonder Ginger mistook Fenster for Shickie; even Ma got them confused without her glasses. Fenster would have made a play for Ginger. He no doubt scared the sweet young thing right out of the house. The "raptured" part was the impressionable young woman's rationalization for her embarrassment. As soon as she left the house, the Hammer must have snatched Fenster.

Damn the Hammer, Shickie said to himself. Damn Thadeus Trout. And damn Rita Rae. She probably had a hand in it. And, *damn*—he clanked his bottle on the bar—how am I going to say a brother-to-brother goodbye to Fenster with him locked up and all these players on the field? The only bright spot on the horizon is the fact that they're not after me now that they're convinced I'm dead and gone upstairs.

Jimmy apparently took Shickie's slamming of the beer bottle as sympathy with his ancestor story. "Thanks for agreeing with me, sir. Isn't it amazing the screwy things people believe?" With a short double take at Shickie's Amish attire, he added, "I mean, to each his own—"

Words to live by, thought Shickie, from a man who dresses in skirts one day, like a movie Indian the next. "So, what are your plans now, my young friend?"

"I don't know. There's a cop car parked by the museum entrance, so I've got to be careful. Both me and my grandfather work for Thadeus Trout. If I get into trouble it could cost Grandpop his job."

"Thadeus Trout." Shickie ran a worried hand across his paste-on beard, pressed his wire-rimmed sunglasses against his brow, and tugged his straw hat further down over his wig.

"Yeah," Jimmy said. "They say he's an unforgiving man."

Shickie left Poncho's feeling decidedly ill at ease. His hand slipped reflexively to the lucky coin in his pocket. No sooner had his fingers brushed metal than the yip-yapping of what sounded like a dog pack caught his attention. One of the higher-pitched yips sounded familiar. He traced the noise to a Chevrolet Suburban parked in a small lot beside a veterinarian's office with "Cataloochee Puppy Farm" on the side. Another yip, and Shickie's heart raced. He ran to the van, peered into one of several windows partially opened for ventilation. Inside he saw tiers of cages and crates, all locked, containing a dozen puppies—mewling, yapping bits of fluff in black, tan, buff, and white—as well as seven adults: a standard poodle, a Dalmatian, two golden retrievers, a collie, a rottweiler, and . . . a tiny Yorkie. The Yorkie Shickie had won from a high-toned breeder in a game of five-card draw at the Lexington Hyatt nine months ago. Shickie's baby boy.

"Houdini!" Shickie practically shouted. So, the bitch had lied about selling him to a tourist lady—she'd sold him to a puppy mill.

Houdini yip-yipped from a small cage in a tier on the far wall.

The van doors were locked, but Shickie easily opened one from the inside with a long reach. He slid in and crouched on the floor, surrounded by a deafening canine din. The Yorkie yips rose to a pyrotechnic whine when Shickie bent close to Houdini's wire mesh door, made kissy-lips and said, "Hold on, buddy, you're as good as free." Houdini whirled inside the cage like a silky dervish, scrabbled, scratched, and thumped at the door to get out.

Shickie retrieved a small leather wallet from a pocket, removed a metal pick and a tiny pry, hovered over the puny lock on Houdini's cage, and . . . voila! He scooped Houdini in one palm, pressed him to his cheek for an energetic doggie kiss, stuffed him into his bib overalls, and slipped from the van to the sidewalk.

He thought about releasing the big dogs, but decided they at least had a meal ticket and were getting laid regularly, and, who knew how soon the owner would return, alerted by the dog pack alarm? "Sorry, guys," he said, and hurried away.

Seconds later, he noticed a man in a brown jump suit leaving the vet's office with a standard poodle on a lead, giving the noisy van a critical stare. Shickie hotfooted it behind the building and patted the squirming lump at his chest. "Welcome home, baby. A lot's gone on since I left for Vegas."

Plato Scopes flew into Director Duckhaus's office. "My mummy is *missing*."

Scowling at the parking lot, less hopeful as each hour ticked by that his high-haired admirer, Maria, might stop by for another heart- and groin-pounding visit, Duckhaus turned to Scopes, narrowed his eyes and said, "Sit down."

"You should have hired another guard like I told you to," Scopes said, "and closed the museum, because someone sneaked into the lab and—"

Duckhaus raised a hand to silence him. "Keeping that mummy in your laboratory was like waving bait for the crazies. We cannot afford another guard. Nor can we afford this notoriety—draws entirely the wrong kind of people."

"Where did you put my—"

"In the past three days I have received—and avoided answering—messages from attorneys representing two Native American tribal groups, the county medical examiner, and the county sheriff."

"You hid my mummy, didn't you? I think it was safer in the lab."

Duckhaus waved the air for Scopes to be still and listen. "You think we'll be compensated by the people who attacked us? The police won't touch a religious cult, short of their roasting and eating infants. They made only three arrests and there's no proof those three were directly involved. Clarence," he continued, "has a broken nose. I wouldn't be surprised to learn he's already called one of those 1–800–L–E–T–S–S–U–E lawyers. Workman's comp? Insurance? Sure to rise. Our employees are scared to death and attendance—"

Scopes bolted from the chair, leaned over the director's desk, and shouted: "*Where* is my mummy?"

Duckhaus looked him in the eye, gave him the slightest of smiles, and shrugged. "I sold it."

"You WHAT?"

"You heard me. I sold it. It was a liability and I turned it into an asset."

"You wouldn't dare. No!" Scopes pressed the base of his palms to his temple, rocking his head. "Please tell me you are joking."

"No joke. Sold. For cash. Five figures, too."

Scopes went rigid. His eyes bugged. "You son of a bitch."

"I'll ignore that. This time, considering your state of mind. I realize you are disappointed, but I acted responsibly, in the interest of the museum. Our agenda is the increase and diffusion of knowledge of buttonhooks and the golden era of buttonhooks—not mummies. I warned you about that thing and look what happened." Duckhaus cocked an eyebrow. "Now, I suggest you settle down and get back to work." He shooed Scopes with a flick of his fingers.

Scopes slumped into the chair and muttered, "*National Geographic.*"

Duckhaus nodded. "I deluded myself, too, but the truth is, they had no interest in our collection."

The scientist rubbed his tearing eyes. "Sold my mummy," he muttered. Then to the director, "Who? Who did you sell it to?"

"To whom," replied Duckhaus, evidently enjoying Scopes's distress. "If you must know, I sold it to Thadeus Trout, owner of the Bible Alive Museum. He plans to put it on display."

Scopes shook his head, eyes unfocused. "You can't just *sell* a *body*, the scientific find of the century, to a tourist trap."

"Can and did. Trout has a deed of sorts. A paper signed by this Reverend Doone promising to either repay a substantial loan to Trout or relinquish a pound of his flesh for each thousand dollars forfeited. Doone paid Trout nary a penny, got himself killed—none of my business how—so Trout feels at—what, twenty-seven pounds?—he owns Doone's body many times over." He chuckled. "I'm not sure I'd want to prove a claim like that in court, but, as I said, it's Trout's problem now. Let him deal with the crazies."

"That mummy is a prehistoric *cave man*, not some loony preacher."

"Not what Trout thinks. And, since I have his check, who cares?"

"You son of a—"

"Ta-tah," Duckhaus raised a bony finger. "I warned you about profanity. If you value your job, I suggest you walk yourself back to your laboratory and resume that privy analysis you began before we were cursed by this mummy."

Scopes gaped, goldfish-like, but no words emerged. He gave Duckhaus a final steely glare, wheeled on his heels, and slammed the door on the way out.

51

Perched on the kitchen counter, back against the refrigerator, Rita Rae muttered a sailor's curse and said, "Trout has him now."

"How do you know this?" Orlando sat cross-legged on the kitchen floor, a cup of coffee balanced on one knee, a Miami dog-racing form in his lap.

She shook the newspaper. "Check out the front page: a picture of that fat toad posing with my Shickie like some big game hunter with a downed pigmy rhinoceros." She held the newspaper at arm's length, squinting, even at that distance, to read the type. "They quote Trout as saying, 'This was a win-win situation. We made a generous donation to the Captain Hook Museum for expansion of their buttonhook collection and, now, spiritually conscious people everywhere will be able to view the remains of the Prince of Light, the Reverend Shickleton Doone, the world's first Rapture, in a suitable venue: the Bible Alive Museum.'

"Suitable? Hah!" Rita Rae shook the paper again. "Suitable for Trout at—would you believe?—ten bucks a head. He'll clean up showing off the shrimp's body, while I, the shrimp's devoted wife, waste away in the shrimp's about-to-be-sold-by-the-bank empty house. It isn't fair."

She flung the paper at Orlando, but two feet out of her hands, the sheets butterflied harmlessly to the floor. "And if I get too pushy," she continued, "Trout will catch on to the life insurance. What we need to do, is steal Shickie out from under Thadeus Trout's piggy snout and drop him on the insurance agent's desk."

Orlando lifted the paper and studied one of the photographs. "This *museo*," he said with a thin smile, "has many doors and many people, not like the one in Pigeon Forge. Your husband is there for the public viewing. Getting him will be easy."

Grandpop McDowd leaned over the breakfast table and tugged the paper from Jimmy's face. "Forget about chasing your mummy for a minute."

"Forget? How can I forget?"

"Do you have any idea how many people have been hanging around the entrance to Mummy Cave—that's what they're calling it now."

Jimmy shook his head.

"What with all the fanfare, it's lots of 'em. National Park people won't let anyone in, of course, so they just mill around and take snaps."

"So?"

"So, I had a little talk with Homer Delaney. They found the mummy on his farm."

A sour look flickered across Jimmy's face. "Stole him, you mean, from the site of his sacred interment."

"The mummy was on Delaney's land, now it's gone is what I mean. And where it's gone from is where my kid friends and me scratched those dirty drawings—what that scientist is calling 'fertility rites' and 'Plice–toe–scene mega–fauna.' Our property has the only other way into that cave—right? Then there's all those crystals and icicles you discovered—"

"Stalagmites, stalactites, calcite, flowstone—"

"That's it. A real nature's fairyland. Stir that all in with what the newspapers, the radio and the TV have been saying, and consider we're closer to Gatlinburg and Pigeon Forge than any other commercial caverns . . . you see where I'm going?"

"Grandpop, I'm not interested in . . ."

"We open that sinkhole of ours, build some stairs, run in electricity, and we got one hell of a tourist attraction. Homer takes a third share, you and me a third each, see? Maybe Mr. Trout would stake us—"

"Trout *bought* the mummy."

"That's why I thought he'd want to invest."

"Trout is a greedy, insensitive, son of a—"

"Doesn't have to be him. We could do most of the work ourselves."

"Not now." Jimmy passed the morning paper to his Grand-pop and tapped the front page. "Here's what I've been thinking: the Bible Alive Museum has my ancestor . . . I'm the night guard. Kind of like the fox guarding the hen house, wouldn't you say?"

"Oh, Jimmy."

Shickie caught the big news on TV, national TV. The mummy had a new home. Trout, he decided, knew how to exploit a story all right, photo ops for everybody. "Behold: the first Rapture," Trout had said, pointing to Fenster's body. "It began right here in Gatlinburg. Though the attraction is not fully complete, we are allowing folks in immediately to accommodate public demand. They say," Trout winked, failing to mention the identity of the referenced 'they,' "that those who have viewed the mortal remains of the Prince of Light will be the first chosen by the Good Lord when the Great Rapture commences in earnest."

His spirits understandably low at viewing his lifeless brother bare-assed on TV, curled up in a velour-draped booth like some freak in a sideshow, Shickie decided to take a walk. He left Houdini in the room with a dog chew and put a Do Not Disturb sign on the door.

Half a block away he said, "Ohmigosh," as he realized he had forgotten his full Amish disguise. He was wearing the laced brogans, rough gabardine trousers, a gray shirt, and suspenders, but forgot entirely the beard, wire-rimmed sunglasses, wig, and straw hat. He looked both ways, saw no one staring, and beat it back to his room with a promise to be more careful in the future. Amish from head to toe this time, he set out again and walked two blocks to a restaurant. A hot breakfast would cheer him up and he would bring a few slices of bacon back to the motel. Houdini loved bacon.

Maury dropped his bagel in mid-bite when he read the headline. The bagel rolled over the Formica and onto the floor, tracking crescents of cream cheese across the linoleum. It was still rolling when Maury reached the phone booth.

"Let me speak to him," Maury said into the receiver, none too happy. "Tell him it's the Hammer."

"Yes?" said an uncertain Thadeus Trout a moment later.

"You *bought* him? I told you I'd bring him to you."

"So you said. I couldn't wait."

"What about my fee?"

"The deal was C.O.D. No delivery, no . . ."

Maury growled.

There was a pregnant pause. Trout finally said, "Hey, why split hairs? I suppose you did him in. The truth is, Doone's far more valuable to me like this than he would have been shot to pieces in an alley. Where do you want the money sent?"

An even longer pause followed. Maury had been sweating collecting the hit fee since he first learned about the mummy. This was entirely too easy. He normally used one of several post office boxes he maintained in Cincinnati, but didn't want to drive all the way home to find Trout had cheated him. But . . . collect the fee face-to-face? Maury had to preserve his image, his anonymity. "I'll call back," he said, and hung up.

He returned to his booth to ponder. The restaurant door dinged as a new customer entered: the Amish chap in the straw hat, straight blond hair, and chin-rimming beard, with the wire-rimmed sunglasses.

Maury considered. The Amish were the people Howard Hughes surrounded himself with in Vegas, weren't they? Honest to the core.

Maury waved. The Amish farmer waved back. Maury motioned him over. "Care to join a senior citizen for breakfast?"

"More like lunch," the farmer said. "It's late." Nonetheless, the farmer slid into the booth, and ordered a double order of bacon, eggs over light, coffee, and grits. The coffee arrived first. When the waitress returned with the food, the farmer grinned at her and said, "We're having a little problem sweetening the coffee, dear. Look . . ." He opened a sugar packet, poured the contents into his cupped right hand, tapped it with his left, and opened the hand. It was empty. Maury smiled, the waitress clapped. The farmer closed the hand again, opened it to reveal a gold Sacagawea dollar. He passed the coin, close-fisted, to the waitress, but when he unflexed his fingers over her open palm, the dollar had vanished. "Check the pocket of that apron," he said. A moment later, she was laughing, saying, "How'd you do that?"

She showed the coin to Maury, who shook his head with appropriate astonishment. The farmer said the coin had been blessed by the Amish pope, made the waitress promise to keep it forever for luck.

Maury decided he liked the man. Maybe the day would work out after all.

They discussed tourists, weather, and crops. Ignorant of all things farmish, Maury merely nodded at the bearded fellow's discussion of the cotton, grass, and mixed vegetables he said he raised. When the farmer put away the last spoonful of buttery grits, Maury said, "Friend, a small favor, I'd like to ask of you. What do you say?"

"Sure. Name it."

"A fellow will be dropping off an envelope for me up the hill at this Bible Alive Museum—an article about the decline of tourism the Holy Land. I'm a bit under the weather today. The walking and stairs are too much for these old bones. How's about I buy your breakfast, drive you up there, you go inside, and pick up my envelope? I'll wait outside in the parking lot."

"The Bible Alive?" A ripple of fear crossed the farmer's face—no doubt concerned about some Amish transgression—but after a fair amount of lip pursing and hemming and hawing, he agreed. "Why not?"

"Deal." Maury shook the farmer's soft hand. He felt for, but detected not a single sugar granule. How did he do that?

Maury phoned Trout to have the cash delivered in care of the Bible Alive Museum. When he returned to the table, the farmer ordered a stack of pancakes crowned with four more strips of bacon. He barely finished half the pancakes and—no wonder with all the food he had already put away—didn't touch the bacon. The farmer wouldn't let the waitress take it away. "I'll have another cup of coffee," he said, "and put the bacon in a doggie bag."

When the farmer finally finished his meal, Maury drove him up the hill.

52

hickie explained to the day guard at the Bible Alive Museum that a package had been left for him. The guard gave him a pass allowing him to leapfrog the crowd, queued like a multicolored snake along the zigzag ramps leading to the entrance. With Fenster on his mind, Shickie barely noticed the faux mud-brick pyramid festooned with plastic plants and flowers. He passed through ornate, faux-bronze entry doors and went straight to the museum office where he retrieved a thick envelope marked, as the old man had said it would be, "Holy Land financial summary for H. Hughes."

Shickie stuffed the envelope in his large trouser pocket and continued to a YOU ARE HERE map which informed him that Fenster had been installed well within the building, beyond a monster of a room labeled Genesis Hall. Simultaneously eager and reluctant to see his brother, Shickie gave scant notice to most of the exhibits, although he did slow to marvel at a lifelike, if somewhat undersized, whale near a big boat floating in a water tank ocean. Nearing the Rapture Room, his progress was slowed by a glut of tourists, apparently all intent on seeing the controversial mummy. Inching along, he saw workmen hanging hastily prepared introductory placards, Biblical quotes, blowups of newspaper articles, even a magic marker rendering by a quick sketch artist of the ASCENSION OF DOONE. Speed marks trailed from the figure's feet as he soared heavenward. A note pinned below promised A FULL COLOR OIL PAINTING OF THE MIRACLE HAS BEEN COMMISSIONED.

As the line crept to the Rapture Room, Shickie heard snatches of conversation ahead: "Euuw, it's a dead guy," from a little boy. "Lord, he's naked as a jaybird under that bath towel," from an elderly woman. "Shameful." And, from another, "Bend down like this, Myrtle, you can see his dingus." "Don't look, honey," from a parent. The first woman, again: "Why, it's no bigger than a peanut."

He read the caption below a chubby stuffed groundhog perched on a plastic log: THE PRINCE OF LIGHT, LESS HIS IMMOR-TAL SOUL, WEIGHS NO MORE THAN THIS WOODCHUCK, A DENIZEN OF OUR BEAUTIFUL GREAT SMOKY MOUNTAINS.

Despite a warning forbidding photographs, a thunderstorm of flashes sparked ahead. Assaulted by the psychedelic flicker-ing, cologne and perspiration-poisoned air, the shoulder-to-shoulder squeeze of bodies, and the dread of seeing Fenster, dead, Shickie felt panic rising like a swarm of angry bees from the pit of his stomach.

When he reached the mummy alcove, he caught no more than a glimpse of his brother, hunched in a fetal curl, pale as candle wax, lying on his side in a purple velour-draped cubicle. Fenster's head rested on a gold-fringed pillow. A baby blue bath towel barely covered his groin.

The glimpse was enough. Rocked by a wave of vertigo, Shickie felt his legs go rubbery. He threw an arm over his chest and sank to the floor. He was kneed in the ribs and kicked in the back before a sinewy teenager in a baseball cap grabbed him by the collar and hauled him to his feet. "Better keep mov-ing, bud. This is worse than a rock concert with festival seat-ing." Another good Samaritan pressed Shickie's fallen straw hat against his chest. Shickie wrapped an arm around it and spun to get another look at Fenster, but the momentum of the herd carried him forward, all the way to the Temple Steps Gift Shop.

He rested against a display case, recovering, blinking at an afterimage of gray, lifeless, dusty flesh. Swallowing back his breakfast, he staggered toward a small sign, ADAMS. Inside a stall, he held his clammy forehead with one hand, gripped the commode with the other, and emptied his stomach. After a flush and several deep breaths, he pressed cold paper towels to his face, checked his beard, adjusted his wig, hat, and glasses, and left the museum in a blue daze.

He felt a tap on his back and heard the old man's voice: "Was worried about you. Did you get it?" Shickie handed him the envelope, waved away the thanks, and beat it to his motel.

He gave the bacon to Houdini and lay on the bed, staring at the ceiling.

The ceiling shimmered, lowered. The walls closed in. "Sheesh!" Shickie sat upright. "I need air." He snagged Houdini from the pillow and ran from the room.

Ten minutes later, he found himself driving into the piney fresh Great Smoky Mountains. He drove higher and higher, eventually parked in an unoccupied overlook. Other than the whir of traffic on the narrow road behind him, he saw not a trace of humanity, only trees and a vista of receding mountains, each ridge a bit softer, more powdery-blue than the one before it. He walked to a rock wall at the edge of a precipice, took a deep breath of cool mountain air, and sat, idly scratching Houdini's ears.

"What a nightmare," he said to the cloud-streaked hills, oblivious to half a dozen deer grazing at ease within fifty feet. "Fenster in Trout's maws, the Hammer lurking, Rita Rae and her greasy boyfriend on the prowl, eager to collect on that million dollar insurance policy she made me take out. Creditors everywhere. Creely Patch and his barbarians taking over the Children of Light, and Ma, who will probably never speak to me again. It's you and me, baby," he said to Houdini, curled against his chest.

Shickie zoned out, began to doze. He jolted awake at Houdini's woofing at a *chick-chick-chick* of a fox squirrel. Shickie watched the rust-tinged rodent clinging to the corky bark of a pine tree, its red tail jerking with each *chick*. The head of a second squirrel appeared at the side of the trunk, six feet below. One darted toward the other, swatted its back with a tiny paw, bounded over it, and vanished behind the trunk. Five seconds later the pair reappeared on a gnarly branch higher up, somersaulting over one another like Chinese acrobats, racing nose to tail to the tree's upper reaches.

A distant memory brought a smile to Shickie's lips: he and Fenster as kids in Sandusky, Ohio, playing tag by the swamp behind the house, right after tying their little sister Nell to the big sycamore at the rim of what they called the alligator pit.

Shickie would have been eight, Fenster seven.

No, not tag. Fenster, as Shickie recalled, had snatched Shickie's coin purse, and Shickie was chasing him, threatening to break his neck.

Ah, innocent childhood.

It seemed like no more than a blink later, though it must have been years, that Fenster, the little shit, spiked Ma's morning Folger's with her sleeping pills and split with the family silver, and sister Nell ran away with the Jehovah's Witness. Then Pa went to work at the cookie factory drunk as a skunk and fell asleep in the coconut shredder between shifts. It was eight hours later that they discovered the accident when the sole of one of Pa Doone's workshoes finally jammed the grater. By then it was too late to recover either remnants of the man or the long ago baked, packed, and shipped macaroons he had become a part of. Kiddies across American were probably still nibbling bits of Pa Doone with glasses of cold milk. Shickie and his Ma held a little service over Pa's sole before they buried it in the backyard. Ma got mean after that.

"Sheesh, Fenster," Shickie said to the forested hills, "Why did you have to show up in Vegas? Why did I have to brag how flush I was?"

A faraway *chick* in the treetops caught his attention. Shickie saw a brushy tail flicking on the topmost branch. He ran the back of his hand under his nose and stared for half a minute at the panorama before him. It was almost dinner time. He looked toward Gatlinburg, hidden below the mountainous horizon, but identifiable by the tiny silhouette of the distant angel blimp, its strobe-light eye—the left one was out again—shining like Venus in a twilight sky.

Houdini wriggled at his chest. Shickie sniffled. "What the hell, Fenster, you date-rape-drugging little prick. The least I can do before I blow this burg is get your dried-up carcass back to Ma in Sandusky. She can plant you next to the parakeets, her thirteen Peteys, and Pa's sole, in that peony bed of hers, behind the septic tank at the edge of the swamp."

53

Maury patted Trout's money in his jacket pocket and did a little soft-shoe shuffle as he left the Lincoln in the motel lot. He hurried to his room, mouth watering in anticipation of a real Manhattan at Cora's Cozy Cove, home, in Cincinnati.

As he began to pack his shirts, conscience nipped the lining of his stomach. He took a double dose of Pepto-Bismol in the hope it was merely the greasy eggs he had for breakfast, but the damnable pangs increased.

He sat on the edge of the bed and reluctantly told himself, Maury Finkle, if you take Trout's money, you're no better than the cheats you've sent to the great beyond. You may have scared Doone to death, but he didn't die by your hands. What if that faygeleh Indian is right, and it's not Doone at all? Or that scrawny scientist? Could Trout be mistaking a caveman for Doone? Ginger Rodgers is a sweetie, but a ditzy shicksa. Is Doone still alive and kicking?

Maury decided he would have to see for himself. He drove back to the Bible Alive Museum, and was soon threading toward the mummy room.

The crowd conveyored him past the Rapture Room before

he could study the small body nestled in the velour, but what he saw sure did look like the photo Trout had sent him. How did he dry up like that?

Jostled toward the next attraction, a gift shop, Maury ran a finger over his neat mustache, and said aloud—an ever more frequent habit, living alone—"Was that Shickie Doone or wasn't it?"

The woman in front of him, wearing a pink sweat suit and white, Easy Spirit sneakers, thought Maury had addressed her. "Couldn't be," she said, turning to face him. "I think the mummy's a fake—you know, like the bat boy in the tabloids?"

"A fake," Maury repeated politely. The mummy looked real enough to him.

"Because," the woman was saying, "I saw the real Reverend Doone only this morning."

"Excuse me?"

"I work at the fudge shop. Mr. T's? Walk to work every morning. I never been to his church, but I'd run into the Reverend regular. Always had a smile on his face, usually invited me to come to a Firefly service—of course, I didn't, being a good Methodist for nigh on—"

"Wait a minute," Maury said. "You knew him?"

"Only by sight and to say a how-dee-doo, but if he was raptured like they say, then he's come back in the flesh, because I seen him this morning. Walking along Parkway near the river. I smiled, but he didn't see me. I had to come up here to see what this hullabaloo was about, him supposedly being a mummy and all. It's hogwash. Not to say that thing in there don't look like him, but then those pictures of the bat boy look real enough, too, don't they? I swear, it's getting so a body don't know who to trust. Course, on the other hand, what if he did go up to heaven and come back with a message from the Lord? Maybe the one I seen this morning was an angel. Although he was real enough looking, no wings or halo or nothing, and he stepped on some chewing gum, scraped his sole on the gutter edge to get it off just like a real man would and—"

"Madam . . ." Maury asked her to describe the man she had encountered.

". . . and a little taller than you. Blue eyes, near shoulder length black hair. Kind of a big nose for a little man . . ."

The description fit. Maury thanked her and wandered into the museum interior to think. He found an empty bench facing a gigantic water tank, shored with crisscrossed two-by-fours. Roped-off stairs rose thirty feet to a gangway leading to a large wooden boat floating in the center. Normally a curious man, Maury paid no more mind to the rude watercraft than he did to the mysterious hoots, growls, and lowings emanating from it, although he did wrinkle his nose at a disturbing zoo smell of biting ammonia. He found a more distant perch to ponder.

After a good bit of thinking, he slapped a fist into his shaky palm and strode back, past the tank, alongside a fiberglass whale, through the Temple Steps Gift Shop, the Garden of Eden Snack Shop, and into summer sunlight. He drove back to his motel at ten miles an hour, scrutinizing every pedestrian.

He flopped onto the bed, his spindly legs dangling over the edge, his gun with the silencer resting on the pillow beside his head. "Shickleton Doone," he said to the ceiling, "if you are alive and walking the streets of Gatlinburg, I'll find you. That twenty grand, I'll earn, fair and square.

"Soon as I get my energy back, I'll visit the space needle with my binoculars and keep an eye on that farschtunkeneh church of yours."

"Betsy, let me out."

Betsy looked both ways, put her mouth close to the heavy door. She tried the knob. "I can't, Ginger, it's locked. I think Reverend Patch has the key."

"He's got me handcuffed to a water pipe."

"No! He told everyone you were meditating on your sinfulness, that you didn't want to be disturbed."

"Yeah, sure. C'mon, help get me out of here."

"I don't know . . . let me think . . . they'll be back any minute."

"The Joneses?"

"They kind of watch everything now. Reverend Patch called the whole congregation to the sanctuary. He has a big announcement to make. Oh, oh, here comes a Jones women in a bonnet—I've got to go. Bye, Ginger."

Shickie Doone, the Amish Farmer, entered the Bible Alive Museum twenty minutes before closing, and walked briskly to Noah's Ark. A perfect hideout, he decided—except for the stench—until the museum cleared and he could snatch Fenster. Houdini, nestled inside his shirt, whimpered at the animal sounds and smells.

Shickie pinched his nostrils and hid in a stall, brushing aside a pair of curious goats, one of which looked suspiciously like the miracle goat he had sent to the Holy Land. He crouched at a porthole. "Shoo!" he said, when the female nibbled his beard. "Shoo!" he said again, when the male gave a randy snort and tried to mount him. Houdini yip-yapped and the goats retreated.

Shickie knew the boy in the skirt at Poncho's was the only guard after hours and that the museum was far too big a complex for one man to watch effectively. He planned to wait fifteen minutes, sneak to the mummy room, clutch his twenty-seven pound brother under an arm, and dash to the rear exit. He would hide Fenster behind a Dumpster at one corner of the parking lot, sneak into the Temple of Light for a surreptitious retrieval of the ten grand taped beneath the desk drawer in his former office, and drive to Knoxville. There, he would pick up a footlocker at a surplus store, UPS Fenster to Ma in Sandusky with a "Sorry Ma—this is the best I could do" note, and, at last, chase the setting sun, a free man.

As he peered through the porthole, he heard a snort at his ear and felt a blast of hot air smelling of overripe cheese. A flinty hoof hooked one of his shoulders and—"Get the hell away from me!" Shickie spun to one side, the billy goat thumped onto its back.

Beah!–a!–a!–a!

Yap! Yap! Yap!

In a flurry of straw and fur, Shickie sprung to his feet, banged his head against a low woody ceiling. "Owwch!"

Frightened peacocks on the prow screeched like eviscerated sopranos, a hyena laughed, something hissed, Houdini barked for all he was worth. "Sheesh," Shickie said, rubbing his skull. He pressed his back against a thick oak beam, heart pounding, waiting for the guard's "Come out with your hands up."

Apparently the jungle noise was business as usual at the Bible Alive Museum, because no one responded. Twenty minutes later, Shickie crept from the Ark and padded toward the mummy room.

Jimmy Feather saw the last of the tourists leave, made his rounds quickly, and returned to the employee canteen for a cup of coffee. The clean-up crew wouldn't arrive for hours. In twenty minutes Jimmy would make his move.

At a blood-curdling scream from the depths of the museum, he dropped his cup. Hot lava seared his bare thigh.

Damned peacocks. How could birds make so much noise? Swing shifts had accustomed Jimmy to the Ark's snarls and grunts, but the banshee yells of those peacocks straightened his spine every time.

He blotted his hand and thigh with paper towels, willing himself to calm down. This is your chance, he told himself. You're finally alone with your ancestor.

He got another cup of coffee, sat, and forced himself to sip slowly.

By opening hour, he assured himself, the mummy would be well hidden on his Grandpop's farm, awaiting proper burial. He would be back at the museum, playing dumb, staring at his feet, "I'm sure it was there last night, sir. Maybe one of the tourists smuggled it out in a stroller or . . ."

With a shrug, he said aloud, "So I lose my job. What's that compared to returning an ancient warrior to ancestral ground?"

He set the cup down and checked his watch. Seventeen minutes to go.

54

C reely Patch climbed onto his throne and stood on the seat, perspiring profusely as he exhorted the white-robed Children of Light to battle. The companion throne belonging to the Witness, Ginger Rodgers, remained conspicuously empty. The Children of Light at Patch's feet formed two groups, the founding Fireflies at one side, and the tall, shaggy Jones clan at the other.

More strident than commanding, Patch declaimed, ". . . will recover the Prince of Light from the Bible Alive Museum this very evening. And God tells me of a *miracle* to follow. He wants me to remain—"

A Firefly asked, "A miracle. Like one of the Prince's?"

Another Firefly added, "Like the time he sent a goat to the Holy Land?"

"We heard about that," said one of the Jones women. "And changing his staff into a snake. The Prince must have—"

"This will be *better*. While I await the divine word here in the Temple of Light, God commands you to recover the Prince from that sacrilegious Bible Alive Museum. March over there and—"

"Like, cut in a diagonal across the parking lot to the back door?" asked a Gatlinburg accountant, one of the more detail-minded Fireflies.

"Skulk like thieves? Certainly not. I want you to leave through our front door in a glorious procession, follow the sidewalk around the block to the museum entrance. Carry trumpets of rams' horns—"

"Don't got any of them," said a Jones. "But little Billy Mike has his bugle."

"Very well," said Patch. "The bugle will do. And carry torches so the townsfolk—"

"You mean our flashlights?" A robed Firefly flicked his on, lifted it.

Patch fluttered his hands impatiently. "Whatever lights up the night sky, all right? Make a show of it. Let the world know our mission will not be thwarted by greedy opportunists. When you reach the ramparts of the Bible Alive Museum, have your young warrior blow a mighty blast and the walls will collapse. I saw that in a vision. You will enter, every man and woman of you, recover the mortal remains of the Prince, and bring him to me."

"And then we'll be raptured?"

"Soon," Patch said.

"Hey," said Goliath Jones, "you been telling us 'soon' since we got here. I gave away our doublewide to the wife's cousin, the furniture, my shotguns, her collectibles—the whole damn Beany Baby collection—everything. We want *up*. This living in tents in the parking lot is getting old. You promised—"

"God promised," Patch said, his impatience growing. "He told me Himself not ten minutes ago: return the Prince to My tabernacle and behold a miracle."

Jones balled his fists. "A miracle would be good," he said, "particularly the kind that gets us to heaven, because we're growing a mite short on patience."

Patch inhaled a resentful breath and held it in. Sweat poured down his cheeks, fogged his thick glasses. He counted to ten silently, extended his arms to form a cross, and resumed his exhortation. "Recover the Prince. Only *then* can the Rapture commence. That is God's will."

A Firefly repeated, "Recover the Prince."

"God's will," chorused two Jones females.

Another Firefly, and then another joined in. "Recover the Prince."

Joneses counter-chanted, "God's will," and stamped their feet.

The tempo and intensity rose until the floorboards of the armory stage vibrated harmonically. The Messenger's throne swayed. Still standing on the seat, Patch lost balance, would have fallen ignominiously onto his backside had he not grasped the wing of the gilded angel at the chair's back.

"Go!" he yelled from the rocking throne. "GO."

Eighty-three strong, the Children of Light streamed into the night. Several Joneses wielded baseball bats. Flashlights flicked on. Far overhead, the tethered angel blimp winked, disappearing momentarily as it drifted from the beam of the searchlight and then sparked back into view.

Below, Little Billy Mike blew a few tentative toots on his bugle. The chant, "Recover the Prince . . . God's will," continued at heartbeat pace.

Half a block away, the mob passed McMullin's Tahitian Luau. Diners recoiled as Joneses—"God's will . . . God's will . . . God's will"—snatched a dozen flaming tiki torches from street-side racks. Their leader, Goliath, ripped an eight-foot spear from the hand of a twice-life-size fiberglass Tahitian warrior and toppled the heroic figure with a hard kick. Tables tipped as tourists scattered. Hot wings, salad bar fixings, fried chicken, french fries, and other Polynesian delectables cascaded onto the restaurant floor.

The mob moved on.

Two good old boys—demolition derby drivers from Valdosta, Georgia, the Galvin brothers, Crash and Burn, scheduled for a death match exhibition in a Knoxville arena the following evening—set down their beers at a nearby bar. "Lookit them white sheets," said Crash. "And them torches."

"Shee-it, boy," said Burn, "it's a Klan march. Let's see what they're up to."

Three University of Tennessee jocks, the same boys who had gotten in a few licks during the Captain Hook Museum parking lot fiasco, set their beer bottles down as the procession passed their street-side bar.

"I smell fight," said one.

"Follow 'em," said the second.

"Yahoo!" said the third.

Rita Rae and Orlando were in Orlando's Caddy, parked near the museum. Orlando had a selection of tools spread on the dashboard, preparatory to picking the lock of the museum's rear door to recover the mummy for the insurance bounty. "It's them," Rita Rae said, "those Fireflies of Shickie's. Some kind of parade." As the procession advanced down the block, around the corner toward the front of the museum, she said, "Great . . . they're after him, too."

"*Muy bien*," Orlando said. "A distraction. *Perfecto*." He put down his burgling picks and hefted an iron pry bar. "No need for the gentleness, now, eh?"

Maury scanned the marchers with binoculars from atop the Space Needle, searching torch-lit faces for the visage of Shickleton Doone. "If you're down there, my friend," he said, "I'll find you. Yes, I will."

Shortly after the Children of Light departed the armory, Creely Patch knocked on Ginger's door. "It's me," he said. "The Messenger."

"Let me out."

"You could have led the congregation to recover Reverend Doone's mortal remains, but, no, not you. You would have traipsed off to some bar."

"Not me," she said from inside. "I'll be good. Let me out."

The Bible Alive Museum rose from the land like a giant, angular wedding cake. Each of its five stories was hexagonal, identical to and smaller than the one below, with two short walls forming points at each end, and two longer walls running parallel to the street. The walls also sloped inward from base to top, so the overall impression was that of a multi-faceted pyramid. Plastic vegetation festooned every level in a Hollywood recreation of the Hanging Gardens of Babylon. At the apex, a propane torch flickered and flashed, complementing the searchlight-lit angel blimp flying over the nearby armory.

Goliath Jones, paterfamilias of the Jones clan, raised a hand at the base of the double entry ramp zigzagging along the imitation mud brick façade of the street side of the pyramid to the entrance. The chanting faded at his sign. Jones motioned little Billy Mike with his bugle to advance.

Surrounded by adults, Billy Mike gnawed his thumbnail. He stared at his sneakers and clutched his mamma's skirts. "I'm scared," he said with a sniffle.

"Son," his mother said, and knelt at his side. "You have been chosen for a holy task. The Lord works in mysterious ways. When Gramps gave you that thing for Christmas, I swore it was Satan's way of punishing me. I see now that the horn and you are the instruments of God." She ruffled his hair, and gave him a sharp swat on the back of the head. "Now . . . you blow that trumpet for all you're worth or I'll tan your butt like you've never had it tanned."

Billy Mike rubbed his scalp and looked heavenward. High above he saw the angel blimp in a black Halloween sky playing hide-and-seek with scudding, moonlit clouds and the blue-white searchlight shaft. He cast worried glances left and right.

Torch-lit adults nodded encouragement, urged him forward.

The small boy worked his way to the side of Goliath Jones, lifted the bugle to his lips and sounded the first memorable notes of *When the Saints Go Marching In*. A bit tinny, a few notes flat, but sufficiently recognizable for some of the adults to hum along.

Faces turned to the museum's front, awaiting crumbling brick and cement, the promised Biblical tumbling of ramparts.

The walls stood fast. Billy Mike blew the *Saints* refrain again.

"Try something else," said Goliath Jones.

Billy Mike sounded reveille. Nothing. And, *The Bear Came over the Mountain*. Nothing. *Three Blind Mice*. Nary a crack appeared in the mortar.

He blew the first six notes of *Jingle Bells*, dropped the bugle on its lanyard, and whimpered. "That's all I know."

"Well, shoot," Goliath Jones said. "So much for Reverend Patch's vision."

"I got a baseball bat," said one of Goliath's cousins. "Me, too," said an uncle.

"The Lord helps those who help themselves. Climb up there and beat the doors in."

The first man took a swing at the twin metal portals bearing a mysterious blend of bas-relief hieroglyphic, Sanskrit, and cuneiform inscriptions. *Thunk*. The second man went to bat. *Thunk*.

They barely scratched the metal, so they swung at the single glass panel in each door. Though not large enough to admit an intruder, the glass proved satisfyingly more susceptible to their blows. A spider web of cracks appeared in one. The crowed cheered. The second pane burst inward. Encouraged, Goliath Jones shouted, "Shoulders to the doors." His compatriots surged forward. "One, two, three . . . heave!" The doors budged perceptibly. By the fifth shove, they bowed inward.

55

everend Creely Patch, wedging a serving tray between his elbow and ribcage, inserted a key into the door lock. He spoke over his shoulder as he turned the knob. "Yes, Father, Thy will be done."

"Betsy?" from inside.

"No, it's the Messenger."

"I don't want to be the Witness anymore. Let me out."

Patch pushed the door open with his foot and entered. "I thought you might be hungry. Look—here's a cup of hot chocolate and some oatmeal cookies."

The fine link chain from the handcuff linking Ginger's right wrist to a water pipe slithered over the bed as she backed against the wall. "Screw you."

Patch set the tray on a bedside table and sat on the edge of the bed. "Profanity is unbecoming of a Christian woman." He motioned for her to sit. "If you settle down, I might be willing to discuss your future."

Ginger sat on the edge of a short stool, her back stiff, her knees pressed together, feet flat on the floor.

"My father chose us." Patch leaned toward her, cupping a

knee with his hairy-backed right hand. He smiled. "If only you had—"

Ginger went rigid at his touch, swatted the hand away. "Get off me, you lecher. Wait till—"

A dark frown replaced the smile. "You're Satan's own hellion, aren't you?" He rubbed the reddened skin of his right hand with his left. "But I'm a forgiving man. Drink your chocolate and take some nourishment and perhaps I'll remove the shackle. Even let you into the sanctuary—if you behave."

Ginger regarded him through slitted eyes. "You promise?"

Patch clasped his hands at his knee. "I am a man of my word."

She looked from Patch to the open door, to the cup and cookies, and back to the door. Ginger smiled. "Okay."

He nodded at the tray.

She lifted the cup and sipped, with a wary gaze at the Messenger, stole another glance at the door, but saw no activity, heard no one. "I guess I was a little disrespectful," she said, brightening. "All this happened so fast . . . the Prince's Rapture, me being the Witness and all."

"Indeed. We must follow the path He sets forth for us." For a moment Patch's eyes unfocused. Then he peered, unblinking, at Ginger through his thick glasses. His eyes, magnified to twice size, bored into hers. "Our destinies," he said, "your's and mine, are linked."

Ginger shook off his stare with a shudder. She covered it quickly with, "If you say so," took another drink of hot chocolate, and ate half a cookie.

He regarded her. "If you do not do what is right, sin is crouching at your door."

"Don't worry, I'll do right."

"You like the chocolate? Sweet enough? I had your friend Betsy pick up the cookies from the little shop down the road."

"Delicious." Ginger drained the mug, lifted a cookie to her lips and nibbled. She looked through the doorway at the empty armory. "Where is everybody?"

"On a mission from God. Recovering the Prince from the

Bible Alive Museum. That greedy, sacrilegious merchant Thadeus Trout bought him from that buttonhook museum." Patch made a fist. "Those Pigeon Forge scoundrels *sold* him. For thirty pieces of silver, no doubt. Trout's put him on exhibit like a sideshow freak."

Ginger scowled.

"I see you share my outrage. I called the man, explained how God wants the Prince enshrined alongside the garments he left behind. Do you know what Trout said? 'Sounds like a good idea, Reverend. Bring the old boy's duds by and I'll hang them up in the mummy chamber.'" Patch stood, a wild look in his eyes. "Hellfire awaits that man."

"It's not right," Ginger agreed. She blinked, rubbed her eyes.

"Poor child, you're tired." Emotions played over his face and he began to mumble. "Yes, Father. The miracle . . . become believers, all of them."

Ginger set the empty mug on the tray with enough of a clack to get his attention. "Gee," she said, stifling a yawn. "That was good. How about unlocking this handcuff? We can go to the sanctuary and wait for the Fireflies to get back."

"Soon enough," he said, with an unfathomable grin. "Sleepy, dear?"

"A little. But if I get some fresh air . . ."

"Rest, first." Patch got to his feet and left the room.

"No, don't go." Ginger struggled briefly against the restraint and slumped onto the bed.

Shickie Doone was not the only one hiding in the Bible Alive Museum after hours. Plato Scopes had darted through a heavy drape into a side room when the recorded "please exit the building" announcement sounded. He stood and looked about. A sign mounted on a five-foot-high, plaster Corinthian column read, IS A MONKEY YOUR UNCLE? EVOLUTION: FACT OR FICTION? YOU DECIDE. CAST YOUR VOTE. Atop the column was a thirty-inch ceramic statuette of an ape seated on a stack of books contemplating a human skull held in one hairy hand.

Intrigued, Scopes next regarded a tall muscular manikin with blond curls and blue eyes with a sign around its neck identifying him as "Adam." To Scopes's left stood a large shaggy ape with a sign that read, "Ape." This was no zoologically described pongid—chimp, gorilla, or orangutan—but rather a model maker's conception of the kind of evil ape cast in a bad Tarzan movie: man-sized, slope-shouldered, beady-eyed, with a drooling, fang-encrusted mouth. To the other side stood a female figure, "Eve," modestly attired in a tasteful two-piece, fig leaf bathing suit. Plastic tropical vegetation surrounded the room, ran between the figures, and up to their knees.

Directly in front of Scopes was a full-length mirror. A box mounted to one side bore an LED counter, three large red buttons, one labeled ARE YOU DESCENDED FROM ADAM? the second, ARE YOU DESCENDED FROM EVE? and the third, ARE YOU DESCENDED FROM AN APE? Three oversized light bulbs protruded from the top of the box; one blue, another green, the third orange, all unlit. Curious to see how the exhibit would demonstrate the infallible logic of evolution to the masses, Scopes pressed the Adam button. He jumped as his vote registered with a *Ding*, the blue bulb lit, and brilliant, ceiling-mounted spotlights illuminated Adam and, simultaneously, Scopes's face. Hidden, semi-silvered and angled mirrors cleverly superimposed the body of Adam over that of Scopes in the mirror before him, and Adam's face became melded with his own. For a captivating moment, Scopes saw himself with blond curls and a buff body, wearing a fig leaf Speedo.

Startled, he released the button, wheeled about, listening for footsteps or a screeching alarm. He heard neither. The drapes at the entrance, intended to keep the room dim during exhibition hours, shielded his actions from patrolling guards.

He again faced the mirror, now reflecting only his own, unimpressive visage. Wanting no part of seeing himself as Eve, but curious about the third option, he raised a finger to the ARE YOU DESCENDED FROM AN APE? button, pushed, saw the orange bulb light, heard another *Ding*—and was immediately transformed into a hairy, hands-to-the-knees ape-man, his face surrounded by ragged fur. Instead of his own mouth—no dentist's dream on the best of days—Scopes saw slavering fangs and huge buck incisors.

With a shudder, he jerked his finger away and again poked the Adam button. *Ding.* He smiled at again seeing his mind's eye image of how he would have looked, had there been a compassionate God in heaven, or at least had he had more aesthetic parents. He grinned, retracted his finger, pressed the Adam button again and again: Scopes . . . Adam, *Ding.* Scopes . . . Adam, *Ding.* Scopes . . . Adam, *Ding. Ding. Ding. Ding.*

Finger hovering once more over the Adam button, he glimpsed the LED counter at the side of the mirror and recoiled in anger. Plato Scopes had just cast seven votes against evolution.

"Bullshit!" he said, and kicked the Corinthian column.

It rocked. Toppled. The ceramic ape fell. The hollow plaster column shattered with a dull KER–ACK–ACK moments before the ape burst beside it like a dropped flowerpot, making a more musical, if no less loud, CLINK–INKLE . . . INK.

Scopes clapped a palm over his mouth. A dozen guards, he knew, must already be unsheathing their weapons.

At that very moment, however, as if that God Scopes knew didn't exist had decided to perform a mini-miracle on behalf of the anthropologist, some out-of-tune horn squeaked near the front of the museum, followed by distracting thumps, breaking glass, and angry voices.

56

L
ike a tin bear in a shooting gallery, Jimmy sped toward the mummy room, away from the tumult at the front door. He stopped, spun on his heels, took six paces back, changed his mind and reversed, again moving in the direction of his dried-up ancestor. What was going on at the entrance? Drunks, maybe, beating on the door. He looked the other way, where the mummy begged his taking. Torn by conflicting duty and honor, Jimmy halted, pivoted, finally did an inconclusive little dance step in place.

"Damn!" He had promised his grandfather not to make trouble—or at least not get caught making trouble. He had also raised his hand in an oath to preserve order and property when the Bible Alive Museum hired him as a guard. On the other hand, the mummy represented everything he had been fighting for. He flip-flopped again at the thought of his ancestor lying helpless and exposed while disrespectful white tourists took snapshots and snickered at his nakedness.

"I'll hide him, then deal with whoever's at the door. No, get rid of whoever's yelling—college kids, probably—and rescue the mummy. When everything's A-OK, I'll duck out, take him to Grandpop's and be back, no one the wiser."

The pounding at the entrance grew louder. Glass broke. "What now?" Jimmy ran to the front doors.

Not just college kids, but a crowd, more of a mob, wearing white robes, carrying torches and flashlights—Ginger's Fireflies, the Children of Light. Jimmy reached for the radio at his waist, realized he had left it in the employee lounge, inside the building, past the entrance. A second pane of glass broke. Though solo, still dressed in his David outfit, and armed only with a nightstick and slingshot, he at least held the moral high ground. He flicked the switch for the outside lights.

Spots bathed the entry portico and exterior ramps in brilliant light. The mob retreated.

Jimmy peered through the small, broken window in one of the door panels, swallowed, gripped his nightstick, unbolted the doors, and stepped outside.

Assuming a wide stance, he made an effort at sounding authoritative. "Stay back. Police are on the way."

"So what?" shouted one of the Joneses. "We're on a mission from God."

Another one added, "Who the hell are you, anyway?"

"Museum guard." Jimmy brandished his nightstick at chest height, slapped the end against his open palm for effect.

One of the shaggy-haired men hooted at him, ran up the zigzag ramp and, before Jimmy could react, grabbed the nightstick and ripped it from his hands. He turned his back to Jimmy, faced the torch-bearing mob, pumped the stick over his head and bowed, grinning. The crowd cheered.

Embarrassed, hot with anger, Jimmy kicked him in the rear end. The sole of Jimmy's sandal caught the man on his left cheek, in mid bow, arms extended, as if preparing for flight. And, indeed, he left the ground, soared six feet in a swan dive, somersaulted down the sloping front wall, and tumbled across the ramp into the mob.

Goliath Jones, half a head above the others, cleared a path through the fallen. "Whoever that is, he's no guard. Look at him, dressed like some big city fairy."

"Am not," Jimmy said, "I'm David, from out of the Bible."

Another man said, "David? He says he's David? Wearing a dress and lace-up sandals? I say he's a Sodomite."

The crowd began a new chant, "Sodomite . . . Sodomite . . ."

Jimmy shouted back, "David, dammit. I'm David."

"David, huh?" Goliath Jones stepped onto the ramp. "I been putting up with David jokes all my life. It's payback time." He made a show of rolling up the sleeves of his robe. He relieved one of his associates of a baseball bat, jabbed it to a point at his right, and said, "I'm gonna send your head right over that fence, Bub."

Jimmy's back bumped the closed doors. He swallowed. No nightstick. No police on the way. The mob waving torches, chanting, growing meaner by the second. He considered retreating but realized by the time he turned to open the door, the big man with the bat would be up the stairs and on him.

His fingers brushed the slingshot, and he remembered scattering Ginger's atheist attackers. If he could keep their spokesman at bay for a few seconds he could retreat inside, lock the doors, and phone for help.

He scanned the pavement for a stone. Apparently Mr. Trout's threats to the janitorial staff had effect because the portico was spotless. The only thing out of place was a wad of pink bubble gum, stuck in a carved lotus flower on one of the entrance portico's Mesopotamian-Phoenician-Graeco-Roman-Egyptian columns.

In one continuous motion, Jimmy yanked the slingshot from his belt and plucked the gum from the column. It was still semi-soft, so he rolled it between his palms into a rough sphere, positioned it in the leather pad, raised the wooden Y, pulled back the rubber, and let loose.

The gum flew like a pink rocket to Goliath Jones's forehead, connecting with an audible *Thwap*. Jones yelped and sank to his knees.

A bonneted woman ran to his side. Apparently confusing the hot pink glop stuck to Goliath's flesh with a bloody hole in his head, she screeched, "He killed him!" and fainted.

Word spread fast: "Goliath is dead."

"The Sodomite shot him."

"Right in the brains."

"—blood all over the place."

Shock turned to rage. Joneses raced past their fallen leader, up the ramp.

Astonished by his aim and the stopping power of Double Bubble, Jimmy stared for several seconds at the fallen Goliath. Too long. He spun to open the door, but the mob was upon him. A hand snagged his kilt and tugged. Another gripped his ankles, a third, his elbow. Three, then four, then five men wrestled him down the ramp.

Goliath, sprawled on the asphalt, picked at his sore forehead and muttered, "Hell, it's only chewing gum," but no one heard him.

The jocks near the rear of the pack slapped palms and shouted, "Fight!"

One of the demolition derby drivers, still convinced he was at the rear of a Klan march, yelled, "String him up!"

Everyone had ideas.

"No, burn him."

"Hang the Sodomite!"

"Hang him, then burn him!"

57

hickie Doone was on his way to the mummy room when renewed shouting at the entrance slowed his pace. Initially, he chuckled, realizing the noise would distract the guard, but the current "Let me go," followed by "Help!" and a series of angry orders to "String him up," "Burn the Sodomite," and "Crucify him" gave him pause. Too long had Shickie cast himself as a victim to ignore the plight of some other poor schmoe about to be drawn and quartered by the masses. The man in trouble, Shickie realized, had to be the guard, the young Indian who Shickie planned to outsmart this night, but who, as Shickie recalled from Poncho's, wasn't such a bad kid, suffering from woman trouble—something else Shickie could relate to.

"Hold on, Fenster," he said, "I'll be right back." Maybe, he thought, as he trotted to the entrance, he could find a phone, call the cops, and put a stop to the lynching or tar and feathering or whatever other untidy end was planned for the young guard. Having done his civic duty, he could beat it back to Fenster, and liberate him.

One peek though the broken panel in the twin metal doors,

however, made it clear if Shickie didn't act himself, the poor kid would soon be toast. He identified the instigators as Patch's Jones clan. They had set fire to a cotton candy cart in the shape of a Babylonian chariot and were fueling it with broken benches and trash from garbage bins, apparently intent on flambéing young Jimmy Feather.

"What can *I* do?" Shickie said. But no sooner did he mouth the question, than he knew the answer. He removed Houdini from his shirt, set him on the floor and said, "Stay." Houdini sat, cocked his head, and watched his master untie his lace-up brogans, slip the overall suspenders from his shoulders, step out of his trousers and Jockey shorts, strip off his shirt, and, finally, remove his hat, wig, sunglasses, and beard. Palming a small item from his trouser pocket, Shickie opened the twin doors and emerged onto the portico as devoid of clothing as the day his Ma screamed, "My God, I went through nine months of hell for *that?*"

Shickie took a deep breath, raised his arms on the top step, and called out, "Children . . ."

A Firefly women gasped. "HALLELUJAH! It's the Prince of Light, come down from heaven to take us up."

Heads turned, eyes bugged, tears streamed. People dropped to their knees and wailed with happiness. Several began to undress, believing the Rapture had finally begun, eager to help it along.

Goliath Jones, a red welt still glowing at the center of his forehead, held Jimmy Feather in a hammerlock, giving him a knuckles-to-the-scalp Indian burn as a warm-up for his impending barbecue. At the appearance of Doone, Jones paused in mid-rub. "Glory be," he said, "Reverend Patch was right about that miracle."

Shickie pointed at him. "Release the young man."

"Whatever you say, Lord." Jones flung open his arms.

Off balance, Jimmy dropped headfirst to the cement.

Shickie motioned. "Come to me, young sinner."

Jimmy didn't need encouragement. He rose to his feet, palming a cut over his eyebrow, and ran up the stairs.

Goliath Jones loosened his belt and unbuttoned his shirt. "We're ready, Lord."

The crowd began to sway, murmuring a rhythmic, "Rapture, Rapture, Rapture."

Jimmy reached the portico, eyed the blood on his hand.

In a near whisper from the side of his mouth, Shickie said, "Get inside, keep the door cracked."

"Children," Shickie said to the assembled, "I returned to commend your loyalty, to say I have been watching you, and that the Great Rapture nears."

"Nears?" said Goliath Jones. He had lowered his pants to his ankles and was about to step out of them. "You mean you're not taking us now?"

"Uh, things aren't quite ready in heaven," Shickie said. "I'll come back soon, okay?"

"Look, we come all the way from Texas and—"

Goliath Jones's wife gave him an elbow to the ribs. "Watch your mouth, dummy. He could send you to hell as easy as heaven."

Jones kicked at the pavement. "I 'spose." He raised his trousers, gave Shickie a sheepish look, and ventured one more question. "How soon is soon?"

"In heaven," Shickie said, with the solemnity of the prophet they took him to be, "soon is seldom the same as soon on earth. But eternity is forever." And, with that, he swept his arms across his chest. There was a brilliant flash of light, a plume of cottony white smoke, and—Poof!—the Prince of Light was gone.

"Ah-ha!" Maury said, binoculars to his eyes, surveilling the Bible Alive Museum from atop the Space Needle. "So, Shickie Doone still walks the earth." He patted the .22 Colt in the holster beneath his madras sports jacket. "And, when you come out of that building? The Hammer will be on you like a hawk. Contract complete, conscience clear."

*　　*　　*

"You okay?" Shickie asked Jimmy as he threw the bolt on the door. He lifted his trousers from the floor, retrieved a red bandana from a pocket, and passed it to the young guard for the cut over his eye.

Jimmy pressed it to his forehead. "Doesn't hurt much," he did a double take at Shickie's shirt on the floor, "but I'm hallucinating. I just saw your shirt move."

"That ain't no hallucination, that's Houdini." Shickie lifted the shirt with one hand, scooped up the Yorkie with the other. He passed Houdini to Jimmy and reassembled himself as the Amish farmer.

The crowd got noisy again, arguing over the why of the Prince's miraculous return, the meaning of soon, and whether the Prince's mummy had disappeared with the Prince. If the mummy had returned to heaven, so the logic was running, recovering him would be moot, but if the Prince left his mortal remains behind again, then, more than ever, the mummy belonged in the Temple of Light.

Goliath Jones again took command, said, "The Sodomite escaped—got inside before the Prince could send him to blazes. Let's get the Sodomite *and* the mummy."

For the second time, the mob advanced.

Shickie pressed the beard to his cheek. "Time to make ourselves scarce." He took Houdini from Jimmy, tucked him in his shirt, and trotted toward the mummy room.

Jimmy followed for ten paces, hesitated, and took two steps back. "I ought to get my radio and call for help. Left it in the lounge, other side of the entrance."

The mob was battering the doors already, chanting, "Get the Sodomite. Get the mummy."

"On the other hand," Jimmy said. "Maybe we oughta hide."

"Smart boy." Shickie put a hand over his solar plexus to hold Houdini in place and broke into a flat-out run.

They rounded a corner as the front doors gave way. Ominous, shifting shadows from the mob's torches lit the passage.

"This way." Jimmy picked up the pace at the sound of a new refrain, "Burn the Sodomite. Burn the Sodomite." He passed Shickie, entered the cavernous Genesis Hall, dimly lit by a single flickering mercury vapor lamp, and headed for Jonah's whale.

Shickie glanced over his shoulder at flickering torch light. When he looked forward, Jimmy was gone.

"In here," Jimmy called from the toothy mouth of the leviathan.

Shickie followed, over the pink tongue, through a matte black maintenance door, and into the belly of the whale.

Junior Trout and his crew were driving to Ponchos when they noticed the crowd outside the museum. They watched from half a block away as the same tanned young man in the skirt who had thwarted their abduction of the stacked blonde, opened the door, backed the mob away, and was subsequently captured.

"Maybe we oughta call the cops," Peaches suggested.

"Cops?" Junior swatted him on the temple. "Us call the cops? They wanna burn the twinkie, let 'em. They want Daddy's mummy, that's another story. I've got a three-fifty-seven in the glove compartment and the museum door keys. We'll go in the back and head 'em off." He slapped the wheel of the Buick. "Daddy is gonna be so damned proud."

"Time to break heads," said Six-pack.

Peaches stopped chewing to say, "Bet your ass."

Junior sped around the block to the rear of the building.

Creely Patch, alone in the Armory Lighthouse, opened the door to Ginger's room. "Hello, dear. How was the hot chocolate?"

He regarded her lying unconscious on the bed, one arm extended, held slightly higher than her shoulder by the handcuff and chain. "No back-talk this time?"

He removed the restraints, set the extended arm at her side, and sat on the bed. "Such a beautiful girl. We're going to be together in heaven, you and I, together for all eternity. Do you know that?" He put a hand behind Ginger's head and lifted, approximating a nod.

"God explained it all," he said. "How you will precede me. Those of little faith need to see another Rapture—and you are the lucky one. I'll follow with the others."

Patch cocked an ear to be sure no one had returned, and ran his fingertips across Ginger's cheek. With a furtive double take at the door, he said, "Alone."

He wiped the sweat from his face, licked his dry lips, and began unbuttoning her blouse.

58

Plato Scopes entered the Rapture Room, draped floor to ceiling with royal purple velour, and slid his arms under the mummy. He lifted, speaking softly as to a baby. "Nearly forgot how light you are. Oh, we're going to make anthropological history, my fine specimen, no thanks to Horace Duckhaus and the Captain Hook Museum, or to this temple of superstition."

The museum preparator had positioned a bolt of velour behind the mummy to keep if from rolling onto its back. Scopes unwound the cloth and wrapped the body round and round, creating a protective, and disguising, shroud. He carried it into the corridor like a rolled carpet, explaining at the sound of distant voices, "We'll just zip out the back while the nuts fight it out up front, eh?"

As he approached the exit doors, however, he heard metallic scraping. One door jiggled in the frame and the tip of a pry bar appeared at chest height.

"Uh-oh." Sandwiched between threats front and rear, Scopes hurried back to the evolution room, hid his cloth-wrapped baby behind the ape, while he hunkered, nerves a-jangle, in the vegetation behind Adam.

*   *   *

Concerned about Ginger, Betsy dropped from the crusade and returned to the Temple of Light. She stepped inside, and, wary of Reverend Patch, ducked behind the Plexiglas display of the Prince's Rapture clothes to listen. She heard the Messenger speaking in Ginger's room, but couldn't hear Ginger. Betsy crept closer, to a thick concrete column, heard Patch say, "It's nearly time, dear."

She soft-stepped closer and peered around the doorframe. Her hand shot to her mouth at sight of Ginger, sprawled on the bed, naked, unconscious. Creely Patch, wearing his purple Rapture Robe, held Ginger's panties in one hand. He wiped perspiration from his face with a forearm, crumpled the pale blue cloth in a fist, and crushed it against his face, sucking air through it in fast, gurgling breaths.

Betsy nearly retched. She clutched her mouth and turned her head. When she looked back, Patch had tossed the panties over his shoulder. His blocky hand hovered over Ginger's right breast. He limbered his fingers like a pianist before a recital, and slowly lowered them.

Betsy gasped.

Patch swiveled his head toward the door.

She ran. "Jimmy," Betsy said. "Jimmy will know what to do."

"How are you doing?" Shickie asked, sitting on a toolbox in the gut of the whale. Napoleon-like, he had tucked one hand in his shirt. Jimmy sat across from him on a five-gallon paint can.

"Feeling a little wobbly." Jimmy examined the bandana. "Bleeding's stopped, though." He peered at Shickie, lit by one of several work lights hanging from the internal metal frame of the cetacean. "You saved my life." He wiped his right hand on his skirt and extended it.

Shickie shook it. "Prince of Light's the name, saving's my game."

"Wait a minute. If you're Reverend Doone, then . . . you aren't . . . that is, the mummy isn't . . . you. I *knew* it. I knew he was my ancestor."

"He's related to somebody, all right."

"You've been in Gatlinburg the whole time."

"More or less, and I'd appreciate it if you'd keep my little secret. There's people I best stay clear of." A muffled shout outside the whale caught his attention. "How safe are we in here?"

"They could crawl right into the whale's mouth and not see that door. This rubber skin is thick, practically soundproof. When the exhibit is finished, they'll have an actor playing Jonah, with whale songs and the sound of waves crashing. The whole thing is on big wood rockers, will roll side to side, like it's swimming. That spiral staircase leads to a blowhole so people will be able to look out and see the Ark and the Six Days of Creation Sound and Light Show. Pretty cool, huh? "

"Trout must have spent a bundle. This whale, the Ark. Hell, the tank it's floating in is huge."

"Makes Ripley's aquarium down the hill look like a farm pond," Jimmy said. "According to the brochure it's 'Big as the Dead Sea'. Oh, Mr. Trout's ambitious. I hear they're calling him the Walt Disney of religion. He spends a lot, but he cuts corners, too. Modifies exhibits from other museums fallen on hard times, skimps on the payroll—like me, the only night guard. That shoring around the flood tank? Building inspectors are making him replace the wood frame with steel, but he's putting it off. Rumors are, if attendance doesn't pick up soon, he's in big trouble. That's why he bought my ancestor. With the buzz on TV and in the papers, and people thinking it's your mortal remains, they're lining up to—"

Footsteps and shouting, muffled by the body of the whale, grew louder.

Shickie rubbed Houdini behind the ears to keep him from barking.

Jimmy shook his head at the sounds outside. "What am I

supposed to do? I'm the guard. But, if they catch me again, I'm afraid they'll—"

"Roast you, or worse. Hey, Trout ought to have half a dozen guards on patrol. You did you duty, kid, put your life on the line for that old goat's property. No . . . we'd better stay put."

"The mummy . . . I can't let that mob get him."

Shickie patted him on the shoulder. "They won't hurt him. They'll take him to the Lighthouse. Plenty of time to recover the little shit later."

"Sir," Jimmy said, "that mummy is not a 'little shit.' He was probably a great warrior and—"

"Some warrior. Scoot over here, let me take a look at that cut."

Jimmy leaned forward. The talisman he wore suspended from a leather thong at his neck, the half an Indian head penny, dropped from his blouse and swung free.

Shickie stared at it in the dim light, lifted it on his palm for a closer look. Reflexively, his other hand dug into his watch pocket, clutched what he knew to be there, but which he was half convinced Jimmy had somehow filched: Shickie's good luck charm, the other half of Jimmy's Indian cent.

59

hickie's voice went hard. "Where did you get this?"

"My lucky penny? My father gave it to my mom. Came from the battle of the Little Big Horn. My dad was a great chief."

Shickie squinted at Jimmy, and again at the coin. He repeated, "Chief," and, "He's around, your father?"

Jimmy shrugged. "Kind of disappeared after I was born. All I know is that he was a great chief."

Shickie's hand dropped to his knee, limp. He stared at the floor.

"You recognized the penny," Jimmy said. "You *knew* him."

"No," Shickie barely paused. "Never knew him. Sorry. I, uh, saw the date. Eighteen sixty-five, year the Civil War ended. I used to collect coins. That would be pretty valuable if it hadn't been cut in half."

"Oh."

Jimmy explained how the Chief had gone on a great adventure before Jimmy's birth, probably a mission for his people, and never came back, had maybe been killed. But somehow, Jimmy could never bring himself to believe that. "He could have been hurt, got amnesia like the stories you hear. I've tried to track him, but I didn't have much to go on. I figure if he wasn't Cherokee, then Sioux or Cheyenne would make sense, but that didn't get me anywhere, either. Mom would never tell me his name. She was real funny about that, said she'd tell me everything on my sixteenth birthday, but then she—"

"What?"

"—died. When I was twelve. Drowned in a flood."

"Drowned?"

"Yeah. I was in school, but Grandpop—his farm's here outside of town—was there. It was black as night one afternoon, raining cats and dogs, tornado weather. The sky opened up over the valley and the sun peeked out, spraying those God rays across the countryside. Mom took her fiddle and climbed into this big oak tree growing at the side of the creek, like she used to do. It had gnarly roots snaking out of the bank and a crooked branch at least thirty feet up, hanging over the water. Had a flat place where the branch veed. You could sit up there and spy on the world and the world didn't know you were there. That was our secret place—Mom's and mine. Grandpop was on the porch that day, said she began fiddling when the waters came up.

"It was still storming in the mountains, see? Whoosh— flash flood. Surrounded the tree, sucked the earth from the roots. It toppled. Flood carried away the tree and my mom.

"They never found her, but there are still stories about people hearing fiddle music during storms down in that valley."

Shickie massaged his forehead, motioned for more.

"With Mom gone, Grandpop took care of me. He never met the Chief. Mom had been trying to break into country and western in Nashville, see? That's where she met my father. He disappeared, she came back to the farm, and that's when . . ."

Shickie remembered Maggie, though he'd had no idea she was pregnant. He couldn't imagine her that way—she'd been wiry as a wet farm cat. Maggie had fiery hair and a temper to match. "Chief" is what she called him, after the Indian outfit he wore hawking phony artifacts to Nashville tourists. With his long black hair he looked pretty convincing, he recalled— more so than most of his artifacts.

He had picked her up in a Nashville bar with a Grand-Old-Opry producer line, actually got her a few gigs during their five-week romance. He'd won the Indian head penny in a game of seven card stud, had sawn it in half with a jigsaw zigzag cut, gave one piece to Maggie, kept the other. Back then, he always gave them something: a healing crystal, a magic stone, a silver charm he'd say belonged to his grandmother. Maggie swore she would keep her half forever, made Shickie promise to do the same. He had, too, though less from the oath than from an uncommon winning streak shortly after.

When he left on his "great adventure," as Jimmy referred to it, Shickie planned to return. Didn't he? He phoned for a while, sent postcards. At least two. The "great adventure" was an extended road trip converting a truckload of phony, prehistoric Indian pottery, "five centuries old from the Spiro Mounds in Oklahoma," into hard currency. The collectors were eager, the artifacts, for once, masterful counterfeits, the documentation convincing, and the profits substantial. With the last artifact sold, Shickie planned a triumphal return to Nashville, but detoured to Vegas to celebrate. He tapped out in twenty-two hours. Thanks to his lucky Indian cent, however, before that same midnight, he met a fallen priest with a dozen cases of holy water bearing convincing Vatican seals. Sold every flask for a bundle and went on a streak. More money, bust again. Next stop: Arkansas, partner in an atomic mud bath in Hot Springs. A year later, he made it back to Nashville, found Maggie's number, phoned. Maggie was gone.

So, she died in a flood. Washed away in the branches of an oak tree, fiddling. It figured. Maggie always had a thing for trees. In fact, Jimmy was probably conceived in one, a humongous beech, as Shickie remembered. He nearly broke his neck falling out of it during one of their more spectacular bouts of amour—would have, if it hadn't been June, with leaves on the bushes below.

". . . left and went out West to . . ." Jimmy was telling him about his life, the travels, the protests, his frustration with never quite fitting in, his recent return to Gatlinburg, his Grandpop's farm, and the current quest for his desiccated ancestor.

Shickie reciprocated but spoke in generalities, said he had been a magician and a promoter, that he founded the Temple of Light as "a beacon to the spiritually bereft, a refuge for lonely souls hopeful of ascending with angels from this vale of tears." How a shrewish wife sold his baby Houdini to a puppy mill, and how heartless creditors had driven him out of town.

"My plan, soon as I recover a few prized mementos from the Lighthouse, is to get away for good. I read about this island in the Pacific where the natives are, like, untouched by modern civilization. They're like Adams and Eves, the kind of people that Frenchman painted in Tahiti. Get this: they worship the airplanes that fly from Guam to Japan or wherever, five miles over their heads.

"Both the Japanese and the allies missed the place in World War Two—or almost. An American C-47 Gooney Bird, full of supplies meant for another island, was shot up over the ocean a hundred miles away. The crew bailed out, was rescued by the Navy, but the pilot made it to this island and crash-landed. Lived there like a king for nearly a year waiting to be rescued. No such luck. He finally sailed away on a double out-rigger canoe, promising to return. Got picked up by a ship and was sent back to the mainland. Outsiders forgot about the island, but the natives set up a trade network of stuff they scavenged from the plane, erected a shrine to the 'great sky bird.' They bring offerings of fruit and natural pearls big as gumdrops, and still speak a smattering of pidgin English. Wild, huh?

"I've been thinking I could charter a plane, see? Mount some speakers, so it flies over first, real low, blaring the Stones—really shake 'em up. Then I bail out with my baby here, my magic kit and a sack full of gewgaws. I'd hire a copra schooner to pick me up a year later. I could live like royalty, have a grass hut full of pearls like Scrooge McDuck's money room before long, huh? I figure—"

He was interrupted by shouts beyond the whale's mouth.

"Better see what they're up to," Jimmy said. "I'm still kind of rocky. How about climbing up to the blowhole?"

Twenty seconds later, Shickie ducked back into the whale's interior. "They ran toward the mummy room, but from the sound of it, they couldn't find Fens—uh, it. They're like army ants, swarming over the place, looking for him."

"What do you mean, 'couldn't find' him?" Jimmy jumped to his feet, a bit too soon. He put a hand on the staircase to steady himself. "He was there earlier, I saw him."

"I'm telling you what I heard. That big one, the guy who dumped you on your head, ordered them to search the place. A bunch just went into the Ark." Shickie grinned. "I hope one of them bends over in the vicinity of that horny goat."

"Goat?"

"Would-be boyfriend. I—"

He was cut off by a distant, but piercing scream: "*Noooo!* That mummy is *mine*. Get your hands off him."

"Looks like the Fireflies found your ancestor," Shickie said, and, like a curious prairie dog, zipped up to the blowhole and popped his head out to see who had Fenster now.

60

Since its humble beginnings, the Bible Alive Museum had grown into a class-A attraction, offering a smorgasbord of marvels to anyone with the price of admission. For Old Testament enthusiasts, there were wax Abrahams, Isaacs, and Elijahs, true to life—so proclaimed the signage—down to hair and eye color; for idolaters, a golden calf, authentic as the one Charlton Heston cast down in the *Ten Commandments*; for the perverse, plague reenactments with convincing stage blood, boils, locusts, flies and frogs; for gamblers, The Genesis Patriarchs: Guess Our Age Challenge, and, for bored kiddies, a Find the Baby Moses in the Bulrushes game.

Visitors climbed a zigzag entry ramp to enter at mid-level an imaginative recreation of the Tower of Babel, a pyramidal Babylonian ziggurat. Once inside the entry gate and beyond the Portal of Free Will, they had several options. One door led to the Elevator of Ascension rising to the apex of the pyramid and Heaven, including the For Those Who Have Arrived Gift Shop laden with designer clothing, name brand crystal, and the Best of The Sharper Image. A second door led to the seemingly endless Purgatory Ride and climatic Descent into Hell in the subbasement, while the third opened into spectacular Genesis Hall, home of the museum's most popular attractions: Jonah's Whale, a Forty Days and Forty Nights Flood tank with Noah's Ark floating at its center, and the Six Days of Creation Sound and Light Show.

Exhibits in the massive hall were spotlit during visiting hours, giving the impression they floated within the limbo black walls, floors, and ceiling. A thirty-foot-plus high dome arching overhead had been artfully painted as an idyllic sky, subtly illuminated during the sound and light show to simulate a transition from rosy dawn to violet dusk.

The floor of Genesis Hall sloped downward to the smaller Hall of Wonders, home of ever-changing attractions, foremost of late being the Mummy Room, continuing a gradual descent past the Temple Steps Gift Shop and the Garden of Eden Café to the ground level exit into the twenty-first century, the parking lot, and the fudge, timeshare, and tee-shirt shops of secular Gatlinburg.

The EVOLUTION: Fact or Fiction? exhibit was one of the first encountered in Genesis Hall. With over a hundred Fireflies and Joneses searching for the mummy this fateful night, it wasn't long before someone wandered into the evolution alcove. That someone happened to be a small, frightened child, one of the Jones clan, separated from her parents. She paid no mind to the broken crockery littering the floor, but, sniffling, walked directly to the full-length mirror at exhibit center. Aware the reflected twin with the worried face looking back at her would be of no assistance, she turned to the Eve figure, took its hand, looked up hopefully and said, "Mommy?"

The hand was cold. Eve remained impassive. The lost child wiped a tear from her eye and moved to Adam. His hand proved no warmer, no more responsive, but to her "Daddy?" he answered: "Go away little girl." Adam's lips hadn't moved, but the harsh order made her drop his hand and take two steps back. She again faced the mirror. Her nose twitched, she whimpered, stuck out her lower lip, and inhaled fitfully, winding up for a full-blown cry.

At sight of the red, prune-face staring back at her, however, she forgot the tears, and, in a moment, giggled and waved. The little girl in the looking glass waved back. The original bobbed left, watched her twin follow suit. She bowed. The twin bowed. Laughing, she—

"Get out of here, little girl," sounded again from behind the Adam figure.

"Will not," she said, and snickered, followed by a pirouette and a quick peek over her shoulder to see if her twin got it right.

"Go away. There are monsters in here."

"Are not!" Making faces.

A hand reached from the vegetal shadows behind Adam, pressed the red button beside the mirror labeled ARE YOU DESCENDED FROM AN APE? An orange bulb flashed, a *Ding* sounded, and a monstrous, snarling ape filled the mirror, obscuring the hitherto laughing twin.

"See?" Adam said. "Now, go away,"

But, instead of running, the little girl froze in place and wailed: long, high, and loud.

"Oh, shit," Adam said. "Just what I needed."

The Jones child's shrill cries at being confronted by the slavering evolution ape brought concerned adults to her side within seconds. The first burly Jones male threw his flashlight at the hairy image, shattering the mirror, initiating more frightened screams from the girl.

Plato Scopes threw his arms around the velour-swaddled mummy and retreated into a dark corner an instant before the mirror disintegrated. Hopeful the Joneses were more concerned with protecting their young than lingering to investigate Darwinian theory, he hunkered amongst the plastic jungle growth and the shards of column, statuette, and mirror.

Unfortunately for him, one of the more attentive Joneses squinted his way. "Hey—who's that back there? What are you hiding?"

"Praise the Lord," a companion said, a short scuffle later, "it's the *Prince*, all wrapped up in purple velvet."

Minutes before, Orlando had thrown his full weight behind the pry bar and sprung the rear doors. He and Rita Rae heard muffled voices ahead, beyond the café.

She shoved his back. "Move. Before they beat us to him. He's up to the left."

They ran up a gently rising floor, passed the When Men Walked with Dinosaurs exhibit and the Make a Wish Wailing Wall. Rita Rae was ahead of him when they reached the Rapture Room. Footsteps and "Return the Prince" sounded not far ahead.

She ran into the mummy alcove. "Empty."

Orlando probed the velour draping. "*Nada.*"

"Hurry. They can't have gone far." She spun to leave, but collided at the doorway with the first of the marchers, who had, in fact, been running toward, not away, from the Rapture Room. Two young Fireflies and Rita Rae writhed on the floor in a tangle of arms, legs, and robes. Rita Rae sat up, ran exploring fingers up and down her beehive cone, found it tilted thirty degrees to the left. She grabbed the braid of the nearest Firefly and tugged. "You little bitch. Crack my hair, will you?" A harder tug and the girl squealed. Within seconds, a bevy of white-robed Fireflies surrounded the combatants, compacted like Tokyo commuters boarding a bullet train. Rita Rae dropped the braid and struggled to her feet.

When it became apparent the mummy had vanished, the mob turned angry and backed Rita Rae and Orlando into a corner. Orlando held them at bay with his flick knife, while Rita Rae taunted them from behind his back.

"Look how she's dressed," said one of the Jones women. "It's Jezebel come to life. Consorting with a son of Ham. What have you done with the Prince, harlot?"

"Harlot? Why, you ugly slug." Rita Rae karate-kicked, imbedding a spike heel in the Jones female's fleshy thigh.

Two Jones males dragged their injured relation away while others formed a mean circle around the woman in red and her dusky companion. Shouts erupted. "Stone the harlot!" "Burn them both." And, from the demolition derby drivers, Crash and Burn, who had worked their way forward, "String 'em up!" and "Hang 'em high!"

The standoff ended with a distant shriek from higher in the museum, perhaps a tiny girl being skinned alive. That high pitched scream was followed by indistinct shouts and a loud, clearly audible, male, "*Noooo!* That mummy is mine. Get your hands off him."

61

*S*ix-pack swung the museum's sprung rear door on its hinge. "Somebody broke in back here, too."

Junior fingered the .357 Magnum tucked in his belt. "If they think they're gonna get that mummy, they've got another think coming."

He led his crew to the Rapture Room. They found it empty.

Peaches said, "They must have got it."

"Well, du-uhhh," Junior said. "And if they get it to that church of theirs, we'll never see it again."

They ran deeper into the museum. Ahead, it sounded more and more like a high school football game, the score even, eight seconds left in the fourth quarter with the ball on the one-yard line.

The whale vibrated from the rhythmic chant filling Genesis Hall, "The Prince . . . the Prince . . . we have the Prince."

Shickie called to Jimmy from the blowhole. "If you're up to it, you'd better get your butt up here."

Jimmy climbed the spiral staircase and poked his head out

beside Shickie. They saw jostling bodies, nearly a hundred of them in white robes, a few in civvies. The Children of Light were passing the velour-wrapped mummy over their heads like a crowd-surfing rocker. Most carried flashlights, a few waved smoking tiki torches. Surging in a triumphal frenzy, they jostled the flood tank and whale. Lesser exhibits were knocked to the floor and trampled. Jimmy and Shickie gripped the edges of the blowhole as the whale shook.

Somewhere, someone tripped the switch that activated the Six Days of Creation Sound and Light show. A deep male voice intoned from hidden speakers, "LET THERE BE LIGHT," and the room (hitherto dimly lit for benefit of the cleanup crew by a buzzing, green, mercury-vapor lamp) glowed flamingo pink as recessed lights illuminated the domed, sky-painted ceiling. The opening notes of Strauss's *Also Sprach Zarathustra* roared through the cavernous space: *Dum—Dum—DUM . . . Ta—DUM!*

In a moment of gallows humor, Shickie said, "What is . . . the theme from Space Odyssey?"

"Real cute." Jimmy pointed to the cloth-encased mummy, "You think they'll hurt him?"

"Nah. Like I said before, they'll take him to the Temple of Light. We'll figure out a way to get him when things settle down."

As if contradicting him, muffled sirens wailed outside in counterpoint to the *Dum—Dum—DUM . . .*

Loudspeakers boomed, "GOD SAW THE LIGHT, THAT IT WAS GOOD," and the world's first sunrise bathed Genesis Hall in peach and yellow.

A skinny man in a lab coat leapt from the crowd, seized the loose end of the shroud, yanked it, and yelled, "He's mine!" The wrapped mummy rolled across heads and upraised hands, unraveling, trailing a purple wake.

Dum—Dum—DUM . . .

At the edge of the mob, Rita Rae shouted in Orlando's ear, "We've *got* to get him away from those yahoos."

Orlando flicked open his knife and began jabbing ribs and backs, mouthing a *con permiso* here, a *perdóname* there as he cleared a path. Poked Fireflies screeched and dropped flashlights.

The ceiling dome darkened. Stars appeared, soon to fade as indigo gave way to azure. "AND GOD MADE THE FIRMAMENT . . . AND THE EVENING AND THE MORNING WERE THE SECOND DAY. . . ."

"The Prince . . . the Prince . . ."

"If they get that thing out of here," Junior said, "Daddy'll bowlingball us for sure."

Peaches jumped for a better look. "It's over there, now. Keeps moving around."

Dum—Dum—DUM . . .

Six-pack barreled his way through thirty feet of mob and stretched. "I can almost reach it. . . . Got it!"

No, not the mummy, but rather the tail of the shroud. He gave it a mighty tug, enough to spin the mummy free of the remaining cloth. Fenster skittered over heads and shoulders like a cork on a storm-tossed ocean.

". . . AND THE GATHERING TOGETHER OF THE WATERS, HE CALLED SEAS . . ."

Noah's floodwaters fluoresced an emerald green from underwater spots as the third day of creation dawned. Startled by the glow, a Firefly on the stern of the Ark lost balance and cannonballed into the tank.

Dum—Dum—DUM . . .

"With all these people after that thing," one of the football players said to his two buddies, "it must be worth a bundle. Let's get it." They lowered their heads like the linesmen they were and rushed. Stomping, gouging, fouling, they cut a swath toward the mummy.

Dum—Dum—DUM . . .

Crash and Burn, the demolition derby drivers, watched the jocks. "Damned if them good old boys are gonna out-do me," Crash said. "C'mon, Burn, let's show 'em what for." Blocky individuals, both, and not adverse to competition, they uprooted a fiberglass palm tree and used it as a battering ram to knock aside white-robed scramblers.

On the third day of creation, hidden track lights illuminated plastic ferns, grass, and jungle foliage—minus Crash and Burn's palm tree.

"AND GOD SAW THAT IT WAS GOOD."

"Yeah, just peachy," Shickie said.

Dum—Dum—DUM . . .

"LET THERE BE LIGHTS IN THE FIRMAMENT OF HEAVEN. . . ."

The vaulted ceiling dimmed, and a projected moon crossed the night sky, already flickering orange from the tiki torches waving below.

Illuminating the battle on the fourth day of creation, a brilliant sun rose in the east—or was it a burst of flame from an exhibit set afire?

Dum—Dum—DUM . . .

Not the tallest man in the crowd, Plato Scopes lost sight of the mummy. He saw it again, stripped of its shroud. Lacking the bulk of the other contestants, he dropped to his knees and burrowed between legs like a toddler navigating a roomful of adults.

He surfaced like the Creature from the Black Lagoon, wrapped both arms around the mummy's waist, and pulled down with all his weight.

". . . LET THE WATERS BRING FORTH ABUNDANTLY THE MOVING CREATURES. . . ."

Dum—Dum—DUM . . .

The fifth day of creation unfolded. ". . . GOD CREATED GREAT WHALES, AND EVERY LIVING CREATURE. . . ."

Jimmy held on to the blowhole, watching the mob whirlpool around his ancestor like ants on a grub. He covered his eyes. "I can't watch."

The mummy resurfaced over the heads of three Joneses.

One of the males reached for the right ankle. Peaches popped from the crowd, wrapped his pudgy fingers around the mummy's left foot.

Shickie said, "Oh-oh," and then, "Wishbone."

Dum—Dum—DUM . . . Ta—DUM!

62

Despite his size, Six-pack was still four feet from the scrum, but Junior, at Peaches side, was nearly to the mummy's thigh. Peaches lost his brief grip on the mummy, but lurched for a more secure hold.

Scopes, clinging to Fenster's waist from below, yelped. His hands flew loose as Orlando poked him with the tip of his switchblade.

"I'm almost there," Rita Rae shouted. "Clear these bozos away."

As the sixth day of creation dawned, Orlando jabbed.

". . . AND GOD MADE THE BEASTS OF THE EARTH. . . ."

Stuck Fireflies yelped.

Dum—Dum—DUM . . .

Shickie flinched, white knuckled the rim of the blowhole. "Damned if it's not Rita Rae with that greaseball. They're after Fenster, too."

"Who's Fenster?" Jimmy said.

"Never mind."

Peaches clawed at the mummy like a drowning sailor at the edge of a life raft. His fingers brushed Fenster's left foot, curled around it for the second time, tightened. A bonneted

Jones woman hooked an arm over Fenster's right ankle. Peaches tugged, the Jones female pulled.

Fenster's legs formed a widening V.

Dum—Dum—DUM . . .

Jimmy's hand shot to his mouth.

Shickie groaned.

With the snap of a cracked potato chip, Fenster's left leg split from his body.

Dum—Dum—DUM . . . Ta–DUMMM!

Shickie said, "Oowwwch!"

Jimmy pinched the bridge of his nose. "My poor ancestor."

Peaches whooped, "I got a drumstick!"

Dum—Dum—DUM . . .

They heard a sickening *kee-raack* as one of the football players ripped loose Fenster's left arm and shoulder. Crash tore away his jaw. A secondary scuffle followed as two Fireflies snapped off fingers. Ten feet away a similar struggle was underway over Peaches's liberated leg. Children climbed the backs of adults to get a piece of the action.

A white-robed Jones woman, stunned, her temple bloodied by a blow to the head from Fenster's jawbone, fell to the floor and crawled aimlessly, keening like a wounded lamb.

". . . OVER EVERY CREEPING THING THAT CREEP-ETH OVER THE EARTH . . ."

A Jones clan boy ran from his older sister, taunting, "Nah–na–na–*Nah*-na. I've got a toe and you've got nothhh–ing."

"Disgusting," Jimmy said. "I'm the guard. I should have stopped this."

Shickie gave Jimmy's shoulder a squeeze, adding, to himself, "Too bad the state early-paroled the little shit."

Dum—Dum—DUM . . .

Rita Rae twined her fingers through the mummy's hair. Goliath Jones wrenched the torso, twisted it so violently that what was left of Fenster's head flew loose. It pivoted in a short blurring arc, anchored by Rita Rae's grasp. One of the football players reacted reflexively, and, in a perfect interception, slapped his palms over the ears, drew the head to his chest, tucked, and ran. Rita Rae held fast. Hair ripped from the scalp. Plato Scopes bobbed for air. A Jones bearing a tiki torch jabbed it at Scopes, missed, and set a robed woman afire.

"... GOD CREATED MAN IN HIS OWN IMAGE. ..."

"This is awful," Jimmy said from the blowhole. He had both hands over his eyes, but spread his fingers to watch. "Just awful."

Shickie shook his head. "Oh, brother."

Dum—Dum—DUM ...

A Firefly housewife held Fenster's lower leg at arm's length for several seconds, stared at it, and, repulsed, flung it in the air.

Twenty feet away, a pack of Joneses snatched at it like maidens at a bridal bouquet toss. Within seconds, a fistfight broke out over chunks of mummified muscle ripped from long bones. Shards crackled under foot. The mob dropped to their knees and scrambled for relics, for souvenirs.

"Gimme a piece."

"I got its calf!"

"... TO YOU IT SHALL BE FOR MEAT. ..."

Orlando stuck the football player cradling Fenster's head in the triceps with his flick knife. The scalped head dropped to the floor, bounced once on the concrete, and rolled between Six-pack's legs. Six-pack saw it, tripped, and fell backward. The skull collapsed under his posterior with an audible crunch. Crash, the demolition derby driver, and Goliath Jones struggled in a brief tug-of-war over the mummy's upper arms. The arms ripped from the torso. Crash and Goliath stumbled, taking three men and a woman to the floor. For an instant, the trunk of the mummy hung in mid-air. Headless, armless, legless, it dropped onto the prone Six-pack's chest.

Dum—Dum—DUM ...

More concerned with what was under him than aware of what had landed on his chest, and, struggling to right himself, Six-pack reflexively threw his arms around the mummy's torso and bear-hugged it to his stomach.

Elsewhere, the mummy's limbs fragmented under scrabbling fingers and hands. Desiccated flakes and slivers clouded the air, showering combatants like gray confetti.

From his blowhole pulpit, Shickie misquoted Genesis 3:19. "Belly to belly and dust to dust."

"You're sick," Jimmy muttered. "You're all sick." And then, "So much for a dignified burial."

Shickie sighed. "So much for being my brother's keeper."

Dum—Dum—DUM . . .

Still lying on his back, Six-pack lowered his chin to see what he had the death grip on. His lips brushed the stump of the mummy's neck. Primal fears of the dead, the boyhood memory of his mother making him kiss the rubbery flesh of Uncle Benny in the casket, the recollection of finding Doone in the freeze-drier, of dumping his body in the sinkhole, and, now, this *thing* coming back to *haunt* him . . .

Six-pack screamed the scream of all screams.

Jimmy pointed. "That's one of Ginger's atheists."

Shickie put his hands to his ears. "Sounds like he finally got religion."

The mob recoiled from the horrific wail. A Firefly choir girl, a part-time clerk in Mr. T's Fudge Shoppe on the Gatlinburg strip, lost her lunch, a quarter pound of semi-digested praline pecan fudge, onto Junior's Hard Rock Cafe leather jacket. In the excitement of the moment, Peaches whirled, slashing a demolition derby driver's shoulder with his Bowie knife. The man shrieked and punched out a bearded Jones. The Firefly who had been set afire howled. The white-robed woman on her hands and knees with the bloody temple sobbed. Rita Rae cursed.

Sun set on the sixth day of creation, "AND GOD SAW EVERY THING THAT HE HAD MADE, AND, BEHOLD, IT WAS VERY GOOD."

63

um—Dum—DUM . . .

Recoiling from the glutinous sludge befouling his prized leather jacket, Junior tripped over a Firefly woman snailing on all fours. He fell backward. His palms slapped concrete and exploded with whitehot pain. He pressed them to his lips and flopped onto his side. For ten long seconds, he lay in an infantile curl.

The frustration of once again failing his father simmered, bubbled over like a stewpot too long on the fire. Junior rose to his knees, eyes stinging, nose dribbling.

"This is so fucking unfair. I find the mummy and the Hammer steals it. Daddy gets hold of it and these crazies rip it up. Why does everything I do go to crap?"

He brushed a tear from his cheek with a sleeve, and was rewarded with a snootful of sick-sweet smelling, semi-digested fudge. "Yu-uck! I've had enough."

Dum—Dum—DUM . . .

"*Enough*, you hear?" Junior reached for one of the McDonald's napkins he kept in his pocket for emergencies, found instead the .357 Magnum tucked in his belt. His fingers encircled the grip. At that moment, the cool knurled plastic felt better in his hand than a college girl's thigh—one more pleasure the world had denied him. "You bastards," he said to no one in particular. "You think you can keep kicking Junior Trout around like some stinking football?"

"Ouch!" He took a boot to the ribs from a white-robed Jones woman chasing either a dried apricot or the mummy's ear.

"That's the last straw." Junior scrambled to his feet, pointed his .357 revolver at the rafters, and shouted, "No more fucking with Junior Trout!"

He fired. Again, and again.

Time and motion ceased. Like Pompeiians caught in the fiery blast of Vesuvius, combatants were fixed in mid-stride, mid-punch, mid-whatever they were doing at the moment, strobed into immobility by the Magnum blasts.

"THUS THE HEAVENS AND THE EARTH WERE FIN-ISHED, AND ALL THE HOST OF THEM. AND ON THE SEV-ENTH DAY GOD ENDED HIS WORK WHICH HE HAD MADE; AND HE—"

Junior fired the last round. The slug took out the ampli-fier, stilling not only Zarathustra, but also the booming voice of God.

"—RESTED————"

Screams, cries, shouts, and moans all faded to a fearful, seemingly eternal, stony silence.

And then, like the start-up of the Big Bang . . . panic erupted. People ran, tumbled, collided with one another, car-omed off the whale and flood tank in a mad rush to get away from the crazy kid with the big gun.

Shickie and Jimmy, neck high out of the blowhole, held on as the whale bucked. Shickie elbowed Jimmy—pandemonium made speech pointless—and nodded to the tank where the stampeding mob had dislodged a ten-foot stretch of two-by-four shoring. A dozen frightened Fireflies who had run from the shooter up the steps and onto the gangway, stopped in mid-stride as a series of oscillating ripples in the water grew into three-, and soon, five-foot waves. Three people tumbled into the water, two dropped to their bellies and hugged the plank walkway. One made it to the lurching Ark, but halted at the bleating, snarling, and crashing of frightened animals inside.

With a reptilian hiss, a stressed seam split, jetting a narrow fountain over the mob. *Kee–rack–rack–rack!* Rivets popped like Chinese firecrackers, and the breach widened, sheeting water in a horizontal cascade halfway across Genesis Hall.

As if some abysmal sea monster stirred within Noah's flood tank, an ominous creaking emanated from it, echoing throughout the room. The tank wall bulged, and, in a heartbeat, disintegrated. A fifteen-foot-high tsunami rolled across the room, engulfing everyone and everything in its path. It sloshed to the far walls, splashed ceiling-high, and rebounded.

The whale rocked like an unstable canoe, shifted, rose from the floor, and spun like a bathtub toy suspended in a chowder of people and shattered exhibits.

Seeking its own level, the floodwaters surged from Genesis Hall down the sloping floor into the Hall of Wonders. Shickie and Jimmy clung to the blowhole as the whale rode the crest of the watery avalanche. They screamed as the whale bobbed into the Hall of Wonders and listed far to one side. They looked straight down for several harrowing seconds before its nose bumped a wall, and it righted. They screamed again when they realized they were on a collision course with the Ark. With a jolt, the whale lodged sideways against a concrete column. The Ark hit the whale's raised tail with a bone-jolting crunch, amputating one of its fiberglass tail flukes. The boat drifted by and the whale rotated in a temporary gyre, surrounded by coughing, cries, and prayers as people clung to debris, treaded water, or swam.

Of a mind the worst was over, Shickie said, "Bottoms up," pointing to a pair of red, spike-heeled feet churning the surface. The feet sank and Rita Rae's head popped into view, wet blond hair coating her neck and shoulders like sun-bleached seaweed. "First time I've seen that woman with her hair down," Shickie said, "and I was married to her for a year."

He recognized a number of his Fireflies, paddling, clinging to flotsam, jetsam, or one another. "Hang on kids," he said, not that they could hear him over the din.

Jimmy shook Shickie's shoulder, pointed to three men clutching one another like Siamese triplets, held afloat by a plastic camel. "Those are the atheists who attacked Ginger."

"Your girlfriend."

"Just a friend," Jimmy corrected. With a worried look, he added, "I don't see her anywhere. I hope—"

"I'm sure she's fine.

"Uh-oh," Shickie said, as the Ark crushed a fiberboard pyramid damming the Hall of Wonders's exit.

Cleared of obstruction, the backed-up water surged through the breach. The Ark flew down what quickly became a rapid-tossed flume into the lower reaches of the building. "Here we go again," Shickie said, as the whale followed. "Hold on."

Jimmy pointed to the top of the fast approaching exit doors, barely visible over rising water.

They were on a crash course with the museum's rear wall.

64

Under a waxy yellow moon in a deep blue sky, fast fading to black, Bobo Jessup was, at last, relieving Holly McAllister of her lace-trimmed panties. Hopeful of privacy, Bobo had parked his Firebird in the empty parking lot between the Bible Alive Museum and the Temple of Light. It had been an exhaustive seduction: half an hour of hand holding and sweet talk, five Jack Daniels'–laced Diet Cokes, pronouncements of undying love, followed by another half hour of inconclusive groping, and, the clincher, Bobo's oath to take Jesus Christ as his personal savior.

An upholstery button bit into Bobo's right kneecap, positioned between Holly's semi-spread legs. Bobo couldn't shift his weight because his left knee was balanced precariously on the very edge of the seat. His arched back cramped again. "If I knew I'd get this far," he muttered, "I'd of stolen Mom's minivan."

Moments before, he had opened the door to straighten his legs, requiring removal of the bulb from a stubborn dome light. His lowered jeans snagged the door handle, necessitating once again taking the Lord's name in vain, and more fumbling. Holly's being unconscious wasn't making things any easier. As if that wasn't frustrating enough, Bobo felt rocky himself from the booze, and wondered if he could get it up again when, if, he ever got Holly into position.

He realized removing Holly's panties would necessitate either cutting them off or backing out of the car. Having no knife, Bobo scooted away from his sweetheart and planted the toes of his hiking boots on the asphalt. "Okay, here we go." He leaned into the car again and, no sweat, pulled Holly's panties down and over her Doc Martens. He groped himself—jig-a-jig, back in business—parted Holly's legs and—

The squeal of brakes and the whoop of a siren no more than fifty feet away drove Bobo's head into the roof. *Bonk*. A spotlight lit his bare behind, cast scarecrow shadows into the interior as an amplified voice boomed, "Get out of the car. Put your hands on top of your head. Now!"

Dizzy from his collision with the roof, not to mention the five whiskey and Diet Cokes, Bobo stumbled out, thinking: Cops. Holly's only fifteen. Run!

It was a valiant start, but the Tommy Hilfiger baggies and Joe Boxers at his ankles limited Bobo's escape to one-and-a-half steps. He hit the ground, hard. As he tried to rise in a weak push-up, he glanced at the rear of the big building to his right, saw water squirting through the half open doors. Fire hydrant? Wha? Before his befuddled mind could make sense of it, the wall exploded.

Bobo's last thought before awakening in the hospital was that God was punishing him for using His name in vain, just as Holly had warned—opening the gates of hell to suck him in.

The prow of Noah's Ark blew the metal doors from their hinges and took out a large chunk of the museum's rear wall. The big boat sailed into the parking lot in a cascade of water, sheet rock, and twisted metal. The whale followed, as did sixty-seven crusaders admixed with the remnants of twenty-one Bible Alive exhibits.

The water bowled a red Firebird onto its side. A police car

skittered and spun like a beer can in a storm drain. The flood pancaked across the lot, would soon gush down the main drag of Gatlinburg and ruin an evening of souvenir shopping for four-hundred-and-fifty-six hitherto high and dry tourists.

The Ark rolled onto its side and slid across the pavement with a metallic screech as nails grated asphalt. The hull split and the broken vessel creaked to a halt. Half a dozen police cars zoomed from the front of the museum to the rear, their headlights illuminating the fallen Children of Light. Water-soaked robes rimmed their dazed bodies as they lay sprawled, limbs akimbo, like a flock of cabbage butterflies struck to the ground by a summer squall.

Noah's menagerie emerged from the Ark two by two, or, more accurately, slithered, leapt, or flew from the wreckage, singly or in flocks, hissing, growling, and howling. A ring-tailed cat, a Mexican coatimundi, bounded over one of the prone demolition-derby drivers and onto a lady cop's face. She screamed as tiny paws wrenched the cap from her head and the animal ran with it into the night. Her partner drew his sidearm but, instead of firing, threw himself under the car as, what he mistook for a six-hundred-pound lion, charged. Noah's lion—in fact, a Great Dane with a mane toupee—gave a powerful wet dog shake of its shoulders.

The mane flew off and landed like a monstrous wad of wet moss—or perhaps a boneless body—on Six-pack's face. For the second time that night, Six-pack wailed like a motherless baby. With a reflexive heave, he flung away the soggy mass and fainted.

Twin hyenas howled in tandem and loped uphill toward the wilderness of the Great Smoky Mountains National Park, followed by the slower-paced aardvark. Bruiser, the Ark's long-domesticated black bear, contrarily, trotted the other way, toward the scent of barbecue at Pig Al's Pit Stop, half a block away. The two autoerotic Barbary apes, apparently turned on by the excitement, shimmied up a tall light pole and did what came naturally.

A dazed Goliath Jones, on hands and knees, robe bunched

under his armpits, batted ineffectually as something bleated behind him, dug horny hooves into his ribs, and showed a determined interest in his posterior.

Peaches, lying across Junior's unmoving body and the plastic camel his crew had clung to during the flood, muttered, "I had the drumstick but they got it away from me," and then, "Oh, man, I think I'm gonna throw up."

Junior moaned but remained unconscious.

With one hand curling Rita Rae's shoulder, the other cupping her mouth to muffle the cursing, Orlando limped from the lot. "Shhhh," he said again. "*Policía,* all over. Not to forget, they look for us still in Kentucky."

Rita Rae walked with a hobbled gait, wearing one shoe. ". . . bastard . . . my favorite pair of heels. The other one's got to be here somewhere. . . ." She swiped a dank strand of hair from a mascara-streaked eye, cursed again, and mumbled, "All his fault, the little fart . . . but I got a hunk of him, here in my purse . . . enough for the goddamned insurance. DNA, Orlando. DNA!"

65

The whale had hit the Ark-torn gap in the rear wall of the museum, ripping a chunk of tail from the body as it followed the boat into the parking lot. Shickie and Jimmy fell from the blowhole into the belly, tumbling like whale lunch in a typhoon. The leviathan spun on its axis twice, and slid to a grating halt, upright. Cowcatcher-like, the open mouth had scooped up three Joneses and one of the University of Tennessee football players. The leviathan was eight feet shorter and its domed head was dented, but the gullet door held fast. Pale orange light spilled through the gap in the tail, illuminating the interior.

Shickie opened his shirt. "You okay, baby?" he asked a trembling Houdini.

Houdini whined and managed a squeaky bark.

Shickie removed his misaligned wig and set it beside his hat, dislodged during the museum exodus. He turned to Jimmy, sprawled on the floor. "How about you, kid?"

"Shook up . . . where are we?"

"Heaven, Hell, or Gatlinburg, Tennessee. From the sirens and the wailing, I'd say it's either Hell or the museum parking lot."

Jimmy staggered to his feet and moved rockily toward the gullet door.

"Whoa—hold on," Shickie said. "We'd better scout the territory before walking into that mess." He shook the spiral staircase. "Broke loose at the top. Give me a hand."

Jimmy held it as Shickie swayed to the top. "Holy moly," Shickie said when his eyes cleared the blowhole. A jaundiced moon in a soot-filled sky washed the scene in sickly yellow light, dimming and waxing as smears of foggy clouds streaked its face. At either end of the lot, two tall sodium-vapor lamps bathed the wet asphalt in reflective cones of Martian orange, while vehicles, people, and wreckage sparked red, white, and blue from emergency flashers. High above, the angel blimp, winking impassively, went supernova as it drifted into the beam of the armory's searchlight.

"It's a war zone out there," Shickie said. "Cops, an ambulance, fire trucks rolling in. Fireflies all over the ground like wads of wet Kleenex. On the bright side, they seem to be moving, most of them."

"Do you see Ginger? She's real pretty, has shoulder length blond hair."

"I see a couple of big-boned blondes with soggy hair to their waists—probably from the Jones clan. I don't see Patch. A car's tipped over, the Ark's on its side . . . hey, there's my buddy the goat, humping that big Texan. Way to go, Billy."

"Ginger. Look for Ginger."

"Sorry. There's canvas, wood, all kinds of stuff like after a hurricane. There's more museum out here than inside. Not a trace of Fenster." Shickie pressed his thumbs to his temples and rubbed. "Sorry, Ma."

"Who's Fenster? Who are you talking to?"

"Wait." Shickie raised his head a bit higher from the blowhole. "There's one of my Fireflies walking around, still dry, carrying a sign like those limo drivers at the airport. It's . . . that cute kid, Betsy. Turn it this way, honey. Shoot. Can't read it. Probably one of my notable quotes about the end of the world."

*   *   *

Maury had done a nervous little dance atop the Space Needle when the white-robed mob and Shickie Doone—oh, yes, he was alive, all right—entered the Bible Alive Museum. Huddled against the evening chill, Maury wondered what they were up to in there. After the mummy, no doubt, but would they come out through the front or the rear? All that ruckus, where were the cops? Didn't the place have alarms? Maury hoped it didn't. No profit in having Doone arrested.

He refocused the binoculars at the rear entrance as a familiar, slender tango dancer in white linen and—ah, yes—Doone's cheating wife, jimmied the door. So, you're after Doone, too, are you?

And, next, the no-goodnik boys.

His fingers thrummed the guardrail—of their own volition, Maury was annoyed to note. Damn shakes.

A few minutes later, he shifted his telescopic gaze to the back lot and a bright blue Pontiac, one of the low sporty models. A kid with his pants down had just backed out of the rear seat . . . Oy! Some hanky-panky going on. Maury saw spread white thighs, a pair of panties discarded. The kid leaned forward for his schtup. Memories of Rose, the cheat, rose to make Maury wrinkle his nose. That bittersweet recollection ended abruptly as his attention was diverted by the whoop of a siren from a cop car flying into the lot. He lowered the binoculars for a wider perspective. More cars out front and . . . what's this? Water spritzing from the rear doors?

He heard the crash from his three-hundred-foot-plus high perch, saw the disaster unfold with the clarity of a helicopter eye in the sky on one of the cop shows: the rear wall blow apart, the cataract propelling—a boat?—from the building, followed by—what now? A big fish? No, a tailless whale, yet. Fascinated, he watched the breaker roll over the Pontiac and the cheating boys' smashed Chevy, the cop car skitter across the lot like a fooz ball, and now, dozens of white-robed crazies flop like beached carp as the water spread and thinned. He watched the water funnel into the street below, saw it toss and foam down the Gatlinburg strip like the Lost River ride at Cincinnati's old Coney Island.

The boat had split along one side. Birds flew out, some screaming like banshees. A pair of big dogs with donkey ears and short rear legs bayed and bounded toward the forest. A lion—no, Maury refocused—a really big dog . . . pigs, furry things of all sizes and shapes—one, a bear, loping toward the city—a big snake, apes shinnying up a lamppost. What the hell are they doing?

Oy!

"Fine show," Maury said. "But where's my mark?" He moved the glasses from carp to carp, recognized none of them. He tracked back to the boat, opened like a split peapod. A few sopping creatures of uncertain identity still hopped or crawled from the wreckage. He shifted to the big fish—a whale, yes, that's what it is, a junior Moby Dick, only black and missing its tail, its jaws chomping robed figures, and—hold on. Maury focused on a black-haired head rising from a hole at the crest of the whale's head, a blond stage beard hanging loose from half the man's jaw, revealing . . . "Shickie Doone, is it? Hoo-ha! Not as pretty as your picture, but it's you, all right."

Thirty seconds later, Maury watched Doone and the faygeleh Indian, still in skirt and sandals, emerge from the whale's mouth. They stepped over several coughing Fireflies, hugged, and parted company. Doone had reapplied the beard, a blond wig, and now wore a round-topped straw hat. "So, my clever friend, you are now the gilgul of that Amish farmer I met at Poncho the 'irates, are you? Well, the Hammer is on to you."

He watched Doone stop to inspect several of the fallen, then move to the armory. The faygeleh waved to a young woman holding a sign, although Maury couldn't quite make out what it said. After a short but animated conversation, they took off in the same direction as Doone.

Satisfied with Doone's destination, Maury patted the pistol beneath his sports jacket. He checked to be certain the silencer was in his side pocket, readjusted his bow tie, and, with a small tip of his hat toward the armory, said, "Time to conclude our business, Mr. Doone. Nu?"

Shickie and Jimmy opened the door in the whale's gullet and slipped out. They found several people sprawled over the tongue, shaken up, bruised, still spitting water, but not badly injured. Shickie moved to prone Fireflies, found no one seriously injured. Jimmy called for Ginger.

Shickie nodded to the Temple of Light. "I've got to run by my office."

Jimmy shook his hand. "It was a hell of a ride. Thanks again for saving me from that mob."

"Shickie Doone is the name, saving souls is my game." Shickie chuckled, but it sounded forced. "Used to be, anyway. Not a word about who I am?"

"Your secret's safe with me."

Shickie looked Jimmy long in the eyes, mumbled something about secrets, placed both his hands on Jimmy's shoulders, and pulled him close into a long bear hug. He opened his arms, held Jimmy at arm's length, and said, "Something I need to tell you, kid."

Jimmy cocked his head, waiting.

"Umm . . ." Shickie screwed up his face, framing the words. "It's, uh . . . that tan of yours. I do the booths, too—the profession demands it—but every time the doc freezes off one of those damned red splotches he warns me I could lose a chunk of my face the next time, or even bite the big one. So, do as I say, not as I do: stick with bronzer in the future, huh?"

"Yeah . . . sure."

Shickie dropped his arms, gave Jimmy a soft punch in the upper arm. "Well, catch you later, okay?" He turned and walked away.

Twenty paces took Shickie to three young men draped like wet noodles over a plastic camel: a Pillsbury doughboy, retching his guts up, a big one barely conscious, and another, out for the count. Something on the thumb of the dead-to-the-world one, protruding from a sodden leather jacket, caught his attention. Shickie walked closer, saw—his star sapphire ring. His, no doubt of it. The one he had recovered from the cigar smoking butcher in the Caesar's poker game in Vegas, the one Fenster had stolen when he date-rape drugged him. And there, wrapped around this pimply-faced twirp's wrist, was Shickie's Rolex, too.

Shickie relieved him of both pieces of jewelry. The kid stirred, moaned, said something about screwing up, and began to sob.

Jimmy watched Shickie, again the Amish farmer, move toward the Lighthouse, pausing as he helped a Firefly to her feet, squeezed another's hand, exchanged words with someone still on the ground. He checked the condition of three men—the atheists.

"Jimmy!"

Jimmy turned. His heart skipped. He saw Ginger's friend Betsy carrying a hand-printed sign: JIMMY—GINGER IS IN TROUBLE. He was beside her in five strides. "What is it? She didn't drow—"

"No. Ginger's been at the armory since Reverend Patch locked her up. He handcuffed her to a water pipe and—"

"Handcuffed?"

"She didn't have anything on. She was, you know, naked. And unconscious. And Reverend Patch was leaning over her. And—"

"That bastard! Did he . . ."

Betsy blushed. "I hope not. I ran as fast as I could to find you. When I saw what happened out here—it's the beginning of the end of the world, I just know it. The Prince said awful things were going to happen and, sure enough, they are. That freak thunderstorm we had, and all the trouble in the Middle East and, I didn't look outside last night, but I'll just bet there was a shooting star. I prayed you'd be on duty tonight and not get killed by the world ending—or starting to end—so I made this sign, and . . ."

Jimmy took her by the elbow. "Show me. Right now."

Betsy led Jimmy into the Temple of Light, to Ginger's room, one of sixteen in the rear of the building. They found the door ajar. Betsy wouldn't look, but Jimmy peered in and shook his head. "Empty."

Betsy stepped to the doorway and stared. She pointed to the floor, nearly hidden by the bed. "Not empty," she said. "Those are Ginger's clothes. All of them, heaped together."

"That son of a bitch! This is awful."

"No," Betsy said. "It's wonderful. Praise the Lord, Ginger's been *raptured*."

66

Oh, happy days," Betsy said. "Reverend Patch told us there would be a miracle tonight."

"Some miracle."

"Don't you see? God must have taken her soul already, but her body wasn't gone yet. Reverend Patch was tempted to do bad things, but then—Poof! I know she's gone, and maybe Reverend Patch, too."

"Betsy," Jimmy grabbed her fleshy arms, forced her to look at him. "It had to be Patch who stripped her. He was about to—you know. Then he must have heard you and carried her off." Jimmy checked the hallway. "Where would he take her?"

"You're wrong, but if looking's the only way to prove it, I'll show you. You'll see."

"Where, Betsy?"

"We could start with his apartment, I guess. That way."

Shickie went straight to his—now Patch's—office on the first floor beyond the sanctuary. He closed the door behind him. The neatness annoyed him. He sat in his swivel chair, cracked his knuckles, said a quick prayer that Patch hadn't done too thorough a cleaning, and removed the second desk drawer. He turned it over—yes! The two envelopes were still taped to the outside of the back panel. He opened one, confirmed the contents: five grand.

He spread his shirt, dropped his chin, and blew hot air on the top of Houdini's head. "We're good to go, baby." After securing both packets in one of his ample overalls pockets, he leaned back in the desk chair, put his feet on the desk and, with considerable satisfaction, kicked three neat stacks of Patch's papers onto the floor.

He tickled Houdini through the fabric at his chest. "Ten grand, plus what's left of the casino payoff, and Rita Rae's ring. Enough for a new start."

A small devil whispered "Vegas" in his ear, but Shickie shrugged it off. Vegas led him to think of the little date-rape drugging fart who, despite his shitty ways, didn't deserve to be mummified and torn to shreds.

Fenster receded from his mind and Rita Rae surfaced, like a message floating to the window of a Magic 8-Ball. *Bitch*, is what this one said. When Shickie first met Rita Rae, she was the answer to all—well, most of—his dreams. A rich oil widow who could write a check, pull him out of debt. Surprise! Hot to trot? Oh, yeah, she knew all the moves. Those first months were as close to heaven as Shickie expected to get. That was before the power shopping started, she began disappearing weekends, and Shickie's luck went south. And, toward the end, when she started the divorce talk—ouch!

Then she sold Houdini. Before Shickie left for Vegas. Casually let it drop over dinner, "Groomer? No, I met a nice lady from up north in town today. She said he was cute, offered me fifty bucks. So I said, 'Sure.' I always hated that yapping and peeing. You oughta thank me."

Thank her? Shickie had wandered up and down the streets, searching, but found nary a trace of Houdini or the mysterious tourist woman. He placed ads, but what was the likelihood of a tourist checking the lost and founds? In a moment of inspiration, he planned the payback, the ring switch—man, she loved that diamond. He executed the scheme flawlessly thanks to an old pal in the jewelry business—not that the switcheroo made up for losing poor little Houdini—and vamoosed for Vegas for what he thought would be a quick comeback.

Houdini wriggled at Shickie's chest, curled into a new ball.

Shickie dropped his chin, whispered, "The bitch sold you to a puppy mill."

His thoughts turned to Thadeus Trout. With a sudden insight, he said, "That SOB set me up. Gave me the junket to Vegas, because he *wanted* me to lose my ass. He didn't want his money, he wanted . . . what?

"The lease on the armory, of course. To expand his frigging museum. Then, why set the Hammer on me?

"Because I was starting to make it big with the Fireflies, had a chance of paying him off. With me out of the way, Patch would run the operation into the ground, and Trout could pick up the lease, cheap.

"Creely Patch. Damn the man. Damn my bad luck." He sighed. "I'm gonna miss my Fireflies. The choir, the sermons, the miracles."

Shickie sniffled. "And, now I'm a daddy. What do you think about that, Houdini? Good-looking kid, even with the phony tan and skirt. Thinks he's an Indian and I'm a big chief. Would break his heart to find out . . .

"Well, that ain't gonna happen, because I'm outta here. Sorry, Ma. Sorry, Fireflies. Sorry, Jimmy Feather. Because, if Trout, or the Hammer, or Rita Rae gets hold of me now—"

He heard voices elsewhere in the building: "I hear him . . . he's on the roof!"

Shickie peered from the doorway, through the open end of the corridor, into the sanctuary. He saw Jimmy and Betsy, the choirgirl from the lot with the sign, running up the metal staircase. Whatever's going on, he said to himself, I'd better make myself scarce.

*   *   *

Oblivious to the disaster playing out in the parking lot below, Patch put a hand on the taut cable securing the angel blimp to the roof. He squinted at the winking angel, lit by the search-light. His gaze dropped to Ginger's pale limp body, lying at his feet. One of her legs was bent awkwardly; an ankle tucked under her other calf. Her arms lay loose at her side. "Yes, Lord," he said. "A second Rapture will convince even the vilest to repent."

He dropped to a crouch, ran open fingers through Ginger's blond hair, haloing her head against the tarpaper. He lowered his hand to her light pubic thatch, brushed it with his finger-tips. His eyelids flickered and closed.

They sprung open at a horrendous squawk. Patch bolted upright, stared wide-eyed, fearful, at the streaming, moonlit clouds. At another raucous croak, he swiveled his head to the right, saw the three vultures rocking foot-to-foot at the edge of the roof, silhouetted against the orange glow of the night sky. Ominous, barely audible *chirk-chirk-chirks* rose from deep within their bodies, and one, and then another, clacked their beaks with the sound of brittle bones snapping. The central bird raised its hooded wings, rustled its black feathers, con-juring images of slithering, antediluvian reptiles, and squawked.

Patch ran at it, waving his arms, "Demons—get thee hence!"

All three birds raised their wings and hissed. The largest, at center, bobbed its fleshy, featherless red head convulsively, opened its beak, lunged at Patch, and regurgitated a wad of viscous green jelly onto his left cheek.

Patch recoiled with a screech, dropped to his knees, obliv-ious of the waxy, fishy curds sliding down his face and neck. He cowered, forehead nearly to the tarpaper. "An evil spirit troubleth me, for I have sinned. I am so sorry, Father. The temptation of a Jezebel . . ."

He mumbled for half a minute, raised his head, and nodded vigorously. "Thou art ever merciful. Yes . . . keep her for me until I lead the ascent of the Worthy."

Patch turned his back on the vultures, shambled to Ginger, and bent over an array of tools belonging to the blimp repairmen. The crew had reeled the angel blimp a hundred feet closer to the roof earlier in the day, preparatory to replacing the recalcitrant blinking eye. A thick, braided wire tether secured the angel to the spool of a winch on the rooftop, and from the winch to a huge U-bolt anchored into one of the armory's roof beams. An electrical cord supplying power to the strobes was intertwined with the tether. A cable ladder rose alongside the cable and cord. Loops of excess ladder lay heaped beside the winch.

Patch lifted a hacksaw, placed its serrated blade against the tether cable, and began sawing, six inches above the winch. His robe, already sullied by the buzzard's last meal, was soon soaked with metal dust and perspiration. Five minutes later he touched the deep cut in the braided wire cable, jerked his finger away, and stuck it in his mouth. "Hot as the fires of hell," he said with a chortle.

Ginger stirred, tried to rise, groaned, and fell back.

Patch gave her a beatific smile. "Not much longer, dear. The world's second Rapture. Who would have guessed a simple girl like you would make history?"

As if swimming though a fitful dream, Ginger's lips moved. She muttered four words, "Be a *star*, baby."

"Soon enough. But first, we'd better get you on the ladder." Patch scooped her in his arms and kissed her lightly on the forehead. "Say goodbye to this wicked earth, child."

Shickie stood in the doorway watching Jimmy and Betsy open the skylight doors and disappear onto the roof. He saluted, "See you, kid." He took one last look around the office and stepped into the hall for his final exit. He nearly collided with a frail old man in a pork pie hat, dressed in a pastel plaid sports jacket, navy slacks, and shiny black penny loafers: the little Jewish guy from Poncho's, the one who bought him breakfast.

"Can I help you?" Shickie said in his Amish voice.

"Yes, indeed. To begin with, you can cut the phony-baloney accent, Mr. Shickie Doone."

Shickie back-stepped. "Zorry, my name is Schwartz." He touched his wig, ran a hand nervously over his beard—still in place. "I think you're mistak—"

"I think not. You're the gonif who cheated his partner, Thadeus Trout, the one who stole his wife's ring. Your name is Shickleton Doone. So let's cut the crap, what say? Should you wonder, they call me the Hammer."

Before Shickie could speak, the little man drew a pistol with a silencer from inside his jacket and shot him. Four times.

67

Patch climbed the flexible ladder with Ginger slumped over his shoulder, and wove her arms and legs through the rungs, ten feet up. He handcuffed one ankle and one of her wrists to the rungs and returned to the roof.

Regaining consciousness in fits and starts like a bulb in a loose socket, Ginger twisted, tugged her cuffed hand. Her eyes opened but remained unfocused. "Where am I?"

Patch lifted the hacksaw. "On your way to heaven, you lucky girl."

The police had cordoned off the parking lot to do a nose count of survivors, although a few, Rita Rae and Orlando among them, wandered away before the yellow ribbon had been strung. Three ambulances, four fire trucks, two TV media trucks, and an animal control van were already on the scene with more on the way. Rescue teams swept the interior. Outside, emergency meds triaged the injured. They encountered broken bones and sprains, dozens of mysterious small puncture wounds, innumerable scuffs, cuts, and bruises, a prodigious amount of water-filled lungs, coughing and vomiting, but, miraculously, no fatalities.

So, this is the end of it, Shickie thought, as he slid to the floor. His life didn't race before him. He mouthed no regrets, felt only pain. His hands moved to the worst of it, came away bloody. He explored with his fingertips. One bullet had nipped his earlobe, another had grazed his cheek, dislodging the fake beard. One had scratched his arm, and the fourth, from the hole in his shoe and the bee sting at the tip of his foot, must have nicked his big toe.

"You sadistic son of a bitch!" He rose to his feet, edged away. "I heard about you—shooting pieces off first for the fun of it."

Maury gripped the butt of the silenced .22 with both hands and fired three more rounds. *Pwop. Pwop. Pwop.* One took out a light switch. Another lodged in the drywall three feet to Shickie's right. The third pinged off a fluorescent light fixture.

Still backing away, Shickie spread his arms. "The world's been trying to do in Shickie Doone for years. Hell, maybe I deserve it. So, go ahead. If you're gonna do it, get it over with, but, please, don't shoot my dog." He removed Houdini from his shirt, kissed him on the nose, and lowered him to the floor.

Houdini circled his ankles, yipping to be picked up.

"Get away from him," Maury said to the Yorkie. To Shickie, "Don't move, cheater." Breathing hard, he advanced.

Shickie back-stepped. "What's this cheater crap? Trout a partner? I owe him money—that's all. Rita Rae wants me dead for the insurance. I took her diamond because she sold my little baby here to a puppy mill. And . . . you know what else? Shooting off pieces? Hell—I think you're just a crappy shot."

Shickie pointed, snapped his fingers. "Houdini? Sic!"

Houdini rabbited to Maury's feet, but instead of attacking, stood on his hind legs and humped Maury's cuff. Maury shook his foot without looking down, raised the barrel and aimed at Shickie's heart.

Shickie didn't flinch. In fact, he froze in place, calculating his odds were better being hit if he moved. The pistol discharged with a muffled pop. The slug struck the floor, ricocheted into the hallway. Shickie stepped back.

Maury rubbed his eyes and stared at his gun hand. His hat fell from his head and rolled across the floor. The barrel wavered. "You're not Trout's partner? Didn't screw him out of two hundred grand? Your wife *sold* your dog? *This* dog?" He glanced at Houdini, still humping his ankle. He looked back at Shickie, confused.

"Bah!" His finger tightened on the trigger. "I don't know who's lying, but a contract is a contract. Hold still, will you?"

Shickie danced away, putting real distance between them. When he saw the barrel raise again, he waved his hands. "Wait! Wait! Let's make a deal."

"A deal you say? What, you think I'm Monty Hall?"

Houdini forgot his love affair with Maury's ankle. Apparently mistaking the dancing and hand waving for a game, he ran from Maury to Shickie and back, yip-yapping.

"I don't know which one hired you," Shickie said, "but they're both lying. I got a little problem with the cards, that's all. Trout doesn't care about the money—and it's nowhere near two hundred grand. I hold a long, cheap lease on this building, see? He wants me out of the way so he can evict my Fireflies and move his museum in. And, like I said, all Rita Rae cares about is collecting my life insurance. Look . . . if you hold off, I'll make it worth your while. No shit. Put the gun down. Please?"

Maury lowered the pistol a foot, but kept both hands on it at waist height. "Stay where you are and I'll listen. No promises."

"Okay, okay." Shickie explained about the loans, the lease, the junket to Vegas, how someone, somehow, had made a mummy out of his dear brother. "Was that your work?"

"No, this mummy business, I don't follow." Maury waved the Colt.

Houdini ran to Maury's right tassel loafer, stood on his hind legs, and scratched Maury's ankle, paws a blur. Maury raised his foot six inches and shook it. "Ruining twenty-dollar silk socks now, are you? No wonder I don't like dogs." Houdini tumbled away, recovered his stance, crouched, and barked. Maury lowered the barrel.

"*Fenster*," Shickie said it loudly to distract the Hammer from Houdini, "was my brother. That's who the mummy is— was. My dear brother, the sweetest little guy you ever met. The light of our Ma's life. Trout bought his body like a side of beef, put him on display for tourists to gawk at, ten bucks a head. What kind of a man does such a thing?"

"Trout's a schmuck," Maury said. "That, I give you."

Shickie rubbed his eyes. "Fenster and I were like twins. And my wife?" He confessed how he'd seen, with his own eyes, Rita Rae, the woman he had hoped to spend the rest of his days with—he pinched the bridge of his nose and shook his head—how he'd seen her with, sniffle, another man.

"Oily fella in the tutti-fruity clothes? His name's Orlando. Sorry to tell you this, but odds are he's schtuping her. I relate, your being cheated by a woman—not that it has anything to do with the here and now."

Houdini ran back to Maury's elusive ankle and jumped at his shin. Maury kept his eye on Shickie, but bent and patted Houdini's head. "There. Now go away, dog."

"See, I'm a victim," Shickie was saying. "I'm a daddy now, too. Not only to that sweet little ball of fur trying to make friends with you. And, no, Rita Rae is *not* the mother. My boy's mama was the first woman I loved. Beautiful girl. Sang like a nightingale, got amnesia, and wandered away. Died in a flood. Tragic. After all these years, my boy just turned up. Looks just like me." He swiped at what might have been a tear. "And now, I'll never get to know him." He sighed. "Life is cruel."

Maury took one hand from the pistol, circled the air with the barrel. "Enough of the krechtzing, already. And you," he said to Houdini, scratching his calf, "have no manners." He crouched, lifted Houdini with his left hand, and scooped him to his waist. "That'll put a stop to ruining the trousers." To Shickie, he said, "Go on with the part about making it worth my while."

"I'm the founder of this fine church." Shickie spread his arms, embracing it all. "Was starting to do well until the cards turned against me. Rapture robes, music, I got them rolling in the aisles with my sermons. You saw my wonderful angel blimp? The strobe eyes? Did you know, people can see her from seven states, maybe eight?"

Houdini scrabbled against Maury's madras jacket, trying to climb higher. Maury lifted him to the crook of his shoulder. "There. Now stop with the pawing, already."

"I tell you, all it takes is a good pitch and a little show. World's full of lonely people, need a fresh kick in the ass to make life worthwhile. That's what I give them. And, you know what? I don't do it for the dough alone. They love me. The Fireflies are my family. I kid you, not. It's a hell of a feeling having all these people think you're the best thing since sliced bread, bringing a little joy into their lives. I'm the Prince of Light, see?"

"Yeah, I hear you're a real k'nocker." Maury lowered the gun. Houdini hooked his front paws over Maury's padded shoulder, stuck out a tiny pink tongue, and lapped Maury's neck. "Oy," Maury said. "Now it's licking, is it?" He moved Houdini out of kissing range to the tip of his shoulder. "This dog, you should teach to behave." He wrinkled his brow. "Where was I? Oh, yeah. I was watching that mishmash in the parking lot, when you came out of the whale's mouth. A real mench, I don't know, but you did go to your people . . . but that's neither here nor there. Get on with this part about making it worth my while."

Houdini scrabbled to Maury's neck, stretched, and licked Maury on the cheek. Maury snaked his head to the side, said, "What, you think I'm a Popsicle?"

"Creely Patch," Shickie said, "the sorry son of a bitch,

took over after I made scarce. He imported this Jones clan from Texas, the ones with the beards, long hair, and bonnets? Patch and the Joneses are screwing up everything I built. My poor Fireflies. There's no more joy in Mudville, I'll tell you that. . . ."

"I met your Patch. Some nudnik, that one." Maury waved the gun. "Go on." Houdini was back to licking Maury's chin. Maury left him in place this time, said, "Must be the brisket I had for dinner."

"Religion," Shickie was saying, "is tax exempt, see? And we tithe twenty percent."

"Gross?"

"Right off the top. Happy to do it for all I give them, too."

Maury, the lower half of his cheek shiny from all the licking, whistled, and scowled. "I thought you lost your shirt."

The corners of Shickie's mouth turned down. "My favorite, baby blue, lucky silk shirt, to be exact. Oh, I was pulling in a bundle, but Lady Luck mooned me. What I didn't lose at cards, I reinvested: the blimp, the searchlight, choir robes. It takes a lot to launch a religion, my friend. But, it's all set up now. Patch is probably flying high, what with all this publicity. A shame I've got to disappear. Even if you don't do me in, Rita Rae or Trout would.

"But . . . before I go, I could hand over this whole operation to you."

"*Me?*" Maury held Houdini at his chin, spoke to his tawny head. "To me, he says. What do you think of that, dog?"

"Sure," Shickie said. "That deep voice of yours? Very impressive. You're a snappy dresser, too. Who knows? If you'd taken a different path, you might have been a real pitchman. You, Mr. Hammer, could be the new Prince of Light."

"Me, I'm a Jew."

"So was Jesus. Besides, the Temple of Light is non-denominational."

"Me, a meshiach—messiah?"

Shickie looked both ways, confided, "I'm not sure I am

either, but I can pull off a miracle now and then and I talk the talk. I shine a little light into people's lives, give them hope. A little practice, you could, too. You're not opposed to singing, a little showmanship? Let me tell you, as the Prince of Light, everybody's your friend."

"Townspeople seem to know you."

"Hell, yes. It's like being some TV star."

Maury replaced the gun in his holster and worked Houdini into his jacket side pocket. He kept a hand on Houdini's head, ruffling the fur at his neck. "No jumping, doggie, it's a long way down." He wiped his cheek with a monogrammed kerchief, adjusted his bow tie, and said to Shickie, "You talk a good line, but can you close?"

"Step into my office," Shickie said, "and we'll work out the details."

"Ginger!"

Jimmy shouted it the moment he cleared the roof door and saw her snared in the ladder. Naked, one arm crossing her chest, one hanging limp before her pale body, blond hair loose and tossed by the wind, she might have been posing for Botticelli's painting of Venus on the half shell.

Betsy clapped both hands to her mouth.

Patch squinted at the intruders, mumbled, "Noisome demons, rising from the pit. I shall finish my course." He bent over the tether and resumed sawing.

Jimmy ran at him, leapt onto his back.

Patch shook Jimmy off, screeched, "Demon, let me go!"

Jimmy grabbed one of Patch's ankles and yanked. Patch grunted, dropped the saw. He kicked, but Jimmy caught his foot and twisted. Patch tumbled, rolled once and was back on his feet, crying, "Spawn of Satan, get thee hence!"

The noise brought Ginger around. "I'm . . . naked."

Jimmy and Patch grappled. Patch broke loose and ran to the tether. He lifted a heavy wrench, held it in a low crouch, and swung as Jimmy ran at him. The business end caught Jimmy's chest, and he dropped to the roof with a grunt.

Patch raised the wrench over his head, shouted, "The angel Michael vanquished the dragon," and slashed down—not at Jimmy, but at the remaining strands of the tether.

The cable broke. Ginger screamed and shot into the air.

68

The lease and the ministry are all yours." Shickie took Maury's quaking right hand in his and shook it. He bent behind the desk. "If Patch hasn't found it yet, I've got a pint of bourbon in the back of this big drawer." He rummaged while Maury took stock of what Shickie had assured him would soon be his.

Houdini lay on the desk, belly to blotter, gnawing the corner of Creely Patch's leatherbound Bible.

Shickie came up with the bottle, took a slug, and passed it to Maury.

Maury eyed the bare neck with distaste, but took a sip. He returned the bottle. "Such a talker. You ever been in the stick game? Furniture?"

Shickie shook his head.

Maury took the bottle for another sip. He ran a hand along Houdini's back. His gaze turned from Houdini to Shickie, from contented to worrisome. "I'm having a crisis of conscience here. I detest double-crossers. I made a deal, a contract—" He set the bottle down and reached into his jacket.

Shickie kicked his chair from the desk, nearly tipped it, stumbling backward. "I signed over the lease. We shook hands.

Drank on it like men. And you're gonna shoot me anyway?"

Houdini danced around the desktop, yapping.

"Don't sell me short," Maury said. "Our deal, it stands. It's my deal with Trout that sours my gut. I took his money and, now, I don't deliver. Trout, on the other hand, cheated me by lying about you being his partner, cheating him out of two hundred grand. The man knows I only do cheaters. That putz."

Shickie remained silent, unsure where this was going, but kept a watchful eye on Maury's hidden hand.

Maury withdrew not the gun, but a large envelope. He removed five strapped bundles of currency and tossed them on the desk. "Trout gets not a penny back. But, for your brother? Scared and hiding in that cave, getting himself dried up? Here's five G's to clear my conscience. I'll keep the rest for my time and good intentions."

Shickie scooped up four of the packets with a single swipe of his hand before Maury finished speaking. "If you insist."

Houdini pounced on the remaining flat green brick, clamped his tiny jaws on a corner, and shook it like a sock.

"Oy!" Maury said.

"Sheesh, be careful, baby." Shickie wrestled the bundle from Houdini's mouth, wiped the doggie spit on his shirt, and tucked the cash in his trousers pocket.

"Now," Maury said, "about our deal. This plan?"

"I'm way ahead of you." Shickie shook a finger at Houdini, who had returned to chewing Patch's Bible in lieu of his relinquished paper chew toy, and said, "*Stay.*"

Houdini dropped onto his belly, legs splayed to the four compass points and resumed chewing.

Shickie motioned Maury to stand. "Follow me to—" he heard the muffled scream of a woman over their heads, ". . . the roof."

As they cleared the skylight doors, Shickie and Maury confronted a surreal tableau etched out of inky shadow by the spooky blue aura of the searchlight. The arc at the heart of the lamp hummed like a sci-fi energy beam.

Ginger was at the far end of the building, naked, her back toward them, snared like a moth in a web, levitating in the twisting cable ladder ten feet over the roof. Jimmy—"Gimme that key!"—was chasing Patch—"Get away from me, demon." Betsy knelt in thick shadow, palms to chin, praying loudly.

Shickie and Maury exchanged glances, trying to make sense of it. "Patch has gone bonkers," Shickie said. "Must have, to chase that naked girl up the ladder."

The ladder twirled and the front of Ginger's bare body wheeled into view. Maury drew a fast breath. "Oy vey! That's Ginger Rodgers."

"Jimmy's girlfriend. Jimmy—that's him, my boy, like I told you." Shickie whistled. "No wonder he's pissed at Patch."

"The faygeleh's your son?"

"The what?" and then, "Sheesh! The tether cable broke. The only thing keeping her from flying to the moon with the blimp is the electrical cord."

Betsy rose from her knees and ran to Maury and Shickie. "Thank the Lord you're here. I was sure Ginger was Raptured—her clothes were in a pile just like the Prince's—but she wasn't. Reverend Patch did it. He handcuffed Ginger to the ladder, and—"

"Handcuffed?"

"See? And he sawed that big wire through."

"Patch *cut* the tether?"

"We tried to stop him. Jimmy's trying to get the keys. Help him."

Patch was at the far side of the roof by the winch, hiding from Jimmy behind the Rapture Gong. He ran out, darted toward Maury and Shickie. Feral terror filled his eyes when he saw them. He spun on his heels and ran in a circle, shouting, "Beelzebub, Moloch, Dagon, Baal. They've all come up." He ran back to the ladder and sprung onto it. "Save me from their hellish claws."

"No!" Jimmy yelled from below. "It'll never hold."

Patch scrambled higher. The ladder, loose at the bottom, bobbed and danced. When Patch reached Ginger, he pushed her aside and climbed past.

With a sudden whine, the winch spun twice, blurring as a gust of wind buffeted the blimp. In an instant, Ginger and Patch flew six feet higher.

Betsy shouted to Patch, "Throw down the key. Please."

"He's over the hill," Shickie said. "Doesn't hear you."

"The ladder, it's loose at the bottom," Maury said. "Wrap it around the winch. If the electric cord snaps, too, the ladder may hold."

"No," Jimmy said, "if it's jerked straight, it could break Ginger's arms or strangle her."

Betsy was on her knees again, mouthing prayers.

"Only one way to save the girl." Shickie reached for the rungs.

"No! Any more weight," Jimmy said, "and you'll all be killed." But Shickie was already six feet up. Hand over hand, he climbed to Ginger, twelve feet over the roof. He hooked an arm around one of the rungs, reached into a tiny pocket below the suspender of his overalls and retrieved the leather pick wallet that had sprung Houdini from the puppy farm cage. A moment later he was working his magician's hands over the handcuff. The bracelet sprung open. He repeated the action at the second cuff and it, too, clattered to the tarpaper.

"You okay?" Shickie, the Amish farmer, asked Ginger.

"My arms went to sleep. I don't know where my clothes went, and . . . I think I'm gonna faint."

"Sheesh." Shickie snugged one arm around her waist, held the ladder with the other. Ginger swayed outward. The ladder jiggled and swayed as Patch dueled unseen tormentors over their heads.

The insulation of the electric cable abraded as it seesawed across the winch spool. The wire sparked. Betsy said, "It's gonna break," to no one in particular. "Please, Lord, bring them down safe."

Jimmy spread his arms. "Jump, Ginger, I'm under you."

Ginger parted her lips to speak, but her eyes rolled to white, her head lolled to the side, and she went limp. Shickie lost his grip, watched her deadfall onto Jimmy.

With a shower of angry sparks and a puff of acrid smoke, the electric cable shorted on the spool. The insulation sizzled and the wire burned through. Snapped. Shickie soared like a rebounding bungie jumper.

He kicked free, fell onto the Rapture gong. *BONG—Ong—ong!*

Loosened from its shackle, the blimp soared. Patch screamed, "Hallelujah!" loud enough to frighten the vultures, still perched at the other end of the building. They hissed and flapped their wings, ran along the rimming wall in bounding strides to gain loft. They leapt from the edge, dropped from view, and appeared seconds later as vague silhouettes flying toward the mountains.

Shickie bounced off the gong in a forward crouch and parachute rolled across the tarpaper. Seconds later, he was on his back, dazed, his wigged head in Betsy's lap, his straw hat kiting somewhere over Gatlinburg. Betsy stroked his forehead. "Are you all right?"

"Nothing broke." Despite a throbbing hip and a badly scraped knee, he managed to hold on to the accent: Nossing broke.

"Jimmy," he said, "and his girl?"

"Ginger. You saved her life. The old man says Ginger broke Jimmy's collarbone when she fell on him. They're both shook up. Say . . . don't I know you?"

Shickie ran a hand over his face, found the beard and tinted glasses in place, the wig askew, but still on his head. He straightened it. Thankful for the dim light, he said, in his The Amazing Schwartz accent, "I'm not from around here. I'm Amish."

At a collective *Oooh—ahhhh* rising from the parking lot, Shickie and Betsy scrambled to their feet. Someone, and then everyone below, had caught sight of the ascending angel and, a hundred and fifty feet lower, bobbing in and out of the searchlight beam, Creely Patch, the Messenger, clinging to the swinging ladder like a center-ring circus aerialist.

Betsy scowled. "That man doesn't deserve to go to heaven."

Shickie blew Patch a kiss. "Oh, yes, he does."

He made his way to Ginger and Jimmy. Ginger, he couldn't help noticing, looked fetching in Maury's plaid sport jacket and a left-behind, repairman's shirt, tied like a diaper around her waist. Maury had tucked Jimmy's right arm into his blouse to immobilize his broken collarbone.

Jimmy staggered upright, said, "I'm fine," and sank to his knees.

Shickie put a hand on Betsy's shoulder. "Why don't you help your friends down to the parking lot? There's emergency people there."

She nodded. "God bless you, sir. I don't know what foreigners like you believe in, but I'll pray for your soul."

Shickie gave her a hug of thanks and turned to Jimmy, once more standing. In consideration of the collarbone, instead of a hug, Jimmy got a cautious squeeze and a lingering look. Shickie ruffled his hair, said, "Go on, get out of here. You're an okay kid . . . maybe we'll see each other again, huh?"

69

hickie enlisted Maury to help him redirect the searchlight so it raked the wall rimming the roof. He unbuttoned his shirt and stepped out of his overalls, removed his disguise, socks, underwear, and shoes. He took something from a pocket and turned to Maury, "You ready for a new career, Hammer?"

Maury straightened his bow tie.

Shickie pointed at the underarm holster. "A prophet shouldn't be packing."

Maury scowled, but removed the rig and set it on the roof.

"What with Noah's flood," Shickie was saying, "the Rapture gong sounding, and the Fireflies witnessing Patch ride the blimp to his just rewards, we've got an audience to die for." He faced Maury, raised a lecturer's finger. "Listen, if you plan on doing any miracles, you've got to be sure you're careful to—what the hell, there's no time for lessons. You're on your own from here on."

He peered over the low wall at the parking lot below. "You're not afraid of heights, are you?" At Maury's headshake, he said, "Good. One last thing, before I check out. It's your show now, but . . . don't just take them, take care of them, hear?"

"Oh, ye of little faith," Maury said. "So, I've shot a few people—cheaters—you think I've got no heart?"

Shickie rolled his eyes. "Forgive me."

"Tell you the truth, I wasn't cut out for the trade I was in."

"Does that mean you're ready?"

Maury nodded and took a deep breath. "I'm ready."

With a quick salute, Shickie turned and sprung onto the wall. Bathed in ten thousand watts of light, he spread his arms like an Olympic diver preparing for a perfect ten.

The newly directed searchlight beam snagged the attention of the spectators. They heard a bang like a cannon shot, saw a puff of red smoke at the edge of the armory roof, and, when it dissipated, a small man standing nude in the light, his legs together, his arms extended to form a cross.

"It's the Prince!"

"He's back!"

The Children of Light, those still standing, dropped to their knees. "Hallelujahs" and "Praise the Prince" erupted like fireworks at a Mexican wedding.

"Now, what's going on?" asked a cop.

"Heads up," said a fireman. "It's a jumper."

"Tilt up," a perky blonde reporter told a cameraman. "Give me a wide shot and zoom in. Where's that parabolic mike?"

"This is *it*," said Goliath Jones, and began stripping. The rest of the Jones clan followed his example, women, men, and children.

From atop the armory, the Prince intoned: "Children of Light . . ."

A cemetery silence fell over the lot as people strained to hear.

"I return for the last time. . . ."

Women sniffled, began to weep.

"Reverend Patch," the Prince was saying, "has risen to meet his maker, borne on the wings of our great angel."

"Hey!" a cop said, noticing the Jones clan shedding their clothes. "We'll have none of that in Gatlinburg."

"I returned to—"

"Rapture us!" Goliath Jones boomed back. "We're ready, Lord."

"Uh . . . not yet," said the Prince. "Soon."

"Soon? How soon? Hey, we come a long way and—"

The Prince shook a holy finger at the bearded man. "Do not dispute me, mortal, or I'll send you to the pit of hell to boil in brimstone for eternity. Do I make myself clear?"

"Yes, Lord," Jones replied meekly.

"Eternity is forever," the Prince reminded him, "soon is . . . less than your miserable lifetime. You Texans . . . Jones clanners?"

"Yes, Lord?" Goliath sounded more hopeful.

"The Rapture for you will happen in . . . what's the highest place in Texas?"

"I guess somewhere in the Davis Mountains," one of the Joneses volunteered.

"Then that's where it will be."

"Oh, man," Goliath said. "That's the middle of nowhere. We thought . . ."

"You thought you'd found a shortcut to heaven? Well, it ain't that easy, big fella. My old Fireflies? Listen up."

The charter members of Shickie's ministry mouthed, "Yes, Lord?"

"You will stay in Gatlinburg. Here, in the Temple of Light. A new prophet will appear to lead you. Soon."

"How soon?" asked Goliath Jones, raising his pants.

The Prince sighed. "In this case, real soon."

The incident commander of the assembled firefighters, speaking softly into his radio, ordered the captain of an aerial unit to fire up his Cummins 350 diesel and move to the armory wall, ladder ready. A rescue team readied a net. Cameramen did focus checks at the base of the armory wall, anticipating the jumper's point of impact.

"Actually," the Prince was saying, "soon is now. Without further ado, I present . . . The Elder. Follow him as you have me. Remember the Golden Rule. Lead good lives and I'll see you up there."

His forefinger pointed skyward. Spectators' eyes followed the invisible line to the moonlit angel blimp, tiny, oh, so tiny, but still visible.

There followed a bang, a flash of light, a puff of white smoke, and the Prince of Light was no more.

Ten seconds later, they heard another report, saw yet another flash, and, this time, a puff of blue smoke. When it cleared, an even smaller man than the Prince appeared, wearing a red pin-stripe shirt, navy slacks, and a red bow tie. The Elder.

The Elder raised his arms, as had the Prince. A hush fell over the crowd. After a suspenseful pause, he spoke: "Have I got a deal for you. . . ."

PART THREE

Redemption

70

With hints of "big news," Thadeus Trout summoned Junior and his crew for the first time since he had bowling-balled them. Junior and Peaches entered the office on crutches, Six-pack, considering crutches unmanly, walked with a skip-hop and one hand on Peaches's shoulder.

"Those broken toes will heal before you know it, boys. We'll have you earning your keep within a month."

Peaches lowered the corn dog he had been gnawing. "So, we're not losing our jobs?"

"Why, no. Although, I don't mind telling you, you had me thinking of either calling the Hammer about you or putting a bullet in my own brain more than once."

"Don't talk like that, daddy."

"Foolish me for underinsuring the Bible Alive. But, who'd have guessed? It's going to be hand-to-mouth for a while, but it's working out. We'll leave the parking lot as is, bill it as an Apocalypse attraction. Add some wailing souls, four bad-assed horsemen, smoke and fire, a few special effects, and it should be spectacular."

"Enough with the Bible stuff," Junior said. "What about our real business?"

"You're worried about finances? About the loans from the fellas up north, are you son? Getting rough, as they are known to do? Well, I did some fast-talking.

"Guess what? They see a future in the Bible, too!"

"Big stinking deal."

"Bear with me. . . . They agreed to write off the loan for a fifty-one percent share of the museum. They're putting up enough money for the restoration *and* expansion into the armory. Soon as I throw a scare into that fumbling old man who's taken over the Fireflies and get him to sign over the lease, we'll be out-Disneying Disney."

"Yeah, sure," Junior said. "What about us? Hijackings, the real stuff."

"That's more good news. The other part of the deal with our new partners is they're taking over the hijackings, the outlet for the hot goods, the loan sharking—all of it. We're straight arrow from here on in. Ain't that grand? Fudge, moccasins, wholesale meat, and the Bible Alive will be our bread and butter."

Junior spat. "That's for shit."

"So . . ." Peaches sounded not entirely as disappointed as Junior. "I guess that means we'll be working in, like, the fudge shop?"

"Unloading sides of beef from semis," Six-pack suggested, with a sour look. He muttered, "Bodies. Cold, stiff bodies."

"No, and no, again," Trout said. "Check out those garment bags."

"Fur coats," Junior said, anticipating the contents. "Left over from that Asheville hijack." He hobbled to a hook on the back of the door and unzipped the first bag. It contained not furs, but a café-au-lait, gold-trimmed skirt and matching blouse. The second bag held a similar outfit, only in baby blue. The third ensemble was pink.

"What the hell's this?"

"Our Bible Alive guard is out, injured," Trout was saying. "Obviously, one wasn't enough.

"You're our new security force. Old Testament heroes. Those are your uniforms. Sandals are in the boxes—plenty of room for those swollen toes. Go ahead, boys, try 'em on."

Horace Duckhaus wore a disturbing grin. "Take a seat," he said to Plato Scopes.

Scopes sat.

"I have good news and bad news. Which do you want first?"

Scopes gripped the arm of the chair. He noticed a legal pad on the director's desk, filled with, from Scope's vantage, upside-down scribblings, a name—Maria—and a numeral, #2, repeated over and over, in script and print, filling the page. He couldn't make sense of either, so he said, "The good news, I suppose."

"Very well. That miserable publicity you garnered with that mummy of yours actually bore fruit. You are familiar with Terrance Hamadi?"

Scopes shook his head.

"You would if you had been paying more attention to button hooks and less to dried-up cadavers. Terrance Hamadi is the owner of the seventh-largest collection of buttonhooks in North America. Man's getting up in years, fearful his heirs will declare him incompetent and sell off the collection." The grin broadened. "You see where this is going?"

Another head shake.

"Hamadi is donating his entire collection to *us*." Duckhaus slapped the desk. "That'll move us from the number three slot to two. Two! South of the Ohio and east of the Mississippi, of course. Nationally, we'll move into fifth place, maybe even fourth.

"Is that an early Christmas, or what?"

"Congratulations," Scopes said in monotone. "And the bad news?"

"Unfortunately, Hamadi isn't giving us a red cent to curate the collection. Really puts the screws to our budget.

"So . . ." Duckhaus extended his arms, lifted his shoulders, and turned his palms up in a What can I do? gesture. "You're out of a job."

Before Scopes could react, Duckhaus added, "I was going to fire you anyway after embarrassing us like you did. Here . . ." He slid an envelope across the desk. "A check for a weeks' salary. Sorry to see it end like this, young man, but I warned you, didn't I? Get your priorities straight, I said. Forget the caves and mummies, but no—"

Scopes crinkled the envelope in his fist. "I have news, too." A near orgasmic smile spread across his face. "When *National Geographic* went strange on me, acting like they never heard of me or Finklestein after the mummy was destroyed . . . those stuck-up, better-than-thou elitists . . ."

His momentary pique faded and the smile returned. "I got a call from—guess who? *Hustler* magazine. *Hustler*! Huge circulation, newsstands, too.

"*Hustler* saw those tabloids you were in such a hissy over, and immediately grasped the significance of my find. Yes, the mummy is gone, but . . . they want to do a feature. Paying me ten thousand dollars for exclusive rights to my photos of the fertility petroglyphs and coprolites."

He stood, put his hands on his hips. "*Hustler* has millions more readers than those sorry scientific journals who've scorned me all these years.

"Not only that, they want a whole series on erotica in the ancient world: Pompeian murals, Moche pottery, Hindu bas-reliefs, Easter Island's phallic statues, Fijian yam dildoes, Alexander's love letters. More.

"So," Plato Scopes tore the envelope in pieces, threw the fragments at Duckhaus. "Screw your firing me—I'm going to be rich *and* famous. I quit."

Maury the Elder bowed deeply to his right. "That was bee–u–ti–ful!" he said in his resonant TV voice. "Let's have a hand for our choirmaster, Miss Rodgers, and the Temple of Light choir."

There were but a few tentative brushing of palms, this being a church and all.

"Did I say 'hand'?" Maury raised one of his to face level, stared at it. He lifted the other, gave it the eye. "Looks to me like God gave us two. Let's use them, what say?" He demonstrated, grinned widely, motioning the congregation to follow suit. "That's it, that's it—let's show these folks they're appreciated." Within seconds, the armory resounded with applause. Maury put his fingers to his mouth and whistled. Several of the younger Fireflies whistled back. He did a little soft-shoe step, called out, "Are we having fun, yet?" The kids stomped their feet. Pretty soon everyone was into it, clapping, stomping, whistling, hooting. Tears ran down cheeks.

Quite a change from the Elder's sermon fifteen minutes before, a dramatic account of Delilah's betrayal of Samson, peppered with admonishments of retribution from an unforgiving, Old Testament God. The Elder concluded with a fiery lambaste against adulterers and cheaters, "who, regardless of creed, color, or national origin, Yahweh will throw into the deepest circle of hell, where the sleek-flanked, steady-handed, Centaur Archers of Retribution will shoot pieces off of them. Nose-less, ear-less, finger-less, everything-else-that-sticks-out-less, the cheaters will suffer through the long hellish night reflecting on their perfidy, only to have their miserable bodies restored in the morning and have the whole shooting off business begin all over again.

"And, now," Maury signaled to Mrs. Binkle at the Casio synthesizer, who pressed the drum roll button. "The moment you've all been waiting for . . ."

He paused, raised his eyebrows, encouraging them to guess. Before anyone spoke, he told them: "The passing of the plate."

There were a few dramatized groans, though, in fact, no one minded pitching in after a show like the one the Elder had just put on. People reached for wallets, opened purses, pressed currency into children's hands to drop in the basket.

"Whoa," Maury said. "Hold on. Put away that paper, forget those bills, because all I want from each of you is . . . a penny."

He faced a sea of perplexed faces.

"That's right. One cent."

Maury stood in place, feet together, face impassive. He stared at the tassels on his loafers while people before him exchanged uncertain looks, began reaching into pockets and coin purses for the modest tariff.

Beat. Beat. Another beat passed while they fumbled for coins. Maury the Elder leaned toward them, and his face came alive as he spoke the words that would become his trademark close: "Ju–usssst kidding about the one cent, folks. I may be old . . . but I'm sure not *craaaaa–zy*."

"That's right," Jimmy's Grandpop said. "You're not an Indian."

"What are you talking about? All these years? Look at me. What about the Chief? What about—"

"Yeah, look at you. Black hair, but your skin? You think I don't know you go to that tanning salon?" He patted the cushion on the worn sofa. His border collie jumped beside him, curled half in his lap. "You, too," he said to Jimmy. "Sit."

Jimmy rubbed his forehead and sank into one of the kitchen chairs. He jolted upright when his bottom hit the vinyl and the shock shot up his spine to his broken collarbone. He was wearing a brace that held his shoulders back until the bone set, but until then, the broken ends scraped with every move.

Grandpop winced with him. When Jimmy stopped fidgeting, he said, "Your mom did call him the Chief, but I never said he was an Indian. That was all your doing."

"You never told me otherwise."

"Yeah, and I apologize. I thought you needed a little hero worship. Kid needs a father he can look up to, even if the father's not there to see. When you set out on your travels, I thought it would make a man of you. And it did. You turned out okay, Jimmy."

"I don't believe this."

"It's true."

"Then the mummy wasn't related to me at all."

"Not unless he was a European like that scientist fella said."

Jimmy sulked. Grandpop went to the refrigerator, returned with a six-pack of cold Budweiser. He set the cans on the table next to Jimmy, popped the tab on the first one for him, and returned to the sofa. He rubbed the dog's belly and said nothing.

Jimmy sipped sullenly for ten minutes.

Into his third can, Jimmy grunted. "Hell, I was never much of an Indian anyway. Always the square peg. My one big coup was getting back my ancestor—what I thought was my ancestor—and I blew that.

"I was planning to visit the Seminoles in Florida. The state's charging them an arm and a leg for airboat licenses. I heard about this Intracoastal Waterway down there, thought we could drain it to protest . . . another bad idea. Ginger said it sucked."

"She's a nice girl. Thoughtful of her to come by and help you out of that brace thing so you can shower and not stink up the place."

"Better her than you." Jimmy took another swallow of beer. "She agrees with you, by the way, about turning our cave commercial."

"Hell, yes." Grandpop sat upright. "With all that publicity? Her being so famous? Scientists saying that those dirty drawings my buddies and me scratched on the walls when we was kids are 'prehistoric fertility rituals'? Everyone and his cousin wanting to see them and exactly where they found the mummy? And there's that wonderland you discovered, the stone icicles and crystals and all. Homer Delaney's excited about it, too, with the cave running through his property. He even offered to go in with us to run power in. I'll bet we could get a loan—"

The doorbell rang. Grandpop answered the door, came back with a Fed Ex box. He shook it, handed it to Jimmy. "Feels empty."

"Kind of like my life." Jimmy zipped the end, pulled out a sheet of hotel letterhead. "Honolulu, Hawaii. Who could that be? . . . Oh."

"Oh?"

"It's from the ex-Prince of Light, Shickie Doone, the man who saved me from the mob, hung out with me in the whale, un-handcuffed Ginger from the blimp ladder." Jimmy read, silently, and then aloud:

> Dear Jimmy,
> Some adventure, huh? I trust your collarbone is keeping you awake at night and your friend Ginger is doing her best to help you forget.
> I'm starting a new enterprise, lots of promise, far from Gatlinburg. When certain parties forget I exist, I may stop back and say Hi.
> Meanwhile, I'm enclosing a little gift, something to remember me by. It may give you ideas—good. On the other hand, if you decide to sell it, don't take a penny less than forty grand retail or twelve to the trade.
> Love and kisses,
> Your Amish buddy.

Jimmy shook the box, looked inside. Halfway down, he saw a wad of toilet paper, layer upon layer wrapped around something hard within. He unraveled the tissue, let it pile at his feet.

"Whoa!" he said when he got to the center. "It's a diamond ring. A really big one."

"I'm the widow Doone," Rita Rae explained to the insurance agent. She was dressed in open-toe black pumps, black mesh hose, a black leather mini, wide black patent leather belt and matching vest over a snug, black mohair, V-neck sweater. A black veil hung from the top of her beehive cone, held in place by crisscrossed lacquered black chopsticks piercing the apex of her do. Scarlet lipstick counterpointed the mourning drag. "And this is my brother, Orlando."

She extended a hand, her fingers tipped by black polish to match her toenails.

The agent motioned them to a loveseat facing his desk. "As I explained on the phone," he said, "without a death certificate I'm afraid the company . . ."

Rita Rae lifted the veil and dabbed an eye with a black hankie. "There must have been a hundred witnesses to what happened to his remains," she said with a sniffle. "Torn apart by barbarians." Another sniffle. "It was awful. But, I understand. You need proof it was him."

"Tangible evidence," said the agent.

Rita Rae gave him the slightest of smiles and reached into her shiny black vinyl shoulder bag. She retrieved a large poly Ziploc and tossed it on the desk. Inside was a wad of damp dark hair. "Shickie's," she said. "From his mummy before . . ." She sniffled, blew her nose in a hankie. "Before those beasts ripped him to shreds."

Orlando patted her knee in sympathy.

Rita Rae rested a palm on the back of Orlando's hand, keeping it in place, and raised her gaze to hold the agent's eyes. "That should be enough for an analysis. DNA?"

"Ah," said the agent. "More than enough to establish identity I should think."

"Good."

"Although, it may not be necessary to give this to the authorities." He poked the poly bag with the tip of a pencil, slid it to the far edge of the desk. "Because I received something in the mail today that should make you very happy, Mrs. Doone."

"A check? Already? You are such a dear." She raised the veil from her face, flipped it back onto the frontal slope of her beehive.

"No . . ." The insurance man nodded to a TV monitor at the side of the room, lifted a remote and pushed buttons. The screen lit, stayed blue for several seconds, and shifted to brilliant blurry white. The exposure and focus adjusted, revealing two feet in flip flops, standing in sand. Sound came on, shouts, happy, indistinct voices, splashing, and, "Here we go," presumably from the operator. The camera moved, rose to reveal a wide hotel and palm tree-rimmed beach. The familiar peak of Diamond Head came into view: Waikiki.

"Okay, now over here," another voice said, and the camera panned swiftly a hundred and eighty degrees across the line of hotels, past a pink rococo palace from the thirties, tall towers, sunbathers, tanned surfers carrying boards, firm young coeds in bikinis, and, finally, a small man in a hibiscus-covered aloha shirt. Shickie Doone.

Rita Rae groaned.

"Hi, sweetie," the familiar face on the TV screen said. The camera jiggled, obviously in the hands of a neophyte, zooming in for a close-up, a bit too fast.

"I know you've been concerned," Shickie said, "but I'm fine. Just needed to get away for a while to sort things out." He was backlit by a salmon sky, tinged with neon red and streaks of pale orange.

Rita Rae chewed a knuckle. Then her face brightened, and she said, "Oh, he sent you a copy, too? It's from three months ago. We had a little spat and—"

"You can zoom out now," Shickie was saying. But the image zoomed in instead, filling the screen with Shickie's already prominent nose.

"Oops." Zoom out.

Waist to head. Shickie had something behind his back. He held it before him. A newspaper. "Closer." Zoom in. The Honolulu paper: headlines, the date, three days old, clearly visible. "Okay, zoom out."

"I'm getting the hang of this, now," from the cameraman.

The view went wide, showing Shickie, full figure. He lowered the paper. "Now, don't you worry about me, sweetie. I'll be home before you know it."

He winked, and—Poof!—disappeared in a cloud of white smoke.

The smoke drifted away, revealing sand, water, and a glorious postcard sunset. The Prince of Light was gone.

71

On a tiny streak of land somewhere in the broad reaches of the Pacific Ocean, no more than a speck on a foldout map, the Sky God pulled a shiny cowry shell from the air. His fingers curled around it. He blew on his fist, opened it. The cowry had vanished. He recovered it from the runny nostril of a giggling, brown-skinned girl, pressed it into her tiny hand and tickled her chin.

The seventy-eight inhabitants of the islet—men, women, and children— mouthed a collective "Aahhhh."

The Sky God nodded in a modest bow and returned to the Game. "Let's see your cards," he said to the three Players. They faced a driftwood crate, draped ceremonially with the brilliant orange silk of the Sky God's Great Wing. Two of the men reclined on the upturned hull of an outrigger canoe, the third squatted on a palm stump, while the Sky God sat on his throne, a corroded fishing chair from the rear deck of an abandoned cabin cruiser run aground a decade ago on the atoll's fringing reef.

The chief's daughter, her back resting against the Sky God's bony shins, sat on the sand stroking the long silky hair of the

Sky God's dog, tiny as a land crab, light enough to ride the wind at the side of his master.

"Too bad," the Sky God said to the Player on the stump. "You've got a jack-high zip."

"Zzzipp!" said the islanders.

The Sky God examined the next Player's cards. "Two, three, five, seven, eight. With a little more luck, you could've drawn a straight."

The islanders scratched their heads and muttered, "Sturr-aate."

The Sky God explained the concept, using his fingers and pebbles to demonstrate. "Three hearts," he said to the third Player. "Two more would make a flush. Flush—all same-same, see?"

"Flusssh."

The islanders understood one word in twenty.

"What do you know?" the Sky God said. "I've got three of a kind again. Queens. I win."

He scooped up nine pearls and his own wager, three bright enameled refrigerator magnets, a Fred Flintstone, a Wonder Woman, and a pickle. He dropped them in his pocket. "Whadaya say to another hand, boys?"

The men nodded, grinning broadly, showing large white teeth.

Being chosen as a Player to sit at the side of the Sky God during the Game brought big mana. The Players got to see the Sky God's magic up close, too. Occasionally, a Player Won and left a Game with one of the Sky God's beautiful tiki-god figurines. The men had bets as to who would get the most tikis from the Sky God. A bride price of twenty-five had been established for the highest-status unattached woman. The leading contender had four, wore them bound with coconut fiber cord across his forehead. Several of the more comely and industrious females wore the god images as pendants, suspended on woven, human-hair leis between their bare breasts. The chief's daughter possessed five of the most colorful. Her father had ten, each unique, heavy in the hand, one more beautiful than the next—a gift from the Sky God when he had drifted down like a feather from the squawking belly of the Great Bird.

"It takes time, fellas," the Sky God was saying. "But not to worry . . . I'll keep dealing till you get the hang of it."

Acknowledgments

Here's hoping Shickie Doone, the Prince of Light, will bless Katey Brichto, Carl Morris, and Ryck Neube for their valuable advice. May his beneficence shine upon my editor, Bob Gleason, and my agent, Eleanor Wood, for their insights and suggestions.

Rick Steiner helped Shickie lose his shirt in Vegas, Mary Katherine Crabb attempted to tutor Orlando in elocution over a long, and, I suspect, energetic weekend, while Elizabeth Murray kindly provided me with fascinating forensic knowledge that I managed to skewer as the mummy tale unfolded. I thank Brian Callaghan for blazing a trail through the thicket of publication, and offer a grateful wink of the angel blimp's good eye to Jerry Galvin, Terry Hamad, Frances Sheard, Curt Tweddell, and those other generous souls who assisted me during preparation of this novel.

And, cheers to Gatlinburg, Tennessee, for its tee-shirt wit and carved candle artistry, its thirty-one flavors of fudge, its garden gnomes and salt shaker bears, its haunted adventures, cars of the stars, micro-wedding chapels, hillbilly golf, and mock chalet motels that serve trout with grits for breakfast and catfish with hushpuppies for supper . . . an island of Americana-gone-wild surrounded by the Great Smoky Mountain forest primeval. The U.S. of A. Ain't it grand?